The Portrait Painter

Fraser Oz

The Portrait Painter is a novel, a work of fiction. The characters, places and events are either the product of the author's imagination or they are used entirely fictitiously.

Published by Fraser Oz.

ISBN 978-0-578-29701-9

APPRECIATION

This book could not have been written without the patience, encouragement and editorial input of my wife, Sara, who has a way of making everything I do seem more worthwhile. I cannot thank her enough.

I also owe a major appreciation to my friend, Kitty Sewell, best-selling author of 'Ice Trap' and numerous other novels, for reading my manuscript(s) and offering many excellent suggestions, almost all of which have been implemented.

I thank Charles Hall, author of the Jack Crain and other novels, for reading and reviewing the draft. I also much appreciate the patience and input of Margaret Sutcliffe and Linda Blench for their patient work, reading the manuscript and recommending various improvements. I should also mention Fr. Mike Gimignani, for his wise counsel.

On my list of helpers and supporters is Heather Bodlak, whose considerable graphic arts and social media skills have helped me to put this project together, finalize the covers and create an online presence with which to promote the work.

Finally, I am honored to be allowed to use, as front cover picture, a painting by Mara Lea Brown, artist, writer and teacher, whose skill abounds in every area in which she applies herself.

PREVIEW

"I looked into his eyes and saw understandable numbness and terror, but I also saw something else. I saw through his present pain into his future."

Cover portrait by Mara Lea Brown

TABLE OF CONTENTS

INTRODUCTION

Most of life is predictable. At least, it would be, if we had a better understanding of how things work and how people behave.

This story is about a man who has unusual insights into the future, and the effect that this gift has on his life. But is such a concept realistic? Maybe it is not as absurd as it seems at first. After all, everything that happens has a cause of some sort, an event or circumstance that is itself the result of other causes. The life of the entire universe is a sequence of cause-and-effect, an infinite matrix of connected events. If we possessed the mind of God or some other unlimited intelligence, we could predict everything that will ever happen.

In other words, our fates already lie before us! We just can't see them. Not usually. But in this story ....

In the words of John Lennon, "There is nowhere you can be that isn't where you're meant to be."

Or, as Goldie Hawn once said, "You often meet your fate on the road you take to avoid it."

CHAPTER 1

Justin

According to my mother, I arrived in the world on schedule. It was the second of June 1991, a stunningly sunny day in the Russian River valley of northern California. Of course, I didn't know that at the time. It seems that I slipped into the world quickly and quietly. Labor lasted a little over two hours, and was accompanied, on mom's part, more by heavy breathing than cries of pain. I, of course, obliged the three women by crying on cue, and then relapsing into a satisfied sleep. I weighed in at seven pounds three ounces and measured twenty-two inches, and all my limbs and other parts appeared in working order. I was declared fit for the world.

My parents occupied a little yellow cottage on the side of a hill outside Guerneville. It sat behind a hedge of vicious thorns upon which I would be impaled many times during my boyhood. There was a short gravelly drive but no garage. The house's one eye-catching feature was a cloud of scarlet bougainvillea which clung to the posts and roof of the porch. It belonged to a couple of out of state retirees who had inherited it a dozen years earlier and were using it for income. It was small and poorly maintained, and so the rent was low, which suited mom and dad well.

I was born in that house, in the master bedroom, although the word 'master' implies spaciousness and an en-suite toilet, neither of which did it have. Indeed, at just ten feet by twelve, the room hardly deserved a title at all. In attendance that afternoon were my grandmother, Mabel West, who was fussing around doing almost nothing, and Mrs. Parris, a semi-retired midwife from somewhere in town, who was doing almost everything: everything my mother wasn't doing, that is.

My father was nowhere to be found. He escaped from the scene as soon as mom's waters broke, having no inclination to witness either his wife's pain or his child's arrival, and, to be truthful, I think mother was glad he wasn't there. Hand-holding, physical or spiritual, were not for him: somewhere along the way he had missed Moral Support 101.

* * *

CHAPTER 2

Alice

Justin's mother, Alice Patricia Gates, was twenty-six when he was born. She had been married to Ernie, a construction worker of some sort, for two unhappy years. He had entered her life when they both showed up at the same open air rock concert. For some reason, which she soon forgot, she had thought him quite good looking. "Well, to be honest," she admitted later, "It was just that we managed to have a lot of fun in a very short period of time, so we decided we might as well get married." Their whirlwind romance was based on parties and concerts and various forms of daring behavior, and was followed by a wild honeymoon which they could not afford. After that, everything went south. Initial domestic bliss quickly deteriorated as responsibilities accumulated and squeezed out the fun. Ernie, she discovered, did not have the stomach for struggling in the trenches of real life. Two years of marriage taught him how much he liked being single, and three months of fatherhood were all he could stand. One day he just left. There was no loud, shouting argument, no physical violence, not even any tears. He just packed up his things and went. To Alice, his departure came as a shock, but she was relieved in a way. Constantly showing love to another human being wasn't really for her either, which made motherhood a challenge. Short, sharp relationships were more to her liking. For better or for worse but not for long, please. Anyway, long before her newborn was old enough to know anything about anything, she and he had become a simple two-person family, Alice and son.

Guerneville claims to be a "charmingly rustic town", population just a few thousand, mostly prospering professionals and contented retirees. There used to be a large hippie community, but time has watched it fade away. Even though the river often overflows and floods the town, its residents like the place and stay. Alice and Ernie moved there when she was offered employment as a second-grade teacher in Guerneville School (K-8).

Alice considered herself a private person. She did not long for friends, nor did she have many. At first meeting, people saw a slender figure, five feet five tall, and weighing a hundred and twenty-nine pounds, with long walnut-brown hair, worn either loose, down her back, or braided and coiled on top of her head. Her eyes were brown, flecked with gold.

Normally she wore the thoughtful expression of an introvert, but she would smile easily at people who spoke to her, which gave her a warm and friendly reputation. One fellow teacher described her as "quiet, kind and gentle," which was about right. She showed no sense of self-importance, and was slow to express her opinions, although she certainly held many. She was content to sit at the back and let others take the limelight, and she would try to do what was expected of her whenever she could. Despite her natural reticence, people who met Alice Gates usually remembered her because of the courtesy, even empathy, with which she listened to them, and because of her smile.

* * *

Once Justin had arrived and Ernie had gone, Alice tried to pull her life into order. It was not easy. She suffered from repeated waves of panic, related to the baby, the home, her job and, of course, money. Not being a confident decision maker, each of these issues would overwhelm her for a while and then recede, rather as waves on a beach come roaring in and then, more quietly, drain away, leaving the empty beach ready for the next onslaught.

Luckily for her, Justin was a much easier child than he might have been. In his early months, he did not cry a lot, and, as he began to grow, he rarely had a tantrum. Unlike so many infants, he almost never threw things, either food or toys, onto the floor. He would play with them instead. In particular, he seemed fascinated by the patterns he could make by stirring his food with his spoon, or by spilling it onto his tray and drawing in it with his fingers.

When people asked Alice how she liked being a mother, she always answered dismissively, "It's OK", which made them suspect that she disliked the role. They were wrong. Her reluctance to talk about it arose, not from any shallowness of character or resentment of her child, but from her inability to describe the amazement she felt at having brought a human being into the world. It was too awesome to explain. Also, her many hopes and fears were far too private to discuss with anyone other than an intimate, and there was no such person in her life. She suffered from a permanent sense of guilt, suspecting that she was not a good enough parent. The truth is that, for her, motherhood was far, far more than merely OK. It did something to her which made every day important in a way it had never been before.

As a single mother, she had to find a way of managing her child, her job and her home. With no mate to lean on, she had to rely on a network of friends, of which she had few, and neighbors, of whom there were more. Although she often wondered, "What on earth am I going to do now?" she always found an answer.

* * *

For his first three years, Justin spent half his days in the homes of well-meaning strangers. Moving frequently from one orbit of care to another, he remained a somewhat lonely boy, whose conversational skills developed slowly. Like his mother, he learned to keep his thoughts to himself.

When he was three, Alice put him into a preschool program at a local church. He was an only child and likely to remain one, and needed to develop some social skills outside the home. He accepted this new assignment placidly but without enthusiasm. If she had longed for him to come home, bubbling with news about what he did each day, anxious to show and tell, she would have been disappointed. Also, her son had inherited her lack of need for relationships. After the first semester, his teacher told her, "Your Justin is a quiet one. He doesn't really like playing with other children, and prefers to be on his own, playing with constructional toys or drawing. In fact, art is his favorite activity, and for his age he is really good."

At home, the refrigerator in the Gates' kitchen did become a gallery for his childish images, but only because his mom insisted that they be put up. Left to himself, Justin would have tossed them onto the pile in the corner of his room.

* * *

It was Mothers' Day, 1988. Alice intended to ignore it, as in previous years. Telling her four-year old that he should appreciate what a wonderful mother she was didn't seem a good idea, especially when she knew the truth. The day would have passed without mention had he not stopped eating his breakfast long enough to ask, "What's Mother's Day?"

She thought quickly and replied, "It is a day for children everywhere to be happy that they have mothers to love them."

"You do love me, don't you, Mommy?"

"Of course I do. You know that."

Justin ate a spoonful of cereal. Then he looked up again and asked,

"Will you still love me after Tina arrives?"

Alice stared at him. What on earth was he saying?

"Justin, who is Tina?"

Without hesitation, and just as natural as could be, he replied, "My sister". He did not add "of course" but it was implied in the way he spoke.

"But you don't have a sister."

"But I will, won't I?"

"I shouldn't think so. I would have to have a husband first, wouldn't I."

"Are you going to get one?"

"I hope not."

"Well, I am still going to have a sister. And she's still going to be called Tina."

Alice was dumbfounded, and had no idea how to deal with this, so she said, "We will just have to wait and see."

This conversation puzzled her. She guessed he was needing a companion, an imaginary one perhaps, one fashioned to meet his needs, a friend who would not tease or bully or insist on winning. Maybe she should buy him a puppy.

* * *

Spring was ending and the school year was coming to its close. As they did every year, Mabel and Fordham West drove up from San Diego for the Memorial Day holiday, traveling a few days ahead of the mad rush and staying to celebrate Justin's birthday. They did not do a lot of grandparenting, but this ritual made them feel good, or at least, less guilty. They were happy not to live any closer.

Alice was exhausted. Her class had been unusually difficult, and the headmaster, on a crusade to have the best elementary school in Northern California, had been making life hard for all his teachers, including her. Especially her. Ever since she had been at the school, he had looked at her with a clear desire, to which she would not and could not respond. In his frustration, his dealings with her often held a touch of unintended meanness. To her mother, that spring, she seemed run down and in need of a rest. In a moment of compassion and guilt, Mabel said, "Why don't you let us take Justin back home with us? It would give you a bit of a break, a chance to catch up." The three adults discussed it for a while, finally agreeing that the boy would go to San Diego with his grandparents, and his mom would follow as soon as school was out, and she was free and rested.

Once the holiday was over, the Wests loaded up their car, strapped Justin in the back, and headed south, leaving Alice to her own devices. It was the first time she had been at home without her child in the four years since he was born, and she found it unexpectedly hard to handle. He was, by most standards, a quiet boy, and the home a normally peaceful place. Yet, once he was gone, the house seemed filled with an intense and oppressive, library-like silence.

For the first few days after school ended she enjoyed sleeping late, catching up with essential chores, and drinking too much coffee. However, she soon began to feel lonely and in need of a change. Before long she was ready to go to San Diego and bring her boy home, even though the prospect of driving on crowded freeways for ten straight hours had little appeal. After thinking about it for two days, she decided to turn the trip into a mini vacation of its own. She would avoid the interstates as far as possible, and meander down the coast. A couple of nights in beachfront hotels, if she could find them, might do her a world of good.

She set out on a Tuesday, passing the Bay Area well before noon, and enjoyed the forests and cliffs of Big Sur. In mid-afternoon she reached San Simeon, just south of Hearst Castle, where the road dropped almost to sea level. There she found a Best Western hotel with a great view of the Pacific and an available room. It was perfect.

Alice checked in, found her room, threw her few belongings onto the couch, and went out again to find the sea. The hotel consisted of three separate buildings around a wide, smooth lawn which stretched down to the beach. Curiously, scattered around the grass were several fire pits, around each of which was a semi-circle of chairs and two-seater benches. She wondered what they were for.

Crossing the lawn, and stepping carefully over the rocks which marked the edge of the property, Alice walked out onto the sand. Standing still for a moment, she took several deep breaths, filling her lungs with the fresh, salty air. It felt so good! Removing her sandals, she skipped across the soft sand to the water's edge, carrying them with her. Without pausing she ran straight into the sea until the small waves lapped around her calves, wetting the cuffs of her capris. A modest breeze cooled her face and stirred the ends of her hair. She studied the view, taking in the vast stretch of ocean. The sense of unwinding, of release from the normal stress of her existence, was wonderful. She drew in great gulps of sea air, stretched her arms wide enough to embrace the entire universe and then hugged them to her chest so as to prevent it getting away. It was a magical moment. Her spirits soared. If the breeze had strengthened enough to sweep her up and carry her away, she would not have minded at all. It was total enchantment.

Feeling wonderfully renewed, she walked the length of the beach, studying the various pebbles and shells she came across, until she found a tall, wide rock, at the foot of a low cliff. She sat down on the sand and leaned against it. Totally relaxed, she closed her eyes and just listened to the sounds of the sea and the birds, and thought of nothing in particular. In less than a minute she was asleep.

Later, she returned to her room, showered, and changed, and headed into the hotel restaurant for an early dinner. Ever since Ernie had left, Alice had largely given up alcohol, but this occasion felt so special she treated herself to a glass of Pinot Grigio. The cold white wine was delicious and refreshing. She drank that first glass, and then another, while she ate a salad followed by chicken tetrazzini. When she was finished and was rising to leave, her server came over, wine bottle in hand, and asked if she was going to watch the sun set. He explained that, shortly before sunset, the hotel lit one or more of the fires on the lawn, and guests gathered round to enjoy their warmth as they watched the sun go down.

"That sounds like a great idea," exclaimed Alice, glancing through the window and noticing that daylight was indeed fading.

"Then may I suggest, Miss, that you take a glass of wine with you? It is sure to add to the pleasure."

Without waiting for permission, he refilled her glass, almost to its rim. Then he smiled at her and wished her a pleasant evening.

Two of the fires were alight, and most of their seats were occupied, but she found a vacant bench at the end of one of the semi-circles. The view was spectacular. A scattering of wispy clouds textured the orange sky. She sipped her wine and watched the sun, lost in her own thoughts and quite unaware of anyone else.

The words, "May I?" made her jump. She turned her head and saw the speaker, a slim, energetic looking young man with a broad, friendly smile. He indicated the empty space on the bench beside her. "Would you mind? Most of the other seats are taken."

Alice glanced along the row. In fact, there were no other vacant seats. She returned his smile. "Of course," she said, picking up her now empty glass from the space beside her, and wriggling slightly to give him more room.

"My name is Tony," he said.

"And I am Alice."

"Delighted to meet you."

"Me too."

The two travelers sat, side by side, watching the sun. At one moment it was a ball of bright fire floating in the sky, then it touched the sea and laid a path of gold across the water directly toward them. Alice wanted to jump up and run along it, toward whatever heavenly Nirvana might be there. Maybe her companion sensed this, for he laid a gentle restraining hand on her arm. Moments later the sun sank into the abyss, completing its nightly demise, and the magic was over.

Tony brought her back to reality with the inevitable questions: where was she from and what had brought her to San Simeon? She found him easy to talk to and did not mind him asking. Somehow, he did not have much to say about himself, except that he lived outside Los Angeles and had interests in the wine trade. These are what had brought him to San Simeon. Mostly they talked about her, about life in California, and about Justin, especially about Justin. Time slipped by. Tony was carrying a bottle of wine and a glass. "What were you drinking?" he enquired, indicating her empty glass, and she told him. He waved his bottle. "This is Chardonnay, but at least it's white." Without thinking, she nodded and let him fill her glass. They continued to sit there, sipping wine, as darkness fell. The fire in the pit gradually dying and the other guests slowly going away. Eventually the evening chill worked its way through Alice's cotton shirt. She shivered slightly.

"Do you want to go in?" asked Tony.

She shook her head. "I am having such a good time."

He responded with the single word, "Here", putting his arm around her shoulders and pulling her against him. She snuggled into his warmth. Their conversation stalled, but they stayed, each thinking private thoughts, staring into the embers of the fire.

Eventually Alice shivered again. With a sigh, Tony gently eased her away from his side and stood up. Taking her hand, he said, "I guess it's time," and helped her stand, which brought her close. She smiled up at him and he kissed her. He had not intended to, but he did it anyway, and noticed that she did not pull away. Hand in hand, they walked across the grass to her building. Helped by the mix of white wines, Alice was quite lost in the romance of the evening and did not want it to end. Tightening her grip on his hand, she led the way into the building and along the hall to her room. Using her free hand, she found her key card in her pocket and opened the door. He held it for her as she led the way in, making sure he came too. It was four years since she had kissed a man, let alone enjoyed anything more. She had been 'off men' and content to be so, but this evening and this kind, thoughtful man had stirred her dormant urges.

Standing face to face beside the bed, they were both unsure about who should make the next move, even though they knew what it would be. Tony was anxious that Alice should feel respected, and she was nervous lest he think she was, in some way, cheap. He pulled her to him and kissed her again. This time she pressed herself against his firmness, ensuring that he felt the pressure of her breasts against his chest. The embrace lasted a long time, ending only when they had silently and mutually reached agreement. He released her. She stepped back and started to undo the buttons of her shirt.

It was almost four when Alice, completely fulfilled and content, slipped into a deep, dreamless sleep. Tony lay, looking at her sweet, untroubled face for ten or more minutes: then he quietly slipped out of the bed, got dressed, and left. When she awoke, Alice turned over and reached for him; but he wasn't there. She was disappointed, but not surprised. During the lovemaking, they had whispered terms of pleasure and gratitude, but carefully avoided the word love. Had it really been a one-night stand? She hoped not: it felt deeper, more meaningful, much more; but perhaps that is all it was. One thing was certain: it was the most beautiful night of love making she had ever known.

She slid out of bed and walked to the window. The sea was still there, the beach, the lawn, the remains of the fires, the bench on which she had snuggled against him. She opened the window and felt the breeze on her bare shoulders, the same breeze which found a piece of paper on the nightstand and blew it away. Alice never knew that Tony had left her a note and a number.

* * *

Alice didn't realize how radiant she looked when she arrived in San Diego, but her mother did. "You look as if your few days off did you a power of good," she said.

Her daughter just smiled and said, "I think they did." More than that she would not say, and Mabel West could only speculate.

"I think she has met someone," she confided to her husband, "But she won't admit it."

"Can't blame her," was his reply.

Alice's evident happiness was tinged with the sadness of knowing she was unlikely to see Tony again. He had told her he was single, and she had believed him. Also, she was sure he really liked her and had felt how good the chemistry between them was. It puzzled her that he was content to waste something that had begun so beautifully. The memory would have to be her comfort as well as her joy.

Within a few weeks she began to feel the changes in her body, to realize she might be pregnant. As the notion took hold she began to panic. She wasn't ready for this. Could she manage a second child? Raising Justin had been about all she could handle. How was she going to find the extra energy? And what about the extra money? Then there was the challenge of facing the people at work, her fellow teachers, her kids' mothers, the headmaster - particularly him. She doubted that she could be fired for becoming pregnant, but she knew how mean people can be, with questions she would not answer, and all sorts of whispered rumors behind her back.

Her parents took the news stoically, accepting it more with sadness than anything else. She notified them by phone from Guerneville at the end of August. Until then she kept her condition secret from everyone, limiting her usually sparse social life almost out of existence. The only person who noticed any change in her was Justin, and he was too young to figure it out. He would look at her when she paled with morning sickness, and ask, "Are you alright, mom?" She would rub his cheek with her hand and say, "Don't worry, sweetheart. Mommy is just a bit off today."

That year, school started in the third week of August. She was sure by then, having missed two periods and taken two positive tests, but nothing was showing. If she could handle the mornings, there was no need to tell the world for another month at least: another two with luck.

Of course, Alice knew she would have to tell Justin sometime, but there was no hurry. She had not forgotten his question on Mother's Day, "Will you still love me?" and wondered how he would take it. What instinct had told him that he was to have a sibling? Had he forgotten all about it since, or would he bring it up again? She knew that, if the baby was a girl, she would call her Tina. She sensed that he would regard any other choice as wrong.

September ninth arrived, her birthday, a Friday. It was years since she had celebrated the event. A couple of friends knew and remembered, phoning to wish her well, and offering to meet for a drink somewhere, but she declined. Mabel and Fordham, of course, did not forget. They sent her a thoughtful card and a huge bouquet of flowers, which they did every year. The day following was a Saturday, and Alice decided that she deserved a lazy morning. She was still in her pajamas when the doorbell rang. She went to answer it. A tiny, cheerful, middle-aged women was on the step.

Behind her, across Alice's drive and entirely blocking the road, was an enormous FedEx truck.

"Morning, gorgeous," said the visitor with a smile, "Here is something for you. I need you to sign." She handed over a stiff cardboard envelope with bright red printing on it. Alice stared at it for a moment, then shrugged her shoulders, signed where required, and said, "Thanks so much"

Back inside the house, she opened the envelope and extracted the single page letter in contained. It was from her father.

> "Dearest,
>
> "Your news has taken us by surprise. You are going to face many new challenges, and we want to help. It is a shame we live so far away, but least we can help financially.
>
> "When your mother and I married and she became pregnant with you, we took out a life insurance, to save the day if anything should happen to me. We have been paying the premiums for thirty years, even though we haven't really needed the policy for a long time. Now we have decided to cash it. The money would have come to you one day, anyway, but we think you are going to need it now. It should be enough to keep you going for quite a while.
>
> "We love you and wish you and your little ones all the happiness in the world.
>
> "Mom and Dad."

Alice looked in the envelope again. She turned it upside down, and out fell a check, made out for $32,000. Alice sat down on the nearest chair and started to cry.

* * *

The holidays came and went. Justin and his mom were able to carry on much as before, with the pregnancy increasingly obvious. Thanks to her parents' gift, Alice was able to take leave of absence from school and focus on her home and family. She had told Justin about the baby just before Thanksgiving. That had taken some courage. She had not forgotten his question, "Will you still love me?", but he took it well, responding with a very serious look on his face as he nodded in affirmation.

"That will be Tina," he said.

After that, from time to time, he would touch his mother's swelling belly and say cheerfully, "Hi Tina."

Alice knew she was not the most affectionate person in the world. Hugging and kissing were not her second nature, yet behind this apparent coolness burned a fire of possessiveness and pride toward her son. In the last four years she had learned the torture of watching him suffer when he caught scarlet fever, and the terror of thinking she had lost him on the day he had wandered off in town and been missing for hours. She would rather die than let anything bad happen to him. Often, when he was quietly drawing pictures or playing with his building blocks, or even just watching TV, she would sit and study him, fascinated by the way he was growing and changing and becoming his own unique self. Alice Gates loved her son in a way words could not describe.

* * *

The baby arrived in March. This time there were four people in the tiny master bedroom: the same three as for Justin's arrival plus one of Alice's few friends, who had asked if she could help. Tina was born at eight in the evening, making much more fuss about it than her brother had, but at least she was noisy and healthy, and everyone was happy. Justin spent the day with neighbors, who brought him home when the drama was over. He walked into the bedroom, looked up at his mom who was sitting in bed, holding the baby for him to see.

"Hi Tina," he said, as casually as if she had been in his life for weeks already. Then he looked at Alice, a concerned look on his face. "You alright, Mom?" he enquired.

CHAPTER 3

Willie

A Jesuit priest once said, "Give me a boy until he is eight and I will have him for life." He knew what he was talking about. By the time Justin moved into third grade, at the school where his mother taught, he was really becoming himself, with his own unique traits of character. The twenty or so children in his class had been together since first grade. By now they knew each another well, and had sorted themselves into various cliques and partnerships. Justin, however, was still a loner. The other kids liked him, but they had given up trying to drag him into their games and mischiefs. He would smile at their antics, without feeling either an urge to take part or a sense of resentment at being left out.

Of course, in the world of growing children, there are always some who think they are called to lead, or at least, that they should be taken notice of. That year, in Guerneville School's third grade, there was Willie Emmett, a taller-than-average red head, the only child of a bombastic father whose favorite saying was "Because I say so", and a timid mother, who seemed to never stop muttering "Yes, dear." For some reason, Willie had accumulated a cohort of three other boys who, even at that age, had learned to be followers and would probably continue in that mold for the rest of their lives. Willie liked to think up mischievous pranks, watch his troop carry them out, and then let them take the blame. Just weeks into the new school year, Willie had decided to expand his power base by recruiting Justin, only to be rebuffed, an unforgivable response. He started thinking up ways to put the quiet loner in his place.

Gerald Foster, the headmaster, ever ambitious for his school's reputation, had decided to show the townspeople what a splendid job he was doing with their school. An Open Day was planned for the Saturday before Thanksgiving. Each class would show off its best work in a classroom exhibit, and then provide two or three promising students to take part in an all-school concert. Three days before the great day, Willie Emmett saw an opportunity to taunt Justin. He called out across the classroom, loud enough to be noticed, "Hey, Justin, is your dad coming to Open Day?"

Having made sure that heads were turned, watching, he strode over to where Justin was sitting at his desk.

Justin looked up at him and said nothing.

"Well?" demanded the bully.

Justin replied quietly, calmly.

"You know I don't have a dad, Willie."

"And why is that? Why don't you have a dad?"

Justin winced at having to answer, and said, "I don't know."

"You are just a No-Dad, aren't you?"

"A what?"

Willie looked triumphant. "A No-Dad. My dad said your dad couldn't stand your mom and left."

The other boy just stared at him, speechless.

"And he says your sister doesn't have a dad either."

Justin said quietly but firmly, "Your dad knows nothing."

Willie was not expecting that reply. His face reddened, as he said, "You don't talk about my dad like that," to which he received the surprising response, "Anyway, you'll be a No-Dad yourself, pretty soon."

"What?" cried Willie, clenching his fists.

"You won't have a dad soon."

"Say that again."

"He is going to go. You just wait and see."

That was too much for Willie. Quick as a flash, his fist flew across the desk and caught Justin's cheek, just below the eye. "You can just shut up," he said, red faced and furious. He hovered over the seated Justin for another moment. Then he let out a long, deep breath, turned and stalked away.

Later that afternoon, when Justin rode home with his mother, she saw the bruise.

"What happened to you?"

"Nothing."

"That is not nothing. Have you been fighting? I can hardly believe it."

"Willie Emmett hit me."

"Why?"

"I don't know."

She gave him a hard look. "I am sure you do."

Her son muttered, "It doesn't matter, anyway."

"It does matter. I want to know."

So he told her.

"What on earth made you say such a thing?" she asked.

All he could say was, "I don't know."

"Did someone say something to you?" she continued. "Did you overhear people talking about Mr. and Mrs. Emmett?"

"I don't think so."

She frowned at her son, shook her head, warned him not to repeat what other people said, and dropped the subject.

I have often wondered, as the years sped by, what made me say that to Willie. I did not know anything about his family, except that he was an only child who lived with both parents. However, the moment he called me a No-Dad, I knew that he was going to be one too. I didn't see a vision or hear some gossip about life in the Emmett home. I just knew that, before long, Willie and his mother were to be on their own. Even now, after decades of such experiences, I find them hard to explain. Back then, when I was just eight, it was impossible.

My previews, as I have come to call them, usually come out of the blue. Certainly, in the early days, I could not have one just because I wanted to. Like dreams in the night, they appeared without warning. They were, and still are, like glimpses through a window as I pass by. I am always certain about what I have seen, but never able to visit that window again. So, when I told Willie that he going to lose his dad, I was totally sure I was right, but I could not explain it, neither to him, nor to my mom, nor to anyone else. Not even myself. I just knew it, and said it because it was true.

* * *

Next morning, third grade's first class was math, which meant Mr. Smart would be in his impatient mood. Generally, he was an OK teacher, but he just didn't understand how boring his students found math to be. There are many brilliant math teachers in the world, but he wasn't one of them. He began the lesson by rapping his desk with his ruler, and everyone stopped talking. He surveyed the room.

"Where is Willie Emmett, I wonder," he said, not expecting a reply.

Justin glanced behind. Willie's desk, two rows back, was vacant.

Mr. Smart was saying something about getting started when the missing student arrived. Some people can open a door quietly and slip into a room, almost without being noticed, but not Willie. He opened the door with a flourish and closed it with a bang, making sure that everyone knew he had arrived. "Sorry, Mr. Smart," he said, his insincerity plain, and turned into the aisle by Justin's desk. As he passed, he whispered, "Hi No-Dad. You are in big trouble now."

Justin had no idea what he was talking about, and it bothered him all through that morning's classes. As soon as they were released for lunch, he caught up with Willie in the hall, spun round to block his way, and asked, "Did you call me that name again?"

Willie grinned in a sort of triumph. "So that's what you are. A No-Dad"

"Well, get ready: you are going to be one too."

Anger flashed across the bully's face. "Don't you dare say that again. You're in enough trouble already."

Not knowing what that meant, Justin said "I am?"

Willie replied, "I told my dad that you said he and mom were getting divorced, and he just went crazy. He started shouting, at me and at mom, real loud with lots of f-words. Then he said he would be round at your house to beat the hell out of you."

"Should I be scared?" Justin asked, not knowing what else to say.

"If it were me, I would be," Willie replied with conviction. "Yes sir! And he said he had a good mind to do something to your mum, too."

"Like what?"

Willie suddenly looked uneasy, dropped his belligerent tone, and said, "Can't say."

With that, he pushed Justin aside and rushed after his friends further down the hall.

The two boys did not speak again until school was over and they were leaving. As he climbed into the bus, Willie caught sight of Justin and called out, "Good luck, No-Dad. You'll need it."

As always, Justin rode home with his mother, but he didn't say anything about Willie. He just crossed his fingers, hoping that Mr. Emmet wouldn't turn up. He hoped in vain. Half-way through supper, the Gates's were disturbed by a loud banging on their front door, sudden enough and loud enough to make them all jump.

"Who can that be?" Alice wondered.

"Willie Emmett's dad," said Justin.

His mother looked at him with a puzzled frown. Then the banging was repeated, and she went to open the door.

Alice had never met Stanley Emmett, but she had no doubt as to who he was. His voice was loud and could easily be heard by the children in the kitchen. Without any introduction or explanation, he shouted at her, "I want to know what the fuck you have been saying to your son about me and my wife."

The man standing on the step was tall, heavily built, with a mat of cropped, greying red hair over his florid face. Behind him, crowding the small driveway, was an enormous bright red pickup, one of those which have been jacked up on extra tall struts to satisfy somebody's oversized ego.

"Are you Justin Gates's mom?" he barked at her.

She recoiled, and said she was.

"Well, I want to know what the hell he thinks he is doing, telling my boy Willie that his mom and I are getting a divorce."

"I take it that you are Willie Emmett's father."

"Of course," he retorted.

"Then tell me why you think my Justin said such a thing. I am sure he didn't."

"I am sure as hell he did. You just ask him."

Alice thought for a moment, then called for Justin to come from the kitchen. Reluctantly, he obeyed. Stanley Emmett glared down at him. Without waiting for Alice to put the question, he demanded loudly, "Why the fuck did you tell Willie that his mom and I are getting divorced."

"Are you?" asked Justin innocently, which further enraged Willie's father.

"Why, you little…I have a good mind to beat the crap out of you, right here, in front of your mother, if she won't do it."

Alice interrupted, trying to cool things down.

"Justin, what did you say to Willie. Exactly, please."

"I told him that he would soon be without a father, that his dad is going away."

Stanley roared, "You little punk! Why would you say such a thing?"

"Because it's true."

The man on doorstep looked apoplectic, but before he could speak again, Justin's mother turned her head to look at her son. "Did you say anything about a divorce?"

He looked up at her and said, quite firmly but not loudly, "No, I didn't."

She studied the look in his eyes. She knew her son usually spoke the truth, and was sure he was doing so then. Even though she was not looking at Stanley, she could feel his fury.

"Your boy is a liar," he roared.

She turned back to face him and raised her voice defiantly. "You don't get to come round here and insult my child."

Justin could not believe his mother was standing up to Stanley Emmett. He knew Willie was a bully who quickly got mad with kids who opposed him. Now he could see where that trait came from. If he had known the story of David and Goliath, it would surely have come to mind. As he watched his mother face that horrible man down, he was amazed and proud.

Alice told him to go back into the kitchen, but he remained rooted where he was.

"I get to go wherever I want," said Stanley, but with a little uncertainty entering his tone. "I'm not going to be bossed around by a woman."

Alice stepped forward, invading his space and forcing him to step back, but not before she had smelled the whisky.

"I think you had better leave," she said.

"No-one tells me when to go," he replied.

"They do now."

Justin, watching closely, saw Stanley start to raise his arm. "He's going to hit my mom!" he thought in alarm, but that isn't what happened. Instead, Alice took another step forward, right up to Stanley, who had to back off again, almost tripping over in the process.

"Go!" she shouted.

He stared at her for a moment, then spun around and strode off toward his truck. Over his shoulder he shouted, "I'm not forgetting this, you bitch, you and your liar of a son."

Climbing up into the high cab, he slammed the door shut and fiddled with the ignition. The red beast's engine burst into life, its four headlights flooding the small yellow house with light. For an instant, Alice was reminded of a dragon, its eyes ablaze. She half expected flames to shoot out between the chromed teeth of its grille as its loud roar shattered the evening peace. The beast quivered, and then, with a clash of gears, it lurched up on its haunches and shot backwards in a rush, toward the narrow road at the end of the drive, just as Nadia Gonzales was driving past.

Nadia was only in her sixties, but she was aging fast and finding that life was becoming far too complicated. Her grandson, Juan, just eleven months old, was in the baby seat in the back of her little Nissan. Her son-in-law had installed it only a week before, and this was the first time she had put the child in it. Darkness had already fallen, and she just could not see a way to secure the straps. "I will just have to drive carefully," she told herself. "After all, it is only a mile and a bit to my house." Nervously gripping the steering wheel, she was on her way home, passing the pretty little yellow cottage with its cloud of bougainvillea, when, suddenly, there was a huge roar and a monster of a truck hurtled backwards out of its drive, right into the side of her car. Goliath kicking David. Her little sedan was hurled up in the air. It landed on its side. The still-moving truck crushed it against the trunk of a tree. The sound of the collision, almost like a clap of thunder, was followed by the screech of grinding metal as the Nissan was destroyed, crumpled like a piece of waste paper before being tossed away. Inside, Nadia was knocked out completely. She could neither move nor make a sound and had no idea what had happened. Behind her, Juan's precious body, now crushed into a lifeless ball, was wedged into the narrow gap between the seats.

From her elevated doorstep, Alice Gates saw the whole thing. She screamed and started to run toward the street, but then stopped and ran back.

Her eight-year-old had not moved. He was staring wide-eyed at the terrifying scene.

"Justin, find the phone. Call 9-1-1 like I taught you. Tell them what happened," she said, before spinning round again and continuing toward the street, where the dragon was still throbbing and growling, presumably its driver still in his place. Behind the truck, pinned against the bole of a tree, was a small gray sedan, crushed almost beyond recognition. Night had fallen and the moon, hiding itself from the deadly scene, hardly helped. Also, the broad tailgate of the pickup was pressed against the car and blocked all view of the interior. Although she could not see inside, Alice was sure that no-one could have survived. All she could do was wait for the flashing blue lights to arrive.

Next day, the accident was the talk of Guerneville. It was Gerald Foster's Open Day at the school, and Alice had various duties to perform. If she failed to show up, he was sure to give her a hard time, however good her excuse. As she drove there with Justin, she wondered about Margaret Emmett and Willie. With Stanley now in custody, it was hard to imagine his wife socializing among the other parents, but she knew that Willie was expected to take part.

As she entered the building she saw Willie's mom, who seemed to be leaving, and called out to her. The two of them were friends in a timid sort of way. After all, Alice didn't have any real friends. She and Margaret had first met when each had a son in first grade, and they had seen each other at twice-yearly parent/teacher events ever since. At that first encounter, each had sensed the other's loneliness, a feeling of isolation arising more from a lack of love rather than of people. Both women were a little shy, having learned that life works better when you don't trust your secrets and feelings to others, and each had a marriage experience which was not to be envied or repeated.

Alice had been free for four years when she first met Margaret, but her memories of life with Ernie were still crystal clear and jagged edged. Willie's mom, on the other hand, was still working for, cooking for, cleaning for, and sleeping with Stanley, which she found soul destroying. The only joy she found in her home was being a mother. Even that had its negative side. Willie was becoming uncomfortably like his dad.

The two women did not meet regularly, and almost never used the phone, so their friendship was tenuous at best. However, they both shopped in the same supermarket, and ran into each other from time to time. When that happened, they would stand and talk about their kids, or whatever was going on in their lives or the community around them. Occasionally they would sit down for coffee in the store's Starbucks kiosk. More than once, Margaret had let off steam, talking about what it was like being married to 'Mr. Right', who had a good job but kept her almost penniless, and whose principal expectations of her related to the bedroom and the kitchen. "Sometimes I wish he would just go away," she had said more than once.

Alice did not respond by talking about her time with Ernie, not because of any loyalty to him but because she feared that talking about Justin's father might somehow force her to talk about Tina's, and that was a firmly closed book. Memories of the brief encounter with Tony were delicious and shameful at the same time: better to not even think about them.

Margaret heard Alice's call and came in her direction. "I have just delivered Willie," she said, "But I just cannot stay, not as things are now."

"Of course."

Margaret said. "I am so sorry about last night. I am sure he shouted at you."

Her friend winced at the memory. "You could say that."

"He accused me of plotting a divorce, and you helping me."

"But that's not true," Alice exclaimed.

"Of course, it isn't."

A moment of silence followed, and a twitch of a smile showed on Margaret's face. "Although the idea has some appeal, I must confess." Then her more somber expression returned. "Still, he should not have come round to shout at you."

Alice observed, "For some reason he thinks I told Justin that you and Stanley were splitting up."

"Which you didn't, of course. And now look at the mess we've got. That poor woman! That tiny baby!" Margaret started to cry: Alice reached out for her and held her in a soft embrace.

"I know," she said.

* * *

Five months passed. Stanley was living at home, on bail and wearing an electronic gadget around his ankle. He was permitted to go to work, but forbidden from leaving the county. Also, a major aggravation, he was not allowed in any establishment which served alcohol, so he was at home almost all the time, miserable and dreading his fate. "The fuckers want to put me away for fifteen years," he said to his wife, "Fifteen fucking years!"

Needing a shoulder to cry on, it seemed natural for Margaret to turn to Alice. Since the accident, the two of them had become closer, looking for each other when they were in town, and even calling one another every now and then in the evening.

* * *

The trial was scheduled for late April. The case was straight forward, with few witnesses. Everyone knew what had happened, and nobody doubted the role that drink had played in it. The conviction for intoxicated manslaughter was assured: fifteen years, maybe out in ten.

Late on the Saturday evening before the trial, Stanley took his massive red pick-up for a final excursion. It roared its way down the Pacific Coast Highway, the hills rising steeply on the driver's left, the cliffs falling to the sea on his right. At one point the road rides high above the sea, with nothing but a wide swath of grass between the pavement and the edge of the cliff. Beyond that, there is a one-hundred-foot drop to the rocks and the incessantly thundering surf, but that could not be seen by the driver in his alcoholic haze. He stared at the grassy patch and the utter blackness beyond it. "The end of the world," he thought. "The end of everything." With a final resolve, he swung the wheel to the right, ramming his foot down hard on the gas. The dragon summoned all of its fury, belched out a terrifying roar, directed the gaze of its electric eyes toward the unseen horizon, and flew off into space.

He was missed that night, in a way, but his wife had her best night's sleep since Thanksgiving and did not trouble to report him missing. Of course, whoever monitors electronic tags would eventually catch on and come round to give her a hard time, but she could truthfully say, "I don't have a clue," and that is what she intended to do.

In the morning she called Alice. "Is there any way I could come round for coffee?" she asked, and soon the pair of them were sitting in the kitchen of the little yellow house while their boys played in the yard outside and Tina was amusing herself with her dolls.

"Are you sure he has gone?" asked Alice.

Margaret replied, "Well, he didn't come home last night, and I just feel he has fled. He has been so dreading the trial. He knows what is going to happen to him. It has made him quite unbearable. One day he has been wild with fury, even hurling stuff around the house at times, and the next he has been really sullen and depressed. It's been really hard, living with him."

"My poor thing," empathized her friend.

"To be honest, if he has gone for good, and I think he might have, I am not going to miss him. Actually, I think I'll be glad."

"What about Willie?"

"I don't know about that. It is weird. When Stan is up, so is he. When his dad gets mad, Willie follows along."

"And when Stanley is depressed?"

"He gets morose as well."

"So how is he handling the prospect of his dad going to prison?"

"Well, I can't quite figure that out. He doesn't say much, just asks questions about the place, where it is, what it is like in there, and so on. As you know, there is a counsellor at the school. She seems to be helping him a bit. When I ask her what she thinks, she says that Willie will be alright. I just don't know if she means it."

Alice fetched the pot and refilled their mugs.

Margaret continued, "One thing I've noticed about Willie. I don't think he has realized how awful the accident was, in terms of Stan being responsible for two people's deaths, I mean. I think he somehow enjoys the notoriety, having his dad in the news, being the center of attention, and that sort of thing."

"And what about you? Have you decided what you are going to do?"

"I think I'm going to leave Guerneville. Go somewhere where people won't keep looking at me and thinking things. I'll probably go and stay with my folks, although I don't know about that. Willie doesn't really get on with them. But until I can get a job I won't be able to afford an apartment, so it will have to do."

Later, when she was leaving, Alice walked her out to her car. She got in and started the engine. Then she wound down the window and called out, "You know, if your boy had not said this would happen, it wouldn't have."

CHAPTER 4

Van Leyden

I was only eight when the dragon went over the cliff. Was I really to blame for what happened? For the deaths of the old lady and her tiny grandchild? Or for Willie's dad's suicide? I have often wondered how my mom felt, when Mrs. Emmett blamed all these things on me and what I had said. What I do know is that my mom never passed the guilt on to me. All she did was tell me to be careful about what I said to other people, and not to make up things about the future. Then she dropped the matter, although for months she seemed sad and troubled, the mother suffering for the sins of her child. How often parents have to do that!

* * *

After Willie and his mom left Guerneville, life went back to normal. Almost normal, that is. One or two of Justin's classmates had noticed the 'No-Dad' incident and realized that something he had predicted actually came true. They started teasing him, asking him to tell such things as who was going to win a Little League game, or whether someone's older sister was going to get pregnant, or if it was going to rain next day. Remembering mother's words, he refused to make predictions for them and they soon lost interest. And when more previews happened, as they did from time to time, he just kept them to himself.

Alice was puzzled by the way her son was developing. Everyone who mentioned him called him 'a nice boy', and she could see why. He was always clean and tidy, polite, and rarely assertive. He always smiled when people spoke to him, a trait inherited from her. He was an unusually quiet child; she could not deny that. The only person with whom he would chatter away endlessly was his sister, whom he clearly adored. From the very beginning, he enjoyed teasing her and making her laugh. At night, Alice would read them stories, and during the day they would play, acting out the stories, dressing up for their parts, building imaginary houses and shops and castles, and generally taking on the world. Theirs was an innocent and happy childhood. Alice bought them a swing and, later, a trampoline, and liked to stand in the kitchen, watching them through the window. It was good to feel that she had brought some happiness into the world by having children.

A few people, principally her parents, remained curious as to who Tina's father might be, but they were never given a clue. For her part, Alice showed no interest at all in men, and the prospect of marrying again was non-existent. Fate had turned her into a single mom and that is what she would remain.

* * *

The months and years came and went in that little yellow house. Justin worked his way through Elementary and Middle Schools, with his sister trailing five years behind. In most respects, he was a very average student, except when it came to art. From the time he picked up his first wax crayon and drew some crooked lines on a piece of paper, he was always content to be left alone with pencils, crayons or paints, and some paper. He did well, of course, in preschool, where such activities are encouraged, but once he entered Guerneville Elementary, with its general curriculum, he began to fall behind. Art was not a major subject there, and the more essential but less visual subjects, such as english and math, did not hold his attention. Quite often, he would covertly doodle on the pages of his workbooks, drawing tiny real-life mages of things he could see around him – a desk, a chair, the partly open classroom door, the chart on the wall. At first, of course, his efforts were rather crude, but they did become more recognizable as time went by. In his last year at middle school he mostly drew people. If he had allowed anyone to look, they would often have been able make a good guess as to who his subject might be. In parent-teacher conferences, Alice would be told things like, "He is really quite smart, but just not too interested," and she would wonder how to encourage him. He progressed sufficiently to keep moving up with the rest of his classmates, but his report card would always say, "Justin could do better."

In due course, he advanced on to El Molino High in Forestville, a fifteen-minute bus ride away, taking his inattentive ways with him. His rather sluggish academic journey continued much as it had at the elementary school until, a month or so into his second year, Justin was enduring a tiresome chemistry lesson. The teacher was Mrs. Juanita Maldonado, a middle-aged lady with a kindly disposition, which she tried hard to hide behind a faux sternness. He was fascinated by her round, olive-colored face, with interesting creases around her eyes and the corners of her mouth, suggesting that she loved to smile, and that, if she had to tell you off, she wouldn't really mean it. For the past three weeks he had studied her during class, and then tried to recall and draw her face when he was home in the evening. The result was definitely a likeness, but he was unhappy with it. Somehow, he could not capture her smile, so he had brought his sketch to school, intending to work on it surreptitiously while she talked about organic compounds and such. At the end of the session, when class was dismissed for lunch, she called him to her desk.

"Were you having trouble concentrating, today, Justin?" she asked.

Avoiding her gaze, he replied, "Not really, Mrs. Maldonado."

"I think you were," she said, sounding more disappointed than cross.

Justin said nothing.

"Look at me, Justin."

He raised his head and saw that she was smiling at him, or trying not to smile. "Which is it?", he wondered.

"I want you to show me," she said.

"Show you?"

"Yes. I know you were working on something while I was teaching, and I don't think it was organics. Show it to me, please."

Embarrassed, Justin put his backpack down and extracted his notebook. He found the page and reluctantly showed it to her. She recognized the image of herself immediately. It covered one entire page and was far from perfect, especially around the mouth, which was blurred where he had been using his eraser, but there was no doubting that it was she. This was the first time Justin had allowed anyone to see one of his sketches, and it made him wriggle with discomfort. The fact that he had been caught, working on it in class, only made things worse. "What is she going to say now?" he asked himself.

Mrs. Maldonado held out her hand and commanded, "Give me the book." Reluctantly, he handed it over. She turned one page, and stared at it, then another, and another, nodding her head as she absorbed what she was seeing. Fortunately, some of the pages were covered with class notes, even chemistry formulae, but there were two other full-page sketches, neither as complete as the one of her, but decently drawn nonetheless and certainly recognizable. One was of a woman who worked in the cafeteria, the other featured Peter van Leyden, the new head of the art department. She finished looking through the book, while Justin stood there, wishing he were somewhere else. She went through the pages a second time, to find the drawing of the art teacher. Showing it to Justin, she asked, "Does Mr. van Leyden know about this?"

He shuddered and shook his head.

"Then I think we should show it to him," she said in a very determined voice, immediately moving toward the door. When Justin did not move, she added, "Come on."

Grabbing his backpack, he followed her into the hall.

Fortunately for Justin, the school maintained a good art department, headed by a recently recruited handsome thirty-five-year-old enthusiast named Peter van Leyden, known throughout the school as PV. He was one of those teachers who saw real promise in almost every child. In Justin he saw near-genius.

They found him in his room, sorting out craft materials. He looked up as they entered.

"Mr. van Leyden," said the science teacher in a rather loud voice, "Have you seen what this young man has been up to?" Without any more words she thrust the notebook toward him.

He looked at it in complete surprise, not immediately saying anything. The other two looked at each questioningly. When he spoke, it was to Justin. "You have quite a gift here, young man."

Trying not to sound as pleased as he felt, Justin replied, "Thank you, sir."

Mrs. Maldonado said, "I am surprised you did not know about that already," which earned the slightly offended reply, "That's because we have not got round to drawing people yet this semester."

Van Leyden looked at his student, holding the book in front of him. "Would you mind?" he asked, and received "OK by me," in reply.

It took him several minutes to study all the drawings in the book. When he was finished, he handed it back to Justin with the words, "These really are very good. How would you feel about letting me work on them with you, maybe after school every now and then?"

The boy's enthusiasm was instant and evident.

"That would be great!" he said, but then another thought occurred. "Although after school might be tricky. I usually ride the bus. Mom would have to come and get me. I suppose I could ask her. She might say OK."

"Why don't you do that, then, and let me know?"

The two teachers looked at each other.

"Thanks for bringing him," said van Leyden, "I do think we have something special here." Juanita Maldonado smiled at him, and then tried to put on her disapproving expression as she looked at Justin. "And you, young man: now you can do your drawing after school, and not during my science class. Got it?"

Alice Gates was delighted that the head of the art department believed in her son's talent, that he wanted to provide one-on-one after school tutoring. She willingly played her part, providing the necessary transport, and the weekly tutorials began, continuing for the remainder of Justin's time at San Molino High.

To Justin, the hour he spent with Peter van Leyden was always the best part of the week. Here was someone who really appreciated his efforts and knew how to encourage, even when his work was not its best. For most of that school year, student and teacher worked together on black-and-white portraits, using pencil and charcoal, progressing on to color only for the final month or so. Week by week, Justin watched his own knowledge and skill grow.

The teacher watched this progress with some pride, thrilled to have a pupil whose natural talent exceeded that of anyone he had previously taught. Leading his protégé to discover and exploit his gifts became close to an obsession. Besides giving Justin undivided attention during the Thursday tutorials, he loaned him books about history's greatest artists, drove him down to the Bay Area on three separate occasions to visit art museums, and tried to develop a friendship with his mother in an attempt to compensate for the absence of a father in the boy's life. For her part, Alice liked the good-looking Dutchman, with his chestnut-colored curls, twinkling brown eyes and broad smile. She did not mind his attentions at all, although romance was on neither of their minds.

The school year ended in early June. PV was leaving town for several weeks. Before he went, he sat down with Justin and gave him some assignments. "I know you love to draw people," he said, "But while I am away, I would like you to sketch places and things instead. Let's see how you get on with landscapes and cityscapes and the trappings of modern life. It would be good to round out your skills a bit."

* * *

On the first Thursday of the new semester, in the middle of August, after school had been dismissed for the day, Justin went along to the art department in search of PV. He carried a large folder containing the work he had produced through the summer. Most of the drawings were in pencil and charcoal, but there were also a couple of painted landscapes and two still life subjects. Mentor and protégé, they spread the work out on a large table. For several minutes, the teacher studied them silently, while the boy stood nervously by.

"Tell me what you think about them," said van Leyden.

"What I think?"

"Yes. How do you feel about your work? Are you pleased with what you've done?"

Justin was embarrassed. "I think so," he said, "But I am sure I could do better."

His teacher smiled warmly.

"Oh, I am sure you will do better one day. We all develop and improve with time, but don't put yourself down. These are all very, very good; quite excellent in fact."

Once again, there was a period of silence as the two of them looked at the work on the table.

"You know, Justin, you are so good at rendering images of things that you can see, I think it is time to have a go at things you cannot see."

"Things I cannot see?"

"That's right. It's like this: a good painter paints what he sees, but a great painter paints what he feels. Study the impressionists, the surrealists, and the modernists. See how their works are far more than plain pictures of things, how they are imbued with feelings. Bright with hope. Gloomy with despair. Gently tranquil or furiously angry. As illogical and confused as life itself. You are going to be a great painter one day, Justin, but first you must learn to paint what you feel. Do you understand?"

"I think so."

"And one more thing. The artist who paints his own feelings into his work can achieve greatness, but the painter who can show, in a portrait, how his subject is feeling … well, he is on the high road to fame."

That conversation was the beginning of a new journey for Justin. It gave him a self-confidence he had previously lacked, and he began to envisage a future as an artist. PV's belief in the young artist empowered him to believe in himself.

The first leg of his new journey was discovering how to paint feelings instead of sights. Initially, his attempts were predictable renderings of nature in its various moods: furiously wild, beautifully tranquil, confusingly chaotic. Later, they became more subtle and more abstract.

His mother, whose choice of artwork usually came in the form of an annual calendar from the National Park Service, was disappointed and mystified. Justin sought PV's advice.

"Just give her time," he suggested, "And never forget, great art speaks different things to different people. Certainly you can tell her what a piece means to you, if you must. But you will do better if you get her to tell you what she sees instead."

"You used to paint such beautiful scenes," Alice once said, pointing at Justin's latest picture. It was a swirl of colors and lines disappearing into infinity. "What am I supposed to make of that?"

He reached out and squeezed her hand. "It is how I am feeling these days," he answered. "Life is a dizzy journey down a tunnel that never ends."

"Well, I suppose that's true," she agreed, a little doubtfully.

For a whole year, the eager pupil concentrated on interpreting experience rather than simply copying whatever he saw. Some of his efforts were successful, others not, but all the way, Peter van Leyden encouraged him to carry on. "You are getting there, really getting there!" he would often say.

During that year, PV forbade his pupil to paint portraits. Of course, Justin did not quite obey him. At home, he worked on a life-size image of his sister, who would never sit still for longer than two minutes, but whom he knew so well that it really did not matter. Then, one Saturday in April, PV showed up unexpectedly on the Gates' doorstep, and Alice invited him in. Although she seemed to avoid men in those days, she had developed a soft spot for him. Justin and Tina wished he would take her out on a date. They thought it would do her good, but it never happened. Anyway, he came into the house, and somehow found Justin his room, working on Tina's picture.

"You know, that is a great likeness," he observed, resting an encouraging hand on the lad's shoulder. "You really have captured some of her cheerful energy." Not a word about not doing portraits!

It was during those months that PV suggested to Justin that he should start listening to music. There had never been much of that in the little yellow house. If Alice had a favorite genre, it was probably 1980's rock, but the radio was rarely on and she did not possess a CD player.

"It is a great non-visual source of inspiration," said the teacher. "Learn to listen, and then paint what you hear."

Time passed by, and he increasingly became a friend to the whole family. He took all three of them to a couple of concerts, one an open-air event on the campus of UC Berkeley, the other a performance by Fremont Symphony in San Francisco. Justin was not sure who paid for the tickets, but they gave him an appetite for fine performances, a preference that never left him. More importantly, they helped him to listen to his own soul, and as he did so his art improved enormously.

Peter had one more musical lesson for his protege that year. Together, they went to a recital at Grace Cathedral in San Francisco.

"No musical instrument has the magnificence and power of a great organ," he said, "And Grace has one of the best there is. It has over seven thousand pipes. In the hands of a master, it can produce the most wonderful sounds you will ever hear."

He was right! Justin had never before heard such soaring crescendos, such thunderous chords, such plaintive echoes. As he listened, with his eyes closed, he saw waves of color and surges of shapes rolling over him. Hearing and feeling and visualizing merged into one indescribable experience. He couldn't wait to go home and try to record it on canvas.

"To paint what you cannot see," his teacher had said. His art underwent a paradigm shift that year.

After the recital, they went to find the organist. PV had known him for years, and introduced him to Justin simply as Mac. Together, they visited the organ. Seated beside Mac on the long bench, Justin was shown the five keyboards, tiered one above the other, the dozens of knobs in ranks on either side, and another whole keyboard made of wooden beams under their feet. He had never seen anything like it, and asked about the knobs.

"We call them 'stops'," Mac explained. "They allow me to press a single key and have the organ play a whole number of notes and chords, or choose what instrument I want the organ to sound like at that time. Look. I'll show you." He pulled some knobs and played a few measures. The sound of trumpets rang out. Then he switched stops and the pipes above them issued a single clear note. "That is a clarinet," he said. He moved his hands to a different keyboard, selected more stops, and delivered the most majestic sound, as if the church was filled with a dozen orchestras.

"One day," thought Justin, "I am going to make music like that."

On the way home, PV and he talked about the performance, shared their responses to the music, and discussed the way their experience might be visualized.

"I had a really good time," Justin said as PV pulled up outside his house. "I really liked your friend, Mac. It's a pity about him leaving."

"Leaving?"

"He is going to take a new job in Washington, DC."

"He is? I didn't hear him say anything about that."

"You didn't?" Justin thought for a moment, then realized he hadn't heard Mac speak about it either. Nevertheless, he knew it was true. That is how many of his previews happened.

PV said, "I think you could be mistaken."

"Probably," Justin responded, regretting that he had raised the matter, and remembering his mother's words: *"Just don't tell people about the future."*

* * *

Justin began his senior year in August 2002. As an art student, he excelled brilliantly, especially when it came to portraits. "Now that you have learned to study the way you feel, it is time to start sensing the thoughts and feelings of the people you paint. If you can figure out what they are thinking about and how it makes them feel, your images will begin to have a depth achieved only by the greatest portrait painters."

While still a high school junior, Justin had begun thinking about college. His grades were good, but not great. He did well in literature and music, and art, of course. Math and science never did hold his attention. Clearly, he was destined for an art school somewhere, or a college with a great art program at least. Alice was reluctant to see him go far from home, and she worried about the cost. Peter van Leyden said he needed to broaden his experience of life in general, not focus too narrowly too soon. As for Justin, he did not know how to choose, and was content to lean on his elders' advice. He just wanted to be an artist.

The three of them compiled a short list of suitable schools, and submitted half a dozen applications, with a preference for the Art Department at the University of California, Berkeley. This appealed to Alice, since it was only a ninety-minute drive from Guerneville and the cost was acceptable. The other five colleges were further away and out of state, which made them much more expensive. PV would have liked to see Justin in some major cultural center like New York or Chicago or Houston, but he rationalized, "Plenty of time when he goes for his Masters." He knew he was going to miss his star pupil, and thought Berkeley at least offered the best possibility for staying in touch.

In September 2003, the three members of the Gates family crammed everything they could into a borrowed SUV to start on the short journey south. PV came round to the house to wave them off.

“By the way,” he said to Justin, “Do you remember my friend Mac, the organist at Grace Cathedral?”

“Sure.”

“Well, he isn’t there anymore. He has moved to Washington.” The teacher paused to see his pupil’s reaction, but all he got was a nod of the head. “You said that was going to happen, didn’t you? What I can’t figure out is how you knew. Mac says even he didn’t know it at the time.”

Justin knew that PV needed an answer, although he hardly had one to give. He shrugged his shoulders and said, “I cannot explain it. I just knew.”

CHAPTER 5

Emmy

Berkeley was a whole new world to Justin. In his eighteen years he had probably not left the Russian River valley more than twenty times, apart from days on the beach at Jenner. The only beds he had ever slept in were in the Guerneville cottage or his grandparents' home near San Diego. University life was an eye opener. The crowded campus throbbed with the intense energy of thousands of eager teenagers, freshly liberated from parental controls, as they rushed around sorting out their academic and social commitments. He did his best to join in, but it wasn't easy. In addition to everything else, there was so much noise: youngsters calling out to one another or just talking too loudly, so as to be heard above the hubbub, and music blaring out of every second dorm window. Justin wondered if he would have done better at a smaller college in a less progressive city or state.

Being six feet tall, and weighing a hundred seventy pounds, Justin stood out among the freshmen of his year. He had straw-colored hair combed straight back, and bright blue Paul Newman eyes that looked at others fearlessly, as well as a jaw that was firm but not too square, and a warm, friendly smile. People noticed him, especially girls.

During that first year Justin lived in a dorm apartment with two other students. Each had his own study-bedroom. There was one bathroom, a small kitchen and a communal area where they ate and socialized. Initially, his roommates were Allan, a Mormon from Utah, who had proven Anglo-Saxon roots, and Shahid, a gentle-natured Muslim from Pakistan. Even though his roommates had good intentions, they did not get on too well. This was chiefly Allan's fault. He denied being a racist, but it was there, deep inside and eradicable. Also, he had a church-driven need to talk about his religion whenever he could. Shahid, on the other hand, managed his faith by shutting himself in his room for prayer, several times a day. Justin, of course, had no religious views. Until high school, the main influencers in his life were his grandparents, nominal Episcopalians who never went to church, and his mom, who had no interest in spiritual things at all. In high school he had been much influenced by Peter van Leyden, whose enthusiasm for medieval and renaissance art might have suggested him to be a Roman Catholic, if anything at all, but he never spoke about such things. He regarded the Church as God's gift to humanity for the sponsoring and preservation of art. Nothing more. In the young artist's eyes, these four adults were all kind and decent people who did not need to be improved by religion, so why should he?

At Berkeley, he did his best to get along with both roommates, but an uncomfortable tension quickly developed between them, due to their religious differences. This led Justin to look for social life elsewhere. He found it, standing in a cafeteria line, next to a tall, dark haired girl named Adriana, a second-year ceramics student from Minnesota, who had a gift for making friends. She invited him to bring his tray to her table and "meet some guys." There were two boys, both sophomores, who were studying geology and had serious passions about climate change, and a freshman, who was majoring in American History which he hated and was already talking about switching, but he did not know to what. And then there was Emmy.

Until the move to Berkeley, Justin had only known the small-town girls among whom he grew up. They were schoolmates and playmates, friends of course, but nothing more. Along with the boys, they came to his parties, and he went to theirs, hardly aware of their sexuality or the promise of an intimate relationship. He enjoyed the company of several but was fascinated by none. The girls in Berkeley were different. Each of them was a stranger who came from an unfamiliar background and usually spoke with a surprising accent. They seemed, without exception, to be more outgoing and assertive than the girls back home, a fact he found quite unsettling.

Emmy's given name was actually Amelia, which she forbade anyone to mention. "Call me Emmy, or just Em," she said. She was a sophomore, studying to become an architect, and Justin was attracted to her from the start. He had not gone to Berkeley looking for romance. That prospect had hardly entered his mind. However, when Adriana introduced Emmy to the group, over a pizza lunch one Saturday, he liked her instantly, finding her easy and interesting to talk to. She was a petite and lively redhead, her hair a blaze of ginger curls, always cut short and usually a little wild. Her face was freckled, her eyes green, her nose cute and her smile infectious. He could not resist drawing a portrait of her, without telling her, and hanging it in his room. They were soon spending a lot of time together, that first semester, never running out of things to say. She had a cute way of listening, her head tilted to the left, and a slight smile on her lips. They became good friends without rushing into anything more serious. It was she, more than anyone, who helped him become at home in the urban chaos of Berkeley.

At Thanksgiving, Alice drove down to collect her son and take him back to Guerneville. He realized that he had been too busy on campus to miss the quieter life of home, but it was good to be back. He enjoyed seeing familiar scenes and faces and catching up with old pals. Being home was a treat, not least because of his mother's cooking, which had never tasted so good. Berkeley offered nothing like it. Yet, while everything in his hometown *looked* as it always had, few things *felt* the same. Justin realized that he had changed. He was no longer the country boy he had been three months before. He had already become a stranger in the place called home. As he tried to explain this to his mother, she said something like "Of course, darling," but clearly did not understand. Even Peter van Leyden, who had been his guiding star for the last four years, was that no longer. Justin had discovered that the universe is full of stars.

* * *

When Justin and Shahid returned to college, they found that their roommate had vanished. There was no sign of him or his possessions, not even a note to say 'goodbye'. Enquiries at the office confirmed that he had moved out, and someone else was on his way in. A few days later, the new arrival presented himself, a twenty-six-year-old international student named Nehal Agarwal, who had come directly from Mumbai, India, where his parents were important in business and civic circles. His accent was extremely strong, but his English was perfect, and he was handsome. Girls would glance at him more than once, taking in his near six feet stature, slim frame, easy flowing movements, and ready but gentle smile. To those who did not mind his race he was an excellent subject for their adventurous and romantic dreams. Like Allan, Nehal had firm religious beliefs, but he was happy to keep them to himself. It took Justin some time to figure out that he was neither a Muslim, nor a Hindu, nor a Buddhist, and he was certainly not a Christian. Yet, he was the kindest of men, the most patient and forgiving person that Justin had ever met, and someone who seemed to think that judging others harshly was a sin. Like Shahid, he liked to close his door and practice his faith in private. In his case, however, his spiritual nourishment came through meditation rather than reciting prayers or reading a book. It was he who taught Justin the basics of Yoga and the inner life, tools which helped to deepen the powers of perception that would eventually help to make him famous. As time passed, the three roommates developed a triangle of friendship which was to survive their four years at Berkeley and many more.

For Justin, the best thing about UC Berkeley was definitely Emmy. They spent hours and days together, and he unfolded himself to her in a way that surprised even him. But one thing remained hidden: his gift for having unexplained, unexpected glimpses into the future. "Don't tell people …." his mother had said. However, during his second semester, he began to feel a need to open up. He wanted to share this last, important part of himself with the girl he was coming to love. He chose an evening walk in the park to broach the subject.

"Em," he said, looking down at her, "Do you believe in fate?"

"Fate?" she echoed, surprised at this turn in their conversation.

"The idea that we can't control what happens to us."

"I don't think I believe that," she said.

"But don't you think that what happens tomorrow is determined by things that happen today."

"Well, I suppose that's true, in lots of cases anyway," Emmy answered. "But many things happen by accident, don't they? Silly things, like tripping up on the edge of the sidewalk, or losing your key. What about sudden, more serious things, like losing one's temper or having a wreck? Think about it. No-one sets out to run a red light, but sometimes they do, and the results can be catastrophic. You know that."

"So, you think that some events in life are purely random. That they couldn't be foreseen."

"Isn't it obvious?" Emmy looked up at her boyfriend. "Why are you asking these things, Jus?"

He studied her face, with its ever-present smile and honest, wide-open eyes. Her affection for him was plain, and it moved him.

"It's like this, Em," he began. "Everything that happens is caused by something that has already happened. And that cause is itself the result of one or more other happenings. So life is a chain of related events. If we were really super-smart, we could see this pattern, and figure out where it was going to take us in the future. Nothing is truly random."

"What about you and me meeting?" she asked. "Wasn't that random, a kind of accident? Didn't we both just happen to turn up at the same place at the same time? No one planned it, as far as I know, although I suppose Adriana might have been fixing us up. I hadn't thought of that. But she didn't invite me that day: I just decided to come."

"An accident?" reflected Justin. "It may have been. But even accidents have causes."

She wrinkled her nose at the thought. "What about the coin toss at the start of a football game? No-one knows which way the thing will fall. They just can't."

"It does seem that way, but a simple coin toss is actually a very complicated event, the result of all sorts of forces working together. If someone was clever enough and knew everything, there might be a way to predict the outcome."

"How?" she responded skeptically.

"Well, how the coin falls depends on which way up it is to start with, with what force it is flipped, how strong the wind is, and so on. If some genius physicist knew all those things, he might be able to calculate the number of spins the coin would make and which way up it would land. The fact that you and I aren't clever enough to do the math, doesn't mean it could not be done. Then the result would be quite predictable."

Emmy thought quietly for a moment. The evening was cooling. She grabbed Justin's arm and worked her way under it. He held her as tight as their walking would permit, until they rounded a corner and found a wooden bench. By unspoken agreement, they sat down. Emmy was ready to change the subject, but not Justin.

"So, you don't believe we can see the future?" he persisted.

"I take it you do," she replied.

"In a way, yes, I do."

Frowning with concentration, Emmy said slowly, "It is all very unsettling."

"Unsettling?"

"Yes, unsettling. It means that everything which is ever going to happen to me, to us in fact, is already planned."

"It's true," Justin conceded. "And lots of people know it. They give it names like karma, or fate, or destiny."

"So, you believe in predestination, do you?"

"Of course."

"Even whether you and I finally make it together."

"Well, yes: but since neither of us knows the answer, we have to go on living, making the best choices we can, in the hope that things will work out the way we want."

“I want them to work out for us, Justin,” she said, stretching up to give him a kiss.

* * *

Emmy had one thing that Justin lacked: a small blue Ford, of which she was very proud. In it, they traveled to San Francisco, to visit art galleries (for him) and photograph buildings (for her) and once drove up the coast to the Oregon border, just for the fun of it. One cold weekend they camped in Yosemite National Park, somehow cuddling up to keep warm but not touching each other sexually. They laughed about that afterward. “It was a near thing,” confessed Emmy, at which Justin merely smiled.

Easter arrived. Through occasional emails and phone calls, Alice had learned that her son had a girlfriend, and she wanted to find out more. “Why not bring her here one weekend?” she asked. So, on Good Friday, the two of them drove the seventy-five miles to the yellow cottage with its canopy of red flowers, and Justin presented Emmy for inspection. If either of the young people was nervous, it did not show, but Alice was clearly tense. Her son had been gone for seven months, and she still missed him. Was this bright, intelligent, and energetic girl going to further the distance between them, she wondered.

Tina, now in High School, grabbed her mother’s arm while the others were outside. “Isn’t she fun?” she said eagerly, “Don’t you just love her?” Alice forced herself to agree.

The Gates’ home did not have a guest space. That weekend, Justin slept on the couch, allowing Emmy to have his room. Alone in that unfamiliar place, she studied the framed photographs on the top of his desk, the row of model windmills on a shelf above the door, and the panoramic landscape bearing his signature which hung above the bed. She even peeked in his closet and stuck her head under his bed. Her boyfriend seemed to be neat and tidy and not interested in accumulating things just for the sake of it. She liked that. Eventually, having learned all she could, she climbed into bed, snuggled under the covers, and wished he was there.

After the visit, on the way back to Berkeley, Emmy glanced at Justin and said, “Well, now that I have met your family, don’t you think it is time you met mine?”

He grinned at her. “Are you sure they could stand it?”

“O yes! They are great people. You will love them.”

“How many of them are there?”

"Just three: my mom and dad, and Grandma Laura. She's the really special one; not that I don't love my parents to death, because I do, but they were always busy when I was small, and she pretty much raised me. She is the loveliest person I know."

Justin responded, "Lucky you, but lucky her too, I think."

* * *

The O'Briens lived in the middle of a subdivision on a steep slope outside Carson City, Nevada. The drive from Berkeley normally took five hours, but Justin and Emma had decided to visit on Memorial Day weekend. They started out on Saturday at seven in the morning, took one break for almost an hour, and arrived just before two.

Emma's father, Ian, was the only child of a cheerful flight instructor from California, who had been in Britain in 1946, helping to end the war. During a weekend leave in London, he and his friends visited a pub. The barmaid who served them had good looks, quick wits, and abundant energy. She seemed able to handle six or more customers at once. For the American, love struck at first sight. Within two months they were married and on their way to a life in the New World. Using a G.I. Loan, the young couple bought a small, struggling motor repair shop in Carson City. They moved into a rented duplex and started working on their version of the American Dream. In due course, they grew their business, bought a house, and raised a child, a boy they called Ian. He grew up, as energetic and cheerful as his father, destined to inherit the family business. When he was twenty-five he married a nurse from the local hospital, named Mindy. In their turn, they had just one child, a daughter whom they named Amelia, a moniker she came to hate.

"Emmy, darling!" exclaimed Mindy, rushing out to meet the youngsters as they pulled into the drive. "We are so thrilled you have come." She flung her arms round her daughter in a tight embrace. Emmy kissed her mother's cheek and struggled free. Panting, she reached out for her boyfriend's hand. "Mom, this is Justin. Isn't he gorgeous?"

Mindy O'Brien stepped back to get a better look. "He certainly is!" she agreed. Then, smiling broadly, she stepped forward and held out her hand. "Justin, you are so welcome to our home."

Glancing at Emmy for encouragement, he pulled her mother to him in a quick, awkward hug. "So pleased to be here," he said. "Any mother of Em's is bound to be someone special."

Mindy beamed at him and then at her daughter. "Let's go inside and meet the others."

There were only two others, Emmy's dad, Ian, and Mindy's mother, Laura. They found the latter in the kitchen, preparing lunch. To see the three women standing together was remarkable: three red heads with descending heights, Laura being taller than Mindy who was taller than Em. Each of them had the same slender figure, a matching oval face, freckles, and green eyes. Mindy moved with similar impatient energy as her daughter, but Laura seemed to be feeling her age.

Once Justin had been introduced and hugged again, Mindy asked, "Where's that husband of mine?" to be answered by a cheerful Irish voice, "Right behind you, dear."

Ian, Emmy's father, walked in through a door that led to the garage. He looked at Justin and said, "Well, I guess I know who you are," and waved a pair of greasy hands in the air. "You will have to excuse these," he said. "I'll just finish up and be in to greet you properly." Then he was gone again.

"That's my man," sighed Mindy happily, "Always up to something. By the way, I am Mindy and he is Ian."

It was a happy weekend. On Sunday, all five of them piled into Ian's SUV and drove thirty miles to Virginia City, a famous relic of Nevada's silver mining days. In the late 1800's it had been the wildest and most successful boom town in the area, populated by all the characters with whom the Wild West movies have made us familiar. Sixty years later, with the mines worked out, there were few fortunes to be made anymore, and the city was more-or-less abandoned. Add on another thirty or forty years and tourism started to revive the place, bringing people to wander the streets and hang out in the saloons, where liquor flowed once more and people relived their dreams of gunslinging cowboys, bawdy showgirls, and the rest.

Memorial Day that year was on May 31st, two days before Justin's birthday. The family and their guest stayed at the house, avoiding the crowds and the worst of the heat, lazing around under an awning, and cooling off in the pool. In the evening, the women prepared a salad of greens and avocados and fruits, and Ian grilled two racks of ribs. Out of nowhere, it seemed, Mindy and Laura produced a decorated cake, and everyone sang "Happy Birthday".

* * *

The young people had decided to return to school on the Wednesday. Em was busy organizing things with her mother, and Justin spent time, out of their way, chatting with Laura. When everything was ready, they got into the Ford and set out, with Emma at the wheel. She avoided the interstate and chose Highway 50, heading into the mountains.

"Are we going somewhere special?"

"We are," was the proud reply.

Reluctant to spoil her surprise, he replied simply, "That's nice."

Em glanced at him. "It's your birthday treat."

"You really are something," he said, and she threw him a happy smile.

After a while they topped the mountain at Spooner Summit and began the long drop down to Lake Tahoe, the deepest and most beautiful lake in America. Although Justin had lived in Northern California all his life, he had never been there before.

"You are right," he said, gazing at the wide blue water and the surrounding crust of snow tipped mountains. "This is amazing."

They pulled off the highway into a rest area and got out to stretch their legs and take in the view. The word stunning does not describe it. They were both overwhelmed.

Emmy hooked her arm though his and gave it a squeeze. "Everyone should have a moment like this," she said dreamily.

A slight breeze disturbed the surface of the lake, the ripples sparkling in the sun as if some lavish cosmic jeweler had covered it with diamonds. The emotional impact of the scene, combined with his feelings for Emmy, left Justin speechless. He pulled her round to face him, encircled her with his arms, and lost himself in the divinest of kisses.

Back in the car, she explained that her mother had packed them a picnic lunch, "Enough to feed a thousand, I think," she said.

"Where shall we eat it?" he asked. "Down by the lake?"

"Ah! That is part of the treat," she replied, and would say no more.

They drove down the long incline to the lake, and turned right to follow the shore for a few miles, before cutting off to the right, climbing a steep road back into the mountains. A few more turns, and they came to stop in front of a log cabin, built onto the hillside, with a view across the treetops toward the lake.

"Here we are," said Emmy in a satisfied voice, switching off the engine and applying the brake. "Come and make yourself at home." Grinning mischievously, she exited the car, skipped up the steps onto the front porch, produced a key from somewhere, and opened the door. Her boyfriend was still standing by the car, unanswered questions running around his brain and probably showing on his face. "Come on," she urged, and disappeared inside.

It turned out that the cabin had been an O'Brien refuge since her parents were young. "Dad and Granddad built it with their own hands," she said.

Without hurrying, they collected the food from the car and a couple of chairs from inside the cabin, and lunched on the porch, enjoying the incredible view. They feasted on salmon salad and chardonnay, with a great array of accompaniments, until they could take no more, and then lapsed into a comfortable silence. They both wanted to say important, intimate things, but weren't sure how to begin. Eventually, Em stood up held out her hand. Justin stood to take it. "And now I have a real birthday present for you," she said.

She led him into the cabin and made him sit on the edge of the bed. Standing close, but just out of reach, she looked directly into his eyes. He had the impression that, although she was smiling, she was trying to look solemn. For Justin, it was an unforgettable moment. How incredibly beautiful she looked, her ginger curls framing her happy face: his own personal sun shining down on him. She was wearing an apple green skirt, straight and short, with a pattern of cream leaves on it. Above that she had a simple cotton shirt, color matched to the leaves. He reached out his hand, but she declined it. Instead, she started to slowly undo her buttons, amused by his reaction as she slipped out of the shirt and dropped it to the floor. She wasn't wearing a bra.

"I told you I had a birthday present for you," she said.

He responded without thinking, removing his shirt, and standing up to pull her against him.

They spent the afternoon in that cabin, and all that night, and much of the next morning, and arrived back in Berkeley at least a day later than they should have. But Tahoe had changed everything, and it just did not matter.

* * *

The following Saturday Emmy and Justin were having pancakes in a student hangout, just off campus. Semester was over for many students, and the place was half empty. They sat by the window and watched what was going on in the street. Suddenly, Em said, "Did you like my family? Really, I mean?"

"You know I did."

"What did you think about my mom?"

"I thought she was lovely. Intelligent and open hearted. Everyone should have a mom like her."

Emmy bit her lip.

"What's bothering you?" Justin asked.

"She may have seemed lively and vivacious to you, but you don't know her like I do. She put on her best front for you, for my sake too, but when you weren't in the room she lowered the façade. She is worried about something. Really worried, I think. I asked her about it, but she wouldn't answer. I asked Dad about it, too, but he told me to ask her, which meant there is something. I even asked grandma, but she wouldn't help. Looking back, I think there was a big secret that none of them wanted to share. That is not normal in our family. Something isn't right, and I don't know what it is. They would not tell me."

He didn't know what to say, because he knew the answer. While under the O'Brien's roof, Justin had one of his previews: he knew what was bothering the family, but didn't know how to tell Emmy, or even if he should.

Emmy noticed his silence, of course. "What's going on, Jus? Do you know something I don't? If so, I need you to tell me."

"What could I know that you don't?" he asked, trying to avoid the issue.

That just made her more suspicious.

"I think you do know something. I can see it in your face. Tell me! I need to know."

Her eyes were open wide. Very wide. She was staring at him in desperation.

"Justin, please!"

With a huge inward sigh, he decided to tell the truth. Later, he realized his whole life might have worked out differently if he had lied, but that was something he could not do.

"Look, Em, I imagine your mom didn't tell you because she doesn't want to worry you."

The pitch of Emmy's voice rose, "About what?"

"About Laura, about your grandmother."

"What about her?"

"It seems she has a brain problem, one that can't be cured."

She looked at him, horror stricken.

"What do you mean, a brain problem?"

"I am not sure I know. An aneurism, I should think."

Her voice suddenly hoarse, Em said, "You can't be serious." Then, before Justin could answer, she added, "Who told you? If they wouldn't tell me, why the hell would they tell you?"

He could feel her horror turning to anger, and reached out to lay his hand on her wrist.

"No one told me, Em."

"Then how can you say it?" She relaxed little, finding comfort in her own next words. "You can't possibly know something like that if no-one told you. You must be just guessing. Why would you guess something like that?"

"Because, sweetheart, I have this gift for knowing things, things that are going to happen."

Emmy stared at him. "Things that are going to happen?" she echoed. "Are you saying that something is going to happen to grandma." Light dawned. "O God! You are saying she's going to die!"

He gripped her wrist, not wanting to let her go, in any sense of the word. "I am so sorry, my love. I just thought you would want to know."

She pulled her hand away and stood up, clumsily and noisily. "If my parents thought I shouldn't be told, who are you to say anything?" There were tears in her eyes as she looked down at him. "I know I love you, but at this moment I think I might hate you too."

Justin stood up himself and stepped toward her, but she pushed him away. "Leave me alone. I need to be alone." She moved toward the exit. "I'll call."

Emmy did not call; not for three days. Justin ached to hear from her. He sent her several emails, attempting to be understanding and reassuring, and trying to avoid applying pressure, but all he wanted was to hear her voice. Finally, early on Tuesday, she rang. Without preamble she said, "Jus, we need to talk. Can we go to breakfast?" Fifteen minutes later he was waiting for her at their usual spot. The blue Ford came to a stop, and he got in. She took off again, without saying where they were going.

"I've missed you," he said.

"And I have missed you: I really have, but I've been having a hard time with this."

They drove a mile in silence. Then Emmy looked at Justin. "I need to ask you something. Do you know when grandma is going to die?"

He shook his head. "I have no idea, although I might expect sooner rather than later…."

"Whatever that might mean," said Emmy, completing his thought for him.

Another few minutes passed. Justin had decided to let her take charge: he would simply be as understanding and supportive as possible. They pulled into a parking place in front of a brassy looking diner which he had never seen before.

"This'll be good. At least it's quiet," she explained. They went in, found a window booth, and ordered coffee.

"I called mom, you know," said Em.

"I thought you would."

"I asked her if it is true. She was horrified that I had found out. It seems that grandma was diagnosed about a month ago. The doctors say her condition is fragile. They expect the aneurism to burst, which will be fatal, but they don't know when. She gets awful headaches, but that is the only warning. According to mom, she is being very brave about it, determined to go on as normal. I asked why no-one told me, and she said grandma wants it that way. Insists on it, actually. It seems she only wants to see me as my normal cheerful self. She wants to remember me with a smile on my face. Mother said, 'Your happiness is the light of her life. She does not want to watch that light go out'."

Emmy picked up her napkin and wiped a cheek.

"Mother wanted to know how you found out. She is quite sure Grandma herself didn't let on, even though we all know you were alone with her while we made the picnic. And, to be truthful, Jus, I think you owe me an explanation as well."

Justin sighed, reached across the table for her hand, and looked into her eyes. God! How he loved her!

"It is almost impossible to explain," he began, "I have what I call previews. I sometimes just discover I know about things that are going to happen. For example ….." He went on to tell her about Willie Emmett, and Mac, the cathedral organist, and a couple of other instances. He finished with a shrug of his shoulders. "I don't know what else to say. These things just come to me. I don't know when they are coming or why they do."

"So, when did you have this preview about grandma?"

"When I was talking to her, on the morning of my birthday."

Emmy shook her head in disbelief. For what felt like an age, she sat, silently staring out of the window. Finally, she turned back to look at her lover.

"If I ask you what is going to happen to us, to me and you, will you have a preview and tell me that?"

Justin shook his head. "You know, although I have had previews about all sorts of people, I have never had one about myself. Why? I have no idea. Perhaps I will figure that out one day, but probably not today."

"If I asked you to name the teams for the next Super Bowl, could you do that?"

"No."

"What about the winner of the next Presidential Election?"

"Not that either."

"Maybe those are too far from home, so to speak. How about the winning numbers in next week's lottery?"

"Not a chance."

"What can you tell me, then?"

"Well, I don't know. I cannot schedule a preview, nor even specify a subject. But I can tell you, my insights are always related to people, people that I have met and spent some time with. So, lottery numbers are out, as are sports games and other things like that."

"But if your previews relate to people you spend time with, well, who have you spent more time with in recent months than me? Why can't you see our future? Or just one tiny bit of it, even?"

"For some reason, these things are never about people I am really close to. Perhaps it is like looking at a building or a large work of art: sometimes you can be too close to see the whole thing."

They continued to talk for a while, getting nowhere. They drank their coffee and forgot to order food. Eventually, Emmy looked at Justin and said, “Anyway, the thing I want to tell you is that I am going home. I need to see grandma again. If I don’t get to hug her at least one more time, I will never forgive myself. And don’t worry, I will pretend I know nothing: she will only see the brightest, most cheerful face I can manage.”

“How long will you be gone?”

“Who knows, Justin?” and adding, bitterly, “Obviously not you.”

* * *

A few days later, Emmy called. “Hi, Jus. Are you missing me?”

“You know I am. How are things over there?”

“They are good. Grandma is behaving normally, except when she has those dreadful headaches. And if she has figured out that I know, she hasn’t said so. She still calls me her little ray of sunshine, even though I am twenty-two.”

“Can I come and see you. I would like to see her too.”

“I don’t think you should do that, although I would love to see you myself. I am not at all sure how mom and dad would handle it. Mother still hasn’t forgiven you for telling me. She would be bound to worry how else you might upset things.”

So the lovers stayed apart, and several more weeks passed, until Laura O’Brien fell from her chair during dinner. The emergency services were summoned, but they did not arrive in time.

“I am going to come to the funeral,” said Justin, when Emmy called to give him the news.

“I am not sure…” she began to reply, but he cut her off.

“I shall be there, Em. I should be proud to stand beside you, to be there for you. But if you prefer, I will be in the back, out of sight.”

She sighed and accepted his plan. “O.K. I will do my best to get mother cool with the plan, but you cannot stay at the house. We already have more relations coming than we can handle.”

* * *

About a month after the funeral, Justin drove himself to Tahoe once more. His mother had taken over her parents’ Buick, and he now had her Chevvy. It was old, and looked it, but it worked. It had driven a hundred and ten thousand trouble free miles: he was sure it would make it to Carson City.

Emma and he had stayed in touch, mostly by email, although there were a couple of phone calls. His need to meet was probably greater than hers. She had so many other emotional mountains to climb at that time. Anyway, they decided to get together at the cabin, it being private and away from her parents, and holding out some hope of reviving their romance. She brought the picnic and got there first. Everything was set out on the porch, exactly as before. When Justin arrived, she ran down the steps to meet him, flung her arms around him, and squeezed until he could hardly breathe. She seemed to be trying to wring something out of him, something that wouldn't come. Of course, they kissed, the kiss of lovers who are longing for passion rather than bursting with it, and then sat down to enjoy the meal and the view.

Inevitably they talked about the future, but managed to do so without talking about *their future*. His prospects were pretty simple: three more years at UC Berkeley, and then on to another Art School for a master's degree. "Peter wants me to go to Rice, in Houston. It is a fine school, and he has great contacts there, so that is probably what I'll do."

Emmy said she was going to take a semester off, stay at home with her parents, and then maybe continue at a different college.

"You'll not come back to Berkeley, then." Justin's disappointment was plain.

She looked at him directly and replied, "We'll see. Maybe I will, but I don't think so."

Making these declarations seemed to clear the air. They were able to talk more easily about their families and about what we had been doing through the summer. Finally, the meal over, Justin rose to his feet and pulled her gently to her feet, intending to lead her inside, but it did not work out. She smiled at him sadly and shook her head. "I don't think so."

After that, they both knew that the gossamer threads of their love had somehow faded away. He looked at what had been the sunshine of her face and saw what her grandmother had feared: the deep sadness of losing the one we love.

Emmy and Justin remained friends, but were never close again. Emails and birthday cards measured the passage of time, but that is all.

CHAPTER 6

Shivangi

Justin was devastated by the loss of Emmy. She was the first person to whom he had felt really close. Her constant cheerfulness had been his daily tonic. He had been able to talk to her about almost anything and let off steam when the need arose. Together they speculated endlessly about the natures of art and science and life, laughing at the same things and hating the same people, mostly politicians and other bigots. She was the perfect complement to his introverted self.

Nehal, his newer roommate, seemed to understand. Without any discussion, he became attentive to Justin's moods, turning out to be a sensitive listener and a thoughtful observer of campus life. Inevitably, he asked what happened to Emmy. He asked it in a kindly manner, a pal trying to help a pal, not a gossip trying to intrude. In answering, Justin revealed his special talent for predicting the future. Of course, he begged Nehal not to tell anyone about it, but his friend had his own relationships and issues to contend with, and at least one leak did occur.

Time moved on. Nehal and Justin continued to dorm together. One day, early in their final year, Nehal came up with an invitation. He had a twin sister named Shivangi, which means beautiful. She was studying at UCLA, majoring in a social science of some sort, and he wanted to visit her. As tactfully as he could, he wondered if Justin might drive the two of them down to Los Angeles in the Chevvy.

"You will like her," he said, "She is really a neat person. Of course, I might be a little prejudiced."

The idea of a weekend away from Berkeley appealed to Justin, and he readily agreed. Arrangements were made, the day came, and they set out. The direct route south largely followed Interstate 5, a boring and tiresome drive. Their conversation roamed over various subjects, and there were long periods of silence, until Nehal began to talk about his family. He was the oldest son in a very rich, high-caste Indian dynasty. Their wealth was derived from a number of trading companies in Mumbai, founded there long ago while that city was still called Bombay, while Queen Victoria was on the British throne and had the title Empress of India. Nehal's father was the grandson of the company's founder, and its current chairman. His dream was for his oldest son to follow in his footsteps, and he wanted him to be prepared. After much thought and, doubtless, prayer, the young heir apparent had been sent to California to study American ways of doing business.

Several generations of Agarwals lived together in a large compound in Mumbai, hemmed in by high walls and strong prejudices. Nehal was the first family member to be allowed out of the country, and that only because of the business. For the rest of the boys, there were plenty of schools and universities in India. As for the girls, well, it was thought they did not really need degrees. Husbands were a more urgent requirement, at least in the eyes of the parents, but the younger women strained at the leash. In particular, Shivangi had always been close to her twin brother, and found life without him very distressing. Just as Nehal was the favorite son, so was she the number one daughter. From the day that her brother boarded his plane for California she begged, reasoned, and sulked, until her father gave in. She could go too.

The boys arrived in LA on a Friday afternoon. They checked into a Holiday Inn Express and called Shivangi. She came over, almost immediately, by taxi. The moment she walked through the hotel doors Nehal let out a small gasp of delight and sprang to his feet. He rushed forward, his face bright with the biggest smile Justin had ever seen, and pulled his sister to him in a hug to end all hugs. Smiling in return, she pushed him back, looked him up and down, and, with obvious pleasure on her face, said, "My, how my little brother has grown!"

Nehal was embarrassed. He turned to look at his friend, and said, "She only calls me that because I am her oldest brother and her twin. I am probably the tallest too. He turned back to look at her again. "It is so good to see you."

It was her turn to glance at Justin, who was still seated.

"And who is this good-looking guy on the sofa?"

"Watch it!" Nehal said with a laugh. Patting himself on his chest, he added, "The good looks are here."

True to her name, Shi turned out to be one of the most beautiful women Justin had ever seen. She was tall and slender, with honey colored skin, jet black hair and deep, soulful eyes. Her mouth was perfect, lips not too wide or full, and she graced herself with a bindi, the red spot on the forehead often worn by Hindu women. Her voice was smooth as silk, and when she moved around in her sari it was as if she were sailing on calm water, not walking step by step on concrete. Incredibly courteous, she rarely interrupted a conversation or raised her voice, but when she did speak she had a firmness of tone which demanded respect.

Her brother apologized and introduced his friend.

"This is my roommate, Justin. He's one of the good guys. We have a lot of fun together, but he is also there to keep me out of trouble."

His sister laughed and said to Justin, "I suppose that keeps you pretty busy," provoking him to look at Nehal and shake his head. "I'll never tell."

The three young people laughed and walked out into the sunshine.

"Let's go for tea and a chance to talk," suggested Nehal, and that became their plan. The three of them piled into the Chevvy and drove into Santa Monica, where they located an Indian Restaurant which Shi knew and said had a good reputation. For more than an hour they drank tea and talked. Mostly, the twins told each other about their comparative lives and experiences in the New World, not forgetting to include Justin whenever they could. Tea-time became dinner-time, and the clock kept turning but they did not notice. Eventually the crowds who had crammed themselves into the restaurant for dinner faded away again, and their waiter started hovering close to their table.

"Good heavens!" exclaimed Nehal, "There's no-one left but us. I do believe they want us to leave."

The account was settled and the trio headed out. The boys took Shivangi back to her lodgings, receiving a promise that she would join them in the morning as soon as she could.

"What did you think of Shi?" asked Nehal as Justin drove them back to their hotel.

"I think she's great," Justin replied, just a little nervously. The truth is, she was as beautiful a young woman as he could imagine, both in appearance and character, but he did not want to focus on that. From the moment his roommate had told him about her, he had feared this might be a set-up. Em was still in his heart, and he did not need any blind dates. Nevertheless, during the following months, Nehal contrived several more meetings between the three of them and watched them closely. In the end, Justin had to speak to him about it.

"Look, Nehal, I am busy trying to finish my degree and am not in the mood for romance. I don't need a girlfriend just now."

"What you mean is, you are still pining for Emmy."

"I'm not saying that."

"You don't have to."

Justin was not the only person to comment on Nehal's match-making effort. As he was taking his sister back to the airport after a visit to Berkeley, she said to him, "I wish you would quit pushing Justin and me toward each other. You know why I can't get interested in him."

"I know he would be a lot better for you than your Indian politician," he retorted.

"But I have been pledged to Aadi since I was nine. Father gave his word."

"Huh! You can escape. You are the light of our father's life. You can twist him round your little finger. He won't force you to marry against your will."

"But it won't be against my will."

"You don't love Aadi. Why marry him?"

"But I will love him. You are becoming too American, brother. Love should be what you do, not what you feel. I will care for him and have his children. In time, I will probably learn to like him."

Nehal shook his head. "I hate to see you wasted on such a guy."

His final push to bring Justin and Shivangi together involved a house party in a rented villa on the North California coast. She invited four of her friends, and he five of his, including his roommate, of course.

"Now, look, Nehal," protested Justin when he received the invitation, but his friend cut him off.

"Just come," he said. "We'll be a great crowd and have a lot of fun. You can spend as much or as little time with Shi as you wish. Besides, the scenery up there is fabulous, and you could do lots of painting."

In the end, Justin agreed to attend.

Those days at Mendocino changed Justin's life, and it was all because of Shivangi. They had liked each other from the time they first met, but she was committed to an arranged marriage in India, and she knew that he could not help comparing her with Emmy. As far as intelligence and culture went, she was brilliant, a star, but she did not provoke the same happy lightheartedness that the young artist had known with his vivacious redhead. Also, she seemed surrounded by an invisible shield of virtue. The thought of approaching her for sexual intimacy seemed out of bounds.

Without speaking about it, Justin and she agreed to draw the line where physical contact was concerned. Once this was accepted, they were able to spend unlimited time together without complications and expectations. Of course, Nehal and his pals, and hers too, could see the pair did have something special going, and they often made suggestive remarks about it, but these were just shrugged off.

The house party was a celebration by eleven young people at the peak of their achievements. Each had either just graduated or come as the partner of someone who had. Each was poised for the next giant leap in life, either into a career or a step further up the academic ladder. Confidence and optimism were in the air. They were an unbeatable generation. This euphoria led to much jovial, occasionally wild, behavior. Shi and Justin hung around together on the fringe of it, observing rather than participating. On the third afternoon, when everyone else was heading for the beach, they decided to stay back.

"Why don't you paint my portrait?" she said. "I think I would like that."

Justin didn't need asking twice. They settled on a location. She would sit on a rock ledge above the beach and stare out to sea. At least, that was the intention, but she chose instead to turn her face toward the artist. As he began to assess her pose, her shape, her grace, her aura, she studied him in return, and he was aware of a strange connection developing between them. He felt that she knew what he was thinking, although he did not know how; and he rather hoped she didn't. He thought her incredibly serene and beautiful. It would be embarrassing if she were to read his mind.

After a while she said, "You remind me of my grandfather."

He replied, "I do?"

She didn't respond at once, and he was busy with his charcoal, so there was a silence. Then she spoke again, "He was a very old man. At least, that's how he seemed to me when I was growing up. Old, and very, very wise."

"And you were old enough to judge his wisdom?" Justin enquired, not intending to be rude.

"Don't take my word for it. He was a Teacher, a Guru, if you like, not in any sort of school, but in the house. All sorts of people came to visit him. He had a special room where they would come and listen to him talk and ask him questions. A lot of people thought him very wise indeed."

Juastin asked what he talked about.

"Spiritual things," she replied. "The meaning of life. Where we come from and what happens when we die. And how we should behave while we are here. He would try to illuminate people's lives for them."

"And I remind you of such a man? I never talk about those things, and people don't come knocking on my door for advice."

"Maybe not now," she said, very seriously, "But one day they will. Nehal told me about your special gift …."

"Which he should not have done," Justin interrupted, a little crossly.

"But he loves you and wants to be your friend. You should not mind." Then she continued her previous thought. "People will come to you because you see things others can't. You know how to listen and hear unspoken words, to watch and see things which cannot be seen, to feel for them in ways that they cannot feel for themselves. People will want to come and sit with you, and let you paint their portraits, in the hope that you will see not only their visible selves, but also the turmoil that is within them, and where it is taking them. You will do a lot of good as time goes by, preparing people for their roads ahead. Indeed, it might be the most important work you will ever do."

Again, Justin was silent. He had stopped drawing, and was staring at her, simultaneously awed and confused. She gave him the sweetest smile, full of understanding. "You know, Justin," she said, "I learn spiritual things through meditation, as I look into myself. You learn them through contemplation, as you look into other people. Very few people can see as deeply as you. You are very special."

Embarrassed, the young artist picked up his charcoal and returned to the task in hand, but he was distracted by what she had said, and could no longer concentrate. After a few minutes, he packed up his things and went to sit beside her on the ledge.

"I should like to meet your grandfather," he said.

With a sad shake of her head she replied, "He is no longer with us, I'm afraid."

They sat silently, watching the waves rolling in on the beach below. Her hand was resting on the stone between them. Very gingerly, he laid his on top of it. She did not push it away, but she murmured his name in a way which said, "Let's not do that."

Was she as sad as he, that their intimacy could only be of mind and heart? He did not know, but he hoped so.

The following day the two of them returned to the ledge, using the portrait as their excuse for not joining the others on a hike into the village. Justin set up his easel and settled into his work, neither of them speaking. He kept looking at the woman before him, trying to trap her serene presence between the layers of his paint. "I will never be able to do her justice," he thought.

As he worked, he found himself thinking about her forthcoming marriage. Nehal had been talking to him about it. Apparently, the man she was supposed to marry had been a boy of twelve when the contract was signed. A dozen years had passed since then. The boy was now a man, and a less-than-admirable one at that. He belonged to a major political family, where ambition and power were more important than truth and justice. He cared a lot about what people thought of him and his prospects, but little about the woman he was to share them with. "He is arrogant and corrupt, and not the least bit suitable for my sister," complained Nehal, words which kept repeating themselves in Justin's brain.

Suddenly, Shivangi said, "Why do you never ask me about Aadi? You and I talk about all sorts of things, and you have shared your memories of Emmy with me, but you never mention the man I am going to marry."

Justin was startled. Was she reading his thoughts? How did she know? What sort of connection was there between the two of them? He laid down his brush and stood up.

"Alright," he said, "Why don't you tell me about him now?"

"What would you like to know?"

"What does he look like? Is he clever? Do you think he is reliable and honest? Most of all, how do you actually feel about him?"

She began to paint a verbal picture, and as it took shape and character, Justin had an uneasy feeling that it was hollow, that there was nothing there. In a strange way, he began to feel that the man she was describing did not exist. Or was it that he was living then, but would cease to exist by the time they were supposed to wed? The sensation was very strong, and Justin was very confused by it. By the time he packed up his easel for the afternoon he was convinced. Shi and Aadi would never be married.

"Justin, you are looking at me rather strangely," Shi said as she climbed down from her ledge and fell into step beside him.

"Oh, am I? I didn't mean to. I'm sorry." Attempting to change the subject, he added, "I have only known you here in California, living the American life. I was trying to imagine you back home in India."

"You will have to come and pay us a visit," she replied. "Then you will know what it is like. Maybe my mother will invite you to the wedding."

"If there is a wedding," thought Justin, but he said nothing.

The house party ended a couple of days later, and everyone went his or her own way. For Justin, parting with Shivangi was hard after a week of such intimacy. He wanted to hold her and say forbidden things to her. At the very end, when they were heading for their cars, she came over to him. In his eyes she saw real sadness and, understanding his desire, she held out her hand. If life had been different, she might have opened the door of opportunity, but it wasn't. Her destiny was sealed. Justin, of all people, should see that. She let him take her hand and pull her toward him. They hugged, with real tenderness but also great uncertainty, and then let go.

Nehal was disappointed that Justin and Shi had found each other, only to let the chance of a future together slip away. He did not try to bring them together again. In any case, Justin was on his way to Houston, while she remained in LA. When her next semester ended, Shivangi packed up the trivia of her Californian life and boarded a plane for Mumbai, ready to surrender herself in marriage to a man she hardly knew.

CHAPTER 7

Houston

When Justin had finished at Berkeley, he left with an excellent degree, a handful of awards, and a host of memories. He also carried with him a dull ache in his heart for Emmy and a sweet but sad memory of Shi. Rice University had offered him a place in its Art History Department, where five years of study and research would earn him a doctorate. After that, there might be a career in the world of museums and art galleries, although he was beginning to dream of a life as a portrait painter instead.

Soon after the Mendocino house party, he loaded his necessities into the back of PV's Chevvy Tahoe, and set out with Peter, Alice, and Tina on a meandering trip across America's southwest. They circled through half a dozen national parks in Utah and Arizona, and followed a twisting route through the splendor of the Rockies into Colorado. Then they sped across the deserts of New Mexico and West Texas to Houston. Along the way, Justin and his mentor roomed together, as did Alice and Tina. The quartet felt and behaved as if they were a complete family. Once in Houston, the two women went sightseeing while PV drove Justin over to the university, with its secluded campus of green spaces and pink brick buildings. They found Registration, located the right dorm, unloaded Justin's goods, and searched for the Art Department in the School of Humanities building.

If Justin's world had expanded when he went to Berkeley, it exploded when he arrived in Houston. Second only to New York for theaters and concert halls, and having over a hundred museums and other cultural venues, his artistic horizons appeared boundless.

From the moment he arrived, Justin really liked the city. Coming from a small country town in Northern California, surrounded by tree covered hills, Houston could have been hard to take. It was huge, seventy miles across in any direction. Two and a half million people lived there. The land was so flat that the only hills were bridges and overpasses. There were twenty thousand miles of roads, many being freeways or similar, and two main airports, which handled tens of millions of passengers a year. In short, Houston was everything that Guerneville was not, and he might have found it repellent, but somehow it was OK.

There were few similarities between UC Berkeley and Rice. The former had forty thousand students, mostly undergrads, whereas there were less than seven thousand in Houston, and most of them were pursuing their masters and doctorates. The Houston campus, set alongside sedate neighborhoods of tree lined streets and solid upper middle-class homes, was greener and quieter than the one in California.

To Justin's delight, the Museum of Fine Art was within easy walking distance. During his first year he spent many hours there, mostly on weekends. When year two began he signed up as a volunteer, and gradually became familiar with the museum's directors. Altogether, he was very pleased with his new life in the Lone Star State. It kept him busy, and he had little need for female company. In fact, during the whole of his time at Rice, he only tried dating twice. One relationship was with a tall, slender, blonde who loved fine music. They went to all the main symphony and grand opera performances for a season. When that was over, so were they. The other was with a cute little librarian, five feet one inch tall and frighteningly full of energy. He knew her for more than a year before giving in to her hints about a date. After that, for three exciting months, they were inseparable, until he realized how exhausted he was becoming and how little art he was doing. Their parting was amicable: she could see that he needed to ease up, which she did not. They woke up together one Sunday morning, had breakfast, kissed briefly, and went their separate ways, Justin to his easel and she in search of another male to consume.

His first year at Rice ended, and he decided to remain in Houston for the summer, but during those months, tragedy struck the Gates family. Back in California, both of Alice's parents died. Mabel went first, taken down by pancreatic cancer. Fordham followed her within a month, probably because he decided to. They had lived together for sixty years, and a widower's life had no appeal. The double bereavement was hard on Alice, but it did occur while school was out, which helped, and Peter van Leyden was very much around for support. Tina was away in Europe, working on a Greek island, and did not come back for the funerals. Justin, of course, was able to make the necessary trips from Texas.

Two blessings arose out of those miserable weeks. When the estate was wound up, Alice had enough money to purchase a modest annuity for life, and her two children inherited the San Diego house, which they sold immediately. Justin used his share to purchase a town house in Sugar Land, a suburb on the southwest side of Houston. He did not know what Tina did with hers.

Another piece of news reached him that summer, which caused him very mixed feelings. An email arrived from Nehal, who was back in the

Mumbai compound under his father's watchful eye. Apparently Shivangi's fiancé, Aadi Arya, had been killed in a road accident, four weeks and one day before their long-delayed wedding. It seemed that the circumstances surrounding the tragedy were unclear, and Nehal thought they were downright suspicious. He promised to explain more at a later date. His sister had taken the news very badly and gone into deep mourning, but he was clearly not so upset. He had never liked the man or the proposed match anyway. The name Arya means 'Honorable'. "If any man was misnamed, it was he," said Nehal in his message.

Justin did not know how to handle the news. He still had the fondest memories of Shivangi. During the Mendocino days they had become so close that they almost surrendered their inhibitions. At least, he had, and he believed the same applied to her. Who knows how the affair might have ended once it had started? It had only been her strength and virtue that kept them apart. She had been pledged to marry a man she did not even like. That was no longer true. He wondered if she was relieved. Was she now free to marry whomever she chose? Would her thoughts turn to him? He didn't know. After several sleepless nights he wrote her a letter, commiserating with her of course, but also hoping it might open a door through which they could travel into a future together. Her reply came about two weeks later. He opened the envelope and read the first words: "My dear Justin," and knew immediately her curtain of restraint was still in place. Further down the page he read, "Who knows where our destinies may lead us, and whether they will cross? Only time will write that story. I don't have anyone here with your gift of seeing tomorrow, and must patiently wait, on my own, to see what happens." In other words, she did not know how she felt, and she wanted him to leave her alone until she did.

The letter was signed, "Your ever-loving friend, Shi."

* * *

Justin spent two years as a full-time student at Rice, followed by three more studying and doing research. He also worked as a part time curator in the museum. Somehow, he found time to paint a couple of dozen portraits and build up a collection of impressionist-style landscapes. At first, the portraits were done at the Art School or in a portrait painting group he joined. The models were either volunteers or poorly paid sitters. Later, people began to learn of his work and give him commissions and he started painting what he called 'real people with fascinating lives'. They came into his studio as strangers, of course, but he soon learned how to put them at their ease. Although there was always conversation, his work required long periods of silence, during which he could study who they were and what they were feeling. Quite often he would get a real conviction about experiences which were coming their way. He usually shared these previews with them, remembering Shivangi's prediction about his life.

Most of those who came to Justin were looking for help with their own lives. However, some wanted to know what was going to happen to somebody else, such as a husband, a child, or a colleague. He would explain to them that he only ever saw into the lives of people who were actually before him. The best he could do was tell them how they were going to be affected by what happened to the other person.

For example, there was Betty. She came to him, asking him to paint her picture as quickly as possible. A lonely widow in her early sixties, wrapped up in too many clothes and hiding behind a great deal of make-up, her insecurities were clear. Justin thought that, dressed more plainly and with fewer cosmetics, she would have cut a striking figure. As it was, she was trying to hide her real self from the world, which was odd for someone who came to have her portrait painted. She explained that lumps had just been discovered in her breasts. She was convinced that she was about to die of cancer. Afraid of being 'gone and soon forgotten', she thought the portrait might work as a permanent and visible memorial. However, it did not take Justin long to foresee that she was going to survive.

"I can't diagnose your lumps for you," he told her, "But I can tell you that you will be alive and thriving next year and for years after that."

"How can you know that?" she asked, urgently clinging onto the new-found hope.

"All I can tell you is that I have a gift for knowing about the future. You can believe me, or not. I wouldn't blame you for doubting, but I promise, you will be able to pick up your phone in one year's time, and two years' time, and maybe more, and tell me that you are still going strong."

"Oh, Mr. Gates!! I certainly hope you're right. You can bet I will be making those calls," she said as she loaded the finished art into her car.

Betty was one of those women who need to talk, to tell others everything about themselves. It was not long before her two children heard of Justin's prediction, and several of her friends. When, two weeks later, biopsy results proved her tumors were benign, there was no holding her back. Justin was being talked about all over town.

Of course, Justin did not have such good news for everyone. Gerald was the middle-aged owner of a troubled real estate company. He had over-borrowed and invested badly. Now he was living in terror that the bank would call in the loans before he could sell the properties, which would have to go for much less than he owed on them, anyway. He did not have time for portrait-sitting, nor any interest in it, but his wife did. A good looking, gold-eyed blonde in her early forties, she bore herself proudly, confident that any rumors about her husband's business were false, and that the bank would never sink his ship. Her fifteen-year marriage had been really good. He had looked after her and spoiled her in every way he could, partly to compensate for their failure to have children, but mainly out of pure love. She looked up to him, trusted him, and could not imagine him as a failure. The state of his business was devastating. His self-confidence had totally collapsed, which was more than she could bear. She looked for ways to boost his morale. As it happened, she attended the same church as Betty, and had learned about the 'Picture Painting Prophet', which is how Justin was being described.

"Perhaps he could assure Gerald that everything will be alright," she thought, and called to make an appointment. Her husband would be horrified at what the portrait cost, but it would be worth it to see his spirits rise and the light come on at the end of his tunnel. The only trouble was that Justin did not see the future in the way she hoped.

"I know how much you want to believe in Gerald and his business, but sometimes our hopes are misplaced," he told her. "They can often prevent us from preparing for a future which cannot be avoided. I don't exactly know what will happen to your husband, but I do know that it is going to demand a great deal of strength and patience from you. You do need to prepare for troubling days ahead."

"Are we going to lose everything?" she asked, on the verge of tears.

"I am afraid there won't be much left." Justin replied.

Justin found the repeated sharing of bad news was stressful. He wished there were more opportunities to tell people that bright days lay ahead. The world, or at least his segment of it, seemed to have far more Geralds than Bettys. Also, his gift was becoming a burden in another way. His phone rang all the time. He changed his unlisted number twice, but it did not help. He received more emails than he could handle, and ended up ignoring them all. Strangers turned up at the door so often that he had to install a security camera and not open the door at times. He would have liked to be a hermit, alone with his paints and canvasses, but so long as he needed clients to paint and a studio in which to work, people would always find him. They came with all sorts of issues. Could he tell them the winning lottery numbers? Would their daughter's marriage work out? Was the longed-for promotion going to come through? Is there really a 'Mr. Right' out there, waiting, or is true love never to be found? Various transgressors, such as tax evaders and unfaithful spouses, wanted to know if their misdeeds would be discovered. One supplicant, Anthony (probably not his real name), paid two thousand dollars for a portrait. Justin sensed his mixed feelings about the project as soon as he arrived in the studio. A slim, baldheaded man in his forties, with a pale countenance, restless eyes, and a nervous air, he was like a deer in the forest which senses the presence of the hunter but can't decide which way to run. As their session proceeded, Justin realized his client was looking for a confessor, but one who could figure out his sin without him having to actually state what it was. It took Anthony over an hour to open up When he did, he admitted that, a month or two previously, he had killed a child in the street, knocking her off her bike with his car. It was a pure accident, he claimed, but he had panicked, and fled the scene before anyone knew he had been there. He was desperate for assurance that he would never be found out. As things progressed, Justin became convinced that Antony would escape the reach of the law, but how he hated giving him that news!

As time went by, Justin acquired a serious reputation as a prophet with both good and bad news. Across Houston and beyond, people began to hear about him. Of course, skeptics abounded, and they weren't shy with their opinions.

"He is just a lucky guesser, that's all."

"Of course, he can't be right all the time."

"Another con-artist."

Other people took him more seriously, and tried to figure out how he could know the things he predicted. Also, Houston is in the Bible Belt, heavily populated with evangelical Christians who regard the Bible as literal truth. They had a real problem explaining Justin. If he had the gift of foresight, did that mean everything is already determined? And, if that is so, what is the point of praying? He was undermining their faith in a God who listens to the requests of the faithful and answers them. And those who noticed that Justin's forecasts were made after spending time with the people concerned said "He is just a brilliant judge of character."

Inevitably, all this talk reached the ears of the media. Several times he was asked if he would appear on local newscasts or chat shows. He always replied, "It is kind of you to ask, but I have nothing to say." One writer, determined to expose the fraud he thought Justin to be, was completely frustrated by the artist's refusal to be interviewed. In the end, he published a long, largely fictional piece in a tabloid newspaper, with the headline: THE PROPHET OF HOUSTON – JUST WHO IS HE? Justin was so insulted that he surrendered, and agreed to be interviewed on ABC's morning show, 'Today'. The anchor preceded the interview with the words, "Today we have, in the studio, the much talked about Prophet of Houston." From then on, that is how Justin was known.

He was often asked, "Where do your visions come from?" to which he replied, "I don't have visions: I have convictions." With this the questioners had to be content. However, it was not quite true. Justin was simplifying the issue for the sake of the media. While most previews entered his mind without any visual component, occasionally he would have a clear picture of what was to come.

During his fourth summer in Houston, Justin completed a large and remarkable picture of a horse. It was commissioned by Hank Harman, a ranch owner with a spectacular spread near Bastrop, two hours west of Houston. The house stood on the crest of a low ridge, facing west. A hundred yards away, on the valley's level floor, was a splendid range of stables, home to a couple of dozen thoroughbreds, of which Hank was either the trainer or the owner. Beyond and to the left of the buildings was an extensive area of green pastures, criss-crossed by white wooden fences, where the horses were exercised. Beyond them, the opposite slope was covered in trees, mostly evergreens, which also crept down into the valley until they reached the back of the stables.

To Justin, Hank was a fascinating character. In fact, the artist would rather have done a picture of the man than his horse. Physically, the rancher was built like Clint Eastwood, tall, skinny and somewhat weather-beaten. His mouth often twitched, ready to smile at the slightest cause, and his silver-blue eyes moved restlessly as he noticed everything around him. He was highly intelligent and superbly educated, but he managed to put all comers at ease, whoever they were.

The subject of Justin's painting was a fine, chestnut-colored mare named My Hero, well known across America for winning the $1 million Arkansas Derby in record time, as well as several other major races. Horses are particularly tricky for artists, especially fit, well exercised animals with muscles in fine trim. Capturing the subtle curves of the body, the precise inclination of the head, the animal's thrusting eagerness and the implication of power its legs, is a challenge. Hank wanted the picture to show My Hero leaping a fence, so the artist had no chance of a static pose.

He watched the horse run and jump many times and took numerous photos. The commission was more challenging than any Justin had faced before. It required repeated visits to the ranch, the last of which happened on a Saturday in early September. Justin had been invited to stay for a splendid barbecue, attended by Hank's family and a dozen other friends, held on the patio and around the pool. As the evening ended and darkness fell, his host walked with him to his car, parked a short distance from the house. The glowing ball of the sun was dropping toward the trees on the far side of the valley, igniting the clouds above with brilliant reds and purples and gold. The two men stood still, side by side, watching in awe.

"I have lived here all my life," said the rancher, "And never got use to this."

"So beautiful," the artist whispered. As he did so, the fire from the sun rushed into the trees, to both left and right, until the whole horizon was burning. Flames spread along the wooden fences, and through the trees behind the stables, toward the Harman ranch. Long Satanic fingers of fire reached out across the valley to grasp the buildings and turn them into a terrifying pyre.

Justin could not move; he could hardly even breathe.

The rancher broke the moment, slapping him on the shoulder. "Well, I guess that's it, then. Thanks for coming. I hope you had a good time." He strode off in the direction of the house, clearly having seen nothing unusual.

Stunned, Justin got into his car and started it up, but he could not drive. The vison of the fire kept burning in his mind. He was afraid to believe its message, but he had no doubt what that was. He had just had a preview. The Harman Racing Stables were going to burn. Nothing could save them.

He did not know what to do. Should he return to the house and warn his client? Hank would surely stare at him in disbelief, then throw back his head and laugh out loud. "Justin, you should stick to your art and leave this fortune telling alone." Justin could see the scene already, yet he knew that he had to try. Someone had to warn the rancher, and he was that one.

Reluctantly, he turned off his engine, got out of the car and went off in search of Hank. He found him, standing with a trio of his ranching friends, joking about something. He began to have second thoughts. Telling Hank was going to be hard enough. Now he had to do it in front of three others.

Hank was surprised to see him, and stepped aside from his group. "I thought you were on your way."

"I had to come back. I have some news for you. Bad news, I am afraid."

The older man could see that Justin was finding it hard to say what he was thinking. Softening his voice, he said, "Well, you had better just spit it out. Something gone wrong with your painting, has it?"

Justin shook his head, then plucked up his courage, looked Hank Harman straight in the eye, and blurted out, "You are going to lose your stables. They are going to burn to the ground."

He dropped his gaze to the ground, wishing a hole would appear and swallow him.

"What the hell are you talking about?" Hank demanded. "What the fuck has got into you?"

Justin tried to explain, and the rancher tried to understand, and neither succeeded. Eventually Justin retreated to his car and took off down the long drive, while Hank stared at his retreating tail-lights, shaking his head in disbelief.

It was exactly one week later, during a brief but scorching heat wave, that a truck, over-loaded with bales of straw, careened off a country road near Bastrop, and hit an electricity pole. The pole went down, the wires entangled themselves with a nearby tree, and a fire started. By the time the truck driver had called 9-1-1, and help had reached the scene, half of the adjacent field was ablaze, and nothing could be done to stop it spreading into the nearby woods. An overnight wind sprang up and drove the flames north and east, eating up everything in their path and heading directly for the valley where Frank Harman lived. For two whole days the fire laughed at the puny efforts of the desperate firefighters. Its flames climbed the side of a hill, burning trees and ground cover alike, until they came over the crest and saw their chance to rush down and feast upon the dried timbers of the stables. Seventy-two hours after the truck ran off the road, the buildings burst into flames. Fortunately, by then, not a single horse remained on the property.

Ten days later, after the fire had been extinguished, Hank was in Bastrop. He ran into a friend, Bert Simmons, a member of the local Chamber of Commerce.

"Man!" said Bert, "You had amazing foresight to get your stables emptied before they burned."

"It wasn't my foresight," the rancher replied. "A guy who is doing some work for me told me what was coming. At first, I thought he was off his rocker, but he was persistent, and I decided to take him seriously. Lucky thing I did."

"How did he know?"

Hank shook he head. "I haven't the vaguest idea. I guess he is some sort of mystic. He thinks he sees things the rest of us don't. Weird, really."

CHAPTER 8

Memorial Day

It was Memorial Day. The tall man with the pleasant smile arose from his seat and approached the front of the plane. Betsy, the senior flight attendant, watched him. Whoever he was, he looked good in his brown sports coat and cream-colored slacks, with his blue eyes, slightly tanned face and straw colored hair. She guessed he could be thirty or so.

"Can I help you, sir?" she asked.

He looked at her and said quietly, "I need to get off."

"Sir?"

"I need to get off this plane."

"May I ask why?"

"Do I have to say?"

"I think you do, sir. The plane is loaded. The door is closed. We are about to depart. If we let you leave, the flight will be delayed, and we will lose our take-off slot. If you have checked bags, they will have to be offloaded too." She nodded her head in the direction of the crowded passenger compartment. "You will inconvenience all those passengers. Not good."

"Please"

"Don't you want to fly after all? To Phoenix?"

"Well, yes. I would like to go to Phoenix. In fact, I need to go to Phoenix. But not on this plane."

"Why not on this plane, sir?"

Justin bent down and said, almost in a whisper, "Because it's going to crash."

Suddenly alarmed, she said, "Is this a joke?"

Justin just shook his head.

Betsy was standing in front of the door, which she had only just closed. She reached for the phone on the bulkhead to her left and pressed some buttons. Almost instantly she was talking to Captain Reed in the cockpit, her eyes remaining fixed on Justin.

"David, I have a passenger here who says he needs to deplane." ......

"I know. I have explained that, but he is insisting." ......

"He says we are going to crash." .....

She hung up the phone

"The captain is coming out to speak to you. He wants you by the cockpit door."

Justin nodded. It was to be expected. He allowed Betsy to lead him away from the front seat passengers, out of their hearing.

The door opened and a short, gray-haired man, wearing a white shirt with epaulets emerged. His face was well tanned, the result of many layovers in sunny places. His eyes showed wariness and a touch of anger. He looked up at Justin, eyebrows raised, and waited.

"I need to deplane."

"Why?"

"This plane is going to crash."

"Why on earth would you think that?"

"I just know."

"How do you know."

"I just do."

"That is not a good enough answer. You must have a reason. What makes you think this flight is in danger? You cannot make accusations like that without cause. It's a criminal offense."

Justin just shook his head.

Reed drew in a deep breath and looked at Betsy. The last thing they wanted was a scene, one that would have the other passengers worrying about their safety. "We had better open the door" he said.

She reached again for the phone, dialed, and spoke rapidly to somebody on the other end. Then she told the two men, "They are bringing the jet bridge back."

The next couple of minutes seemed to last forever. David Reed said to the flight attendant, "Keep him here. Don't let him talk to anyone."

He did not want to continue talking to Justin, not in that place, not within the hearing of other passengers. If they heard talk of a crash, there could easily be a panic. So he told him, "I don't want you to say another word, not to anyone. Understand?"

Then he went back into the cockpit, closed the door, and got busy on the phone.

The other two stood in awkward silence in the cramped exit passage, until a gentle bump rocked the plane. The jet bridge had arrived. Reed emerged again from the cockpit and Betsy opened the aircraft door. Justin was hastily ushered off the plane and up the jetway. He was motioned to an area where there were no waiting passengers, and made to sit down. Almost immediately an electric cart arrived carrying two TSA personnel, closely followed by another with a pair of armed police.

Justin started to speak but Captain Reed silenced him with a gesture, adding, "Just a minute." He went over and had a low-voiced conversation with the new arrivals. A few minutes later FlyAir's Station Manager, Rick Stevens, arrived, embarrassed at being the last to get there. He had been with the airline forever, or so he sometimes felt, and was responsible for ensuring the safe and timely departure of all flights, as well as the implementation of the airline's security procedures. This new development challenged his job performance. He was not pleased.

He shook hands all round and jerked his head toward the seated Justin, "Is this the guy?"

Reed nodded, "That's him"

The station manager stepped over toward Justin. "Now, everyone is here. Why don't you tell us who you are and what you think you are doing?"

"My name is Justin Gates. I am an artist and I live in Sugar Land."

"I need to see your ID."

Justin produced his driver's license and handed it over. Rick Stevens took a copy of it with his cell phone, then walked over to the podium and checked with the flight records. Everyone waited, talking in hushed tones, but not to Justin. The Station Manager came back and said, "Now, you had better tell us what is going on."

Conscious that everyone else was standing, Justin rose to his feet. "It's very simple," he said. "This plane is going to crash on its way to Phoenix. That's it."

"That's it? That's all you have to say?"

"I don't know what else there is."

"Well, you could tell us why the hell we should believe you? Or don't you have a reason? FlyAir's safety record is impeccable. Every passenger is security screened. Bags are X-rayed and cargo inspected. There isn't a single reason to believe the flight is unsafe. If you know different, you need to tell us. And tell us now."

The senior TSA man asked, "Why would you think this flight is in trouble? What do you think is going to make it crash? Give us something real to go on."

Justin reluctantly shrugged his shoulders. "I can't give you what you want. Sometimes I just know things, things that are going to happen, and in this case, I know this plane will never make it to Phoenix. It is going to crash."

Staring hard at him, the officer said, "You do know that interfering with airline operations like this, making terrorist threats and so on, is a serious offence. It can land you in prison. For a long time."

Justin said nothing.

One of the policemen asked him, "What did you say your name is?"

When Justin told him, he asked, "And do you paint pictures of people?"

Those gathered around were startled by the question, the change of subject, but Justin replied simply, "Yes, I do. I am a portrait painter. That's true."

"And you painted the one of Mayor Spencer, the one that was in the news recently?"

Justin just nodded.

The officer, whose last name was Clemmons, looked at Rick, "My wife told me something about this guy. He was on the news. He paints pictures and tells fortunes, and they generally come true. She says."

Rick Stevens thought hard for a moment, then looked at those around him. "It's no good," he said. "We're going to have to deplane everybody. And all their bags. And any freight. This plane has to be thoroughly inspected. Until that's been done, we cannot afford to let it go anywhere. Personally, I don't believe a word of what he says, but we need to take all possible precautions. If the flight should take off and then get into trouble, there would be more than hell to pay. Hmm. I suppose there is going to be hell to pay anyway."

Justin was taken to a room, somewhere deep in the airport terminal, in an area which the traveling public never see. It was a plain room with an oblong table in the center, and two pairs of upright chairs on opposing sides, and could easily have served as a setting for a police-station scene in a crime movie. There was a reflective window in one wall, and a small black camera tucked up against the ceiling. That was all. Justin sat at the table, alone, with a paper cup of cold coffee in front of him.

No-one had treated him badly, certainly not as if he were a suspect in a crime, but there were suspicions, questions. Many had been asked, others just hung in the air. He could see them in the eyes of the people who came and went. To them, he was an enigma. They could not make him out. In their experience, he was a first.

The FBI seemed to be in charge. Their lead was a not-unpleasant blonde woman called Gwen, in her forties perhaps, a harassed working mother, if Justin had ever seen one. She spoke to him in a kindly way, sounding more like a social worker than an inquisitor, asking penetrating questions, and expecting answers, but not aggressively. The same could not be said of her sidekick, a nervous young man called Greg, a scrawny character with an irritated scowl on his pale, unhealthy face. He had a habit of interrupting her line of inquiry with his own, mainly sarcastic, questions.

At one point, Justin was left alone for more than thirty minutes. When Gwen came back, he asked if he could leave. She shook her head, "We need to keep you here, for now. When they have checked the plane over, that's when we'll decide what to do with you. For now, you have caused a huge amount of trouble for hundreds of people, and we need to get to the bottom of it. Also, we may yet charge you with interfering with airline operations or making a terroristic threat. I can tell you one thing: you are already a very unpopular guy. You are likely to find that out big time once you get out of here. If you do get out of here, that is." She offered to get him a coffee, but he declined, so she pulled up a chair and sat down facing him.

"Tell me again, just how did you know that the plane was going to crash? We have been researching your background. It does seem that some pretty credible people have been impressed by your predictions, but this story of a vision is really hard to take."

In fact, the FBI, the TSA, the HPD (Houston Police Department), and God knows who else, had gone to their records, computers, databases, and files, to see what was known about him. His driver's license gave his name as Justin Fordham Gates, resident of Sugar Land, Texas. Other official records showed he had been born in Guerneville, California, the child of Alice and Ernest Gates. He had been educated at local public schools, then the University of California, Berkeley and finally Rice University in

Houston. After graduating from there, he seemed to have largely disappeared as far as official records were concerned, except for his driver's permit. The military had never heard of him. Nor had the police. He never even had a parking ticket. At some stage during this time he must have settled in Texas, because in 2011 he showed up in Fort Bend County property tax records as owning a home in Sugar Land.

The most fruitful source of information was the Houston Chronicle, who unearthed a whole trove of items about him. One of these concerned someone who had recovered from stage four cancer, and had described that as a miracle attributable to Justin Gates. Apparently, he had predicted it even though the doctors had given up hope. There was also a piece about a rancher near Bastrop, who saved his livestock and many of his possessions from the great fire because of a forecast by the artist. Numerous other mentions were found, among them several stories in which he was described as The Prophet of Houston. The most recent news item, however, had nothing to do with predictions. It concerned the presentation of a portrait of the Mayor of Houston, which been commissioned to hang in City Hall. Justin, of course, was the artist.

* * *

That evening, HPD officer Al Clemmons had finished his twelve-hour shift and was at home, having supper with his wife and telling her about his day.

"Actually," he said, "I met someone at work today that you are a fan of."

"Me? A fan?" she responded. "I'm not anyone's fan as far as I know."

"His name is Justin Gates. You told me about him once."

"Oh him! The guy who sees the future. How interesting. What is he like?"

Al had to think about that one. "He looks like a regular guy, I suppose. There's nothing much to say. He speaks quietly, doesn't say a lot."

"What does he look like?"

"Well, he is tall, with light brown hair and blue eyes. You would probably say he's good looking."

"Was he telling fortunes?"

"That was the problem. He had a forecast for an entire plane load of people."

"How exciting!"

"That's not my word for it. He said the plane was going to crash, and they were all going to die."

Al's wife was horrified and yet intrigued. She continued to ask questions about the incident, but there wasn't much more that he could tell her, and soon they let the matter drop.

* * *

Gwen came into the room once more, and took her seat, Greg at her side. She studied Justin's face for a while, trying to figure him out.

"Look, Justin, we can't decide what to do with you. You do realize, of course, that you have caused an enormous amount of trouble, and incurred tens of thousands of dollars in expense. Your suggestion that flight 728 was going to crash, unsupported by any evidence at all, sounds a lot like a terrorist threat. Believe me, the backroom guys have been looking into who you are, where you come from, what you do, how you show up on social media. If anything is known about you, you can be sure they have found it already, or soon will. To me, I must say, you just don't seem like a terrorist, or even a crazy person. Except for this fortune telling thing, that is."

Greg interrupted her.

"Here's what I don't get. You can't be much good at telling what's going to happen, because that plane is still here, on the ground, going nowhere, and safe. It did not fly, and it did not crash. You got it wrong, didn't you?" he said, almost triumphantly,

His partner gave him an irritated glance.

"Greg does have a point, you know." She took a deep breath, pausing for thought. "Why don't you tell us about this gift of yours. How does it work? Do you always get things right? What made you believe that this particular flight was in trouble?"

"I had a preview," said Justin.

"A what?"

"A preview."

"What the fuck is that?" asked the sidekick, scornfully.

How often have I been asked that question, without the expletive of course? Everyone wants to know what my previews are like, but they are so hard to explain. I don't fully understand them myself. In a way they are like dreams, coming out of nowhere, passing through my conscious mind in an

instant, and then are gone again, but I hate the words 'dreams' and 'visions'. They suggest something out of this world, whereas my previews are, in fact, very real. To me, at least.

Justin answered, "They are actual glimpses into the future, a chance to see something that hasn't yet happened. Let me ask you, Greg: have you ever been riding in a car, with another one coming at you from the opposite direction? For a really brief moment, you can see into that car and its occupants, and then it is gone. You can't see them anymore, but you know that they were there, they actually passed by. They were real."

Gwen spoke, "People in a passing car, I can get. It is there, on the road. But the future isn't a car and there isn't any road. You can't blame Greg for thinking it is all nonsense."

Justin looked at her.

"Then think about this," he said. "Do you ever dream at night? Isn't that seeing things without the use of your eyes, or hearing things without the help of your ears?"

Greg butted in again. "Yes, but that's just dreaming. Nobody takes it seriously," he said.

Justin nodded in agreement.

"Yes, and I have dreams, too, and they are different. My previews aren't dreams, but they are insights which come to me in that sort of way."

"So, what is the difference between a dream and one of these previews you mention?" asked Gwen.

"That is hard to explain. When you remember a dream, you know it was just a dream. When I have a preview, I know it's not a dream, it is about something real: I just know it."

Greg spoke up again, his tone full of scorn. "Like you knew flight 728 was going to crash? Only it wasn't." He slammed his hand down on the table, as if he had said the last word, as if he were closing the door on the matter.

The three of them sat silently for a minute before Gwen said, "Tell us again, exactly what happened, from the beginning. We still aren't convinced."

Justin sighed wearily. "I suppose it began in the waiting area. At the gate. I was early, as I usually am. Then here comes this woman ..."

"What woman?" barked the impatient sidekick.

"...this woman. She came and sat in a seat, sort of opposite me, just a short distance away. I could see her quite clearly."

Another pause. Another prompt. "And? Was there something special about her?"

"Well, she reminded me of my sister."

"Your sister?"

"Yes. She had the same color and style of hair, the same shape face, the same figure. She walked the same way and sat down just the way Tina does. I think her eyes might even have been the same blue."

"So?"

"I just looked at her. Stared at her, I suppose. She noticed, and it made her smile. It was exactly, exactly the way Tina might have smiled. I was embarrassed to be caught looking at her like that, but it was hard to turn away. So, I took my sketch pad out of my bag, and began to draw her face."

"And that was what you call your preview?"

"Oh no. That came later. After we boarded. I had an aisle seat half-way back."

"Yes. 28C. We know that."

"She boarded after I did. Her seat was two rows ahead, on the opposite side of the aisle. I watched her find her seat and put her bag in the overhead bin. I remember she was wearing blue jeans and a white shirt. Then she sat down, and I was happy about that because I could keep my eyes on her without a problem. That's when it happened."

"What happened?"

"I had my preview. I saw the plane falling out of the sky. Hitting the ground. Exploding into a million pieces. And then, there she was, lying there among the wreckage. Quite perfect but definitely dead."

Justin seemed to choke on his words and stopped to collect himself. The others were silent too, as if they could see what he was seeing, feel what he was feeling.

"That's when I knew I had to get off the plane," he said.

"What I don't understand," said Gwen. "Is this. If you could foresee the plane crashing, why didn't you tell everyone to get off the plane? Or at least raise the alarm with the crew? Why save just yourself? For heaven's sake, you were so taken with this woman, but you did not even try to save her."

"You just don't get it, do you? I had seen the future. The future. Something which was going to happen. If I had raised the alarm, and people had panicked, or the flight had been cancelled or something, then the plane would not have flown, and the crash would not have happened. Then the future wouldn't have been the future, would it? And so I wouldn't have seen it in the first place."

Gwen frowned, confused. Her partner snorted again. Justin just waited. He had tried explaining his previews before. It wasn't at all easy.

"I just had to get off by myself," he said.

Then Gwen had an idea. She asked to see the drawing Justin had made while waiting for the plane. He took the sketchbook from his briefcase handed it to her. She was surprised: it was quite beautiful. It showed the head and shoulders of a young woman, probably in her twenties, who was looking off into the distance, a slight smile on her lips. She seemed to possess a calm contentment which Gwen could almost feel.

"Do you mind if I borrow this for a moment?" she asked and, without waiting for a reply, rose and took it from the room.

Fifteen minutes later she returned, carrying Justin's sketchbook and some papers. "Here is your book back. I hope you don't mind; I made a copy of it for our files." She handed over the original drawing, laid the copy on the table, and placed a photograph beside it, a security camera image of passengers who were boarding flight 728. In the center of the line was a woman, quite clearly the same woman as in Justin's drawing.

Gwen commented, "That is a remarkable likeness. Yet you had never seen her before. Isn't that right?"

"Yes, it is."

"Does the name Annabel White mean anything to you?

Justin thought for a moment and then shook his head.

"If she was seated two rows in front of you across the aisle, that is probably who she is. She was on her way to Palm Springs via Phoenix."

In the end, they decided to let Justin go. The plane had been cleared of explosives or other threats. There was no sign of mischievous intent on his part, and therefore no reason to hold him. He was released with a warning not to leave town. "We doubt that this is the end of the matter," they said.

He was escorted out of the terminal at eleven thirty-four that evening, the exact time that FlyAir flight number 439 fell out of the sky, over Palm Springs in California. That plane had not been on its way to Phoenix at all.

* * *

I don't remember the drive home. The events of the day had worn me out. Once in the house, I grabbed a snack and fell into bed, but I could not sleep. How could I have been so wrong? I kept asking myself. My preview had been quite clear: the girl, the plane falling and disintegrating, and then her lying there amid the wreckage, I saw it all as if I had been at the scene.

It bothered me, too, that I had caused so much trouble at the airport. Telling the flight attendant why I wanted to get off had ruined the day for so many people. To cap it all, my preview had been wrong: the Phoenix flight never even took off.

How could I have been so wrong?

On top of that, I was troubled again by the never-resolved question of Stanley Emmett, who, eighteen years before, had killed an old lady and a baby, and finally himself, all as a result of me telling his son, Willie, about my preview. Three people died because I spoke up. Would they still be alive if I had kept quiet? I will never know. It did look rather like it.

Now, nearly two decades later, things had been reversed. By speaking up, had I saved over a hundred lives? What would have happened if I had kept quiet? Maybe they would all have died.

While I was still a child, my mother had advised me not to tell people about the future, but was she right?

Finally, of course, I drifted into sleep, quite unaware of the disaster at Palm Springs.

* * *

Someone was ringing his doorbell, and banging on his front door. His clock showed one minute to six. Who wanted to disturb him at such a time? He struggled off the bed, wondering if he had even slept an hour. He grabbed his robe, and went to see. Two men were standing there, wearing suits and ties and looking agitated. One of them, the tall, broad shouldered one, was waving some sort of badge. His short, skinny companion was peering into the room, trying to see if there was anyone else around.

The taller one spoke, "Are you Justin Gates?"

Justin nodded sleepily.

"We're from the FBI. Sorry to disturb you, sir. We need you to come with us."

"Why?"

"You'll find out. Please get dressed and we can get going. There are people who are anxious to see you."

If they had offered their names, he had not caught them. He mentally christened them Big Boy and Little Boy.

"Am I being arrested?"

"No, sir. That's not it. It's just that you are needed very urgently in Houston."

Before long Justin was dressed in blue jeans and a sports shirt and riding in the back of their Chevy Tahoe, heading for the city.

"Now," he said, "Please tell me what is going on."

Little Boy was driving. His companion turned to look at their passenger. "It has to do with last night's plane crash. That's all we know."

Justin froze. His words were a hoarse whisper. "A plane crashed?"

"It did, sir. But it happened too late for the nightly news."

"I didn't see that anyway. Tell me, do you know which airline it was?"

"FlyAir, I believe."

"Yes, it would be," muttered Justin, and saw the way the two of them looked at each other. That was, they thought, an odd response. Suspicious even.

Nothing more was said until they arrived at the FBI's Houston office. He was led inside, security-checked, and taken upstairs.

Big Boy led Justin into a large conference room, where six or seven agents were gathered around a long table. He recognized just one of them, Gwen, from yesterday, looking as tired as he felt. She attempted a smile. Several people were talking at once, a serious discussion clearly taking place.

"Mr. Gates," announced Big Boy. Conversation ceased and everyone looked in his direction. Justin was motioned toward a vacant chair.

At the head of the table sat a white-haired man, a professorial type, with a high forehead and intelligent gray eyes behind rimless spectacles. He looked straight at Justin and spoke in a clipped Boston accent. "Mr. Gates,

I am Denis Maynard, the head of this FBI division. Thank you for coming. I understand you are the cause of all that trouble yesterday."

"I suppose I am," said Justin, "I did not intend to be."

"Intend or not, you inconvenienced a great many people and caused a vast amount of expense, but that is not why you are here. Well, not exactly. We want to know if you can tell us anything about last night's disaster in Palm Springs."

"Palm Springs?"

"Yes. Palm Springs. You know what happened there last night, I presume."

Justin shook his head in denial. "Your agents said something about a plane crash. That is all I know."

Maynard stared hard at him for a long moment, then turned to the man on his right and said, "Frank, why don't you fill him in?" which Frank did. It seemed that a FlyAir jet, flight number 439, had taken off from Houston at 6.15 the previous evening, destined for Palm Springs International Airport. There were 78 passengers and seven crew on board. Everything was perfectly routine. The aircraft stayed in touch with air traffic control as normal. With good weather and favorable winds, an early arrival was expected. The pilot and the control tower were coordinating, following procedures, when the plane suddenly disappeared from the controller's screen. Nobody at the airport saw it happen, but a couple who were taking a walk on a nearby golf course heard an explosion and turned in time to see an enormous fireball falling from the sky. "It was terrifying, quite apocalyptic." they said.

When agent Frank had finished, Maynard spoke again.

"Does any of this surprise you, Mr. Gates?"

Justin thought for a moment, then answered, "Few things surprise me."

Maynard opened his mouth as if to reply, then thought better of it. Instead, he looked at Gwen. "Over to you, then."

Gwen was sitting across the table from Justin. In front of her was a stack of papers. She extracted two pages and, reaching across, placed them face up in front of him. The first was her copy of the picture he had drawn on the previous day while waiting for his flight. The second was the photograph of the same woman standing in the boarding line.

"Do you know who this person is."

"I have no idea. I told you that yesterday."

"We hoped that sleeping on it might have refreshed your memory."

"I am afraid not. I have no idea who she is. She just looks a lot like my sister. That is all I know."

"Would it help if I told you her name? According to her ticket she was Annabel White. Does that ring a bell?"

Justin shook his head.

Gwen reached into her stack again and extracted another photograph. It was very similar to the one already on the table, showing the same woman standing in a similar but different line of passengers.

"This time we see Ms. White as she was boarding FlyAir 439, the flight that crashed. We presume she is one of the casualties. Maybe we will be able to identify her remains. Time will tell."

Justin looked at the three pictures but said nothing.

"You say that you had a vision of a plane going down, a plane in which she was a passenger. You just seem to have identified the wrong plane."

Still no response from Justin.

Maynard rubbed his chin thoughtfully, as if pondering a difficult decision.

"You see, Mr. Gates, this is how things stand. A plane was brought down. It was either an accident or a deliberate act. Evidence suggests an explosion occurred, but that is all we know right now. If, as we suspect, criminal intent was involved, then someone must have known about it ahead of time. You seem to be such a person. Was there anyone else? Well, that question is still unanswered. For now, you are the only person who knew. But how did you know? You claim you had a vision. That is hard to believe. I know you spoke to my colleagues yesterday, but please tell me directly, now. Exactly when did you decide that the FlyAir flight to Phoenix flight was in danger?"

"Soon after I boarded the plane, while I was sitting in my seat."

Maynard spoke to the agents around the table. "We need to take note of three things. Number one: it is unlikely that anyone with prior knowledge of the crash would board in the first place, unless he was a suicide bomber. If that were the case, it is unlikely that he would try to get off again, so we must conclude that Mr. Gates here did not anticipate the disaster when he went aboard. That supports his contention that he knew nothing about any plot to bring the plane down. Two: the only explanation he gives for his behavior is that he had a vision of some sort, which defies credibility, and makes us suspect that he is hiding something." Maynard paused to look at Justin. "Are you hiding something, Mr. Gates?"

Justin just shook his head.

Maynard continued his remarks. "Well, we will doubtless see about that later. The third thing is this: It is hard to see how Mr. Gates could have brought down a plane in Palm Springs when he was here in Houston, expecting one to crash in Phoenix."

One of the others spoke up. "Maybe he managed to get a bomb aboard the plane, with a timed detonation or something. Perhaps he intended suicide and then chickened out."

"But he never was on the Palm Springs plane, the one that crashed," Frank pointed out. "In any case, the explosion did not occur until long after the original flight should have landed in Phoenix. The timer theory doesn't work."

Another of the team contributed, "He might have had an accomplice in Palm Springs," and then realized the absurdity of his words. "But if so, why did he predict that it was a Phoenix plane that would crash?" he asked.

Everyone was silent for a moment. Maynard spoke again,

"Mr. Gates, for the time being we are going to accept that you had a vision and believed it. That was then, but what about now? Do you think that you made a mistake?"

"A mistake?" said Justin. "I don't know what to say. My previews are usually correct, but I see these pictures of Ms. White and I wonder. Maybe what I saw was something that was going to happen to her, rather than to any particular plane. Perhaps whatever plane she ended up flying in would be the one to go down."

Frank, glancing at his boss, said to Justin, "Do you agree that you caused all of flight 728's passengers to be deplaned?"

"I suppose so."

"That resulted in Ms. White being on the Palm Springs flight instead?"

"So it seems."

"Then what would have happened if you had stayed on the Phoenix flight and said nothing?"

"I cannot say, but I think that plane would have been the one to go down.

She would have been on it. And me too."

Maynard spoke up again.

"Mr. Gates, perhaps you do have a unique insight into these things, which we do not. I think we need to keep you around until the plane has been more completely inspected and we can decide how to move forward. I have a feeling we may want to consult you further. Do you have a problem with that?"

"I suppose not."

"Events like this often involve national security. You might learn things which cannot be divulged to other people, not even the person you sleep with. Will you be OK with that?"

Justin nodded. "I am not sleeping with anyone, anyway."

"Since you are not a government employee, we will probably ask you to sign a paper which binds you under the Official Secrets Act. Can you handle that?"

"Sure."

Maynard then said to Gwen, "Why don't you take our visitor to find some coffee? In fact, I'll bet he hasn't even had breakfast yet. You might need to feed him too."

Gwen pushed her chair back, rose, and looked at Justin, jerking her head as if to say, "Come with me." They both left the room.

As they were standing, waiting for the elevator. Justin looked at her carefully. "Can I say something personal to you?" he asked.

Startled, she looked up at him. "I suppose so."

"I know you are really worried about something. Yesterday, you were struggling to concentrate. I saw that quite clearly, and I sense it is happening again today."

Gwen said nothing, but made a rueful expression and nodded her head, so he continued, "Maybe you have a child, a son perhaps, who is much on your mind at the moment."

"How did you know?" she whispered.

Avoiding her question, Justin asked one of his own. "How is he? I know you are worrying about him."

With a deep sigh, she said "I wish I knew. I have been trying to call him for the past few days, but he never picks up. He is in Florida, staying with his father, and that is not a good place for him to be."

"How come?"

"Well, to my mind, his dad is a bad influence. His home is a mess, and so is his life. If Danny wants to slide off the rails, he'll not be stopped. He might even be helped."

Justin touched her elbow lightly, a reassuring gesture. "You shouldn't worry. He isn't impressed with his father's example. Before long he will be back with you. He is really a quite sensible young man."

At that moment the elevator doors opened. Gwen whispered, "I hope you are right" and they stepped inside. The presence of other people put an end to the conversation. They did not speak again until they were in the cafeteria, where she left him, promising to return when he was needed. "I hope we won't be too long," she said.

At the buffet, he loaded up a tray with coffee, toast and eggs and found a seat at a table from which he could see the television. A gray-haired Hispanic man was reading the news.

"......... Confirming again, FlyAir Flight 439 to Palm Springs crashed as it was coming in to land, with eighty-five passengers and crew on board. There were no survivors. We will bring you more news on this disaster as soon as it breaks."

"And now to another story, also involving FlyAir Airlines. For that, we go back to Jenny Lane, live, at George Bush Intercontinental Airport.

The picture changed to show an attractive young woman with shoulder length, wavy black hair, wide brown eyes and an easy, relaxed smile. "Yesterday afternoon, FlyAir flight 728 was scheduled to leave for Phoenix at 2.40. It was supposed to be an on-time departure. All the passengers were on board and in their seats, and the door had been closed, when one passenger, who was apparently afraid of flying, asked to be let off again. It is reported that he said the plane was going to crash. The crew opened the door and allowed him to go, telling the remaining passengers that there would be a short delay to the departure. Fifteen minutes later the captain announced that the plane was being taken out of service, because of a technical problem, and everyone would have to get off again. One of the other passengers, who was seated in the front row, claims to have heard the passenger who wanted to disembark, speaking to a flight attendant. He is sure he heard them discussing about a possible crash. The flight was cancelled, and the passengers rebooked on other FlyAir flights."

The picture on the screen reverted to the news anchor in the studio.

"The downing of the flight to Palm Springs makes us curious about this earlier incident. We have asked FlyAir who this particular passenger was, or at least to comment on the matter, but our calls have not been returned."

* * *

Six miles away, Mary Jo Clemmons was watching the same program. She felt a touch of pride: they might not know who the passenger was, but she did. With hardly a thought she picked up her phone and called the TV station. Maybe they would give her credit for helping them with the story.

* * *

It was more than an hour before Gwen fetched Justin and took him back to the meeting room. There were just two people waiting for him, Maynard and his assistant, Frank.

Maynard spoke. "You have presented us with quite a problem, Mr. Gates."

Justin nodded. "I suppose I have."

"The crash of an airliner, such as happened in Palm Springs, is a national disaster. There is going to be a major investigation. It will probably turn out to be a criminal act by a person or persons unknown. In that case, finding the culprit will be our number one priority. We will need all the help we can get. At this stage, all we have is a mass of wreckage in Palm Springs, . . . and you."

This last statement was not quite true, but the FBI was not ready to go public with what else it knew.

Maynard continued, "You might be the only living person to have had prior knowledge of this event, which is probably the worst terrorist act on American soil since nine-eleven. People will need to know how you came by that. Your story about having what you call a preview is hardly credible."

Justin responded, "Well, I cannot change it, can I?"

"Only you know that."

There was an awkward silence. It was Gwen who broke it.

"I gather that, by spending time with people, you can see into their lives in some way. Is that correct?"

"Yes, but not all people and not all the time."

"So which people can you work with?"

"That is hard to answer. I connect easily with some people, less easily with others, and not at all with the rest. I am sure it is the same for you. Aren't there some people with whom the chemistry is really good, and others where there is no chemistry at all?"

"Yes, but I don't see into anybody's future."

Maynard asked, "Have you ever had one of your previews, as you call them, with someone who was not actually in the same room as you? If you saw them in a photograph or on television, for example?"

"I did once watch a TED talk," answered Justin, "And as I watched I began to see into the speaker's life. Quite alarmingly, really. But, normally, I do need a direct connection with the real person."

"How about if the person isn't there, but you had some intimate possession of theirs, would that work?"

Justin smiled, "You mean, am I like a bloodhound who needs to smell someone's clothing in order to set out on the chase?"

Maynard looked amused. "Well, I had not thought of it that way, but yes. What is your answer?"

"I don't have an answer. It has never happened."

"Then let me ask you something else. How far into the future can you see?"

"I am not sure I know that, either. Usually weeks or months. I did once have a preview of something that might not happen for several years, but that was a special case."

"Can you see what will happen tomorrow?"

"That can happen."

"What about later today."

Justin just nodded.

"Good. Then I have just two more questions. One is this. If you can see into someone's future, can you also see into their past? Can you see what happened some time ago?"

"I don't know. It has never arisen."

"That is a shame. If you could, you would be a wonderful asset for the FBI. You could tell us if our suspects really are guilty. That would save us half our work, but I suppose it is too much to hope for."

Justin said nothing, just smiled.

"OK. My last question is this: does your gift give you the power to know when someone is lying?"

"I am not sure about that."

"That is also a pity. We could really use you if you could."

Maynard finished questioning Justin and he was dismissed, escorted by Big Boy who was to take him back to his house in Sugar Land.

* * *

Sugar Land is a city, twenty-five miles southwest of Houston. Justin lived there, in a subdivision called Grants Lake. The lake itself is a three-acre man made pond, surrounded by single family homes and condominiums. His place was a 1200 square feet townhouse, with one and a half floors. All principal living areas were downstairs, with guest accommodations on the upper level, which consisted of a bedroom, a bathroom and a wide balcony overlooking the sitting room below. Justin was very fond of the house and had made the entire second floor into his studio. That is where he was at work when the doorbell rang. He put down his brushes, wiped his hands on a rag, and went down to see who it was. It was the female reporter he had seen on the FBI's television on the previous day.

"I am Jenny Lane." she said in a soft, midwestern accent, "From KHOU TV. Are you Justin Gates?"

"I am," he replied.

Justin normally avoided news reporters. In his experience they were troublemakers. Once, during his California days, one had interviewed him and then published a wildly inaccurate story, filled with exaggerations and lies, which made him sound like an Old Testament prophet. For the next few months, he was bombarded by news media and countless individuals who wanted their fortunes told. Many people asked him to tell them which horses might win which races, which politicians would lose elections, and which teams would triumph in their various championships. He was once offered an all-expenses-paid trip to Las Vegas if he would help a high-rolling gambler to break the bank. When he moved to Texas he hoped he might escape such attention, and at first he did. But then he was able to help some of his portrait clients with previews into things that were troubling them, and it all started up again. This business with the plane crash would only make matters worse. This reporter's appearance on his doorstep proved it. "Never encourage them, and perhaps they will leave you alone," was his rule. Ms. Lane's arrival should have made him wary, to say the least, but that is not what happened. Instead, to his surprise he was actually pleased to see her, in spite of the microphone she was holding. Was it something about the tone with she spoke or the way she smiled as she did so? He did not have time to figure that out. She was still speaking.

"Can I ask you a few questions about an event on Monday at the airport?"

Instead of saying, "No comment," he found himself saying, "Of course."

"We have a report that you boarded a FlyAir flight for Phoenix. Is that true?"

"Yes, it is. I was on my way to a meeting."

"But you decided, at the last moment, to get off the plane again?" Jenny made her statement sound like a question.

"Who told you that?"

"I can't tell you that, but it is true, isn't it?"

"Yes."

"And that was after the door had been closed?"

"Yes"

"Why did you decide to deplane?"

Justin had to think before replying.

"I found I was uneasy about flying."

"Are you normally afraid of flying?"

"Not usually, but on this occasion I had a strong feeling that the plane might crash. I decided to get off."

"Did you tell the crew that the plane was going to crash?"

"Actually, I did."

"Was that before they opened the door to let you go?"

He nodded.

"So, they must have believed you? That the flight was doomed?"

"I can't say what they believed, only that they let me go."

"Did you know that, after you left, all the other passengers were made to get off? The flight was cancelled, and everyone had to find other ways of getting to wherever they were going."

"I did hear that, but it was after I had gone."

"FlyAir says that the plane was taken away and thoroughly checked for safety, and everything was as it should be. So, you gave a false alarm."

Justin just looked at her.

"Do you feel responsible for all the trouble and inconvenience the other passengers experienced?"

"Well, I feel pleased the flight was abandoned. If they had continued on that journey, they would have all been killed."

"So, you still believe that?"

"Oh yes."

"And now you know that a different FlyAir plane did crash, in Palm Springs, that same evening. Do you think there is a connection?"

"Connection?"

"Do you think the Palm Springs disaster is related to the event you were involved in, earlier in the day?"

"Should I?"

"Some people say you have a reputation for seeing the future. They even call you The Prophet of Houston. I take it you know that."

"I know what people say."

"Is it true? Do you have a psychic gift?"

"It has happened from time to time."

"So is it possible that you had a glimpse into the future, and foresaw a plane going down, but got the wrong plane."

Justin sighed heavily, "I don't know. It is possible, I suppose, and it does trouble me. But there is nothing I can do about it."

Jenny Lane opened her mouth to start her next question, but Justin cut her off. He raised his hand, gesturing toward her microphone.

"Let's just leave it there, shall we?" he said, trying to smile. He stepped back into his doorway, intending to end the interview.

Taken aback for only a second, she nodded in agreement. Bringing her microphone back to herself, she turned to face the camera. "That was Justin Gates, the passenger who warned the airline that one of its planes was going to crash. By doing that, he may have saved more than a hundred lives. This is Jenny Lane in Sugar Land, returning you to the studio."

She walked over and said something to her cameraman, who was already lowering his instrument. He moved off in the direction of the van and she returned to Justin.

"Can I call you Justin?" she asked.

"Why not?" he replied.

She spoke tentatively. "I want to ask you something."

"More questions?"

"This is personal, private, off the record. No camera. No mike. Just between you and me."

Justin was wary, but she seemed sincere, and he liked her, so he said, "OK"

"I am fascinated by this gift you have for seeing people's tomorrows. I would love to sit down and talk to you about it, maybe over a coffee sometime."

The idea of spending time with her appealed to him, not because he wanted to talk about himself but because an hour with her would be a pleasant change from his normal solitary routine.

"We could do that. I think I would like it too."

She gave Justin her business card and he recited his phone number to her, which she immediately entered into her iPhone. She gave him one more smile, said "Bye, then," and left.

Back at her office, Jenny Lane's editor asked her to build up a story about this mystic portrait painter from Sugar Land. From the studio's databases she found all the stories and articles which the FBI had also unearthed, including the item which named him as the painter of the mayor's portrait. She called City Hall.

"That picture was commissioned and paid for by Gary Brewer," a public relations assistant told her.

Jenny knew who Brewer was, a well-known billionaire philanthropist in Houston. As a young man he had inherited a modest oil fortune and multiplied it many times over through shrewd investments in software start-ups. She got his phone number and placed a call. He wasn't available, so she left a message, and later in the afternoon he called her back.

"Ms. Lane?" he inquired in a rich baritone voice, "How can I possibly help our favorite TV station? I certainly hope you haven't found out anything sensational about me."

"Good afternoon, Mr. Brewer. Thank you for returning my call," she replied. "Actually, we are looking for information about someone called Justin Gates."

"Dear me," came the cordial response, "I hope he is not in trouble."

"Oh no! Not at all. We are just looking for background information from people who know him."

"Well, I can tell you he is a fine young man and a great artist, too."

"How long have you known him?"

"About a year, I should think. My wife and I celebrated our fortieth last year, and I wanted to give her a portrait of our daughter, Maddie, to mark the occasion. I asked around, among people I know, for a recommendation, and his name came up. I hired him and he did a great job."

"What do you know about him as a person?"

"Well, I think he is one hundred percent straight forward. He was always very respectful to my wife and daughter. A very reliable guy, too; always showed up when he said he would. I don't have anything but good to say about him."

"That's great! Do you know if he has a family, or where he comes from?"

"I am pretty sure he is single, and he doesn't strike me as a woman chaser or anything like that. He lives in Sugar Land or somewhere. That is where he has his studio. As to where he comes from, I want to say California, but I am not too sure."

"Does anything else come to mind about him?"

"I don't think so, except that he saved me a hell of a lot of money. More than I paid him for the portrait, actually."

"How so?"

"We are talking about last year, when he was working on Maddie's picture. It was August. She had just gained her doctorate at UT in Austin and was on top of the world. She and Jim had got engaged and were planning a fancy wedding in the Caribbean. It was the only thing she could talk about. Mavis and I had never seen her so happy. She must have been talking to Justin about it, during her sittings, because he mentioned it to me. He said it was great to see so much excitement and he hated to pour cold water on it, but she was heading for a huge disappointment. I asked what on earth he was talking about, and he said that the wedding was not going to happen."

"Good heavens! How did you respond to that?"

"Well, I was mad at first. I asked him why he would say such a thing. He was as cool and calm as could be. He said he had a gift for seeing the future, and Maddie should be prepared, or at least I should be. He could not tell me why the wedding would be called off. In fact, I don't think he knew. It was still eight months away, but we were already doing a huge amount of planning, and I was committing to many thousands of dollars. For some reason I could not get his warning out of my mind, so I went ahead and took out cancellation insurance, and I am mighty glad I did."

"And what happened?"

"Ten days before the wedding some drunken fool ran a red light and smashed into Jim's truck. Maddie wasn't with him, thank God, but he was almost killed. They life-flighted him to the hospital, where he only just made it. He was still in a coma on his wedding day. Of course, it was an accident; no-one could have foreseen it. But Justin did."

"So, Justin turned out to be some sort of prophet, did he?"

"I guess you could say that. He certainly had the foresight, and the courage to tell me about it. Smart guy."

CHAPTER 9

Jenny

Justin had just finished a commissioned portrait. The following week he would call his client, deliver the painting, and collect the balance of his fee. He was satisfied with the work and delighted about the money, but his real pleasure would come when he saw her reaction. Also, with this project complete and paid for, he could afford to take time creating something different: maybe a surrealistic image to reflect America's moral and political disarray, he thought. He selected a canvas and placed on his easel. Then he picked up his sketch pad, grabbed a folding chair, and walked down to the lake, his favorite place for meditation. Seated beside the water, he watched a procession of ducks swim, smooth and graceful as skaters on ice, across the glassy surface. He studied the way the reflections of the clouds were rippled by their progress, and felt himself relaxing. Gradually thoughts about his new painting began to accumulate, and he started sketching them in his book. That was when his phone rang. His first instinct was to ignore it, but his creativity was already disturbed, so he reached into his pocket for it. Putting it to his ear, he said, "This is Justin."

A cheerful female voice on the other end greeted him with "Good morning, Justin. How are you today?" The voice was vaguely familiar, but he could not quite identify it. Whoever she was, she sensed his hesitation, so she added, "This is Jenny, Jenny Lane."

Justin's spirits rose. "Hi there!" he said. "It is good to hear your voice. How are things?"

There followed a little getting-to-know you chatter. Then Jenny said, "Actually, I wanted to speak to you. I have something to ask."

"Oh? What would that be?"

"I wondered if you might be free tomorrow. I am thinking of going down to Kemah to watch the boats, and would enjoy some company. If you would like to come, that is."

The invitation was unexpected, and Justin's first instinct was to accept, but his wariness about talking to the media got in the way. He hesitated before answering.

Jenny continued, "I promise to be a friend and not a reporter. Anything we talk about will be strictly off the record. I just think we could enjoy each other's company. I mean, I could enjoy yours. I should not guess how you might feel."

Justin took a deep breath and made his decision. "Actually, I think I feel the same. I would be pleased to come along."

"That is great," Jenny responded. "I know where you live, of course. How about I pick you up, maybe around one or one thirty?"

"That will work. I will be ready and looking forward to seeing you again."

"Super! See you then." She ended the call.

* * *

Kemah is a waterfront community, thirty-five miles south-east of Houston, situated where Clear Lake empties itself into Galveston Bay. There are nineteen marinas in and around the lake, with seven thousand boat slips, giving it the third largest concentration of pleasure boats in the country. Access to the broad waters of the Bay and, beyond that, into the Gulf of Mexico, is through the Kemah canal. The south side of the canal is home to the Boardwalk, a large leisure resort, with many restaurants and other attractions. Justin and his companion checked in at Landry's, a restaurant with wide water views, and asked for a table by the window. After a twenty minute wait, a table was found, and they were seated, able to watch the people wandering along the Boardwalk and the boats passing through the channel behind them.

Jenny said, "As a portrait artist, I'll bet you enjoy people watching." But Justin wasn't looking at the passersby: he was looking at her. Their eyes met in a fleeting moment of unexpected intimacy, which was over as quickly as it occurred, but which left its mark on both of them.

Justin studied her face as she quickly averted her gaze. Her complexion was exceptionally clear, her brown eyes wide and honest. He judged her to have a kind and open personality, possessing neither meanness nor guile. Her nose was, perhaps, a little small, but her raspberry-red lips were perfect. When she smiled, which she did often that afternoon, she literally sparkled.

"Justin," she said, trying to recapture his attention.

"Oh, I'm sorry," he said.

"You looked far away."

"On the contrary, I could not have been closer. You know, you have a very beautiful face. You will have to let me paint your portrait one day."

She blushed, and reached out to touch his hand. Nodding in affirmation, she said, "I think I would like that."

Without realizing it, he was beginning to fall in love. Who wouldn't have fallen for a girl with a smile like that?

The afternoon was a huge success. It was Jenny's date, and she led the conversation, but in a gentle and tactful way. That was fine with Justin: he was enjoying the best female company he had known since losing Emmy. They talked about all sorts of things, getting to know each other, finding out where they came from, how they liked to spend their time, and so on, and staying away from anything controversial. Evening came too soon, and they drove back to Sugar Land.

Justin noticed that Jenny made no attempt to use one of the available parking spaces, but pulled up against the curb, directly opposite his front door. Clearly, she was not expecting to stay.

"Why not come in for a glass of wine or a cup of coffee?" he suggested, but she declined. Smiling and shaking her head at the same time, she said, "Not today, but I certainly hope we can do this again."

He said, "Me too," and meant it.

Without warning she leaned across and kissed him quickly on the cheek. He responded by giving her the lightest possible kiss on her lips. Then, slightly embarrassed, he turned to open the door and step out. Leaning back into the car, he said, "Let's make it soon."

Inside the house, he poured himself a glass of wine, stretched out in his big recliner, and closed his eyes. It had been a really good day, even more so because Jenny had not asked any reporter-like questions about his gift, or predictions he had made, or people he had helped. He knew she must be curious about such things, and that they would discuss them one day, but on this occasion she had kept her promise to not be a reporter. He appreciated her for that.

It would be hard to say who had enjoyed their lunch at Kemah more, Jenny or Justin. When they parted, they both knew they wanted to repeat the event. She called him on the Monday to thank him for his company. That call lasted almost an hour and ended with a promise to get together on the next Sunday.

"I chose Kemah last time," she said. "You can choose this time."

"OK," he replied, "Shall I come and pick you up?"

"Driving into the city is a real pain, especially when you don't know where you are going. Why don't you let me come for you?"

Justin shrugged. "That would work."

"Great. I will be there, say, about noon."

* * *

Two days before their next date, the news broke. Some weeks previously, the President of the United States, had received a letter, dated April 1st. threatening a terrorist attack somewhere in the country. Although the FBI, the CIA, the NSA and the DHS had put all their resources into tracking down the sender of the letter and figuring out if the threat was real, nothing useful had been learned. The Administration had decided to keep the matter under wraps, but CNN obtained a leaked copy and broadcast it to the world.

Dear Mr. President,

We, the parents of United States servicemen and women, whose lives have been lost on overseas battlefields and through suicide after their return home, call upon your administration to put an end to all overseas involvement in other countries' wars and to bring our troops home.

We are ashamed that our country has put uniforms on the backs of our sons and daughters and then considered them suitable to be killed to further American political, economic, and commercial interests. The blood of our children is not the currency with which our governments should pay for their various policies. It is no longer enough to say that our young people knew the risks they were taking. By putting on their uniforms they did not become dispensable. Every one of them was innocent of bloodshed until our country put guns in their hands and told them who to kill. Not one of them deserved to die.

We demand that you, as Commander In Chief, immediately order the recall of all overseas combat troops and implement it before the coming Memorial Day. Should that not happen, a catastrophe will occur which will be as painful and unforgettable to America as the downing of Pan Am 103 over Lockerbie in 1988 or the destruction of the World Trade Center in 2001.

We regret undertaking this initiative, but we believe that our young people deserve to live.

Respectfully

The Memorial Day Group

April 1, 2019

Although the letter did not specify what the catastrophe would be, it was now being assumed that the downing of FlyAir 439 fulfilled the Memorial Day Group's promise. The news channels and the papers outdid themselves in covering the story. Only two facts were known: the letter had been received, very early in April, and the plane had been shot down, but there was no limit to the theories and predictions which were being made. Above all, there were two questions on everyone's mind: what would the President do about the troops, and what would the Memorial Day Group do next? Would they plan something even worse?

As Sunday approached, Justin realized he knew nothing about Jenny's social and political views. He hoped that their time together would not be spoiled by this news, important and frightening though it might be.

Sunday arrived and she was exactly on time. He was watching for her and walked out to meet her in the street. A friendly hug just happened. He kissed her cheek and said, "I am so pleased to see you again."

There was an awkward pause. She said, "Shall we go?" and he replied, "Sure. Just let me lock up." He turned to walk the few steps back to the house, and realized she was following. He looked at her, understood her intention, and said, "Do you want to come in for a moment?"

"Why not?" she said with a smile.

Inside the house, she looked around and said, "This is nice."

His town house had a main room with sitting and dining areas, at the back of which was a bar-height counter separating them from the kitchen. To the left was a pair of double doors, leading into the master bedroom. The main living area had three large windows and a high ceiling, creating a light and spacious feeling. A staircase led up beside one wall to an open landing, on which she could see an artist's easel and other furniture. A door led off that landing, presumably to a bedroom and perhaps a bathroom.

Jenny grinned at Justin. Indicating the landing, she said, "Is that where you work?"

He nodded. "Sometimes."

Without waiting for an invitation, she said, "Shall we?" and headed up the stairs. He followed.

Once on the landing, she could see there was an unfinished painting on the easel, mystically merging the shapes of skyscrapers collapsing onto the prone figure of a naked man. The sky was aflame with the setting sun. To Jenny, the colors were amazing, giving a sense of the whole world being on fire and mankind being consumed by it. When finished, the picture was going to be both stunning and alarming.

To one side of the easel there was a mobile table with drawers, on which were all sorts of paints and brushes, the tools of the artist's trade. Against the wall was a rack containing canvasses, standing on end. She pulled one out, a really elegant portrait of some woman. She pulled out others, taking time to study each one, sometimes asking questions and sometimes not. When she had finished, she turned to him with a happy but serious look on her face.

"You know, these are very good. I am impressed."

He just grinned, slightly embarrassed because he had wanted her to say that. She turned back around and saw there were two doors to the left. One was closed. That must be the bathroom, she surmised, because of its location in the corner. The other was open, revealing a bright room with a large window. In one corner, next to the window was another workstation: easel, paint wagon and stool. Behind the door, against the wall that faced the window, was an upholstered couch and a rather ornate upright chair. Various rolls of fabric were leaning against the wall in the corner. There were several lampstands scattered around, and a small stereo player on a table in a corner.

"Ah! This is your portrait studio. The scene of your success."

"I don't know about that."

She hooked her arm through his and squeezed. "I do."

For a moment, she held on to him and neither spoke. Then he asked,

"Would you like a coffee or a wine or something?"

She hesitated, measuring the moment. Then she gave him a bright smile and said, "Maybe we should go in search of that lunch we talked about. If you have decided where we are going, that is."

They drove southwest, away from Houston, eventually swinging straight south until they reached the coast. The terrain was as flat as a pool table, and the pastures just as green. They passed several herds of Texas Longhorns, brown and white and lazy in the sun. The road ended at Surfside Beach where they found a parking spot in front of the restaurant Justin had picked.

"This place serves the best catfish I've ever eaten," said Justin. "I hope you like that. If not, they have plenty of other choices."

They had to wait for an outdoor table but were seated eventually. Their meal was served at a leisurely pace which suited them, and it was after four when they finished. Leaving the car where it was, they walked onto the beach, holding hands.

"Justin, can I ask you something?"

She had already asked him dozens of questions: he wondered why she suddenly needed his permission.

"Of course."

"I have tried very hard to not be a reporter when I am with you, and I promise I am not being one now, but I am so curious about something."

"Which is?" he asked, knowing the answer.

"How is it you know things that other people don't? I would like to understand."

"Off the record, right?"

"Absolutely."

"Well, I am sorry to disappoint you, but I don't know how it happens. It just does, and not all the time, just occasionally."

"Is that all you can say?"

"No. I could say quite a lot and, if we stay friends, I imagine I will."

"I hope we do stay friends," she said, squeezing his hand.

Justin replied, "Then think about this. If we were riding in the car, up into the Rockies perhaps, the mountains would block our view. We would not be able to see what is on the other side. But that doesn't mean there is nothing there. Actually, there is a lot there, waiting to be discovered. Well, I sometimes think of the future like that. It is already there. We just have to take our time discovering it."

Jenny thought for a moment.

"That would mean that the future is already determined, already fixed."

"Exactly. We cannot see it, but that does not mean it isn't there. I sometimes say that the future has already happened, meaning that it is already laid out for us."

"So, should we give up worrying about tomorrow? All our efforts to figure out the best way forward, even for our own little lives, are they a waste of time?"

"Oh no! Not at all. They are what makes life interesting. They help us to grow as people, and life is more satisfying when we get things right. In any case, sweating our way through is part of the future that we cannot avoid. We don't have a choice."

"That is deep," said Jenny.

They went down to water's edge, took off their shoes and walked in the surf. It was a perfect afternoon. By mutual but unspoken agreement they turned to face each other. Jenny flowed into his embrace, and they kissed. Justin held her, immersed in the moment, time standing still. Then, suddenly realizing what he was doing, he released her, an embarrassed look on his face.

"I am sorry," he said, "I think I forgot myself."

She gave him her most radiant smile. "No, Justin. I rather hope you just found yourself."

He seemed a little confused, so she tugged on his arm. "Come on," she said, and they started walking again. It occurred to Justin that he had never been this contented with a female companion since his days with Emmy. He looked down at her. She noticed, and asked, "What?"

Caught off-guard, he said, "Nothing," but he did not mean it, and she knew that.

"I think we are good together," she said, putting his thoughts into words for him.

This new-found involvement with the intelligent and pretty news reporter was both unsettling and irresistible: he was not sure where it was leading, but he was prepared to see. Impatient, even.

It takes a good hour to drive from Surfside back to Sugar Land. They were in Jenny's Jeep Wrangler, and she was driving, so her concentration was more on the road than anything else. It was Justin's job to find subjects to talk about. He asked her what she had been working on lately. She replied, "My editor is trying to keep your story alive. He wants me to think up new aspects of it. Something different."

"My story?"

"Well, not yours really. The story about Flight 943. Did you see, on the news, that someone has claimed responsibility for it?"

"You mean the Memorial Day Group?"

She nodded. "That's the one."

"Do you think they really exist? No-one has ever heard of them."

Jenny maneuvered her way round a farm wagon full of pigs.

"My opinion, for what it's worth, is that they really are a new outfit, and their cause is what they say it is. They are Americans who are sick of our endless war in Afghanistan, and furious that we have sent in so many of our troops. But how the group came into being, and who leads it, I don't know where to start on that."

"What do you think about their mission statement?" Justin asked.

"Are you asking if I think that they are going to shoot another plane down, or something as bad, because the President did not comply?"

Justin stayed silent, allowing her time to think. After a minute or two, she continued.

"How can he do what they ask? Every administration from the beginning of time has agreed: you cannot negotiate with terrorists. Once you give in to them, there is no limit to what they can demand or what the country might have to do."

Justin pressed the issue. "So, you don't expect troop withdrawals in the near future?"

"No, I don't. In fact, I think they are less likely now than they were before this happened. How can he bring them home? He has only just sent more out. If the President brings them home any time soon, he will be marked down as weak, as cooperating with terrorists, and as unfit to be Commander in Chief. I suspect they are stuck over there, wherever they are, for a good bit longer."

Her passenger did not respond immediately, so she asked, "What do you think, Justin?"

"Do you mean, what is my opinion as a concerned citizen? Or are you asking for a prediction, based on my reputation for seeing the future?"

Jenny had to think about that.

"I guess I would like your rock-solid forecast, your preview as you call it. But I will settle for whatever you say."

"Then let me say, as a regular, largely uninformed member of society, I don't have a clue what he might do, although I think you might be right. A hurried withdrawal would be a real sign of weakness. As for me making some magical prediction, I am afraid you are out of luck. I have not had a preview about this, and I don't expect one. In fact, I am sure one will not come."

Slightly surprised, Jenny asked, "How can you be so sure?"

"Because I never see the results of remote events. Every preview I have ever had has come after I have spent some time with the person concerned."

"Do you mean, to have an insight into this, you will have to spend time, one on one with the President?"

"I suppose so. And let's face it, that is not likely to happen."

When they got back to the house, Justin invited her in. They spent the rest of the evening sitting very close to each other on the couch watching a couple of movies. As before, Jenny was sensitive to her companion's mood. She felt that their relationship was becoming very special, and would be all the better for not being rushed. Unlike other male companions she had known, he made no physical advances, and yet she felt that threads of intimacy were entangling them, binding them together.

It was past midnight when she looked up at him, pulled his face down to hers, and kissed him. With a sigh, she said, "It's late. I ought to be going."

He didn't say "You are probably right." Nor did he say, "You could always stay." He just let her make her move in her own time. When they were disentangled and standing up, he kissed her once more and said, "Let's do this again."

CHAPTER 10

Nehal

On Memorial Day, Justin had caused the FlyAir flight to Phoenix to be cancelled, saving a hundred or more lives. That should have made him feel pretty good, but it did not. The same action had led to the deaths of eighty-five others on their way to Palm Springs. That generated more guilt than he could bear. He was still living with that conflict when Nehal called. He was coming to visit.

* * *

Justin waited patiently, watching hordes of arriving passengers ride down the escalator and start looking around for the correct carousel. Baggage Claim was a noisy place, large and echoey, and the air was vaguely foul with the odors of several hundred human bodies. As usual, over by the back wall, there was a scattering of unclaimed bags, clumsily grouped together, like lost children, waiting for someone to tell them what to do. Why were there always so many, he wondered. Had they all arrived at the wrong airport? Or had they been forgotten by their impatient, scurrying owners?

For the umpteenth time he looked at the screen. The British Airways flight from London had landed on time. He glanced at his watch. How long would it take his friend to de-plane, conquer passport control, and make his way through the terminal? It did not matter: Justin enjoyed people watching. His eyes followed a tall, bean-pole of a man, with a pale, unhealthy complexion. He was patiently shepherding a small, plump, sunbaked woman with black hair and matching eyes, who looked as if she had spent her whole life out in the fields somewhere. It was the oddness of their pairing that attracted him. The man guided her through the crowd with great tenderness. A son, perhaps, caring for his mother? Or even his grandmother? But a grandmother's hair would be more gray than black, wouldn't it? They stopped at a carousel, and she leaned her head back to look up at the young man's face. She said something, and he replied. Justin could not hear what was said, but whatever it was, it made her smile. They obviously shared a close bond of family or friendship, and he was happy for them. Justin's only living relatives were his mother and his sister, and they lived two thousand miles away. He rarely saw them, let alone their smiles.

"But at least I have Jenny," he said to himself. "At least, I think I do."

As for friends, real friends, the sort who have shoulders you can cry on and who are actually pleased to see you when you show up, he had almost none. Except for Nehal, that is.

"Justin!"

He heard his name, and spun around. There, pushing his way through the crowd, was the friend whom he had not seen since they parted ways, that summer in Montecino. Not long after that, Nehal had returned to the family home in Mumbai, to fulfil his role as heir to the Agarwal empire. Many years had passed, but they had kept in touch, mostly by email, and were fairly up to speed on each other's lives. The prospect of a reunion was exciting.

Justin raised a hand high, and grinned widely as his friend approached. They embraced, and then stood apart to look at each other.

Nehal spoke first. "It is so good to see you, my friend." Noticing Justin's lean figure and clear complexion, he added, "But how have you managed to stay so young?"

Nehal's six foot frame had filled out generously since their student days, although he was still strikingly handsome. Justin punched him lightly in the stomach, "By not living quite as well as you, I think."

They laughed and pushed their way through to the carousel.

Soon they were in Justin's car and on their way into Houston. When Nehal had emailed Justin to announce his visit, he explained that he was coming to the city on business. "My meetings are all at the Four Seasons, so that is where I will be staying."

"How is it that you are still single?" Justin asked is his friend, once they were out of the airport and on the highway. "Surely the Agarwal empire requires you to breed an heir and successor? Someone will have to take over from you one day."

"Hang on!" exclaimed Nehal. "My father hasn't died yet! He is still in charge. Then it will be my turn. But you are right. My father is always on my case about it, but I keep resisting. I like the American method."

"The what?"

"The American method. Fall in love first. Marry later. In my country it often works the other way around."

"As your sister told me," Justin said. "I had to admire her discipline, her dutiful dedication to her marriage contract, but it made me sad."

"It made me sad too. I rather hoped she would fall in love with you. You would have made a much better brother-in-law than Aadi."

"I don't think that was ever on the cards."

"Well, she ended up with neither of you."

"She hasn't found anyone else, then?"

Nehal shook his head. "Not yet." He made a wry face. "And never will, I think."

"How so?"

"I think she is dedicated to walking in our grandfather's shoes. Although she has a great job right now, with the World Health Organization, she is becoming a mystic and a teacher. She spends all her spare time in meditation and study, and it shows. Already she has a reputation, and people often come to her. Before long she will take over his room, and his work, and forget about her career."

Justin glanced sideways at his friend. "Maybe that is her destiny."

For a couple of moments they drove on in silence, which was broken by Nehal.

"She did send you a message, by the way."

"Oh?"

"She was very impressed by your ability to see the future. Apparently you knew that she would never marry Aadi, long before she did."

"How did she know that? I never told her."

Nehal shrugged his shoulders. "I don't know that. She never said. But you must have communicated your thoughts somehow."

"She must be very perceptive."

"She sends you a big Thank You. Knowing about things in advance enabled her to be prepared. It saved her from wasting too much time and energy getting ready for a wedding that would never happen. And it made the whole thing easier to bear."

"I'm glad she feels that way."

"She hopes you are still helping people to handle their tomorrows. She says you have a real gift for doing good, even when predicting something bad."

Justin smiled at his friend.

Once Nehal had checked in at the hotel and found his room, he came down to the bar, to find Justin sitting on a sofa, in animated conversation with a pretty, dark haired young woman.

"Aha! Who do we have here? You didn't tell me about this," he said. "If I had known we were to be in good company I would have worn a tie."

Justin laughed and his companion looked a little embarrassed.

Standing up, he put his arm round Nehal's shoulders and said, "Jenny, I want you to meet my very good friend, Nehal Agarwal. We have known each other since college, but he lives nine thousand miles away. You might think he has been trying to avoid me!." He grinned happily and added, "Nehal, please meet Miss Jenny Lane, Houston's number one ace television reporter."

Jenny stood up and took Nehal's hand.

"Justin has told me a lot about you," she said with a welcoming smile.

"Don't believe a word of it," was the predictable reply.

Justin suggested they all sit down again.

"How long are you staying?" Jenny asked.

"Just a couple of days," said Nehal, "This is a flying trip for business. I have to be in New York the day after tomorrow."

"It is a shame you can't stay longer," she responded.

Nehal sighed.

"I know. Maybe another time. I really want to come back for a few days, and let this fellow here prove he really can paint a portrait."

Jenny smiled affectionately at Justin as she said, "Oh, you don't need to doubt that: he's the best there is in Texas! In anywhere, in fact!"

After cocktails in the bar the trio exited the hotel and strolled a couple of blocks to a Mediterranean restaurant that Jenny liked.

"After all, the Med is half way between us here and you in Mumbai," she said. "It should be a good compromise."

The food proved as excellent as she had promised. They enjoyed a long, leisurely meal, and left only when the waiters started closing down for the night.

"I don't know about a compromise," Nehal commented. "That was a meal to remember."

He took Jenny with one arm and Justin with the other, walking between them.

"This has been a wonderful evening, with you two very special people. We will have to find a way of getting together again."

Jenny looked up at him.

"Were you serious about Justin doing your portrait?"

"I was and I am. Years ago he painted a really fine picture of my sister, Shivangi, which she gave to our father. He has said, several times, that he would like a matching one of me."

"I hope you make a date to come back soon, then," she said.

"I think I will," was the reply.

CHAPTER 11

Previews

"So, you are the Prophet," said the girl with the spikey orange hair, gazing at Justin in wonder. She turned to Jenny and added, "You were right about his good looks," which made Jenny blush and Justin shake his head.

"I hate that term," he said.

Orange-head and Justin had just been introduced by Jenny, as she showed him where she lived.

"This is Binnie, my roommate,"

He looked at the hair, the wide, pale gray eyes which studied him through spectacles with blue frames and huge lenses. She had a wide mouth filled with sparkling, orthodontically corrected teeth, thick, brightly made-up lips, and an over-large nose. Everything about her was startling, but her voice was pleasant. He already knew that she was the primary tenant of the apartment and Jenny had rented a bedroom there for at least three years.

"I needed somewhere to stay, and she needed a roommate," she told him.

Binnie worked as a receptionist at a public relations firm in the city.

"I think she is very good at that," Jenny explained. "She just loves talking to people. Spend an hour with her and you know all the latest news or, I should say, gossip. We aren't the best of friends, but we get along well enough."

They spent an hour in the apartment, getting acquainted, and then Justin took the two girls to eat at a nearby Italian diner. Afterward, when it was just the two of them again, he and Jenny, they laughed about the evening.

"I never heard so much in so short a time," laughed Justin, "And such an inquisition! She doesn't mind what she asks or says, does she?"

"You'll get used to it," replied Jenny.

"That remains to be seen."

"I would like to entertain you, cook for you, that sort of thing," Jenny said, "But maybe I could mostly do it at your house. That might work better"

"I know what you mean. My kitchen is at your disposal."

* * *

The following Sunday Justin and Jenny decided to stay close to home. She asked him to show her round the Museum of Fine Art.

"I have been there once," she said, but I went there knowing very little about art, with someone who knew even less. Going with you will be an education."

They met at the museum, she getting there on the Metro-rail, and he by driving up. For two and a half hours they toured the galleries and looked at the various exhibits. Afterward he asked her which artists had impressed her the most.

"Maybe I liked the impressionists best. They painted intelligible pictures without being slaves to the scenes they were looking at. I enjoyed the way their presentations made me think about what they were thinking or feeling as they painted."

"That's very good," Justin replied, "You are about to be promoted to Art Critic for your TV station."

"I hope not," Jenny said, with a laugh, adding more seriously, "Some of the twentieth century art really worked for me, too. For example, there was that large Picasso, which didn't make much sense graphically, but was somehow stunning all the same."

They continued to discuss her experience as they walked to the car, but when they got in, Justin changed the subject.

"I am curious to know what Binnie thinks about your boyfriend. Did I pass the inspection?"

"Oh, she thinks you are terrific," was the reply.

"That's good, I suppose."

"She thinks that you are hugely famous and enormously rich. In fact, according to her, by finding you I have done fantastically well for myself."

He glanced across at her. She was studying his expression.

"Famous? I suppose so," he said. "Rich? Certainly not. In spite of that, I do hope that I am fantastically good for you. Or not too bad, at least."

She reached across and patted his knee.

"I don't know how I could have done better."

* * *

On another Sunday. Justin took Jenny to Galveston for lunch. They dined in a beachfront restaurant, feasting on oysters followed by shrimp etouffee, accompanied by chilled Chablis. Emerging from the building, they meandered along the seawall, watching the antics of the swimmers and sunbathers, and talking about nothing in particular.

After a while they lapsed into silence. Jenny pulled on Justin's arm to make him stop and turn to face her.

"Can I ask you something?" she said.

He was amused. "You often do," he said.

"This is serious," she continued, "And you might think I am being very rude, which I don't want to be, but I do want to ask."

"Ask what?"

She looked into his eyes, "You do know that you are very special to me, and that I think the world of you."

"But?"

Jenny averted her gaze. "But I need to ask you, do you always tell the truth?"

Justin was taken aback. He already treasured the bond of trust that had developed between them. Was it now in jeopardy?

"I think you need to explain," he said.

She looked into his face again. "I do love you and trust you: you have to know that. But I wonder: how can you be honest about your previews, to the people concerned? I mean, don't you sometimes have to lie a bit, to shield them from knowing what's coming their way?"

Her companion shook his head. "I hate telling lies," he said, "But I admit, it can be a problem. For example, not long ago I was dining with friends in Houston. I was placed next to an expectant mother, and talked to her quite a bit. ……."

Jenny interrupted. "So, if you saw that something really bad was going to happen to someone, like their baby dying perhaps, you would be willing to blurt it out and not bother about the consequences?"

"I would try to avoid telling her the bad news, but I would not tell her that everything was going to be good when I knew it wasn't. Once I start doing that, I will lose all credibility, and my own self-respect."

"So that situation has never arisen?"

"Not quite as blatantly as that. There have been a couple of times, though, when I have pretended that I did not have a preview, when in fact I did. I suppose you could call that lying: what do you think?"

Jenny hugged him. Still looking into his eyes, she said, "I think I love you for not wanting to hurt someone."

They started walking again.

"I have another question for you."

"Oh yes? Another needle to stick into me?"

"No, sweetheart, I am not trying to needle you, just to understand you a little better."

"Then ask away."

"Do you only see bad things? Don't you ever have previews of good things happening to people?"

"Of course I do, and I tell the people concerned. Sadly, they often fail to take me seriously. They think I am just giving them well-intended, but uninformed encouragement."

They saw an empty bench, facing the sea, and sat down.

"What I mostly see," said Justin, gazing into the distance but not seeing it, "Is people's feelings."

"How do you mean?" asked Jenny.

"If someone is taking exams, for example, I will probably not see their actual results, but I might well see their happiness or sadness when they learn how they did. Similarly, if someone is facing surgery, I might have a preview of the relief they will experience when it is over, or of their misery if things don't work out. The stronger their feelings, the more clearly I might see them and understand what is going to happen."

"So, people who don't have much in the way of feelings, presumably you can't do much for them."

"That seems to be true."

Spending Sundays together became their ritual. The two of them, artist and news reporter, gradually explored their part of Texas, visiting everywhere they could reach within the day. Over the next few months Justin visited more restaurants than he had entered in the previous five years. Also, sometime during that summer, they started a habit of Wednesday evening dates, too. Most often, Jenny would come to Sugar Land, and they would prepare a meal together. These occasions developed into long and precious evenings, during which their knowledge of each other deepened and their appreciation of each other grew. Week by week, their mutual respect and affection expanded into a love which would hold them together for ever.

CHAPTER 12

Tony

Six months had passed since flight 439 had crashed into Palm Springs and Jenny Lane had walked into Justin's life. He was at work in his studio when the phone rang. He picked it up and opened the call.

"This is Justin."

The caller was clearly male. He spoke with a slight accent, Italian perhaps, and sounded middle aged. "Are you the portrait painter."

"People say so."

"Do you undertake commissions."

"I do. That is how I make my living."

"And do you only paint in your studio, or are you able to go to wherever your client is?"

"I can travel if necessary. Why? What do you have in mind?"

"I live in California. Would you be willing to come out here if I paid your way? I need you to come and paint a portrait of my daughter."

"Why did he say 'need'?" wondered Justin, but he did not ask. Instead, he addressed the caller's question. It would not be the first time he had travelled out of state, although he did prefer to stay within driving distance of home.

"Possibly," he said.

"I could fly you up here, to Palm Springs. Would you have a problem with that? I will certainly make it worth your while."

"I guess that could work. By the way, how old is your daughter, may I ask?"

"Twenty-two."

"And she is willing to sit for me, for this portrait?"

"No problem."

The caller gave his name as Tony White. He provided Justin with an email address, and asked for a message proposing a fee and timescale for the project. An hour later Justin sent him a quotation. He could travel any time at two weeks' notice and would need to stay for up to a week: painting in oils can be a slow process. The proposal was accepted immediately. Justin was to appear at Houston's Hobby Airport at noon on the Thursday of the following week. A private jet would be waiting. Accommodation would be provided while he was in California.

* * *

If Tony's call had come as a surprise, so did the one which followed a week later.

"Is that Justin Gates?"

"It is."

"You don't know me." The caller spoke with an accent vaguely reminiscent of Guerneville. "My name is Craig Long. I work in the offie of the State Attorney for Riverside County, California."

Justin sighed. He wanted to say, "Oh no!" but thought better of it, and stayed silent.

"I need to sit down and talk with you about the crash of FlyWay 439, and what you know about it."

"Everything I know has already been told repeatedly to the FBI here in Houston."

"I am sure it has," said the caller, "But the investigation has moved along since then, and I have questions which they did not think of asking."

"I can't imagine what they would be."

"You will understand when we meet. I would like to set up a date for me to fly out to Houston. We can meet in the FBI office. You are familiar with that, I think. Will that work for you?"

"I suppose so, if it is absolutely necessary, but I am about to leave town on a trip. It would have to wait until my return."

Sounding a little put out, Craig said, "How long will you be away?"

"At least a week. I have a portrait commission in Palm Springs."

"Palm Springs!" exclaimed Craig. "That is just down the road from my office. Would you be willing to meet here instead?"

Justin thought for a moment. "I could probably do that, if my client doesn't mind me leaving the job for a few hours." Then something occurred to him. “Am I going to need a lawyer for this?”

“Oh no!” The response was intended to be reassuring, although it sounded a little forced. “You are not in any line of fire, so to speak. No-one is accusing you of anything.”

They discussed the possibility for a few minutes. In the end it was agreed that Justin could take time off from his painting at Tony White’s house, probably on the following Monday. Other details would be confirmed by ‘phone once he arrived in California.

* * *

Flying in style was a new experience for Justin. He had never coveted luxury, but he was grateful on this occasion because it allowed him to carry his canvases and supplies more easily than on a public airline. At Hobby, private planes use a small, exclusive, general aviation terminal, away from the crowded main facilities. There are no lines to wait in, only minimal security procedures to contend with, and no cramped coach-class seats to squeeze into. It was a rare treat to be alone in the splendid cabin with its soft leather and polished walnut and a deep comfortable armchair by the window. There were two pilots up front, and a slim good looking young man with blonde hair to serve him a lunch of cold sliced meats and salad, plus whatever drink he might want. He chose coffee.

Justin was looking out of the window as they made their final approach into Palm Springs. He looked at the distant hills and then down at the valley beneath, with sprawling subdivisions and a sparkling blue swimming pool in almost every yard. Then, as they came lower and closer to the airport, he saw the scorched ground and burned-out homes where Flight 439 had ended its life and those of the eighty-five people on board.

The plane landed, bumped gently on the concrete runway, and taxied to the general aviation terminal. The young steward opened the door and lowered the steps. “Don’t worry about your baggage, Mr. Gates. We will take care of all that.” Twenty minutes later he was riding in the front passenger seat of a shiny red Range Rover, up into the hills south of the city. They pulled into a curved driveway and stopped next to a short flight of stairs. These lead up the hillside to a long, low, single-story home. Followed by his driver, Justin ascended, to find himself on a paved terrace with a spectacular view across a wide valley toward distant hills. He looked around. The house itself seemed to be made of glass, with floor to ceiling windows along its entire length. At one end of the patio was a swimming pool, shimmering bright blue in the afternoon sun. At the other end, there was an arrangement of furniture, a table with chairs for eating, and several loungers for relaxing. This was obviously the comfortable home of a successful man.

A voice interrupted Justin's thought. He turned to see his host approaching, a slim, energetic looking man, probably in his late fifties, with silver-gray hair, brown eyes, a slim white moustache, and a wide, generous smile.

"Tony White, Mr. Gates. Please call me Tony. I shall call you Justin if I may. Welcome to my home."

"Please do. I am happy to be here. And I must thank you for your excellent travel arrangements." replied Justin. He looked at the house and the panorama it commanded. "You certainly do have a beautiful place."

"I must admit to loving it myself. Now, Andrew here will show you around and find you your room. Please feel free to make yourself at home. Mi casa es su casa. *(My house is your house.)* Take whatever time you need to freshen up. I have some work to finish, but we can meet here on the terrace for drinks at about six, if that's OK with you."

Andrew, it turned out, was the name of the young man who had been the steward on the flight and the chauffeur on the ride from the airport. He showed Justin around the house, ending in an extensive guest suite. There were two bedrooms and a connecting bathroom. "Mr. White thought you might like to work in one of these rooms and sleep in the other."

Justin said that was more than he needed. Andrew left him with a promise that his bags and supplies would be brought in immediately. He was as good as his word, bringing them all himself. He was turning out to be Tony's right hand man in all sorts of ways.

* * *

At five minutes past six Justin walked out onto the terrace. The temperature was high, over ninety Fahrenheit, but that did not seem to worry Tony White. He looked totally relaxed in shorts and a light cotton shirt. Justin was glad he had dressed casually too, summer slacks and a short-sleeved shirt.

"Come over here," called Tony, greeting him with a smile.

"Curious," thought Justin, "I am sure I have seen that smile somewhere before," but he could not remember where.

Tony was reclining on one of the loungers. A second one was close by, and a low table was between them, with a huge umbrella for a sunshade. An ice bucket containing a bottle of white wine had been set out, as well as pitchers of water and juice. Justin fell into the unoccupied lounger and followed his host's example, choosing iced pineapple juice. He wondered when the daughter was going to appear. Not immediately, it seemed. He was curious to see the girl whose portrait he was to paint. As yet, she did not even have a name.

It was clear from the start that Tony White liked to be in control. He began the conversation with, "So, Justin, tell me about yourself."

"What would you like to know."

"Oh, just whatever you feel like sharing. For example, where were you born? Where raised? Which schools did you attend?"

It was like an interview. Like? Heck, it was an interview. The interviewer appeared relaxed and friendly, but he clearly had an agenda. Justin, as interviewee, felt vaguely uncomfortable, although he was not sure why. Through a series of apparently casual questions, with enough momentary breaks for humor or anecdotes from Tony, Justin found himself giving an almost complete biography. Tony seemed interested in every aspect of his life.

"Tell me, Justin, do you have any particular ambitions or goals?"

Justin thought for a moment before replying, "Not really. I am fairly content with my life as it is."

"Have you never wanted to marry, and have a family?"

"No. I have had a few girlfriends over the years, but nothing serious. Except one, that is, and that was a long time ago."

"Anyone special now?"

Justin pursed his lips as he considered his reply.

"Perhaps," he said.

Tony laughed.

"You don't like to admit it, I can see."

"It's not like that. It is very new, and I am not sure where things are heading."

"But you like her, and are hoping things might work out."

It was Justin's turn to smile.

"I guess so."

"Well, tomorrow you can start on the portrait. The sooner you get it done, the sooner you can return to your sweetheart."

As they talked, Justin gradually became used to Tony's charming but domineering presence. The artist in him observed how Tony's facial expressions changed frequently as the conversation progressed. At one moment he appeared curious, the next amused, then fascinated, then distantly thoughtful. "It would be a challenge to paint his portrait," thought Justin.

Time sped by, until Andrew appeared and announced that dinner was ready. Tony rose from his seat and indicated in the direction of the house. "Shall we?". Justin followed him into the cool of the interior. Earlier, he had seen a splendid dining room with a table that could easily seat ten, but they went to a smaller table at one end of the spacious living room. It was set for just the two of them. Still no sign of the daughter.

As he sat down, Justin said, "Is your daughter not joining us?"

Tony replied, in a rather clipped manner, "She cannot be here this evening."

They were served a meal of cold avocado soup, followed by salmon in an orange sauce, accompanied by a fine Chardonnay. Dessert was a spread of cheese and fruit. Andrew acted as waiter. When Justin congratulated his host on the excellence of the meal, Tony said, "I am glad you enjoyed it." He turned to Andrew and said, "Could you ask Jose to spare us a moment?" A minute or two later the door from the kitchen opened and the chef appeared, a cheerful rotund figure in spotless whites.

"Ah! Jose. El Sr. Gates aquí quiere decirte lo que piensa de tu cocinaste." (*"Mr. Gates here wants to tell you what he thinks of your cooking."*) Tony watched Justin to see his reaction as he spoke this Spanish.

Justin almost choked on the cheese he was nibbling. He did not realize that Tony was going to put him on the spot. Fortunately, he knew enough of the language to catch the meaning, and quickly rose to the occasion. "That was the most delicious meal I have eaten in many months. I can see why Mr. White values your service. Eres un gran cocinero. *(You are a great cook)* Muchas gracias, Jose."

The cook's round, florid face broke into a huge grin. He bowed and muttered, "De nada. De nada."

Jose beamed. Tony seemed satisfied. He dismissed Jose and asked Andrew to serve coffee outside. They returned to the terrace, which was now in darkness save for the light spilling out from the windows of the house. The air was fresher and cooler than before. Andrew appeared with a coffee pot and cups, accompanied by small macaroon-like cookies.

There were two unexpected items on the table, a small black remote control and a large white envelope. Tony picked up the remote and aimed it upward. A line of overhead lights beamed down from the edge of the roof, illuminating the entire patio. Coffee was poured and cookies selected.

"You have been very patient, Justin. I know you have been itching to see Bella, to get started on studying her, getting to know her, in anticipation of your work tomorrow."

"I cannot deny it," the artist replied.

"Well, please understand, she cannot be here. She passed away just recently."

Justin stared at his host, speechless. He could see that his host was pleased to have startled him with the news.

With a satisfied smile, Tony opened the envelope and extracted a single eight-by-ten photograph. "This is the most recent picture I have of her. I take it you have painted portraits from photographs from time to time." He handed the picture to Justin, watching him closely. He recognized her at once. She was the girl he had studied and drawn while waiting for his flight on Memorial Day, the one whose death he had foreseen. Anabel White!

Justin was stunned. His mouth opened, but no words came out. For thirty seconds he just stared at the picture, wondering what was really going on? This could not be a coincidence. Finally, he lifted his gaze, looked across at Tony, and asked "Why?"

"Why what?"

"Why am I here? Why are you doing this?"

"You know why you are here, to paint her portrait."

"Why me? There are plenty of excellent artists right here in California."

"Nevertheless, I chose you. I have studied your work. You paint very sensitive, perceptive portraits."

"Thank you for the compliment, but I don't believe that is the real reason."

"What other reason could there be?"

"You tell me."

"Listen, Justin," said Tony, a little bitterness creeping into his tone, "I know what you did, back there in Houston that day. You sent my Bella onto Flight 439 and she was killed. If you had kept your mouth shut or minded your own business, she would never have switched flights and would still be alive. I figured that, since you took her away from me, you would be the perfect person to bring her back to me in the form of a portrait."

Justin took a deep breath as he tried to decide. Should he try to explain that she was destined to die that day whatever plane she was on? He had no doubt about that himself, but persuading her father might not be possible.

"Tony, I am so terribly sorry that she died, but you have to believe I did not send her to it. In fact, I did not even speak to her. What I did was to leave the plane myself because I thought it was going to crash. I did not share my concern with anyone else except the crew."

"So you were busy saving yourself but not concerned about saving other people."

"I told the crew on the plane. The airline decided to take everyone off that plane and re-route them on other flights. That is how your Bella ended up on 439. I had nothing to do with that."

"I want you to paint this portrait, Justin. I want you to study her picture. In fact, you will find many pictures of her in your rooms. I want you to look at them all. I want you to really get to know her. You have a special gift for empathy. I believe you might even come to love her. Then you might realize the pain I have because of what you did."

Justin found it hard to look at his host, let alone return to normal conversation with him. He quickly made his excuses and retired for the night. He was emotionally exhausted. Fortunately, there was a deep spa tub in the bathroom. He filled it nearly to the brim, lowered himself into it, closed his eyes and drifted into a semi-sleep.

He remembered Anabel as she had been in the airport, relaxed, reading her book, patiently content. She had the coloring and the bearing of his sister: that is what caught his eye. He had wondered what she was reading that enabled her to escape so completely from the bustle and hype all around her. He also recalled how he had boarded before her, and taken his seat in row 28, next to the aisle. She had boarded a few minutes later. He watched her come down the aisle toward him, stop two rows away, stretch up to place a bag in the overhead bin, and then lower herself into her seat, not ten feet away. For some reason, at that moment he had closed his eyes. That was when the preview hit. He saw her fly, still strapped in her seat, hurtling to the ground as the exploding plane disintegrated all around her.

The preview had departed as quickly as it had come. Justin remembered being horrified, frozen in his seat, yet with a desire to leap out of it and rush over to her and say something that would save her. But he knew that nothing could. On previous occasions, if he had dared to warn people that bad things were coming their way, they would usually try to avoid them. Never once did anyone succeed. In fact, the attempt to evade that destiny always became part the process by which it was fulfilled. As someone once said, "You often meet your fate on the road you take to avoid it."

That day, in Houston, there had been nothing he could do to save Tony's daughter. All he could do was remove himself from the plane.

Being brought face to face with his role in Annabel's tragedy was devastating. Justin did not know how to handle it. He was not even sure that he could paint the portrait now. Lying there in the bath, he tried to get rid of the confusion, to empty his mind of all thought. For the longest time he hardly knew what he was thinking about. Maybe he slept, he wasn't sure, but eventually he pulled himself together, climbed out of the tub and went to bed. His sleep was instant and deep. He woke to find the sun streaming in through the window, making him squint. He struggled out of bed and headed for the bathroom, where he splashed his face with cold water. As he shook off the last of his sleep, he realized that he needed to go ahead. The commission to portray Bella was an honor to him: it was also his opportunity to memorialize her.

* * *

Breakfast was served on the terrace. The ubiquitous Andrew offered Justin a choice of juices and fresh fruit, cheeses and breads and almost any cooked foods he might like. Justin chose scrambled eggs alongside an English muffin, with a bowl of fruit salad on the side. Plus coffee, of course.

Tony was nowhere to be seen. Andrew said he was away for the day, somewhere on business, but would return in time for dinner. Justin understood that he should retire to his temporary studio and get started. Lunch would be at whatever time he liked, but thirty minutes notice would be appreciated in the kitchen.

"One thing," said Andrew, "You are going to be here for several days, of course. Tony wants you to feel relaxed, at home, able to come and go and move around as you might wish. He says he cannot imagine you at your easel, painting continuously for eight or more hours a day, every day. There is a spare car in the garage. It used to be Bella's. You are free to use it if you wish."

"Actually," Justin said, "That would be really useful. There is something I forgot to mention to Tony, last night." He told Andrew about the call from Craig Long and his need to go to the DA's office in Riverside.

"I can't see that being a problem," was the response, "But I will talk to Tony about it, just in case there are any issues. Perhaps you would like me to liaise with Long on your behalf, since I know my way around here."

"Now that is an offer I won't refuse!"

Returning to the guest suite, Justin set about organizing his workspace. In the second room the bed had been pushed to one side and a canvas tarp spread over the carpet. Tony had promised to provide an easel, and it was there. The rest of his art supplies were to one side on a folding table, plus a roll of paper towels, a pitcher of water and a large book. The more comfortable chairs which had been in the room on the previous evening had been removed, replaced by a single upright wooden chair. Clearly his host did not want Justin to sit on his fine furniture in any paint-stained clothes. Tony (and Andrew, he was sure) had tried to think of everything.

Justin was curious about the book and went to pick it up. It turned out to be a thick photo album, the story of Anabel, told in pictures. He took it into the bedroom, stretched out on the bed, and began to become familiar with her life.

After an hour or so, Justin began to sketch out possible ideas for the portrait. The one thing that he and Tony had not discussed was what sort of portrait was wanted. Should it be full length, or just head and shoulders? Would a side profile serve better than a full face? Should his subject be standing or sitting? In what setting should she be placed? The only clue to his host's preferences was on the easel where someone, presumably Andrew, had placed a stretched and primed canvas, measuring twenty-four inches wide and forty-eight tall. Justin was to paint her full length.

He went in search of Andrew. "I am in need of two things," he told him. "One is a large pot of coffee, the other is some good advice."

Andrew looked a little perturbed. "Coffee is no problem. I am not so sure about advice." He suggested that Justin wait for the coffee on the terrace. It took just a few minutes, and came with a plate of cookies. There were two mugs. Andrew sat down and poured coffee for them both while Justin explained his problem about composing the painting. His helper said he could not help. "I have no idea what Tony would like," he said. "We have never talked about it."

"Maybe you could tell me about your boss's relationship with his daughter. There has been no mention of a Mrs. White. Did Anabel have a mother or was Tony a single father? Has she lived with him her whole life? I have seen pictures of her in the album, playing tennis and golf, but not with her father and not with anyone who might be her mother. There are vacation pictures from many places, so she has obviously traveled a lot, but her father rarely appears in the pictures and, again, never anyone who might be her mother. I don't want to make you tell me things you shouldn't, but the more I understand her life the better my work will be."

Andrew gazed over Justin's head, seeing unseen things in the distance, considering how he should answer. After some moments he looked directly at Justin and said, "All Mr. White wants is for you to show what a beautiful woman his daughter had become. But I can understand that the more feeling you have for who she was, the better your work will be, so I will tell you this. There used to be a Mrs. White, and she was Bella's mother. The three of them were a close and happy family, I believe. I was not around in those days, but I am sure that is correct. Mrs. White contracted cancer about twelve years ago, when Bella was ten. Her father was devastated. He never tried to replace her after she died. He and his daughter were very close. She never wanted for anything, yet, to me at least, she seemed quite unspoiled. She and her father traveled widely. The reason you don't see him in the pictures is simple. He was always behind the camera. He loved to take pictures of her. She gave him more pleasure in life than anything else. You can tell that from the size of the album. Anyway, she went away to Louisiana State University on a full sports scholarship, to study law. Her ambition was to be a public prosecutor. She was on her way back here when you met her, changing planes in Houston. That is about all I can tell you. I hope it is some help."

"That is great, Andrew. Thank you so much. I have just one more question. Do you know if Mr. White has a favorite picture of Bella?"

"He does have one in his bedroom. I can fetch it if you like."

Andrew went away and was back almost immediately. He held a gold framed photograph of Anabel. She was leaning against a stone wall somewhere, tall and slim, smiling at the photographer. Her affection for him was clear. She was dressed in white pants and a brown silk shirt, which beautifully complimented her wavy blonde hair. Justin studied it for a full minute.

"I don't think I can let you hang on to that," said Andrew.

"That is OK. I do appreciate you showing it to me, however. And thank you again for sorting out my things and setting up the studio. You are a great help. Quite invaluable to your boss, I should think." He handed back the picture and stood up. "I have work to do. Would it be alright if I took the coffee with me?"

"Don't do that. Let me bring you a fresh pot."

"If you wish. That would be great."

Tony arrived home in time for dinner, which was served in the dining room. The meal was simple: fruit salad, followed by filet mignon with roasted veg. While they ate, they talked about varied things, wandering from one subject to another apparently at random, although Justin suspected his host had, as always, some sort of agenda. Once the meal was finished, they relocated to the terrace, where Andrew brought coffee and cheeses and Tony chose the next topic of conversation.

"Andrew told me about your proposed meeting with the DA. I don't see any problem with it, but you might be wise to have an attorney with you. I could arrange for one, if you like."

"Craig Long said that would be quite unnecessary, and I think I believe him. Thank you all the same. It is a kind offer."

Tony grimaced, clearly not used to being turned down. He continued as if he had not heard Justin's reply. "Tomorrow, I will take you into town to meet my attorney. He is expecting us at eight thirty. Your appointment is at ten, and the Federal Building is close to his office, so he will walk over there with you. You can call Andrew when you need to come back to the house."

Then, as if the matter was closed, he changed the subject.

"Would you mind if we talked about what happened in Houston?"

Justin had been expecting the subject to come up.

"You mean, leading up to the crash that killed Bella?"

"That's right."

People ask me about that all the time, and I understand their curiosity. Normally I try to avoid in-depth discussions. Few inquirers are capable of understanding, but Tony was different. His daughter had died when the plane went down. Perhaps he still wanted to blame me, although, if that were the case, his friendly welcome would be hard to explain. He deserved an answer, an understanding of my role in her death. In fact, although almost six months had passed since that dreadful night, I was still having trouble coming to terms with it myself.

"I don't mind talking about it. What do you want to know?"

"I want to understand how you came to know that Bella was going to die that day."

Justin told him exactly what happened, beginning with the moment he first saw her, waiting for her flight, and included as much detail as possible. Tony studied his guest's face as he talked, trying to get behind the words and understand the experience.

"So, you had a vision? How else could you describe it?" he asked, when Justin was finished.

"I don't like that word," the artist replied. "It was more like a memory of something which was yet to happen."

"That doesn't make sense to me."

"When you remember something, you often visualize it even though you cannot see it. You never call that dreaming or having a vision. The experience is too real, and you know the truth of it. That is how it is with my previews."

"Justin," said Tony, "Yours is an amazing tale, and I am fascinated to meet you. When I first learned of your role in Bella's death, I was mad as hell, assuming that, in some way, you had caused it. Since then I have read and watched everything I could about you. I even had someone make inquiries, as the saying goes, and you came across as being exactly what you say. I became convinced that you were not responsible for what happened to her, although the question of whether you could have saved her continued to bother me. We needed to meet, you and I, for me to find the answer."

He paused, to sip his drink. Then he changed the subject.

"Through my research I have learned a lot about you, but there is nothing like seeing someone face to face. I am pleased to have you here, under my roof. And if you are as good an artist as people say, I am excited to have you do her portrait. By the way, how is it coming along?"

"Quite well, I think. Do you want to see?"

"No, thank you. I would rather wait until it is finished. I find an incomplete image of my daughter to be a confusing concept."

He raised his voice, "Andrew!" and the ubiquitous young man appeared at once. "Fresh coffee. And brandy, I think."

* * *

Next day, at dinner, Tony led the conversation again. He loved to travel, and gave fascinating accounts of safaris in Africa, mountain climbing in the Himalayas, deep sea diving off the Great Barrier Reef, and running with the huskies across Alaska. His enthusiasm for adventure was infectious, and Justin enjoyed listening. Then, the meal over, they adjourned once more to the terrace and the conversation became more serious.

Tony said, "You know, of course, that they have caught the guy who shot down Bella's plane."

Justin nodded. It had been all over the news. "Matthew Carne they call him. He is some sort of city employee in California, a quiet and respectable sort by all accounts. An unlikely suspect, by all accounts. No obvious connection to terrorism."

"It seems his parents are, or were, US citizens, who immigrated from Afghanistan decades ago. They were over there, visiting for some family event, when the Taliban bombed the village where they were staying. They, and their other son, were among the casualties. That might figure into his motive somehow."

"What do you think is going to happen to him?"

"Well, of course, there is going to be a trial, and they will want to put him away for life. Some will call for the death penalty. But they have to convict him before they do anything else."

Justin asked, "Is that going to be a problem? Isn't it a foregone conclusion?"

"There is always a chance of acquittal. I hear he has a series of alibis, whatever what that means. Obviously the feds think they can get round them. We have to wait and see. One odd thing: there is no obvious connection between him and the so-called Memorial Day Group."

"So he could be a one-man terrorist cell, calling himself that."

"Given the enormity of the crime, that seems a bit unlikely. If nothing else, he would have needed help in obtaining and learning to handle the missile, not to mention finding the funds for such an operation. That cannot have been cheap. The case might contain a few holes."

"But I imagine the deck is pretty much stacked against him. He has already been convicted in public opinion, thanks to the media. I wonder when the trial will be."

"It's sure to be in the new year. We'll know soon."

"After all the publicity, do you think a fair trial is even possible?'

Tony thought for a moment. "Don't forget, this is the United States. Many an innocent man has been found guilty in our courts. Carne's problem is that this case is politically red hot. The powers that be, from the President down, are desperate for a conviction. We know that there must be other conspirators, but it's possible they won't be found. If Carne was involved, he will know who they are, and might cut a deal by turning them in. But what if he is innocent? If he knows nothing, he won't be able to name anyone, so he will have no bargaining power. In that case, he is the only suspect. If the case against him is credible, he could go down for the whole thing."

"That is preposterous!" exclaimed Justin. "You mean that, if he is guilty, he might cut a deal and almost get off, but if he is innocent, he is likely to go to prison for the rest of his days?"

Tony nodded. "That's how it is, or at least, it could be."

* * *

Working in oils is a slow process. The paint has to be applied in layers, each of which must be at least partially dry before the next is added. Justin worked for several hours each day, but there were long periods when he could not work. At such times he relaxed in his room or beside the pool. He swam a little, but sunbathing held little pleasure for him. He would rather stretch out in the shade with a book. Tony was never around during the working day, although he usually appeared for cocktails at six. Andrew was always somewhere to be found, if needed, but Justin was largely left on his own. A couple of times he took advantage of his host's offer and took Bella's car for a drive.

On Monday morning, Tony kept his promise. He drove Justin into Riverside and introduced him to his attorney. Isaac Stern appeared to be an easy going, fatherly figure, tall, with white hair and gray eyes which smiled at the newcomers through a pair of rimless glasses. But his relaxed, easy-going manner disguised a sharp intellect and a massive accumulation of experience in the courts. Tony performed brief introductions and left, having told the attorney to take good care of his friend.

"Let's sit here," said Isaac, indicating a small conference table. "We don't have long, and I need to understand a few things before we get there."

He already knew what the main issue was, having spoken not only to Tony, but also the prosecutor's office. Now, he needed to understand the situation from Justin's point of view. Fortunately, he was a patient listener.

If he found Justin's tale hard to believe, he did not show it. The discussion lasted for half an hour, and then they set out for the meeting with Craig Long.

From Justin's point of view, it was all a waste of time. They met with two lawyers and a secretary present, but Craig did all the talking. Clearly, he was familiar with everything Justin had said to his FBI colleagues in Houston. There was nothing he could add concerning flight 439 and its demise. Then, as the meeting was drawing to a close, the second lawyer spoke up. He wanted to know if Justin had ever been to the Laguna Beach area, on the coast, south of LA, and whether he knew anything of someone called Matthew Carne or his wife. Justin answered "No" to all such questions, which was the truth. He had no idea what they were talking about. With that, Isaac and he were free to leave.

* * *

Apart from a brief conversation about the style and format of the portrait, Tony showed little interest in the project and did not visit the studio to monitor progress. He said, on day one, that he did not want to influence the work, preferring to wait until it was complete.

On his fifth day, Justin had stopped work early and was relaxing on the terrace when the Jaguar purred into the driveway below. A few minutes later Tony appeared. The two of them greeted each other and, right on cue, Andrew appeared with wine.

"How are you coming along?" asked Tony.

"Good news," said Justin, "I think I have finished. Would you like to see?"

"Congratulations! I certainly would. Let's go."

They rose from their chairs and carried their glasses to the studio. Justin had moved the easel to the corner opposite the door so that the picture could be viewed from a distance. As soon as Tony stepped into the room he stopped, stunned.

"That is amazing!" He spoke slowly, staring at the image of his daughter. He paused for a long time, then walked further into the room and moved around, viewing the picture from different angles. "It is brilliant. You are quite as excellent as I was told."

Anabel, better known as Bella, was smiling at him. She was perched on a low stone wall, leaning backward a little, supporting herself on her left arm. She wore a light, modest summer dress of purple and pink, knee length. The lower part of her legs could be seen, one ankle crossed over the other, her feet encased in gold sandals that matched her hair. Her blue eyes showed a particular kindness, or was it affection, for the person at whom she was looking.

"Quite beautiful!" murmured Tony. "Yes."

He turned to look at the artist. "I hope you are as happy with your work as I am."

Justin turned to look at him, and then looked away. There were tears in Tony's eyes, and he did not want to embarrass him.

"I was privileged to paint this. The more I worked on it, the more I felt that Bella looked like my sister, Tina. It was a strange sensation, but it made me feel very close to her in a way."

"There is a reason for that, you know."

"There is?"

"I have been waiting to tell you. Bella is Tina's sister."

Justin turned and stared at Tony, speechless.

"It is true. Come back to the terrace, and I'll tell you the story."

Two minutes later they were back, sitting under the shade of the big umbrella. The artist gazed at his host expectantly. Stunned by the news, he had still not spoken.

"Maybe we should start," said Tony, "By you telling me what you know about where your sister came from."

"That is easy," replied Justin, "I know nothing. Mother has never said who Tina's father was, or how they got together, not to me nor anyone else."

Tony studied his wine. "Twenty-six years ago, when I was younger and wilder than now, I attended a business conference at a seafront hotel near San Simeon. It was the sort of place where you can relax, enjoy the ocean, and forget the world. That's when I met Alice. I don't think either of us was looking for anything, but we found ourselves sitting next to each other, watching the sun set. It was very romantic. We just started talking. You know, she was a very beautiful young woman. She probably still is. Anyway, we drank wine and talked for hours, and didn't want the evening to end. She told me a lot about herself, and her home in Guerneville, and about you, of course. She was so very proud of you. You were her reason for everything. I am sure I told her a good deal about myself too, but I cannot recall. The sun went down, and night grew dark and chill, but neither of us was ready to quit, so we moved indoors. Next morning, we woke up and went our separate ways. Really, that is all there is to it. Looking back, I cannot be very proud of my behavior, but nor do I regret it. It is one of the most precious memories I have."

Justin interrupted, "But surely you exchanged phone numbers or something?"

"Actually, your mother was still asleep when I left. I scribbled her a note and added my phone number, but I never did hear from her." He looked up at Justin. "I know this can sound like a cheap, one night affair, but I want you to know that it was a very special and memorable event in my life. I was getting over a relationship that had ended, and wasn't ready for a new one, but Alice really needed someone. I don't think anyone had ever shown her real love, certainly not in years. I never forgot her."

Justin could not help staring at his host. "I don't understand. If my mother affected you like that, why didn't you try harder to make something of it?"

"I don't really know," was the reply. "The encounter was surreal, but I was in my early twenties and ready to take on the world, but not someone who already had a family. Also, you must remember that I did leave her my number, and she chose not to call. I don't think either of us thought that she might have become pregnant. We just went our separate ways. It wasn't until much later, when I was married and had a daughter of my own, that I had to go to Guerneville on business. My appointment was in a client's home. There was a portrait hanging on his wall. It was an intriguing work and I said so. That is how I learned about a young artist called Justin Gates who lived in the town, and that made me remember a delightful, if rather sad, young lady called Alice Gates. I asked my client if he knew the artist's mother's name. He checked with this wife, who confirmed it was Alice. The fact that she now had a daughter did not come up, although I did learn that she taught at the local school.

"In 2009 I went through Guerneville again. My wife had passed away by then. On an impulse I went by the school and, long story short, caught up with your mom. That is when I learned about Tina. Truthfully, I was embarrassed to have fathered a child about whom I knew nothing. I asked Alice what I could do, how I could make up. She said she did not need my help, and I should go away. She was quite clear that she did want me around and I respected her wish, whatever her reason.

"Then, a few months ago, Bella was traveling through Houston, and you saw her. Even then, you only came to my attention because you got yourself into the news. Surely, I thought, there cannot be two portrait artists called Justin Gates. I just had to track you down. The rest you know."

Tony fell silent. He took a deep breath, carefully set his wine glass on the table, and looked at his guest.

"Unbelievable," was all Justin could say. "Quite unbelievable."

* * *

Next day, Tony and Justin met on the terrace for breakfast. The portrait was finished and Justin needed to return to Houston. He assumed he would be sent back in the jet, although that seemed an unnecessary luxury.

When they had eaten, it was Tony who raised the subject. "I hope you know, Justin, you have been a welcome guest. It is a pleasure to have you under my roof, and you should feel free to visit whenever you like, but I imagine you are itching to get back home now."

"If you wouldn't mind. I thought I could catch a regular flight at the airport."

"That would work for me," said Tony, "Especially since the jet is tied up this week. I will have Andrew make arrangements. Would tomorrow be OK?"

"That would be fine by me."

"Before you go, Justin, there is one more thing we need to discuss. It is something that matters a lot to me. I want to ask you for a very big favor."

"Oh?"

"I want you to come to California and stay with me, here, during the trial, whenever that might be. I have plenty of money and can afford to pay you well for your time, but I shall need you by my side."

"I am not sure I want to be at the trial."

Tony leaned forward, looking his guest straight in the face, and said in a taut voice, "Remember, this is all about who murdered my daughter. Nothing is more important than watching the culprit brought to justice, but I am not sure we are going to see that done. The trial could end with the wrong man going to jail, which would leave the true villain out there, free and clear. It could also set Carne free, even though he might actually be guilty. Some justice that would be! Now, you Justin, have more insight into the dark souls of men than anyone else I know. Also, you have shown a strange, almost mystical connection, to the events surrounding Bella's death. I want to have you here with me when this all comes to a head, and we can figure it out together."

"I don't know, Tony, …." Justin began.

The older man continued to press his point. "I would be surprised if you stayed away, given your intimate involvement in the crime and the fact that your prediction may have led to the murder of your sister's sister, my Bella. not to mention the nearly one hundred other people who died. I can't imagine you not attending." He settled back in his chair to reduce the pressure of the moment, but still he added, "Think about it." It was an order from a man who was used to getting his way.

Justin reached for his coffee and contemplated the brown liquid before he replied. Then he looked at his host, "I suppose I could attend. It might help us both to find some closure. I take it that you intend to be there yourself?"

"Of course."

"Then I'll do it."

As it turned out, there was a direct flight that afternoon. Justin called Jenny with the news.

"Wonderful!" she exclaimed in delight. "What time will you land? At which airport?"

He gave her the details.

"I am so excited," she said. "I can't wait to see you."

Justin was quite moved by her response. He had to swallow hard before he spoke.

"You know, Jen, I have missed you so much more than I expected. It has been a whole new thing for me."

"I am so glad!"

Six hours later, there she was, waiting patiently by the baggage carrousel. Justin wanted to run across the hall, grab her, lift her off the ground, whirl her round in a circle, and make a real spectacle of himself. Instead, he walked over quietly, hugged her gently and whispered, "God, I missed you."

She kissed him, long and sweet, and said, "Missed you too."

Almost since Kemah, he had known that there was something special between them, something which had become increasingly important to him since, but only then did he realize that he wanted it to never end.

It was well into the evening when he landed, since Houston is on central time, two hours ahead of Palm Springs. Jenny offered to celebrate his return by taking him to eat at a favorite restaurant, but he suggested Chinese take-out had more appeal.

"We could enjoy that at home. Just the two of us. That's what I think I would like."

"Me too," she said happily.

Later, seated on the couch, with the wreckage of their meal on the coffee table in front of them, Jenny raised a question which had been in both of their minds. Christmas was approaching, and she wondered how Justin intended to spend it.

"I had thought of going back to California, to Guerneville," he said. "What do you have in mind?"

Jenny looked suddenly, and unusually, coy. "Well, to be honest, I was hoping we might spend it together, just you and me. Together."

Justin's face broke into the most enormous smile. He reached out and pulled her against him, then used a hand to raise her chin so that their lips almost touched. "Together it shall be." He kissed her, gently. "But I am not sure about the 'just you and me' bit. I was rather thinking that I might take you to California, and introduce you to my mother and my sister …." He took a deep breath, and added, "As my fiancée."

"Oh," she gasped.

"Is that all you have to say?"

"Oh no!" she replied, and he saw tears in the corners of her eyes. "You just took me by surprise. I was lost for words."

Justin smiled again, gently mocking. "A news reporter, lost for words! Well, I never!"

She punched him gently in his ribs. "Stop it! You can have all the words you want. How many ways are there for saying YES? I love you, Justin. You must know that. I give you every YES I can, in every language and in every way."

The two of them stood, just inches apart, studying each other's face, knowing what true love really feels like.

Jenny did not go home until the sun and risen on anew day.

CHAPTER 13

Liz

It was a Monday morning in February. Justin reluctantly set his art aside to work on his taxes. The final return would be left to his accountant, but he had to assemble and sort the various papers. It was an annual chore that brought him no pleasure, and the phone call came as a welcome diversion.

"This is Justin," he said.

"Are you Justin Gates, the artist?"

"I am. How can I help you?"

"I have a project to discuss with you."

It was a woman's voice, clear and articulate. Justin visualized someone of English descent, the product of a good home and a fine education.

"What sort of project?"

"Perhaps I could come and explain it to you, face to face."a

"You cannot tell me over the phone?"

"I would rather not. It's a little complicated."

"Well, you are welcome to come here if you wish. I live on the edge of Houston."

"I know where you live. Would you be available on Thursday?"

"I believe so."

The caller gave her name as Liz, agreed to come at 3pm., and would say no more.

Three days later, she arrived, exactly as promised. Justin opened the door and invited her in. Her appearance matched her voice, sophisticated and constrained. Wearing a mid-blue pants-suit over a white shirt, she appeared to be a Caucasian of middle height and weight, with brown eyes, well made-up face, and hair pulled back into a ponytail. In spite of her evident good manners, she greeted him without a smile. He noticed the sadness in her eyes and the anxiety creases at the corners of her mouth.

Justin offered her a choice of drinks, and she settled on water.

"Shall we sit here?" he asked, indicating the living room, "Or do you need to be in the studio?"

"This will be fine," she replied, lowering herself into a couch.

There was an awkward pause, as if she did not know what to say next.

"Whose portrait do you wish me to paint?" asked the artist.

"No-one's really," was the surprising reply. "When I said I had a project to discuss, it was not about painting."

Justin looked at her, eyebrows raised, forcing her to continue.

"I understand you are some sort of mystic," she said.

He did not respond.

"Aren't you the man who predicted the Palm Springs disaster last year?"

Justin shifted uncomfortably in his chair. "So people say, although that whole thing is complicated. Anyway, how would my role in that tragedy bring you to my door?"

"I haven't told you my name yet, have I? It is Elizabeth Carne. My husband is facing trial for shooting down that plane."

Justin did not know how to react.

"You need to know he's innocent. He did not bring that plane down. In fact, he had absolutely nothing to do with it." she continued. "The point is, he has already been tried in the media and found guilty. People are out for his blood. Now the real trial is about to happen, and I just can't handle it. In fact, the stress is destroying me, more and more each day."

Her calm demeanor began to crumble. "I need to know what is going to happen."

"And you think I know?"

"Yes. I have read about your special gifts. I know what happened last spring when the plane came down. I'm hoping you have enough insight, now, to know how the trial is going to turn out. Will they acquit him or put him away for life?" She wiped away a tear. "Night after night I lie in bed, knowing they plan to convict him, and throw away the key. And yet I keep telling myself, there has to be room for hope. I know he didn't do it. He was asleep in our bed at the time. They just won't believe me."

Elizabeth Carne was sitting, crying quietly, on his couch, and Justin had not the slightest idea how to help.

"Elizabeth ..." he began.

"Please call me Liz: everyone does."

"I am worried about something. Please tell me that you didn't fly all the way here from California, just to see me."

"Actually, I did."

"That might not have been clever. I don't think you understand how my predictions work."

"Then tell me."

"This is not a grocery store. You can't just walk in and say, 'A can of forecasts, please,' and expect me to reach up and grab one off a shelf."

"Well, how do they work? I need to know."

"First of all, I have never made a prediction without first being in the presence of the person concerned. You want me to tell you what is going to happen to Matthew without even meeting him. That can't be done."

Liz Carne wiped her tears and said in a plaintive voice, "Isn't there any way for you to help?"

"Also, please understand, my insights don't arise upon request. I usually need to spend time with a person, getting to know them. I paint portraits as you know, which means spending hours studying faces and trying to meet the people behind them. Then, once in a while, if that happens, I might see things about their lives that they can't see for themselves."

"Like into their future?"

"Yes."

"Then I want you to paint my portrait."

"When?"

"Starting right now. Why not?"

"I am not sure I have the time, and even if I do, there is no guarantee I will be able to tell you what you want to know."

"Please, Justin. Please. You don't know how desperate I am. Please."

After some discussion the project was agreed. Liz would return next day.

"Then we'll see what we can do," said the artist.

* * *

Liz arrived on time, and they started straight away. Instead of working upstairs in his studio, Justin had set up an easel in the living room and proposed to portray Liz sitting back on the couch.

"You looked so tense yesterday," he explained, "I thought this might help you to relax a little."

They spent a while deciding exactly how she should sit, what she should do with her hands, and so on. When he was satisfied, and was sure she could sit comfortably for an extended period, he brought out a camera and took several photos. "To allow me to continue working after you have gone," he explained.

He worked steadily for the next four hours, almost without pause, occasionally releasing Liz from her pose, allowing her to get up and stretch her legs.

As the afternoon passed, she became increasingly curious about Justin's progress, but he would not allow her to look. "It's better not to see the work until it's nearly done," he said. "You might be tempted to change the way you are sitting, or smiling, or something, which could be a problem for me."

Just before five, without warning, the front door opened and in walked an attractive young woman with wide brown eyes and shoulder length hair. When she saw Liz, she stopped moving, smiled happily, and said, "Oh, hello. You must be Liz."

"Hello to you, too," Liz responded, not having a clue who the newcomer might be.

Justin laughed at the awkward moment.

"Liz, let me introduce you to my fiancée, Jenny. I have already told her who you are."

Jenny walked over to him, kissed his cheek, and said, "Happy day, sweetheart." Then she turned to look at the half-completed painting, "Not bad," she commented, "I do believe you might out-do yourself .... Again."

Justin grinned at her affectionately and started packing up his brushes and supplies. "I guess that will have to do for today," he said.

Jenny sat on the edge of the couch and looked at their guest. "Tell me, is he treating you properly? Has he shown you around? I'll bet he hasn't even taken you down to the lake yet."

Liz shook her head, and Jenny said, "Typical artist! One track mind. Come on then. Let's leave him to get cleaned up and get ready to take us out on the town."

"On the town?" echoed the visitor.

"Well, not exactly, but we could certainly go somewhere for a wine and a bite."

Half an hour later, when Justin was ready, the three of them walked to Casa Perez, a local restaurant, where the owner greeted them like old friends. When he saw that Justin and Jenny had brought a stranger, his smile got broader than ever.

"Ah! Any amiga of Señor Gates is more than welcome. He is a great and famous man! We are honored that he eats here." Then he pointed his finger at Justin, "And you, my friend, are honored that I feed you!"

Daniela, the waitress, seated them in their usual booth by the window, and they got busy ordering wine and food. As they ate, they got to know one another, talking about their various lives, jobs, and families. It was a pleasant enough time, but over-hung by the cloud of Liz's problem. Toward the end of the meal, she looked at Justin.

"Can I ask you a question?"

"Of course."

"You mustn't be shocked. I am not trying to be rude."

"OK. What is your question?"

"Have you ever made a prediction that did not come true?"

"I don't think so. I hope not."

"Then, when you say something is going to happen, we can be sure it will?"

"It seems to work out that way."

"In that case, is it possible that, by predicting something, you actually cause it to happen?"

Jenny spoke. "Are you suggesting that he brings things about, just by the power of his imagination?"

Liz replied, "It seems possible."

Justin stared at her, horror stricken. "That is ridiculous!" he exclaimed. The idea that he was responsible for the events he predicted was scary, to say the least.

Jenny said, with a frown, "So are you suggesting that, by predicting the crash of 439, he is responsible for all those people being killed?"

"I didn't say that!" Liz protested.

"But isn't that what you meant?"

Liz continued, "I am not sure what I meant. I am just puzzled by the fact that impossible things seem to happen where Justin is concerned, and I am trying to have an open mind. He does have some mystical connection to the future, which even he cannot explain. He claims to have a vision, tells someone about it, and then it happens. What is more, he says it ***always happens***. That is pretty remarkable .... and unique, don't you think?"

Justin was hardly listening to her. He was remembering a voice he had first heard when he was eight years old. "If your boy had not said this would happen, it wouldn't have." Now, he leaned toward Liz and said, "So, you think I make self-fulfilling prophecies."

"In a way, yes."

"Well, let me tell you about the first prediction I made; and, by the way, I hate the word prophecy. Anyway, I was only four years old. I don't even remember making it, but my mother insists I did. I told her that she was going to give me a baby sister, and a year later that is what happened. Now, how could that have been self-fulfilling?"

Jenny re-enforced the point. "Could a four-year-old boy induce his mother to get herself pregnant by the power of his will? Hardly likely!"

"Please forgive me," said Liz. "I was just trying to make sense of things. After all, what a wonderful gift it would be, how much good someone could do, if they had the power to imagine things and then watch them happen."

Justin was studying her face. "So, you actually came to Texas hoping to persuade me to imagine a world in which your husband is acquitted of bringing down that plane," and Jenny added, "Wouldn't that mean Justin was, in fact, responsible for the crash itself, since he predicted it?"

There was a long silence between them. Then Justin picked up his wine glass and proposed a toast, "Anyway, here is to Matthew. May his innocence be proved and his life restored." The three of them clinked their glasses and drank.

Liz looked chastened. "I am sorry, I did not mean to ... "

Justin stopped her with a gesture of his hand. "Don't worry about it, but please do remember: until or unless I receive a preview, a vision as you call it, there will be no prediction, not even for Matthew. As for the power to make something happen," he shook his head, "I just don't know anything about that."

It was, of course, ridiculous to suggest that I was responsible for the crash of flight 439, but the very fact that someone could think it was terrifying.

Liz called for an Uber to pick her up at the restaurant, the others waiting with her until it came.

"There goes one very unhappy lady," observed Jenny, as the car drove away.

"I agree," replied Justin. "Hers was one of the saddest faces I have ever had to paint. Still, I hope you would be that sad if I were facing life in prison."

"She came, hoping you would say there would be an acquittal."

"I know."

* * *

Almost two weeks passed. Jenny arrived at Sugar Land for their Wednesday night date. She found Justin upstairs, in his studio, perched on a stool, studying the picture of Liz, which he had just finished. He glanced at his fiancée and said, "Hi, Sweetheart," but did not rise from his seat.

She came up to him and kissed his cheek. It was clear he was distracted.

"Boy, that is an enthusiastic welcome!" she teased. "Is something wrong?"

"I'm sorry," he said, "I was just thinking about this." He nodded toward the picture on the easel.

She turned her head to look at it herself, and gasped.

"Justin," she said, "Are you sure that is how she looked?"

"I have had a big problem with this one," the artist admitted. "Three times I tried to paint the sadness we both saw in her face, and just could not get it right. So, I thought I would paint, not the misery she was feeling, but the happiness she was longing for."

"Well, you did a brilliant job at that. She looks beautiful and radiant. Amazing. Is it finished?"

"I think so. I don't really want to alter it again, but now I don't know if I can send it to her. How do you think she will react, Jenny?"

"Hmmm. That is a hard one, but you do have to send it. Not only have you been paid. You also have a promise to keep."

"I was thinking of sending a message with it, saying something like, 'I have attempted to paint the real you.' Do you think that would help?"

"I suppose it might."

* * *

Liz's doorbell rang twice. She dropped her book and ran to see who it was. A tall, skinny man wearing a brown UPS uniform was standing there, clutching a hand-held computer, which he thrust toward her. "Sign here, ma'am, please." She did so, and he fled.

Leaning against the doorpost was a large rectangular box, almost three feet square and six inches thick. "Can I even lift that?" she wondered.

Her impatience gave her strength, and she hauled it into the living room, fetched a sharp knife, and opened it up. The picture, in a sturdy gold frame, lay face down in its container. Excitedly, she eased it upright, saw the image for the first time, and stared in amazement. When she had commissioned the picture, less than three weeks previously, she had known she was not looking her best. In fact, she had not looked either healthy or happy for several months, yet here was a picture of a vibrant, healthy, smiling woman. It was undoubtedly she, and yet not in the slightest like the version of herself she had presented when she went to Houston.

She leaned the picture against a chair and looked in the box again. There was a plain white envelope, which she opened. The note inside did not say, "I have attempted to paint the real you." In fact, it was not from Justin at all. Instead, it said, "I hope you like this. If you want to, please feel free to call. Warmest. Jenny." A phone number was included.

Liz looked around the walls of her living room, then walked over to the one opposite the window, lifted down the Lakeland scene which had been hanging there since she and Matthew moved in, and hung the new portrait in its place. Then, a glass of wine in hand, she lay back on the sofa and studied it. Justin had certainly done a masterful job. She looked out at herself from the canvas, eyes smiling, cheeks slightly flushed with excitement, and a smile that was almost a laugh. To be sure, it was a flattering image in a way, and yet she felt (or was it hoped?) that it was an insightful picture of who she really was. But how did he come to paint her in that mood, when she had been so totally not that way when she and he had met?

She reached for her phone and dialed the number she had been given.

"This is Jenny."

"Ah, Jenny, this is Liz Carne. I received Justin's picture and thought I would give you a call."

"Well? What do you think? I hope you like it."

"Like it? I love it! As a piece of art, I think it is brilliant. As a portrait, it is so totally flattering. I wish I really did look like that."

"I know what you mean. If I can be honest with you, Liz, I was a little surprised, myself, when I first saw it."

"Why do you think he painted me like that?"

"Why do you think?"

"I don't know. That's why I called you. You know him better than I. I thought you could tell me."

"I think he expects you to be and feel happy and relieved, when all this nightmare is over."

"I am not sure it will ever be over."

"I am sure he wants you to believe it will, that things will come out alright in the end."

"Do you mean …?"

"That Justin does not want you to give up hope."

"Do you mean, he thinks they'll find him innocent?"

"Not guilty, you mean."

"Yes. Does Justin believe that an acquittal is possible?

"An acquittal? Of course."

Liz could hardly contain her excitement. "Can I tell Matthew what Justin thinks?"

"That might not be a good idea. Justin would need to see your husband face to face before telling him that he's going to win."

"But his predictions do always come true, don't they?

You can believe it."

"Oh, Jenny! Do you really believe that?"

"You never know about tomorrow, of course."

"But Justin does! Tell him I love the picture, and I am going to take it as his sign that Matthew's going to be OK."

They continued chatting for a short while. Liz was excited, believing that all would be well for Matthew and her. Eventually, when the call ended, Liz drained her glass and refilled it.

Fifteen hundred miles away, Jenny frowned and thought to herself, "I hope I haven't said the wrong thing."

CHAPTER 14

The Judge

Ever since the debacle of Memorial Day, when the world had learned of Justin's connection to the disaster in Palm Springs, the media had made his name known across the country. Much to his displeasure, he had become even more famous than before. In the weeks immediately following the crash, he had been bombarded with phone calls and doorstep visitors, many with microphones in hand. The fact that he had identified the wrong FlyAir plane did not seem to matter; in fact, it made the tale more interesting. To all such inquirers he said as little as possible, and gradually the attention faded, but by then the Prophet of Houston was known everywhere.

The Carne trial was scheduled for the first week in April. The media were preparing their audiences, rehashing details of the event, discussing what was known of Matthew Carne, and finding or inventing whatever background pieces they could. Two days after Liz received her portrait a phone call came into the office of the San Francisco Chronicle and was patched through to the news desk. The caller was female. She spoke excellent english with a clear, mid-western accent; obviously a well-educated woman. She did not want to leave her name, but she did wonder if the paper was interested in the Carne trial. Of course it was. Then it might like to know that the Prophet of Houston, who had foretold the defendant's crime, was now predicting his acquittal. The caller would not say how she came by this information, but she swore that it was true.

Brad Sumner was a rookie reporter, but his editor was pleased with him and thought he had good potential. He was given the assignment: locate and contact the Prophet and find out if the rumor was correct. His first two calls to Sugar Land went unanswered, and he left messages. They were not returned. He would have done better had he not identified himself. As it was, they made Justin aware that a journalist was after him. He could not imagine why, since he had lain low and not made any public or significant predictions recently, but he was always wary of reporters. When Jenny arrived for their usual weekend together, he told her he was concerned.

"Some reporter from San Francisco has been trying to reach me," he said. "I don't know why but I don't like it. With the Carne trial now only days away, the media are looking for anything they can find connected to the crash of 439. I don't have anything to tell them, but they understand what I do, and are likely to twist whatever I say."

"Since you predicted the crash, I suppose they are hoping you will forecast the result of the trial."

"They can hope, but I'll not be doing that. As I told Liz, I have never met her husband, so I have no basis for a preview."

"But you do believe Liz is going to come out of all this happily. Isn't that what her portrait is about?"

"True," sighed Justin, "But I was careful not to tell her what I believe."

"Why would that have mattered?"

"I don't need her to be telling people and start up the whole media thing again."

Thinking about her conversation with Liz, Jenny began to feel uncomfortable. "Well, let's forget about it for now. Maybe the reporter doesn't really have anything and will drop it."

Justin made a doubtful face, but changed the subject anyway.

"How about some wine?" he asked.

* * *

Wednesday being their regular date night, Jenny had cooked a meal at Justin's house and stayed for the night. They had made love lazily and beautifully until the small hours and were still asleep when Jenny's phone rang. She looked at the screen: it was her editor.

She sighed, gave her fiancé an apologetic look, and said "Hi, Bill".

Justin watched her as her expression became more and more horrified.

"No!"

"I cannot say …."

"Yes, I am with him now …."

"I am not sure that he has an answer …."

"This could be really tricky, he and I being engaged …."

"No. No. I would rather handle it myself …."

"Well, of course, that would be great …."

"Sure. I will call you back …."

"Yes. Very soon."

She ended the call and turned to look at Justin.

"Don't tell me," he said.

"It's in this morning's news, in the papers and on TV. The Prophet of Houston has spoken. Matthew Carne is to be acquitted," she said.

"How can they say that?" Justin's voice was taught with anger. "I have said no such thing." He reached for the remote control and turned the TV on. The first station he selected was already discussing the case. Across the bottom of the screen ran a large banner: CARNE TO BE ACQUITTED.

The anchor of the morning show was speaking. "This report comes from a usually reliable source. We have not yet been able to verify it ourselves……"

"Nor are they likely to," muttered the prophet.

"……We have reached out to Mr. Gates, but he is yet to get back to us."

Jenny looked at him sharply. "You can't avoid all reporters," she said.

"And why not?" he demanded.

"Because I am a reporter."

"Not with me, you're not."

"Sweetheart, you know I never take our private life into my work, but things are different right now."

"How so?"

"Because you are big news this morning, a topic of real public interest, and I am engaged to you, and my editor knows it. He just called to say he cannot avoid the subject. Either I will give him a story or he will put someone else on it."

"And I will avoid him, just as I am avoiding all the others," replied Justin, defiantly.

Jenny did not respond immediately. He could see she wanted to say something, but was hesitating

"You don't like that idea?" he asked, more gently.

"He wants me to be the only reporter in the country to get the story: a real exclusive."

"And great for your career, I suppose," said Justin bitterly, completing the argument.

She made a face which somehow mixed guilt and defeat, like a child who has been caught with her hand in the cookie jar.

"Why can't we work on this together?" she asked. "Let's figure out a story for Bill. We can agree on it between ourselves. I won't say anything you don't want me to. And you let me handle all the reporters who call or show up at the door."

After some thought, Justin agreed. "But I want you to stay here, until the fuss dies down. You can't be my shield if you are charging all over town on other assignments.

"I will have to ask Bill," she said.

Bill agreed, provided that she came up with Justin's story within the next hour.

"The next three," she insisted. They settled on two: television news is an impatient business.

By the time the camera crew arrived, the two lovers had agreed how to handle things. She would interview him out of doors, beside the lake. He would admit to being the Prophet of Houston, deny having made the rumored prediction, and say that, since he had never met Matthew Carne, there was no way to have done it anyway.

"Have you any idea where this story came from?"

"None at all," he would reply.

No mention would be made of Liz, her visit or her portrait.

* * *

Easter had passed. The date for the Carne trial was approaching. Jury selection was scheduled for the coming Wednesday. Tony had suggested that Justin should arrive on the preceding Friday and bring his fiancée with him. "It is about time I met her, and I am sure she deserves a weekend away," he said. Justin wasn't quite sure why, but Jenny said it sounded like a great idea. Besides that, thought the artist, one does not turn down invitations from Tony White lightly. He called to accept.

"That is excellent! Don't worry about a thing. Either I or Andrew will meet you off your plane. You will stay at the house, of course."

True to form, Tony White had taken care of everything. Their flight landed at Palm Springs early in the afternoon. Andrew was there with the Range Rover. Before long they were at the house, standing on the terrace, and Justin was introducing Jenny to the splendid view.

"Mr. White apologizes that he isn't here to greet you," said Andrew. "He has business all day but will be back in time for dinner. Please make yourselves at home." Looking at Justin, he added, "You probably remember where your rooms are."

Justin took his fiancée's hand and led her inside the house. Everything was as he remembered, except that his portrait of Bella was now hanging prominently on the wall behind the grand piano. Jenny stopped when she saw it, grasped his hand, and exclaimed, "That's the one you painted! It is just beautiful." She held him there while she studied it, then, looking at him, her eyes shining, she added, "I am so proud of you."

He took her to the guest suite, where the temporary studio had been turned back into a second bedroom. He observed drily, "I see that the beds are made up in both rooms. Tactful, don't you think?"

She was still holding his hand, which she squeezed affectionately. "But not necessary."

They sorted out their things and returned to the terrace, where Andrew brought them chilled Perrier and fruit. They swam in the pool, lazed on shaded loungers, and held hands as they talked. By the time they heard Tony's Jaguar on the drive below they were totally relaxed, lost in the luxury of the place, the hospitality, and their love.

"That will be Tony," Justin observed.

Jenny leapt to her feet. "Oh no! I can't let Tony greet me in my bikini."

"I don't see why not," responded her fiancé, standing up. "You look really great." But she was already on her way into the house, and he followed.

When they emerged from their room, dressed in casual shirts and pants, they found their host in his favorite chair on the terrace. He rose to greet them, pretty well ignoring Justin as he reached out to grasp both of Jenny's hands.

"Welcome! Welcome to my home. I hope everything is as you would like."

His greeting set the tone for a very pleasant evening. The matter which had brought them together was not mentioned until the meal was finished and they had moved into the living room. Andrew poured coffee for the three of them and quietly retired. Justin also excused himself and left the room for a few minutes.

Tony was in a thoughtful mood. Jenny chose to sit at the end of a long sofa, and he picked a nearby chair. "It's strange what twists and turns our life journeys take," he said to her. "We never know what is around the next corner."

"Sometimes Justin does," she said quietly.

"Ah, yes! Of course. But he is unique."

"I was thinking that the crash which killed my Bella was as awful as it was evil, but it brought Justin into my life, which I think will prove to be a great blessing. I feel that I have lost a daughter, but maybe, perhaps, found a son."

"He would be touched to hear you say that."

"When the plane came down, killing my daughter, I was so angry that I could have strangled whoever was responsible. At that time, of course, no-one knew who to blame, but Justin's role in getting her onto the plane made me mad. I didn't understand it, and he was a convenient target for my fury. Only later did I realize that he had been trying to save her, and the other passengers, from a plane that he thought was going to crash. I began to make inquiries about him, and learned what a great artist he is. I also discovered his connection to a woman I had loved and a daughter I had never known. I still don't know her, by the way. So, I invited him to come and paint a portrait of Bella, which he did. I hope he will agree that, in doing so, we became friends."

Justin appeared in the doorway. "Absolutely," he said.

Tony continued addressing Jenny. "Then they arrested this fellow, Matthew Carne, and charged him with bringing down the plane, but I'm not convinced he is guilty, and if he is, whether or not they will convict."

Jenny looked at him. "Why the doubt?"

"I have an uneasy feeling that they will acquit him. In fact, Justin and I talked about that some time ago. The American justice system is far from perfect. Every year, hundreds of guilty men and women go free, and scores of innocents end up in prison." His voice hardened with emotion. "If Carne did, indeed, murder my Bella, I want him locked up for the rest of his miserable life. In fact, I would like him to suffer an even worse punishment, if one could be found. However, if he is innocent, I want him set free, and the real killer found. I am determined that she should be fully and properly avenged."

"Why do you doubt that he is the one?"

"Matthew Carne is just an ordinary, middle class American. He has no criminal record, and no apparent interest in terrorism. Also, I have heard that he has an alibi for the night in question. Obviously, if he was involved at all, he must have had accomplices, including someone who knew how to procure and operate a missile. In that case, he could turn them in and cut a deal for a lighter sentence, but he has not done so. So, either he has associates whom he is unwilling to name, even though that may bring him a life sentence, or he doesn't, because he was not involved in the first place.

"Never forget, Jenny, that this was a crime with major national and political implications. The pressure on the FBI to solve it quickly has been enormous. It would not be the first time they have offered up the first viable suspect they could find."

"If they convict him, you won't be satisfied?" asked Jenny.

"Nor if they acquit him." Tony answered.

"Then you just can't win."

"That's how it seems."

Tony walked over to a credenza and poured himself a single malt whisky, offering the same to his guests, who declined. As he returned to his seat he said, "As you might imagine, I have been thinking a lot about all this, with the trial approaching, and then your fiancé throws his own wrench in the works by predicting an acquittal." He looked across at Justin, who was shaking his head from side to side. "I take it that you did predict Carne's acquittal."

"Actually, I didn't."

Tony was surprised. "Then how ....?"

Justin replied, "We don't actually know, although we do have an idea." He looked at his fiancée and said, "You tell him."

She responded, "About Liz Carne, you mean?"

A surprised Tony exclaimed, "Liz Carne, Matthew's wife?"

"That's right."

"How on earth does she come into things?"

Jenny took a deep breath and dived in.

"A couple of weeks ago, Justin received a phone call, quite out of the blue."

She continued to tell how Liz had come to Houston, looking for a prediction, and ended up asking for a portrait. "Justin says she had the saddest, most miserable face he has ever been asked to paint."

The story continued, without interruption from Tony, until Jenny had described her phone call with Liz.

"So, you did not say that Justin had made a prediction, but she ended up believing he had."

"It seems that way, although I'm sure I stressed that he had not. I clearly remember asking her to remember that."

Justin spoke up. "It is hard to believe that she would call the newspapers with this story."

"Well, if she didn't, who did?"

"We don't know."

"Maybe she told a friend who let it out."

"She swears she told no one. Jenny called to find out."

They talked around the subject for a while, but found no answer. In the end, they decided to retire for the night.

* * *

It was Sunday evening. Jenny was due to catch a morning flight back to Houston next day, and the three friends were enjoying early evening drinks on the patio, reclining on three loungers grouped round a low table. Cool drinks and various pastries were on hand, but hardly touched. Tony stood up, reached for the tray of goodies, and offered them to Jenny. She smiled and shook her head, so he tried Justin, with whom he had more luck.

"By the way," he said, putting the tray back on the table and taking an éclair for himself, "I have been meaning to ask you, Justin: how is your mother these days?"

"She seems to be doing well, thank you. Her parents died some years ago, and left her some money, so she only has to work part time now."

"I have often wondered," said Tony in an off-hand manner, "If you ever told her that you and I had met."

Justin made a rueful expression. "I was going to, but I chickened out. I am not sure how she will react to my discovery of something which she has kept secret for so long. Maybe reminding her of a former love would not be kind."

Tony looked a little disappointed, but he said, "You may be right."

Justin continued, "The trouble is, I think that Tina might like to know who her father is. In fact, she probably ought to be told, but telling her without telling mom could lead to some seriously hurt feelings down the line."

Jenny looked at him and said softly, "Why don't we go there and tell them both at the same time?"

Justin smiled at her. "As a woman, do you think that's the thing to do?"

She nodded. "I do."

"We will have to figure out when," he replied.

Early next morning, Justin took her to the airport in Bella's car. Standing on the sidewalk outside the terminal, she clung to him.

"I don't want to go," she said.

"I know," he replied, and pushed her away a little so that he could look at her face. "But I love you so much that I will still be close to you. And we can call each other, of course." He pulled her against himself again and their lips met in a soft, tender kiss. Then they parted, Justin standing by the car watching her disappear into the terminal.

* * *

The trial was big news. On Wednesday morning, the live media were all over the place, except in the courtroom, from which they were excluded. Selected reporters were allowed inside, without cameras or recorders. Jury selection was expected to last three days, with the trial beginning in earnest on the following Monday. In the courtroom, the front row behind the defense table was reserved for people with special interests. Two seats were allocated to the defendant's wife and a friend. Tony had pulled some strings and secured two more. The rest of the rows were occupied by potential jurors. On the prosecution side, several rows had been reserved for relatives of people who had died in the disaster, although not many attended. More were expected in the following week. A few curious members of the general public were seated behind them.

Liz Carne arrived shortly after Justin, accompanied by a friend, and took her seat two chairs beyond his, directly behind where her husband would sit.

"Hello," she said, "I wasn't expecting to see you here."

"You could say that I've a vested interest in the case," he replied. "Your visit to Houston only increased it."

"Oh," she said, and fell silent.

"What did you think of the portrait?" he asked.

"I told Jenny what I thought," she replied, a little nervously. "I am sure she told you."

"She did."

"Do you really think I will look like that one day?"

"I am sure of it."

There was a tense silence, which ended when Justin asked, "Have you shown it to many people?"

She shook her head. "Not really. It is too awkward to explain, under present circumstances." Then she noticed a look of concern on his face and reached out a hand to touch his knee. "But don't worry, I have never told anyone what it might mean. Jenny was very strict with me about that."

Just then, people started arriving and moving around in front of them. She withdrew her hand, and he smiled at her.

"Thank you," he said, "I knew you wouldn't."

The prosecution team arrived to take their places at the table on the far side of the room. Leading them was a tall, slender, very professional looking woman in a tailored gray pants suit. Justin already knew who she was, Sandra Fulbright, United States attorney. With her came two assistant US Attorneys, Craig Long and someone he did not recognize. Before sitting down, Craig glanced around the courtroom. As his eyes scanned the defense side of the room he saw Justin and did a double take. He leaned down and spoke quietly to his boss. She turned round and stared at Justin.

At that moment, Matthew's lawyer, Paul Simpson, arrived, accompanied by a small, smartly dressed Hispanic woman, presumably also an attorney. Paul acknowledged Liz with a nod of his head and a slight smile and took his seat at the defense table in front of her. No sooner had he seated himself than Sandra Fulbright came over and whispered something in his ear. The two of them looked hard at Justin and then moved away, out of earshot.

Liz leaned close to Justin and whispered, "You do still feel that this is all going to end well, don't you?" she asked.

Suddenly, a loud voice commanded "All Rise" and Her Honor Judge Alicia Hamilton appeared. To Justin, the portrait painter, she looked like everyone's mother. She was of average height and build, perhaps a little on the heavy side, although that was hard to tell because of her judicial robe. She had short, wavy black hair and a soft, tired face, and interesting brown eyes.

She took her seat, and everyone was instructed to sit again. The case was announced, and Matthew Carne was brought in. He looked at his wife and mouthed a silent "Hello" before sitting beside his attorney. Justin could see him in profile only: not well enough to study his face.

The case was called, and the proceedings began. Immediately, the prosecutor and the defense attorney said, in unison, "Your Honor, may we approach?"

The judge was clearly surprised, but agreed with a beckoning gesture. The crowd in the body of the court watched as judge and attorneys huddled across the judge's wide bench. Ms. Fulbright explained something to the judge, which caused her to look at Justin for a long moment. She spoke to the lawyers again, quietly, and then addressed the assembled audience in a loud voice: "The court will be in recess for fifteen minutes."

The judge retired through the door behind her seat and the two attorneys disappeared through a door at the side of the room. Moments later, a uniformed marshal came in through that same door and approached Tony.

"'Morning, Mr. White," he said, which made Justin wonder if everyone in Riverside knew Tony. "Would this be Mr. Gates here?" He indicated Justin, who said, "That's me,"

"I have to ask you to come with me," the officer said.

Justin looked at Tony with a puzzled frown, and received the advice, "You had better go."

Leaving by the side door, he followed his escort through a couple of short passages until they came to a heavy paneled door. They entered without knocking. The marshal announced Justin by name and left, closing the door behind him.

The room was clearly the judge's sanctuary. There was a deep pile carpet on the floor, bookcases on every wall, and a window facing across the room toward the door. In front of the window was a credenza and a heavy mahogany desk. The judge was standing behind the desk, and the two attorneys were standing in front of it. In one corner of the room sat a middle-aged woman with slumped shoulders and a tired face, ready to operate a strange little typing device, the instrument on which all court proceedings are recorded.

Everyone except the clerk remained standing. Alicia Hamilton addressed Justin. "You, I take it, are Justin Gates from Houston."

"I am, ma'am."

She studied Justin silently, in a not unkindly way. When she finally spoke, it was with a firm, low pitched voice that demanded attention.

"Then let me explain what is going on here. Our concern, as you know, is the upcoming trial of Matthew Carne, who is accused of a terrorist act and many murders. Ms. Fulbright here is a United States Attorney and is the prosecutor in the case. Beside her is Mr. Simpson, Mr. Carne's defense lawyer. You are here because you appear to have disrupted our attempts to offer him a swift and fair trial."

Justin opened his mouth to speak, but the judge held up a hand.

"If you let me ask the questions, I think we will get through most efficiently. To start, please identify yourself, stating your name, address and occupation."

Justin did so.

"Are you the person who is known as the Prophet of Houston?"

"Some people seem to call me that."

"And are you a prophet."

"I would not say so."

"Then why do you have that name?"

"I cannot say."

"Oh, I suspect you can, Mr. Gates." The judge paused for thought, and then said, "It will help us all if you would take these proceedings more seriously, and not skirt round the edges of the issues in hand. I ask you again, why do people call you the Prophet of Houston?"

Justin answered with a sigh. "From time to time I have received unexpected insights into future events, and have shared these with the people concerned."

"And have these prophecies come true?"

"They have."

"Every time?"

"So far they have."

"Have you had such an insight into the outcome of the trial before us?"

"No, ma'am, I have not."

The judge frowned. "It is tempting to question the credibility of your predictions and, indeed, of yourself as a prophet. But whether your activities are credible is not the issue. We have two problems this morning. First, that a significant percentage of the American public do think you are credible, that what you say will happen. And second, that the popular media have told the world, including those good folk who may become jurors in this trial, that you have predicted a not-guilty verdict. I ask you again: have you made such a prediction?"

"No, I have not."

"Then why are there headlines in the papers like this?" The judge reached onto her desk and held up a newspaper with a banner across the top of the page, CARNE TO BE ACQUITTED? I take it that you have seen this already?"

"I have, but why the paper came up with that is beyond me. I don't see how I could have made such a prediction: I have never met Mr. Carne."

"So you only make predictions about people you have met."

"Correct."

"Then let me ask you this: did you, or did you not, make a prediction last year relating to the shooting down of FlyAir flight 439 over Palm Springs."

"In a way, I did.

"In what way?"

"I actually thought that a different plane would be brought down."

"So, you made an inaccurate prediction."

"What I was predicting was not the crash of that specific plane, but the death of one of its passengers in a crash. Initially, she was on a flight to Phoenix. That is when I had my preview. Only later did she transfer to the Palm Springs flight, the one that crashed."

"I see. Well, we can set that confusion aside for now. Answer me this. Did the publicity which followed that prediction make you very widely known, and was the title 'Prophet of Houston' given to you as a result."

"I think some people may have used the title before then."

"So, are you aware that, however modest you might be, your statements on matters of public interest can affect public opinion. You do realize that, don't you."

"I can see your point."

The judge sounded irritated. "No, Mr. Gates. Seeing my point is not enough. I want you to know that, in the eyes of this court, you have attempted to interfere with the proper administration of justice by the things you have said."

Reluctantly, Justin said, "I suppose so, but that has never been my intention."

Sounding like a schoolteacher reprimanding a fifth grader, the judge said, "In life, what we intend and what we achieve are often not the same." She indicated the two attorneys. "These two fine lawyers have already submitted a motion to the court, alleging that a fair trial is no longer possible because of this." She stabbed the newspaper with her finger. "We are about to start selecting our jury. Several dozen potential jurors have already been summoned. Every one of them has likely read about your so-called prophecies. Who can blame the prosecution for arguing that the jury pool has become tainted, and an impartial jury could be impossible to find."

Justin looked confused. Saying nothing, he just shook his head in denial, although what he was denying was unclear.

"So, Mr. Gates, I am going to impose on you something which is commonly called a gag-order. From this moment on, you are absolutely forbidden to discuss the case of Matthew Carne with anyone, anyone at all. You are prohibited from making, either implicitly or explicitly, any predictions relating to Mr. Carne, his alleged crime, his associates if he has any, or any other aspect of this case. And you are to refrain from expressing any views about the conduct of the trial or its likely outcome. This order will be in force from now until Mr. Carne has been tried, and if convicted, sentenced. Do you understand me?"

"I believe so."

"You should be aware that any breach of this order will result in you being brought back to court, whereupon you will be cited for contempt and very probably sent to jail. Do I make myself clear?"

With that, the brief meeting in the judge's chamber was over. Everyone returned to the courtroom, and jury selection got under way.

* * *

Questioning potential jurors is as boring as it is important. By four o' clock on that Wednesday Alicia Hamilton was ready to call it quits for the day. She adjourned the proceeding until the following morning. Tony and Justin made their way toward the exit and the street. As they emerged, they were greeted by an array of cameras and microphones, with reporters shouting questions at them.

"Are you the Prophet of Houston?"

"Are you Justin Gates?"

"Were you forced to be here today?"

"What did the Judge want?"

Justin did not know how to respond. He looked at Tony for help, but at that moment a tall, slender female, dressed in a gray business suit, came from behind and pushed her way between Justin and his friend. With her black hair coiled on top of her head and a face with almost no make-up, Sandra Fulbright looked as if she meant business and had no time for anything else. Facing the assembled crowd, she said,

"I am United States Attorney Sandra Fulbright, lead prosecutor in this case. Mr. Gates is alleged to have made statements which could adversely affect the impartiality of the jury, and he has been silenced as far as any more such statements are concerned."

The waiting newshounds started aiming their questions at her instead, and she responded by painting as dark a picture of 'the Prophet' as she could, and saying how the government would not allow his misleading remarks to interfere with securing Matthew Carne's conviction.

Justin and Tony hovered behind her until the hubbub died down and they could escape.

* * *

CHAPTER 15

The Trial

Jury selection commenced, a monotonous procedure which was expected to last for the rest of the week.

When the court recessed for lunch, Tony asked Justin for his thoughts. "I presume that, as a student of people's faces, you at least get something out of it."

"Maybe, but not too much," was the reply. "The main thing is that I cannot see Matthew's face. I can't read his eyes."

"I will have to see what can be done about that," was Tony's response.

* * *

After the court adjourned for the day, Tony took Justin for a drive in the hills behind Palm Springs, and found a small taverna, a cream colored stucco structure with dark wooden beams showing, perched on the side of a steep hill. It reminded Justin of photographs he had seen of Switzerland, although the Californian terrain was not nearly that green, and there were no snowcapped mountains in view.

"This is one of my favorite places," he said. "They serve excellent, home-made food in a very simple style. It's good, occasionally, to escape the sophistication with which we normally surround ourselves. Let's sit here on the porch for a while. We can go inside to eat later."

Their arrival was noticed by the owner, Manuel Chicas, who came bustling out to greet them and take their drink orders. When he went back in, Tony explained: "He comes from the south of Spain. His grandparents moved to Mexico to escape the civil war in the nineteen-thirties. He was born and raised there, but preferred to make his fortune this side of the border. I don't think it is much of a fortune, but he has created a delightful restaurant all the same. He gives a lot of pleasure to a lot of people. I hope he lives to be an old man."

They spent the next hour enjoying the evening air and talking about the day.

"What do you think?" asked Tony.

"About the outcome?"

"No. It's too early for that, but at least you have had a chance to see the defendant, to get an impression of him. And I know how important such things are to you."

"Yes, but I have not been able to read him yet. He sits with his back toward us. I really need to see his eyes. They are the doorway to his soul."

Tony White said, enigmatically, "I am working on that."

As the evening began to cool, they went inside the restaurant. The host, who clearly knew Tony well, did not ask them what they would like. He simply began serving them a series of what, in Spain, would be called tapas. Each was a small portion of something delicious. There were calamari, empanadas, ham croquetas, goat cheese with plum sauce, shrimp stuffed avocado, and other dishes that Justin could not name. It was a delicious and memorable feast.

* * *

Next morning, instead of going straight into the courtroom, the two men waited in the lobby for Liz and her friend. Tony took Liz aside and spoke to her quietly. As a result, she and her friend changed seats, placing her next to Justin. When the defendant was brought in, to sit at the defense table, he leaned over the bar to greet his wife, who said hurriedly, "Darling, I want you to meet our new friend, Justin. He is the artist who recently painted my portrait."

By his response, it was clear that Matthew knew about the Prophet of Houston and his wife's dealings with him. He said, "I gather you have been trying to help us," he said. "I should thank you for that."

Her Honor was not pleased with this interaction. She said, in a stern voice, "Mr. Carne."

Embarrassed, Matthew hurriedly turned round and sat down.

* * *

"It was a strange moment," Justin reported to his fiancée on the phone that evening. "I don't know what Liz said to him. Maybe he already knew about the portrait. Whatever it was, he glared at me, sort of challenging me, I felt as if the whole weight of his future was in my hands, as if I had control of what happened to him. Nothing could be more absurd."

"Gosh!" exclaimed Jenny. "And did you get any new insight into things?"

"Not really. I need more time with him."

"But what about the portrait? What about your promise to Liz that everything will turn out well in the end?"

"But that is not what I promised her. In fact, I didn't promise her anything. I just painted her future happiness. I did not say how or when that would happen for her. That would be more than I know."

"Well, she thinks….." Jenny began, but Justin cut her off.

"Let's talk about something else," he said.

While Justin was talking to his sweetheart, Tony White was making calls of his own, tracking down Paul Simpson, the defense attorney. They talked for quite a while. When the call ended Tony gave in a deep, satisfied breath.

"That should do it," he said to himself.

* * *

Jury selection continued next morning, Friday. After two and a half hours the onlookers were weary of it, and lawyers were also in need of a break. The judge announced a one-hour recess for lunch. Tony immediately hustled Justin out of the courtroom into the lobby, where they waited impatiently. A few minutes passed until they were joined by Paul Simpson. He looked at the artist and said, "Come with me."

Justin was surprised, and looked at Tony for guidance. He received a nod of encouragement and a one-word command. "Go."

As he and the lawyers walked through various doors and corridors, Paul explained. "I understand you need to meet the defendant. I am going to request an attorney-client meeting and take you along as a temporary associate. We will have to be quick. Tony says that what you see in Matthew will be more important than what he says. It will certainly be easier for me, anyway, if you let me do the talking. Just tell me if there is anything you would like me to ask or say."

Justin said, "Just talk to him about the way things are going, or how he feels about the trial in general. That should give me an impression of who he really is."

* * *

Matthew Carne seemed amazingly calm, given the circumstances. His black hair and dark skin, deep brown eyes and clean-shaven face suggested a mid-east heritage, but when he spoke, his accent was pure California. He appeared to be an honest and straightforward character, probably about twenty-seven or twenty-eight years of age.

It was clear that he and his attorney were friends. Their brief conversation seemed frank and focused. For Justin's benefit, Paul asked him to talk about himself. He revealed that he was an accountant, married for seven years, without children. He had lost his parents a year or two previously and there were no other close relations. Talking about his family seemed to make him uneasy, and Paul moved swiftly on, asking him about the crime for which he was being tried. On that subject he was less hesitant, speaking convincingly, insisting that he knew nothing about it. He was easy to believe, although Justin felt that, behind all the words, there were unspoken reservations. "What might he be hiding?" he wondered.

As the time for the visit was ending, Paul stopped asking questions and prompting opinions. Instead, he outlined how the trial might conclude, what the possible verdicts might be, and what could happen to Matthew as a result. Justin watched watched him very closely and became convinced that he was innocent. He laid a hand on Paul's arm, a sign that he wanted to interrupt.

"Just tell me, Matthew, why you don't take the easy route out of this mess?"

"I don't know what you mean."

"Oh, I think you do."

Matthew stared at Justin. "If you think there is an easy way out, you must think you know what it is."

"Perhaps I do. Perhaps you and I both do, and maybe Liz as well."

Matthew looked quickly at his lawyer, who was staring at the artist with a puzzled frown. Then he turned back to Justin.

"I am innocent. That is all you need to know about me. That is all the jury needs to know, too."

* * *

That evening, Justin called Jenny, as he did every evening.

"How is it going?" she asked.

"Pretty much as expected," he replied.

"Do you still think he is innocent?"

"I don't think I ever said he was, but, for the record, I have major doubts about him being guilty."

"Why?"

"I looked into his eyes and saw understandable numbness and terror, but I also saw something else. I saw through his present pain into his future. I saw him standing beside himself, a free man. It was very strange."

"So what does that mean?"

"I think the defense attorneys are right, and we have a case of mistaken identity. Matthew is not the terrorist who brought down the plane, but he looks like him."

"You mean, there is someone out there, who looks like him, and with whom he has been confused."

"That's right."

"Do you think Matthew knows this look-alike stranger?"

"Probably. I think it will turn out to be his brother."

"Isn't that a bit far-fetched?"

"Maybe, but not impossible."

"I didn't know he had one."

"Nor did I until today. I still don't know it really, but my preview tells me it must be true. Actually, I don't think anyone knows, except maybe Liz."

"If Matthew had told people, he might already be a free man."

"Perhaps turning his own brother in was too hard. Which is worse, to spend the rest of your life in prison or to escape by condemning your own flesh and blood to be there in your stead? Jesus Christ said, 'Greater love has no man than this, that he lays down his life for his friend', or, in this case, his brother."

"So what are you going to do, Jus?"

"Nothing."

"Because?"

"The future doesn't need me to. It is set and I can't change it."

"But you do think that, in the end, the truth will come out and Matthew will go free."

"I do."

* * *

He tried to smile sympathetically. “I wish I could tell you how I feel, but, as you probably know, the judge has forbidden me to say anything to anyone.”

Liz shook her head. “I didn’t realize,” she said.

$$

Monday arrived. The courtroom was packed, although the judge and the jury had yet to appear. The various attorneys were at their tables, but not the defendant. Everyone expected things to start promptly at ten-thirty, but that did not happen. Instead, a marshal came and spoke to the attorneys, first at the prosecution table and then the defense. They immediately got up and left the room through a side door. The marshal then studied the people in the front row, identified Justin, and told him that he was also required.

They all found their way to the judge’s chambers. With five lawyers, Justin, one marshal, one court reporter, and the judge, the room was packed. Everyone, except the reporter, was standing, with Her Honor, Alicia Hamilton, behind her desk. Her face was flushed and taut with fury as she glared at Justin. Clearly, he was the center of attention.

“Mr. Gates, what do you have to say about this?”

She held up a sheet of paper, normal letter size. Justin had to step forward to see what was on it.

“Never mind, let me read it aloud. Then everyone will know.” She adjusted her glasses. “This is a printout of a message which is being tweeted across the nation as we speak. It has already been shared twenty-one thousand times. The message originates with someone who calls himself Barking Dog. Goodness only knows who he might be. Here is what he says. ‘The Prophet Speaks Again. Justin Gates, the renowned Prophet of Houston, who is known for making accurate predictions about peoples’ lives, is attending the trial of Matthew Carne, who allegedly shot down an airliner last year. The prophet spent half an hour with the prisoner yesterday. Then he called his fiancée and said the man is innocent and will go free’.”

“I will ask you again, Mr. Gates, what have you to say about this?”

Justin stared, open mouthed, at the judge. He could not come up with a single word.

“I am not surprised you are speechless. There is nothing you can say. Do you have any memory at all, Mr. Gates? Last Tuesday I bound you under a gag order, forbidding you to make or publish any prediction in the

Matthew Carne matter, and here we are, now, discovering that you have been to see the prisoner and then broadcast your opinions across the entire internet. You have blatantly broken the undertaking you gave to the court." She glared at him, and then, glancing behind her, she sat down heavily in her chair, laying the offending document on the desk before her.

"Well?" she demanded.

Justin stared at the paper. He did not use social media, had never written a tweet in his life, and did not know how such things happened. He just shook his head in disbelief.

The judge spoke in a menacingly low voice. "I am waiting for your answer."

"I can't say anything. I have never seen it. I don't know who wrote it. It is pure fiction, anyway."

"Do you deny renewing your prediction about the outcome of this trial."

"Since I never made one in the first place, I could not have renewed it. Could I?"

"Don't play games with me, Sir. You are in very serious trouble."

She turned the paper toward herself and started to read. "'The prophet spent half an hour with the prisoner yesterday. Then he called his fiancée and said the man is innocent and will go free.'"

Redirecting her gaze toward the befuddled artist, she asked, "Is that true, Mr. Gates?"

"I am afraid it might be, your honor."

"Do you admit making such a phone call?"

He hesitated before answering quietly, "Yes, Ma'am."

Alicia Hamilton said to the assembled company,

"Less than a week ago I imposed a gag order on Mr. Gates in relation to this trial. Here is strong evidence that he failed to observe it. In fact, he appears to be admitting it. Since he is here without legal representation, I am detaining him pending the arrival of his attorney, at which time I intend to place him in custody for the duration of the trial. That would appear to be the only way to secure his silence."

She directed her gaze at the marshal. "Please take care of Mr. Gates."

The officer stepped over to Justin and, grabbing his arms, secured him with handcuffs and led him away.

I couldn't believe what was happening. Someone had leaked this story to Barking Dog, whoever that might be. Who would do such a thing? The only person who knew what I thought about Matthew's future was Jenny, but surely she would not betray me, but who else was there? The longer I sat in that jail and thought about it, the more certain I became that the impossible had happened: my fiancée was responsible for my plight.

It was past eleven when order had been restored in the courtroom and everyone was in his place. A voice commanded "All rise" and the judge walked in. Things finally got under way. Formalities were completed, and Sandra Fulbright stood to address the jury. She reminded them of the facts of the case, already well known of course, before summarizing the evidence she was to present.

"Today, you will learn how Matthew Carne, acting either alone or in concert with unnamed accomplices, carried out this heinous crime, the worst terrorist act in the United States since nine-eleven. You will hear how, for reasons known only to himself and his possible accomplices, he decided to try and force the United States government to abandon its defense commitments to countries around the world. He attempted to do this by threatening a major unspecified act of terrorism. The administration, as they always must, refused to respond to this terrorist demand. As we will show, the defendant somehow managed to procure a surface to air missile, probably importing it directly from Pakistan. He then bought a used Winnebago motor home, the previous owner of which will be in court to identify the defendant as the purchaser. The defendant took the motorhome to a workshop and had it customized, the purpose being to make it serve as a missile launch platform. The owner of that workshop will be in court to identify the defendant as the person who ordered and paid for that work. On the evening of Memorial Day last year, he drove the motorhome to Palm Springs, parked it in a lot behind a law office there, and waited for FlyAir flight 439 to appear overhead, as it made its final approach to Palm Springs International Airport. When the plane came into sight and into range, he fired his missile, which streaked toward its target, totally destroying it and the lives of all eighty-five people on board. Following the success of his dastardly mission, the defendant destroyed the motorhome, hoping to leave no evidence that could connect him to his crime. Fortunately, he failed, and our law enforcement agencies were able to identify the motorhome and its former owner. After that, it was only a matter of time before Matthew Carne was identified, arrested and charged. He now stands before you, awaiting your verdict and the sentence of this court."

"The defense will doubtless argue that we have arrested and charged the wrong man, but their claim will fail in the light of the positive and definitive identification of Matthew Carne by four credible witnesses, none of whom has anything to gain from identifying the wrong man. In addition, we will tie him to the scene of the crime by presenting, in evidence, a laptop computer which belongs to him and was found close to the wreckage of the Winnebago after the event.

"The conclusion is inevitable. Matthew Carne, alone or in concert with others, yet to be identified, conceived, planned, and executed this crime, the worst act of terrorism carried out in this country since the World Trade Center was destroyed on September eleventh, two thousand and one.

"It will then be your duty to find him guilty, as he surely is, and to send him to prison for as long as the court shall decide, presumably the remainder of his life."

She sat down, and Paul Simpson took her place in front of the jurors.

"The prosecution has already stated that the defendant had no known reason for committing this horrendous crime, and that is true. They cannot identify a motive, for the simple reason that Matthew Carne has never had anything whatsoever to do with shooting down FlyAir flight 439 or any other airplane. Also, as we will prove, he could not have been in Palm Springs at the crucial time, because he spent that evening and the entire night at home with his wife, which is more than one hundred miles away.

"You will learn from various witnesses that he is a man of impeccable character who has never been in trouble with the law, not even to the extent of receiving a single parking ticket. You will learn that he is a loyal and generous, natural born citizen of these United States, who makes repeated donations to many charitable causes. He has no affiliations with political or socially radical organizations, and is the last person one might suspect of violent, terrorist activities. During the course of this trial, you will notice that the prosecution is quite unable to produce any evidence to the contrary. Mr. Khan is here because of mistaken identity, plain and simple. It will be your privilege and duty to declare him innocent and set him free."

Tony White had been puzzled by Justin's removal from the courtroom, and was more than worried by his failure to return. He slipped out of his seat, pushed past the people in his row, and walked back up the aisle toward the door. A marshal was standing there, a silent sentry in case there should be any disturbance. Tony whispered to him. "What have they done with Mr. Gates, the person who was sitting by me?"

The marshal pushed the door open and jerked his head as if to say,

"Outside."

The two of them moved into the lobby, where the marshal explained that Justin was now in custody. At first, Tony could not believe it, but when the marshal opened his cellphone and showed the offending tweet, he had no choice. He stood still, stroking his chin in thought.

The marshal enquired, "OK, Sir?"

Tony nodded absentmindedly, and the officer disappeared back into the court. Then he pulled out his own phone and made two calls. The first was to Isaac Stern. The second to Jenny Lane.

Back in the trial, Sandra Fulbright was introducing her first witness, a three-star army General, Abe Holland, who had overseen the investigation into the crash. He confirmed the shooting down of the plane, the places where its pieces fell, the numbers of casualties and so on.

The next witness was a short stocky, red-faced soldier with straw-colored hair and a permanent squint. In response to the prosecutor's questions, he confirmed that the FlyAir jet was brought down with a Pakistani made surface to air missile, known as an Anza-III. Its launch tube was found among the wreckage of the Winnebago. Also, not far from that wreckage, investigators had found a severely damaged lap top computer. That was produced in evidence and shown to the jury. The witness recognized it and confirmed where it had been found.

Sandra Fulbright then called for a seedy little man called Niles, an obvious nerd with pebble-lens glasses on his pointed nose, to come to the stand. She helped him establish that he was a fingerprint expert, and asked him about fingerprints on the laptop. He said there were many, not all legible, but two of the prints matched fingers on Matthew Carne's right hand.

Paul Simpson jumped in to cross examine.

"How confident can you be in attempting to identify a person from the prints of just two fingers?" he asked. "One-hundred percent or less?"

"Well, certainly not one hundred," was the reply, "but I could be …."

"Thank you. Less than a hundred. Now, tell the jury how many other prints there were and to whom they belonged."

"There were at least fifty individual prints. I do not know whose they were."

"But they all belonged to the same individual?"

"I would say so. At least, that is most of them."

"And would you also say that the computer is far more likely to have belonged to the fifty-print person than to whoever left only two?"

The witness hesitated briefly, before saying, "I would."

After he finished his evidence, the judge adjourned the proceedings for the day.

* * *

Being locked away in a cell was something new to Justin, something of which he had never dreamed. He was alone, with no-one to talk to and nothing to do. He tried to sleep, but that did not work. Thoughts about Jenny and what she had done tormented him constantly. How could she bring herself to betray him like that? And why would she? It didn't make any sense at all. He had been so sure of her love, but now this. Those first hours in the cells under the Federal Courthouse were the worst he had ever known.

After a while Justin was taken from his cell and placed in a small interview room where, to his surprise, he found Isaac Stern waiting.

"I suppose Tony White asked you to come," Justin guessed.

The lawyer nodded. "He was hoping I could get you out of this mess," he said. "But I told him that what happens next is entirely up to the judge. She could lock you up or let you go. As I understand things, she is furious about your behavior and is determined to detain you until the trial is over. That could be at least a week."

"How about me promising to keep quiet, to say nothing to anyone about the trial?"

"She will say you can't be trusted to keep that promise. After all, you have admitted that you told your fiancée, which was a breach of her previous gag order. And it is a problem that you are too famous and too many people believe what you say. She just doesn't want you stirring things up anymore."

"So what happens next?"

"When today's session of the trial is over, she will call us into the court. I will try to persuade her that you have learned your lesson and are prepared to toe the line. Then she will decide. But I must be honest. You need to be prepared for the worst."

And that is what happened. The day ended with Justin Gates, the so-called Prophet of Houston, being locked away in Riverside's Robert Presley

Detention Facility, where he would be held until the judge ordered his return to court, presumably when the trial was over.

The next day, Tuesday, saw the trial continue, with testimony from more prosecution witnesses. First up was a retired rancher named Hal Stampley, the former owner of the Winnebago. He identified Matthew as the person who had come to his ranch to look at the motorhome, and later met him and his wife at a workshop called Ron's Repairs, where he completed the purchase with $23,000 in cash.

Hal Stampley was followed by Ron Powell, owner of the workshop. Like the Stampleys, he also identified the defendant as the person who bought the motorhome, ordered various alterations, and took possession when the work was complete. In answer to the prosecutor's questions, Ron described the work in detail, and produced photographs of it all, which were displayed to the jury and the court on video screens. They included shots of a new sliding roof and a substantial metal platform beneath it. When asked about the purpose of this work, he said the defendant claimed to be an astronomer who needed a purpose-built mount for his telescope.

"Would you agree," asked the prosecutor, "That, with the roof open, someone could stand on that elevated platform and be in a perfect position for observing an approaching aircraft?"

"I would say so."

"And would you agree that such a person would be in an ideal position for aiming and firing a shoulder mounted missile at such a plane?"

Paul leapt to his feet, calling out "Objection!"

"Yes, Mr. Simpson?" asked the Judge.

"The witness is being asked for an opinion. Furthermore, it is being assumed that he has knowledge of operating military weapons, a matter which has not been established."

"Objection allowed. The jury will ignore this question."

Ron went on to confirm that Matthew had arrived on a motor bike when he came to collect the finished vehicle, and that a motorcycle rack had been added to its rear bumper at his request.

While Stampley and Powell were giving their testimonies in the trial, Jenny Lane was sitting, miserably curled up, in a window seat on a Boeing 737, heading for Los Angeles. It was the first flight she could find that would take her anywhere near wherever Justin might be. Isaac Stern had said that he could not meet her, but that he would arrange for a car to pick her up at the airport and bring her to Riverside. He would also book her a room at the Hyatt, if he could get one, and offered to buy her dinner later that evening.

The call from Tony had come as a complete shock. Although she used Twitter quite often, she had not yet come across the tweet which had caused all the trouble. The terrible news shook her to her core. "No!" she cried out. Several of her colleagues in the newsroom turned to see what was happening. They saw her standing by her desk, telephone to her ear, visibly shivering, and shaking her head in disbelief. Slowly she absorbed what was being told her, and she sat down and began to ask questions.

"Are you sure?"

"Where is he now?"

"Are they really going to put him in jail?"

"Can't Isaac do something about it?"

"I have some money saved. What about bail?"

"Have you any idea how he is handling all this?"

After she ran out of things to ask, all she could think of was going to him. Having thanked Tony and ended the call, she barged into her boss's office, interrupting a conversation with another reporter. Without waiting to be asked, she blurted out, "Bill, I have to go to California."

Shocked by the intrusion, he asked her why, asked her what about her job, and asked her how long she would be gone. None of her answers pleased him, but he saw the state she was in and agreed to let her go.

Then she ran down to the TV station's in-house travel office. They had found her the flight and booked it for her.

* * *

That night Jenny could not sleep. She tossed and turned in the hotel's luxurious king-size bed, tried dropping off with the lights off and then with them on. She helped herself to an over-priced nightcap from the refrigerator, which did not help at all. All she could do was fret about what would happen when she saw her fiancé. She had been anxious enough before her meal with Isaac, but then it got worse. He told her he had made her an appointment to see Justin. "That's how they do things there. It is for ten-thirty, but I am not sure he will want to see you." Her stress reached screaming pitch. She looked at the attorney aghast.

"You can't mean that," she gasped.

"I am afraid I do," he replied.

Next day, fifteen minutes before her appointment, Jenny entered the front door of the Robert Presley Detention Center in downtown Riverside and asked where she should go. Slowly, she was processed through security and administration, until she found herself sitting at a table in Dayroom 2, waiting for her man to appear. A door opened, and there he was! Since childhood she had known the phrase, 'my heart leaped for joy'. Only then did she discover what it really meant. However, the excitement only lasted for seconds. He did not look like the Justin she knew. Not only was he dressed in a prison jump suit, but he had a hollow, vacant look on his face.

"Oh my God!" she thought, "What has this done to him?"

He walked slowly toward her, not at all pleased to see her, it seemed.

"He really thinks I did it," she realized.

She had a huge impulse to leap to her feet, run round the table and fling her arms around him, but the rules were strict. No human contact.

"Justin," she murmured as he sat down.

"Hello," he said. "I'm surprised you have come."

"How could I not?"

"After what you did …."

She jumped in, "But I didn't."

Justin shook his head. "It had to be you. There isn't anyone else. I didn't say a thing to anyone but you."

Jenny started to cry. "Sweetheart, I would never let you down like that."

"Then who?"

For five minutes they talked around the subject, getting nowhere. Finally, Justin stood up. Looking down at her, he said, "You had better go now. I don't see how we can ever trust one another again."

He turned toward the approaching guard and was led away.

Jenny wished she were dead.

While this drama was happening at the detention center, things were moving along at Matthew Carne's trial in the District Court, only a couple of blocks away. The flow of witnesses continued, on and off the stand, as they testified to what they thought they knew. Together, they established that the Winnebago had been parked in a lot behind a law office in Palm

Springs. It was from there that the missile had been fired. Also, it was clear that the motorhome had been destroyed by explosion and fire at about the time of the crash. Finally, it was proved that someone, who could well have been the defendant, had been recorded by security video, on those premises just before and again, just after that explosion.

Step by step, the prosecution explained how the crime had been conceived, prepared and executed, by the defendant, Matthew Carne, who had been identified in court by several live witnesses. There was no shred of evidence that anyone else had been involved.

The prosecution's case was rested at four forty-five on Wednesday. The judge adjourned until 10.30 a.m. next day.

* * *

At nine twenty that evening, a Southwest Airlines flight landed in Houston, delivering a despondent Jenny Lane back home. She took a taxi to her apartment, closed her bedroom door, slid under her duvet, and cried herself to sleep.

CHAPTER 16

The Verdict

Thursday arrived, the day for the defense to present its case. Paul Simpson called his first witness, Josh Hammerly, a business associate, who declared that Matthew was lunching with him on the day when the missile was allegedly being collected from the docks. Next came Martin Vinson, a client whom he had been visiting when, according to the FBI, he was buying a motorhome sixty miles away. Then there was Delia Thompson, an associate from Matthew's office. She clearly remembered that the two of them had worked on a special project for the whole of the day when Ron Powell said the modified Winnebago was being inspected and handed over. Sandra Fulbright cross examined all three witnesses, but failed to shake any of their stories.

The final alibi witness for the day was the defendant's wife, Liz Carne. She took the stand late in mid-afternoon, and was sworn in. Paul began with questions aimed at establishing the length and happiness of the Carnes' marriage, her personal admiration for her husband's character, and her incredulity that he could have been involved in such a crime. All her answers were predictable and satisfactory. He then moved on to talk about Matthew's social and political views. She confirmed that he never showed any interest in political matters or the Afghan war, was not religious and had absolutely no connection to any Muslim cause. Her performance was stunning. It would be hard to believe that her testimony was contrived.

Finally, Paul moved on to talk about Memorial Day.

"What can you tell us about your husband's whereabouts on that evening?"

"He was at home with me."

"Are you sure?"

"I am."

"What were the two of you doing?"

"Watching television."

"Can you remember what you watched."

"No."

"Did you go to bed together?"

"We did."

"At what time?"

"Probably about eleven."

"So you are perfectly clear that, between nine o'clock and ten o'clock on Memorial Day evening, your husband was with you in your house. Remember, you are speaking under oath."

"That is the truth."

Paul Simpson looked at Judge Alicia Hamilton.

"No further questions, Your Honor."

She looked at the clock, glanced at the prosecutor, and said, "Cross examination will begin at ten tomorrow morning. Court is adjourned."

The next morning, Friday, Liz Carne returned to the witness box to face Sandra Fulbright, more nervous than she had been the previous day. That proved unnecessary. The prosecutor quickly saw that questioning the defendant's wife was doing more to solidify his alibi than undermine it. She quickly said, "No further questions," and Liz's ordeal was over.

Paul Simpson returned to the floor, calling several character witnesses. Together, they portrayed Matthew Carne as a thoroughly respectable and reliable member of society, honest, trustworthy, generous, and non-political as far as anyone knew.

The case for the defense was completed soon after noon. The judge called the lead attorneys to the bench, conferred with them quietly for a moment, and then announced to the court that closing arguments would be heard on Monday. She sent the jury home for the weekend.

Justin, of course, was kept in his cell.

* * *

Monday morning arrived. There was much excitement in the courtroom. Every available seat was filled. Bereaved relatives crowded together with members of the public and hordes of reporters. The marshals had to twice remove people from the seats reserved for Liz Carne and her friend. Even Tony White lost his privilege and had to jostle with the rest of the crowd.

Precisely at ten-thirty, Her Honor Alicia Hamilton walked majestically into the room and took her place at the bench. Everyone was seated and things began. The judge addressed the jury.

"Today the prosecution will make their closing arguments, summarizing their case. Then the defense will respond. After that, I will give you your instructions and send you away to review the case and consider your verdict. I urge you to pay close attention to every word that is said this morning. Your ability to deliver a fair and proper verdict will depend upon it."

She looked at the prosecutors. "Ms. Fulbright?"

For an hour and fifteen minutes the lead prosecutor reviewed the case and the evidence which had been given. She outlined the dastardly nature of the crime, showed gruesome pictures of the crash, and generally tried to rouse the jury to righteous anger. As for the defendant, on whom she was casting the blame, she had little to say about him personally, little that could help her case. His apparent lack of motive was obvious. The worst she could have said about him was that his parents had immigrated into the country from Afghanistan, before he was born. She chose to remain silent on that issue.

When she sat down Paul Simpson took his place before the jury. He stepped right into the gap left by the other side.

"Members of the jury," he began, "You will have noticed already that the prosecution has not been able to undermine the defendant's fine character, nor suggest any motive that could have caused him to commit this crime. All they have established is that someone who looks very much like him is to blame." He did not mention the fingerprints on the computer.

For the next hour the jury watched and listened as the attorney worked on their sympathy for his wrongly accused client. When he sat down, there was a buzz of whispers around the room. However, the judge had little interest in her audience's reactions, and recessed the proceedings for lunch.

She began the afternoon session by reviewing her instructions to the jury, and saying that they would be sequestered, accommodated in a suitable hotel, if necessary, from that moment until they had reached a unanimous conclusion.

That evening and all next day, the news media found plenty to discuss regarding Matthew Carne and his trial. Opinions were strongly divided. The key questions were clearly, was this was a case of mistaken identity and had the defendant been at home with his wife at the crucial time? The prosecution witnesses had been very convincing, but was their testimony strong enough to convict? America waited while a dozen men and women thought and argued about it. A guilty verdict would have to be unanimous.

If they could not agree among themselves, the judge might have to declare a mistrial.

* * *

In their search for new and original material, a number of newscasters brought the Prophet of Houston into the discussion. The rumor was that he, who was renowned for accurate predictions, had said that Carne would be acquitted. Various opinions about Justin and his work bounced around the airwaves, but it was all speculative nonsense.

The jury retired shortly before four on Monday afternoon. Next day, at fifteen minutes after noon, they sent word that they had reached a verdict. The court was reconvened at two.

"Members of the jury, have you reached your verdict?" asked the judge.

The foreman stood. He was a middle-aged man, dressed in a cheap suit and crumpled white shirt. His tie was loosely knotted, and hung low beneath his unbuttoned collar. He looked uncomfortable in his moment of prominence, and his voice was too quiet for many to hear. "We have, Your Honor."

"Will you please read your verdict to the court."

He looked at the paper in his hand and read, "We find the defendant, Matthew Carne, guilty of murder in the first degree."

There was an outbreak of conversations the room, with a few faint cheers, and the judge called for silence.

"It would help the court if you could speak more loudly, Sir."

The foreman complied,

People started clapping and cheering, but Liz Carne was silent, burying her face in her hands. The judge called for order, asked the foreman if the verdict was unanimous. He said it was. The twelve jurors were then told to state their decisions individually. One by one, they each said "Guilty".

The judge addressed the defendant, who was made to stand with his attorney at his side.

"Matthew Carne, you have been found guilty of one of the worst crimes ever committed in America." She continued to outline the heinous nature of his offense, the harm it had done to America, and the court's intolerance of such things. A properly formed jury of the his peers had determined his guilt. The court would set a date for sentencing in three months' time. Since Federal law mandated a sentence of life without parole, this seemed an unnecessary delay, but procedures are what they are.

Once the judge had finished, Matthew was returned to his cell. He had remained silent throughout the proceedings, with a sad and confused look on his countenance. As he was taken away, he glanced at his wife and tried to smile, which reduced her to tears. Her Honor then brought the proceedings to a close and left the room.

Back in her chambers, Her Honor agreed to see Isaac Stern and Sandra Fulbright. The former asked if Justin Gates might now be released and his opposite number said she did not mind. The judge agreed, adding that he had turned out to be a pretty poor prophet anyway.

A couple of hours went by as formalities were completed, and Justin became a free man again.

* * *

The outcome of Matthew Carne's trial was big news. The whole affair, from the shooting down of the plane to the conviction of the man who did it, was covered over and over again, from every possible angle. Some commentators remembered that the Prophet of Houston had played a role in the disaster itself, initially predicting a crash but naming the wrong plane. Then, as the Carne trial approached, it was said that he had predicted a not-guilty verdict, another spectacular error. So much for prophecy! Some commentators were thoughtful and objective, but the majority seized the opportunity to mock him, painting him as either a fool or a conman, or worse.

In the face of this treatment, Justin remained in his Sugar Land town house, silent and isolated from human contact as far as possible.

Twenty-two miles away, Jenny just ached for him, for what she guessed he was going through, and because he ignored her attempts to reach out to him.

* * *

Two weeks passed. Matthew Carne and the FlyAir plane disaster became old news. People found other things to talk about, and Paul Simpson was back in his Laguna Beach office, working on other matters. Business was ending for the day and his receptionist was about to leave when the door opened, and a visitor walked in. She looked up at him and her jaw dropped.

"Good afternoon. Is Paul Simpson in? I need to see him."

Pulling herself together, she leaped from her desk and rushed down the hall to her boss's office.

"You have a visitor," she said.

"I do?" he responded. "Was I expecting anyone?"

"Not this one."

"Well, show him in."

In a very strange voice, she said, "I'll do that."

A moment later, Matthew Carne walked into Paul's room.

Or someone who looked exactly like him.

* * *

"Come on in, Mike," Paul rose to greet him. "I have been expecting you."

Michael Khan stopped in mid-step. "You were?"

The lawyer walked round his desk, hand outstretched. "It just had to be you."

They moved over to the armchairs in the corner of the room, and sat down.

"Everyone here thinks you died in that explosion," explained Paul, "But there never was proof of it. No-one was ever able to find or retrieve any remains, not of your parents or yourself. The only proofs of death we were able to get were in the form of State Department documents. They were sufficient for estate purposes, but far less than absolute proofs. Everything went to your brother, of course. How you are going to re-open that issue, well, that is a question."

Michael Carne, Matthews twin brother and look-alike, smiled sadly. "I don't think we are going to worry about that. I intend to turn myself in, confess to my misdeeds, and get Matthew released. After that, I won't need any inheritance anyway."

There was a brief silence, and then he continued, "You really were expecting me? You actually figured out that it was I, not Matt, who shot that plane down."

"To me, your brother's innocence was a given. I have never doubted it. I don't know anyone less capable of such a crime. The case against him is almost entirely based on identification by a series of witnesses. There is no clear motive, no background of terrorism, nor of religious extremism. In any case, he has alibi's for the night of the event and also for all the occasions when the witnesses say he was with them. We clearly had a case of mistaken identity."

Matthew picked up the story, "And who could be a better look-alike candidate than his identical twin brother?"

"Exactly!"

"Except that his twin brother was dead."

"And then, one evening, with the help a large brandy, I suddenly had an inspiration. What if the brother was not dead?"

"So what did you do?"

"What could I do? The State Department had supplied documents to establish that you were. I could hardly go to Afghanistan to research, and no-one was going to believe that would be worthwhile anyway. Everyone except Liz and I believed that the feds had done their duty and Matthew must be guilty, however unlikely that might seem."

"But you kept wondering."

"I did." There was another pause, before Paul went on, "So tell me how you come to be alive after all."

"I don't really know," Michael said, with a sigh. "I don't recall the explosion. It was apparently an American air strike, probably a bomb dropped by a drone. My parents and I had just arrived in the country. We landed at Kandahar and were met by one of my cousins. He was driving us back to the family compound, in the hills, about an hour and a half away. It seems that the village we were driving through was a known Taliban stronghold, when the US Air Force decided to use it for target practice. That is all a complete blank to me. I just have other people's word for it. From the time we left the airport until I woke up six weeks later, I was out of it. It is likely that the blast threw me out of the truck. I was found, crumpled up, in a ditch fifty yards away."

"So who took care of you? And why? After all, you were an American."

"But at least I looked a lot like them. My folks were Afghans, don't forget. Anyway, the group I was with were fervent Jihadists, and I was at least nominally a Muslim. I think they started out by thinking I could be used as a hostage, that they could sell me back to the Americans for big bucks. A lot of that still goes on, you know. But as time passed, I began to see the world through their eyes, to be infected by their hate for the West in general and the US in particular. I could not forget that it was an American bomb that had killed my parents. I gradually became one of them. That is when I dreamed up my plan for taking revenge on you Americans, a plan which might even help drive you out of Afghanistan for good."

The conversation continued, with Mike explaining how he had sold his ideas to his Taliban group, and how their leaders had agreed to fund and help the plan. He described his training in the use of shoulder-mounted surface-to-air missiles, and the detailed plan for sourcing one in Pakistan and shipping it to California. And he talked about what it had been like to arrive back in his native country, with such a vicious plan to carry out.

"I was quite taken aback when I got here," he said. "Figuring things out in a cave in Afghanistan was one thing. Being here, trying to live like a normal American, with my new found hatred in my heart, was hard. It took me two months to get everything together and pull it off. Then I fled."

"And what about Matthew?" asked Paul. "Didn't you worry about him?"

"Why should I?" came the reply. "I did everything possible to make it the perfect crime. I covered all my tracks. There should not have any way for people to identify me. I still don't know how they got on my trail."

"I can help you there. You did a good job blowing up the Winnebego, but the Feds managed to find its chassis number, embossed on a piece of the wreckage. From that point on, it was good old fashioned police work."

Mike shook his head. "Even so, they should not have been able to charge Matt. He knew nothing about anything. Certainly he did not know I had been back in the country. When I heard he was to be tried, I thought of coming back and turning myself in."

"So why didn't you?"

"Because I was sure he would be acquitted. I could not believe an American court would convict him. Only when I realized I was wrong, did I decide I had no choice."

"Now that you are here, what do you want from me?"

"I want to confess. Matthew is innocent, and needs to be set free. You are the attorney. You will know how to go about it."

"The first thing we are going to need is your confession."

"I have that already," said Michael, pulling a wad of papers from his pocket.

"And the second is a new attorney for you."

"But I want you."

Paul shook his head. "That is not allowed. I cannot speak for your brother and also for you. It would be a conflict. But don't worry. I know just the right person."

* * *

"You want to do what?" exploded the judge, glaring at the three lawyers who were seated on the other side of her desk. They were Sandra Fulbright, Paul Simpson and Harvey Tubin, Michael Khan's new attorney.

"We need to reopen the Matthew Carne trial," said Sandra.

"Why on earth would we do that?"

"Because the man is innocent, your Honor."

"Innocent?" Alicia Hamilton was indignant. "You came to my court, accused him of mass murder, proved his guilt to the satisfaction of twelve good jurors, and now want to say he is innocent?"

The prosecutor looked at Paul Simpson, the defense attorney, for help. He addressed the judge.

"It turns out that Carne is as innocent as we always said he was. He did not shoot down the plane. His brother did."

"Are you playing games with me?" asked the incredulous judge. "His brother?"

"That's right. His brother. Ten days ago, I was in my office when in walked someone who looks so like Matthew Carne that I thought it was he."

Paul rose and stepped forward. He placed a pair of photographs on the judge's desk. They could have been two pictures of the same man. Returning to his seat, he went on to describe his encounter with Michael Khan, his selection of Harvey Tubin to represent him, and their subsequent discussions with Sandra Fulbright. She picked up the story.

"So we checked his fingerprints against the ones on the damaged laptop. They were a perfect match. And we showed pictures of him and of his brother, Matthew, to some of the witnesses. It is clear that they could have identified either brother as the culprit. As you can see, the similarity between the two men is so close, it is uncanny. Anyway, the new Mr. Carne has written a full confession. We have a copy here for you." She passed a several-page document across the wide desk and continued to speak. "In fact, he has provided so many details of the plan to bring down that plane, it is impossible to doubt his involvement. The only question is whether his brother Matthew was involved at all. We believe he wasn't and should be cleared of all charges."

For several minutes the judge sat behind her desk with a frown on her face, reading Michael Kahn's confession. Then she looked up and said, "I need a few days. No-one is to hear a word about this until I say so. Got that?" She consulted her computer. "We will meet here, in this room, at nine-thirty next Friday morning, and decide then how to proceed."

Paul broke the news to Matthew, still in the detention center in Riverside, and then to Liz.

Matthew's response was surprisingly quiet. He seemed to have mixed feelings.

"I can't believe it," he said, "But I know it has to be true." He was seated opposite his attorney, staring at some far place, and shaking his head. "Mike. Alive. No. I never would have believed it."

"Even though you knew that there had to be someone out there who looks a lot like you?"

"I had grown so used to the idea that he had died in that explosion. Now he has shown up. I don't know what to think."

"You might think about getting out of here. About going home to Liz. About putting this whole nightmare behind you at last."

"You are right, of course. Still, you must admit, it is a lot to take in all at once."

"Would you like to see Mike? He is still a free man. At this moment you, he and I are the only people who know the truth."

Matthew thought about that one.

"You know, I am not sure. It will have to happen, I know, but I am just not ready yet."

Liz, of course, was ecstatic. It was like coming out of a dark, foggy tunnel into a paradise of bright sunlight, a garden of Eden, a place where the air was filled with symphonies of birdsong, and life was a complete joy. He was sitting on the couch in her living room when he told her. Her face brightened up, her eyes shone, her smile was glorious. She looked exactly like the image in the portrait over the fireplace. Amazing!

* * *

Lawyers and legal affairs take their time. With attorneys earning hundreds, or even thousands of dollars an hour, it is not surprising that they drag things out. At least, that is what Matthew thought as he remained in custody. But all things do come to an end, and two weeks after Paul and

Sandra had dropped their bombshell on the judge, Matthew Carne was back in court. His was the second hearing of the day. The first had been the arraignment of his brother, Michael, who had pleaded guilty to the crime of bringing down FlyAir 349 and killing eighty-five people. A plea agreement had been reached, and was accepted by the judge, meaning that he had given up all rights to any appeal. After he was taken away, to await the formal confirmation of his fifty-year sentence, Matthew was brought in. According to the rules, he arrived in handcuffs, but left as a free man, fully vindicated, his innocence established once and for all.

Matthew's exoneration was huge news all over the country, and swiftly landed on Jenny Lane's desk in the TV newsroom. She could hardly handle it. On the one hand, she was ecstatic for him and for Liz. She was excited that the portrait of a so-very-happy Liz was justified. Although Justin and she appeared to have parted for good, she was totally delighted for him, that he had been vindicated. Her only sadness was that she could not run to him, fling her arms round him, and share his relief. Frustrated by their lack of contact, she sent him several emails, congratulating him and sharing various bits of news about it all. Justin's failure to reply to even one of them upset her more than she could admit.

CHAPTER 17

Heartache

After Matthew Carne was cleared of any involvement in the FlyAir 439 disaster, Justin's fame soared. Who was this man who could see tomorrow so often and so clearly, even when everyone else doubted what he saw? Requests for interviews abounded. Two offers arrived, from professional biographers, to immortalize him in print. Thousands of people emailed, telephoned, and mailed letters, all begging for his help in one way or another, either to ease their anxieties or to make themselves (and him) rich. He was submerged in communications he neither wanted nor needed. It was all too much to handle.

As if being overwhelmed by the attentions of others was not enough, he suddenly found himself besieged by self-doubt in a way he had not previously known. The fact that he had given all his love and trust to one woman, only to be betrayed so badly, really shook his self-confidence. It began to appear in the quality of his work. His first attempt at a portrait, after his return from California, was so disappointing that he would not let his client have it. To make that situation worse, he knew that the middle-aged banker who had commissioned it had really done so in the hope of a prediction regarding his retirement. Justin had nothing of the sort to offer. A second client appeared the following week, a successful actress, who wanted to enhance her own ego with a full-length portrait of herself. He felt quite unable to start on the project and had to feign sickness.

"Perhaps we could reschedule for next month," he said.

Justin and Jenny did not speak to each other for more than a month. For her, there was anger and shame, as well as a deep, deep longing for what there had been between them before. She was angry that the situation had arisen, that some unknown person had created the Twitter storm, and she was being made to carry the blame. She was furious with her fiancé for so readily doubting her, and with herself for lacking the courage to go to him in an effort to put things right. Instead, she threw herself into her work, using it as a distraction. That was better than lying on her bed and feeling miserable. To make matters worse, she found no comfort at home. Binnie seemed to be always around but surprisingly lacking in empathy.

Down in Sugar Land, Justin was not faring much better. He was mad at himself for being mad at the woman he loved, unable to understand his inability to forgive her for the betrayal. He realized she had not intended to harm him, or at least, he hoped that was so, but the wound was very deep. Making it worse was the worry that, if things did not improve, his skill at painting his usual insightful portraits might have faded, along with the ability to receive his previews. They were so mysterious in nature that any self-doubt on his part became a curtain though which he could not see into someone else's soul. The tide of true love, upon which Jenny and he had been riding so high, had turned. The ocean of contentment and hope, which had been carrying them into a future together, had faded away. Life seemed emptier and lonelier than before they had met.

It took a scrap of paper and an untidily written note to turn the tide and bring it in again. It was a Sunday, and Jenny had slept late. She walked into the kitchen, hoping her orange-haired roommate might have already made coffee. She was out of luck. Looking around, she saw a note, stuck on the refrigerator door with a magnet. In keeping with Binnie's constant, over-the-top optimism, it read: 'Wake up, Sunshine, Today is going to be your day. PLEASE ENJOY IT! I'll be back later."

Jenny muttered, "Huh!" and tugged the note off the door. It, and the magnet, fell to the floor. She bent down, picked them up, threw them on the table, and started making coffee. Mug in hand, she sat down, and glanced again at the note. Binnie's writing was as bold and startling as everything else about her, but the message was simple and to the point. Jenny grimaced, and, for no good reason, turned the paper over. She could see it had the remains of perforations along one edge and recognized it as the counterfoil of a check. Vaguely curious, she wondered who was sending her roommate money. It turned out to be the San Francisco Chronicle. Intrigued, she read the details.

Payee: Ms. Brenda McSwain

For: Carne trial article.

Amount: $5,000

Jenny frowned. Putting her mug down, she studied the paper again and again. Why on earth would that famous newspaper send such a sum to a no-account receptionist in a Houston PR firm? What did Binnie have to do with the trial? Why was she submitting a story on it to the newspaper? Why the San Francisco Chronicle? A suspicion began to form in Jenny's mind. Could Binnie have been the one who leaked the story about Justin's supposed prediction to the paper? How would she have known about it, anyway? Jenny was certain she had not told her. The more she thought about it, the more it seemed that Binnie was the source of the published story. But what about the Tweet? According to reports, that was originated by someone who called himself Barking Dog. Could he and Binnie be one and the same? Adopting a nickname like that would be typical of her unconventional roommate.

Jenny had kept a copy of the original article. She fetched it from her room and read it carefully. The piece was attributed to a reporter named Brad Summer. On an impulse, she called the paper in San Francisco and asked for him. Of course, he wasn't there. He was either off duty, it being Sunday, or out on assignment. She left a message, wondering whether she would hear from him before Binnie returned. When her phone rang, barely ten minutes after she left the message, she knew the answer.

Brad spoke with a pleasant Southern accent. Maybe he comes from Alabama or Georgia, she thought. Yes, he authored the article. Who was asking, he wanted to know? When Jenny identified herself, he seemed to hesitate before speaking further.

"How can I help you?" he asked.

"Let me be blunt, Brad. I want to know if you are Barking Dog? If not, do you know who he is?"

"Don't you think that, whoever he is, he uses that name to remain anonymous?"

"I don't care what he wants. I think you are Barking Dog, and I want you to know that, by sending out that tweet, you have ruined two people's lives."

The reporter sounded genuinely surprised. "I hope I haven't," he said.

"So you admit that's who you are."

"I suppose so, but ruining lives was not my intention."

"How did you come to write the original article?"

"Some female called McSwain called it in, offered it to us, for a price. I don't know how much we paid. That is not my department. But I did speak to her, and she satisfied me that she knew what she was talking about."

"And what about the Tweet? Was she paid for that, too?"

"Oh no! Once the judge had put that gag order on your fiancé, the paper would not touch it."

"But you would?"

"I guess so. You see, Ms. McSwain called me directly, asked me to put it to my editor. When he turned it down, I thought it was too good a piece of news to waste, so I sent it out on Twitter. I've used Barking Dog a few times for projects like that."

"Well, Brad Summer, I hope you can sleep easy in your bed, knowing that you have ruined my marriage and Justin Gates' career."

Angrily, Jenny hit the END button and killed the call.

Binnie did not arrive home until after ten that evening. She swung into the apartment, humming some unrecognizable tune. Her evening must have been fun: she looked flushed with pleasure, and greeted her friend with a cheery, "Oh! Hi!"

Jenny, who had endured twelve hours of frustration and mounting anger, brought her down to earth with a single word.

"Bitch!"

Binnie stopped in mid-stride and stared. She had never heard such a word from her roommate.

"What?"

"Why did you do it?"

"Do what?"

"Sell that story to the paper."

Sudden silence, then "Oh."

Binnie sat down across the table from Jenny.

"I heard you talking to Justin. Your door was open, and you were lying on your bed."

"But you couldn't hear what he said to me."

"True, but it was pretty clear from your responses. He was telling you that Carne was innocent and was going to go free. That story at that time was worth money, and I was broke. Besides, I thought the publicity would help Justin with his fame and fortune."

"Well, you were wrong. And then you went and tried to sell it to them again, even though the judge had put a gag order on Justin."

"But I didn't know about the gag, I swear. Not until Brad called me back to say the paper was turning me down because of it. Then I knew I had to shut up on the subject."

"But you still let Brad Summer put it out on Twitter."

"No, I didn't. You are wrong there. It never occurred to me he would do such a thing. I assumed he would just forget it."

"Well," said Jenny, less angry but still very bitter, "Whatever you did, I lost my fiancé, and you probably ruined his life too."

Next morning, she packed a bag and moved out of the apartment.

* * *

More than a month went by. Justin was at work in his studio. Still unable to grapple with portraits, he was working on an overlarge abstract in wild greens and blues and whites with spears of red running through, an attempt to express the torment in his soul. It wasn't working.

He had almost entirely given up using his computer. Never one for Facebook or Twitter, he only used it for emails and letter writing. Once the deluge of messages started, following the Carne trial, he just closed it down and put it away, so he never saw the emails that Jenny sent. Only later did he learn about them, and realize how hurt she must have felt by his lack of response. One guilt chased another through his life in those days. Deep down, he was aching for her, to see her smile, to hear her voice, to feel her touch, to close his eyes and breathe in her sweet scent. But the wound was very deep, and he wasn't prepared to beg.

The doorbell rang. He was not expecting a visitor and did not appreciate the disturbance. He kept on painting. The bell sounded again, and he tried to ignore it, but it sounded once more. With a sigh of reluctance, he put his brush down and went to see who the intruder was. He did not hurry down the stairs. Perhaps the caller would give up and go away before he reached the door, but that is not what happened. He reached the door, released the latch, and pulled it open. And there she was! He had not seen her in almost two months, and the sight of her almost moved him to tears. Her usual self-confidence was missing, replaced by furrows of anxiety across her brow and an unaccustomed sadness in her eyes. Even her sweet, kissable lips were quivering. She didn't look like her normal self, but it was she, and the sight of her overwhelmed him. In an instant, his straight-jacket of misery and loss was stripped away.

The two of them stood still, just taking in the sight of each other.

The drive from Houston to Sugar Land had taken Jenny nearly half an hour, thirty minutes of thinking about what she was doing, how she would feel when he opened the door, wondering if he was still frozen against her, or if his anger might be ready to thaw. Would he be pleased to see her?

She didn't know. If he would give her a chance to explain, to tell him that she had always loved him and would never have betrayed him, and that it was all Binnie's fault, then maybe the gulf between them could be bridged. She hoped so desperately, praying that, deep down, he still loved her.

What should she say first, when he opened the door? If he opened it, that is. As she drove, Jenny had thought up one opening gambit after another. Nothing seemed quite right. And then, suddenly, there she was, on his doorstep, ringing his bell. Once. Twice. Three times. Perhaps he wasn't home. Perhaps he was refusing to answer. She did not know. Should she turn and leave? She was about to give up when the door began to open, and she saw him, and completely forgot everything she had thought she might say.

Justin, of course, had no warning of her visit. Ever since he returned from Riverside he had been longing to see her, to feel her hand in his, to know that there still was love between them. But his anger still burned fiercely. He knew he needed to forgive, both for her sake and for his own, but he just could not. Frustrated by his own obstinacy, he had decided that she would have to make the first move, or there wouldn't be one. After all, she was the one who had broken their bond, wasn't she?

The suddenness of her appearance on his doorstep quite threw him. He was conflicted inside. His need for her was at war with his anger at what she had done. He stared at her, unable to react to her arrival. And then she smiled, in her unique, delightful, bewitching, intriguing way, the smile by which she had begun to win his heart so many months before. The dam broke. All the pent-up regrets and longings were released. He stepped forward, snatched her hand, dragged her into the house, and wrapped himself around her. God! How good that felt.

Jenny struggled free and pulled Justin onto the sofa.

"Jus, I have to talk to you," she said.

"And I to you," he replied.

"Just listen. Please. Just listen. It wasn't me. It was Binnie."

@"What was Binnie?"

"Binnie sent the stories to the newspaper. She overheard me talking to you on the phone and got the wrong end of the stick. She thought she could make money by telling the world what she thought you had said."

Justin gazed into his fiancée's eyes. "And I have been blaming you all the time."

"How could you not?" she replied.

"Because I should have known you better. I need you to forgive me for doubting you. I just didn't know what else to think."

"I know."

"After we parted, I was lost," he continued. "I couldn't paint. My previews went away. I had nothing left. I need you, Jenny. That's all there is to it."

"All?"

"No, not all. I love you with all my heart. We belong together."

"Yes," she said. "We do."

CHAPTER 18

Sophie

For Jenny, the reunion with Justin brought overwhelming joy. His insuppressible smile spoke more than anything he might have said. She had been so afraid that he would continue to blame her, or want to punish her in some way, for the misery she had unwittingly caused, but one look at his face told her not to worry. Her man loved her, whatever had passed between them.

For Justin, things were a little more complicated. He had absolutely no doubt that he wanted her, needed her, could not do without her. But his anger, instead of evaporating as he thought it would, morphed into guilt. How could he have doubted her? Could he ever be worthy of her if he lacked faith in her goodness and love? What sort of loving husband could he be when he had so readily thought she had betrayed him?

Jenny sensed his troubled spirit, and was patient and generous with her love and understanding until he healed. Meanwhile, he began to take up his charcoals and his paints again, and welcome clients into his studio once more. To his relief he discovered that neither of his gifts, as a painter or as a seer, had deserted him after all.

Since falling out with Binnie, Jenny had been essentially homeless, camping out in various friends' spare rooms or on their couches.

"Why not move in with me?" asked her fiancé. "We are destined to be together soon enough, anyway."

Jenny looked around her. His little townhouse was bright and pleasant and comfortable, fully adequate as a bachelor pad cum studio, but perhaps she and her things would prove too much. Justin watched as she studied his home, and read her thoughts. Putting his arm around her shoulders in a reassuring hug, he said, "I know, but we can make it work. And when the wedding is behind us, we can start looking for somewhere better."

And so Jenny moved in, and took over his computer and his phone, booking his clients and making sure that he was never too busy, but always busy enough. For the rest of that summer, Jenny kept working and Justin kept painting and an aura of deep contentment pervaded the little townhouse near the lake. And, one after another, all sorts of people found their way there, to sit for the mysteriously talented artist who knew how to paint so well the things that could be seen, and sometimes discern those which could not.

And among them was Sophie. She came for a portrait. It was a Monday, and they brought her in a wheelchair. She was tiny and frail, shriveled away, you might say. Justin had never been asked to paint someone who looked so sick. Normally he asked clients to climb the stairs to the studio, but there was no way for her to do it. True, she could not have weighed more than eighty or ninety pounds, so anyone could have carried her up. But she didn't want that.

She might have looked like a candidate for a 'Help the Aged' calendar, but she had enormous energy. Not the sort of energy that helps you run upstairs, of course. What she possessed was inner strength, the sort that radiates, empowering those around to feel wiser or stronger or more creative, just because they are near.

"You can call me Sophie," she said, speaking clearly and precisely, but not loud. "I know I look old and past my best, but I don't want any flattery. Paint me just as I am, in this darned wheelchair."

Her eyes were bright blue. They shone out of her graying skin to grab your attention. Her hair was gray, too, but whiter than her skin, pulled back from her face and gathered somehow behind her neck. Her lips were thin and pale, and her teeth were old, but her smile was real and infectious, although perhaps a little sad.

"And if I don't like it, I won't pay for it," she added.

One of the women who brought her said disapprovingly, "Mom!"

"No, Sally," she said, "We want something honest, or we don't want it at all. Anyway, you two run along and leave me with Mr. Gates here." Then she turned to the artist. "When should they come back?"

"Two or three hours would be good," he said, and then made a mistake, by adding, "If that isn't too long for you."

She glared at him. "Don't you start," she said.

Justin could not guess her age, but her daughter looked old enough to have her own wheelchair. Sally and her friend, whom he took to be a nurse of some sort, made their way out of the house, and left him in sole charge of Sophie. Or was it the other way around?

They agreed on the style of portrait, the background, the angle from which he would look at her, what she would do with her hands, and so on. Then he brought an easel and other necessities from upstairs, and got started.

"Tell me a bit about yourself, Sophie," he began, but she cut him off.

"We don't need to do much talking. I want you to concentrate. Do a good job. This is the first and last portrait I will ever have. I want it to be right."

"At least tell me why you have decided to have this done, after all these years," he said.

"You just figure that out for yourself, young man."

They settled down to their tasks, he working at his easel and she sitting as still as she could, not looking straight at the artist, but a little to his left. He placed a vase of flowers on top of a cabinet, to give her something on which to focus, to help steady her gaze Then, as always, he began by sketching an outline using a charcoal pencil.

It wasn't long before she turned her head to face him directly.

"What is it about you, Justin?" she asked, adding "Is it OK to call you that?"

"It's my name. Feel free."

"Well, what is it that makes you different?"

"I didn't know I was," he replied, trying to avoid the question.

"O come on! You know perfectly well what I mean. How is it that you see into other people more deeply than they see into themselves?"

"I don't honestly know. It is just a gift, I suppose."

"Don't you feel, sometimes, that you are invading their privacy?"

"Maybe, but they don't have to come to me, do they?"

He needed her to resume her pose, and pointed his pencil toward the vase.

"I know. I know." She muttered, readjusting her gaze.

"I didn't come because I wanted my fortune told," she went on. "Well, not really. But I have read about you many times in the paper or listened to news reporters naming you, and I was curious. I am old and past my expiry date, and could go at any time. I wondered whether you could see a future for someone like me."

"Sophie, you don't sound as if you are on the way out. You still have tremendous strength."

"Huh! You say things just like the rest. But I don't think you are like any of them. Now, get on with your drawing or painting, or whatever you are doing."

After that, she settled down, looking toward the flowers but not seeing them. Neither spoke for almost an hour. Occasionally, she would look in Justin's direction again, which would enable him to see into her eyes. Each time, when he needed her to resume her pose, he pointed his pencil or brush to direct her. She would give a sly grin and obey.

The eyes, it has been said, are the windows into the soul, and Justin has found it to be true. In her case, they showed both uncertainty and sadness, not surprising for someone so near the end of her days. He wondered what she was thinking about as she sat there, but was reluctant to enquire. Experience had taught him that clients will speak when they need to. That way, what they say is directed by their emotions, not his questions.

Eventually, Sophie sighed quietly, glanced at him quickly, and looked away again. Then she said, in a voice so quiet that it could hardly be heard, "Are you scared of death, Justin?"

"Are you?" he responded.

"I wonder if I should be," she answered.

Their silence resumed. After all, he was an artist, not a counselor, and experience had taught him that she would open up if she wanted to. He would not pry. A few minutes passed, and then she resumed her whispering.

"The worst thing is the not knowing."

"Not knowing what?" he asked, quickly clarifying, "Not knowing what lies on the other side?"

"Well, that, of course, but I think I worry more about what happens here, on this side."

Justin was busy with his brush and didn't say anything for a minute.

She spoke again, her voice still hard to hear. "I worry about the mess I may be leaving behind. About what you could call my legacy. Not the money and stuff, you understand, but the impact I might have made, over all these years. I wish I had stood for something. Something real. Something big. Something good. I don't think my life has amounted to much, and I regret that now."

Not knowing how to respond, the artist concentrated on his canvas. He was not too sure whether, by whispering, she was talking to him or not.

Perhaps she was addressing some private god of her own. He rather hoped so.

"When I was a child," she continued, speaking more loudly, now looking directly at him, "I was taught to believe in Heaven and Hell. Do good, and you end up in one. Do bad, and you end up in the other. We used to go to church, and those preachers knew all about hell." She gave a bitter laugh. "They could describe it with great relish: fire and brimstone, whatever they are. Interestingly, they were far less eloquent about heaven, much less sure what that is like." She paused for breath, and then mused, "When you think about it, it is kind of funny how little preachers know about Heaven."

"You don't believe in them now?" Justin interjected.

"Do you?" Sophie countered, pausing to think. "Until a year or so ago I would have said that no intelligent person could. Since no one can say where the fire is burning, or where the heavenly music is to be heard, I refused to waste time thinking about them."

"But now?"

"But now I am not so sure. I am very near the end: I know that. And I find myself worrying about such arrogance. Perhaps it is possible, after all, that we do receive our just rewards. In a way, that would make sense of having been alive."

"So, what do you think could be on the other side?"

Her reply shocked him. "That is what I'm here to find out."

"How can I tell you that? What makes you think I know, anyway?"

"Over the years I have met preachers and priests, mystics and fortune tellers, philosophers and theologians. None of them know. Some tell me my body will be resurrected one day." She laughed sourly and pointed at herself. "Who would want this one back again? Then there are those who say I am going to be a disembodied spirit, although what that is and where it might exist is beyond me. Beyond them, too, I think"

Putting his brush down, he looked at her. "So why do you think I know better than they?"

"Simple," she said, "You see the future. All they do is speculate about people in general. They are all talk, all theory, about mankind as a whole. You deal with real men and women, individually, one by one. You are the only person I know, who can tell someone what is going to happen to her down the line. And, according to what people say, you are always right. If anyone knows what's going to happen to me when I die, it has to be you."

He walked over and squatted down in front of her wheelchair. Taking and holding her hands, he looked into her face and said, as gently as he could, "Sophie, I hate to disappoint you, but I have nothing to offer. I don't always receive previews of my client's lives, you know, and I don't have one today."

"Ah!" she exclaimed, extracting one bony hand and thrusting a finger at him, "So my future is a blank to you, is it?"

The prophet nodded.

"But," she demanded, with the air of a triumphant prosecutor, closing her case in a trial," Is that because you have drawn a blank on this occasion? Or because..." She drew in a deep breath. "Because my future truly is a blank? Because there really is nothing on what they call the other side? Because there is no other side after all?"

Justin finally understood. "And that is why you came, not to find out what happens to you when you die, but to be assured that nothing does."

The frail old lady with the piercing eyes and troubled soul said simply, "I needed to know."

"And now you do?" he asked softly.

She nodded.

"I think I do."

Then she closed her eyes, and her head fell forward. For a moment Justin thought that she had died; that, having learned it was safe to leave, she had indeed gone. He was frozen where he knelt. He could not move. He had no idea what to do, and was only saved from his panic by a sound behind him. The front door opened, and in walked Sally and the nurse.

Sophie must have heard the noise, because she began to stir. Slowly, she raised head and looked at her daughter.

"I guess I'm tired," she said. "Let's go."

Then she turned to the artist and said, "I'll be back the day after tomorrow. Same time. We need to get this job finished. Before I die, that is."

He already had plans for the next three days, but couldn't bring himself to contradict her.

"OK," he said.

* * *

Two days later, Justin's phone rang. It was Sally.

"I am sorry to let you down," she said, "But mother won't be coming today. Monday's outing was really too much for her. She has been sleeping almost all the time since, and the doctor says her heartbeat is very weak. She may not be able to come again, ever."

"That is such sad news," replied Justin. "I do hope it wasn't my fault that she went downhill so quickly."

"Oh no! Please don't blame yourself. She has been fading for quite a while now. This is one more step along the way. Besides, although she seemed to take a hit physically, she seemed to gain strength mentally. I can't quite explain it, but her spirit seems stronger, more courageous since Monday. You must have said something quite special to her."

"I would like to think that. Please give her my love, and wish her well for me."

Sally hesitated, "About the portrait…"

"Just don't worry about it."

"I was wondering, is there any way for you to finish it, even if she doesn't come?"

"Maybe I could try."

"Please do. For some reason it means a very great deal to her."

After the call ended, Justin walked over to where the half-finished image of the frail but spirited old lady rested on his easel. He sat down on the nearby couch, leaned back, and studied his work. Then, with closed eyes, he dreamed of something new and different. He picked up the phone and called Sally back.

"I think I want to start the portrait again," he told her.

She was alarmed. "But I told you, mother cannot stand another trip to the studio."

"That is no problem. I have a very clear image of her, enough to paint her again, but I do need your help if you don't mind."

Surprised, Sally asked what she could do, and he told her.

"That should easy enough," she responded. "Just give me a day or so."

"I will wait for your call."

Justin put the phone down. Standing up, he took the picture of Sophie off the easel, and replaced it with a clean canvas. Then he started work.

It took Sally two more days to gather the things that Justin wanted and to deliver them to Sugar Land, and another ten days for him, working between other jobs, to complete the new portrait. When it was done, he called Sophie's house and arranged to visit. The following afternoon he appeared on her doorstep, a wrapped parcel in his hands. Sally was waiting for him.

"Mother is not so good today," she said, "But she insisted on getting out of bed to greet you."

The front door opened into a lobby, from which another door led into the living room where Sophie was waiting. She was lying back in a large, over-stuffed armchair, one that could have accommodated a very large and jolly Santa Claus. Her small and fragile frame was almost lost among its cushions. Even though she was wrapped in a pink, fleecy robe, there seemed to be almost nothing of her. Nothing of her body, that is. She still had the fierce blue eyes and the radiant personality that forbade sympathy.

"Ah! My dear artist!" she greeted her visitor, her voice faint, but determined.

"Sophie, how are you?" he replied.

She gave a small laugh. "Better not to ask."

"It's good to see you."

"That is as may be," she replied enigmatically.

There was an awkward silence, and then she said, "Let's see what you have brought me."

Justin looked at Sally. "I have brought the portrait. It would help if we had something to stand it on. A dining room chair, perhaps."

She glanced at the only other person in the room, the nurse who had helped deliver Sophie to the studio a couple of weeks before. Within a minute, a straight-backed chair was produced and stationed where mother and daughter could see it clearly. Justin carefully unwrapped his work and put it in place.

Sally reacted with a heartfelt, "Good Heavens!"

The nurse said "Wow!" and shook her head from side to side.

They both looked at the old lady, who was sitting, very still, staring at the picture. For four whole minutes, no one said a word. Then the old lady looked at the artist.

"That is not what I was expecting," she said, words that could have been a criticism, but weren't.

Sophie sounded more like she had been expecting bread and been given cake. Someone who had been expecting a seat in coach but had been upgraded to first. Someone who had won a gold medal when she had thought she would come in last.

The entire painting was a portrait of a person and, at the same time, a brilliant study of radiant light. The central figure was, of course, Sophie, perfectly recognizable, yet painted in white, cream and gold. No gray. No dark shadow. Nothing to suggest age or physical decline. It was amazing. By his choice of colors, the artist had managed to portray her inner beauty rather than her outward frailty, not denying her age but allowing her to appear radiant in spite of it. She exuded a peace and certainty about life, as she looked at the faces gathered around her. True, she was shown in her wheelchair, but this was rendered in shades of silver and gold, and managed to suggest a chariot in a victory parade, or even a throne, rather than a means of carrying the sick. All around, kneeling and seated on the floor, and standing behind, was a crowd of boys and girls and young men and women, all with happy and loving expressions on their faces.

Although he suspected that Sophie already understood, Justin felt he should explain. He said, "Sally told me."

"What did you tell him?" Sophie asked her daughter.

"I told him about the family."

"Why did you do that?"

"He told me that he didn't want to just paint an old lady at the end of her journey. He wanted to show the real you, the person you have always been. So I told him about the eighteen of us children who you rescued and took in, fostered, and adopted, and about all the grandchildren and great grandchildren too. I told him you have been the lovingest person on earth." As she spoke, Sally wiped a tear from her cheek.

Sophie turned to look at Justin again.

"You have done something amazing," she said. "Now, I want to see the picture more clearly."

The nurse moved the chair toward her.

Slowly, patiently, her gaze travelled across the canvas, looking at each of the painted figures, one by one. The others in the room watched and waited, Sally and the nurse found chairs to sit on, and Justin stood awkwardly to one side. Finally, when she had finished, Sophie looked up at him and said, "Very clever."

He smiled but did not reply.

Sophie looked across at her daughter. "Did you already see this picture?" and received a negative shake of the head.

"You know, he …" she nodded in Justin's direction, "… has painted eight figures whose faces I can see clearly. I recognize each of them. There are your brothers George, Harry and Mark. There is your sister Ann, and her three youngsters. And you, of course. All of them as they used to be, years ago. I can see that, but beautifully and accurately painted."

She looked up at the artist again. "These are so good. How could you paint, so accurately, seven people you had never seen?"

Sally interrupted. "I did lend him some photographs, mother."

The old lady nodded, and continued speaking to the artist.

"I hope you are not going to charge me for nine portraits instead of one," she said with a smile.

He just shook his head.

Then Sophie addressed her daughter once more. "There are, I think, more than a dozen others in the picture, less clearly shown, who could easily be your other siblings or their children. This is not really a portrait of me, it is a portrait of our whole family. It is wonderful."

To Justin she said, "What made you do this?"

He drew in a deep breath. "You wanted to know what was on the other side, and this is it."

Sophie frowned. "I thought we agreed there is no other side."

Justin crossed the floor to her chair, and knelt down so that he could watch her face closely.

"When Sally told me about the way you created this family, I knew that your life has been a fountain of goodness, goodness which flowed into the hearts and lives of eighteen young people who might otherwise have been unwanted and lost. Also, I am sure that the same goodness is flowing from them into their children and grandchildren and generations yet to be born. The goodness that has been your life lives even now, in them, and will continue to live in their children, and in their children's children. You came to me because you wanted to know what is beyond this life." He leaned across and laid his hand on the picture. "Sophie, this is what is beyond."

CHAPTER 19

Mr. President

A couple of weeks after presenting Sophie with her picture, Justin was at home, working in his upstairs studio, and Jenny was busy with her computer on the dining table. It was a Monday, a regular workday. Their calendar was blank, and they were not expecting anything unusual, certainly no callers. But with Justin's notoriety there was no predicting who might turn up on their doorstep. Usually, surprise callers were anxious people, hoping for a miracle insight into their future, and this could be seen in their faces. However, the young woman who rang the Gates' doorbell, on that particular morning, was different. She was perfect. At least, a fashion magazine editor might have thought so. She had elegantly styled, shoulder length, auburn hair surrounding a precisely made-up face. Her burgundy pants suit was made of expensive looking velour, and her high heeled boots looked as if they had just stepped out of a storefront in Rome. Her evident self-confidence suggested she would be more used to giving advice than receiving it.

"How can I help you?" asked Jenny as she opened the door.

The visitor gave her name as Roxy Parker, and she needed to speak to Mr. Gates.

"Can I tell him what this is about?"

"I would rather tell him myself."

"Then you had better come in, while I see if he is available."

A few minutes later, Justin came down the stairs from the studio. The two women were standing, talking to each another, and he joined them.

"Ms. Parker? You wanted to speak to me?" he asked.

Roxy looked sideways toward Jenny, and answered, "This is rather private."

Justin refused to take the hint.

"Let me introduce my wife, Jenny," he said. "She and I have no secrets."

"Well, let me ask both of you, please do not mention my visit to anyone, nor what I have come about."

"This sounds mysterious," Jenny observed.

"Conspiratorial," was Justin's comment.

"Not really," Roxy said with a smile, trying to put them at ease. "It's just that I work in the President's private office in Washington. I handle certain confidential matters for him. We don't want them talked about. Can I rely on your discretion?"

Jenny just nodded, while her husband spoke for them both.

"I should think so."

"I am bringing you an invitation from the President of the United States, to meet with him in the White House."

Jenny was impressed. "Justin! That is quite an honor."

He looked at her thoughtfully. "Is it?" he wondered.

That obviously irritated Roxy, whose smile chilled as she said, "It certainly is."

Justin watched her face carefully.

"Did you come here, all the way from D.C., just to invite me to dinner."

"I didn't say anything about dinner. I think the President has a meeting he would like you to attend."

"Would it be about the election?" he asked.

His visitor nodded. "I believe so."

"Ah! Yes! It would be."

"Then I take it you will come? All your expenses will be covered, of course, and we will put you up in a first-class hotel."

"Do you have a date in mind?"

Roxy did not need to consult her calendar. She had all the information in her head: not only the date of the meeting, but the times of suitable flights too.

Justin did not write anything down. He merely stated, unenthusiastically, "I need time to think about this."

Roxy was clearly put out. She had been expecting an immediate 'yes'.

"How long will you need."

"Well, your meeting is in two weeks. How about I let you know by this coming weekend."

"You know, Mr. Gates. People don't usually turn down personal invitations from the President. He may not be happy with your response."

"Oh! Don't worry about that. I am sure he has far more important things to worry about than me."

"But he is particularly interested in you, and what you might have to say."

"I am sure he is," said Justin.

The conversation ended there, and Roxy Parker left.

When they were alone, Jenny looked at her husband.

"You were kind of rude," she said. "That's not like you. Not everyone gets invited to the White House."

"It's a trap, Jenny. I'll bet it's a trap."

With that, the artist went back to his studio.

* * *

That same afternoon, the President called his election campaign manager, to boast.

"You've heard about this fellow they call the Prophet of Houston? Well, I have invited him to the White House."

"What on earth for?"

"It's a smart move, Sid. Half the country thinks he is magic, infallible. They write about him in the papers all the time. We need him to be on our side, to let the world know that he predicts a landslide for us. People love to ride with a winner. Once he stands beside me and says I'm going to be reelected, thousands, hundreds of thousands, even millions of votes will come our way. That alone might be enough to sweep us over the line."

"I can't believe there are so many simple-minded voters."

"Of course there are. People are fascinated by the weird and the unlikely. They love anyone who claims to know the future. That's why they read their horoscopes. Hell, Sid, that's why they believe the polls. They hunger to know what can't yet be known."

The man on the other end of the call was silent.

"What's wrong with that, Sid. Come on! You are usually so upbeat about these things."

"I was just thinking, what if he does not endorse you? Maybe he won't believe you'll win."

"Nonsense," the President scoffed. "How can he not support me? Just think. If I put him up before the cameras and he proclaims that my reelection is a sure thing, he will be seen by half the people in America. Within a month he will be overwhelmed with invitations and offers and will be able to name his own price. Within a year he will be richer than he ever dreamed possible."

His friend inserted a note of caution. "Has it occurred to you that he might not be interested in money?"

"Don't be ridiculous!"

"No. Seriously, my friend, such people do exist."

"Why?"

"Oh, I don't know why. I don't follow their thinking. But they are out there, and mostly they don't vote for us. Maybe he doesn't vote for us either. You might be giving him the opportunity to forecast your defeat. Then where will those million votes go?"

"Give me credit, Sid. I have already thought about that. In fact, one of the reasons for inviting him is to muzzle him. It already occurred to me that, if he is out there, saying whatever he wants to the world, and isn't on our side, he could do us a hell of a lot of damage."

"Do you know how he leans politically?"

"I will strap him down with the official secrets act and executive privilege. Unless he tells our story the way we want, we will stop him talking about the election at all, let alone prophesying against us."

* * *

That evening Jenny, dressed in her sapphire-blue nightgown, was sitting at her vanity, doing mysterious things to her fingernails. She glanced up as Justin entered the room, watching him in the mirror. How tall and lean and totally handsome he looked! She smiled at him, that mischievous, private smile which was reserved just for him, and which always turned him on.

"Hi," she said.

He responded with, "I've been thinking. Perhaps I'll say 'No'."

She spun round on her stool to face him.

"You can't be serious!"

"I think I can," he replied.

"No-one says 'No' to the President."

"Oh, I'll bet they do. But if not, then I will be the first. Someone has to be."

"But why would you do that? It is a great honor to be invited to the White House."

"Maybe, but I have a bad feeling about this. It might not turn out too well, either for him or for me."

"How come?"

"I might have to tell him things he won't like, and by all accounts, that is not what one does with this guy."

"Maybe you should go anyway. You might be needed."

"By whom, for Heaven's sake?"

"By Uncle Sam, or whoever it was that said, 'Your Country Needs You'."

* * *

Ten days later, Justin found himself staying in a lavish hotel somewhere in Washington; he had no idea where. On the previous evening he had been met at Reagan International Airport and chauffeured to the hotel. This morning, he had been picked up, exactly on schedule at nine thirty. A man in a dark suit and plain blue tie met him in the lobby and took him to a waiting limo. There was another passenger already there, a small, compact, rather boyish figure who spoke with a European accent of some sort.

"Good morning, Mr. Gates, and welcome to the nation's capital. I am Miguel Anders, and I work for the President. He has asked me to take care of you and put you at ease. He wants you to feel relaxed and, in due course, able to speak your mind freely."

Justin gave a small laugh. "Relaxed, you say? At ease, when faced with the most powerful man on earth? That's a challenge."

The younger man nodded. "I know," he said, "It can all be a bit daunting at first, but you will soon get used to it."

“Maybe. Maybe not. We will see.”

“Anyway, in this traffic it will take us a few minutes to get there. Let me tell you what you should expect and how it is all going to work.”

For almost ten minutes the limo crept along with the rest of Washington, with Miguel talking non-stop and Justin trying to take it all in. Finally, the young man stopped in mid-sentence and said, “Here we are.”

The car pulled up at some gates, clearance was issued quickly, and Justin arrived at the command center of the free world. At least, that is how Miguel described it.

There was a lot of waiting around, offers of coffee to drink (“no thank you”) and magazines to read (“how kind”). The small waiting room was empty when Justin arrived, but three other people appeared, all in time for the scheduled 11 a.m. meeting. There was some nervous, polite conversation, with everyone avoiding the “why are you here” question in favor of observations about the White House and its protocols. Eventually a smartly dressed middle-aged lady, with blue hair and too much makeup, appeared and said, “The President is ready.” It was eleven forty-three. She led them along some passages and into the Oval Office. Justin’s companions stared around at the room, trying to take everything in, to get used to the idea that they were really there. They appeared as new to the experience as he. Six or seven other people were already in the room, clearly more relaxed and at home. The newcomers were told where to sit, and more waiting began.

The purpose of the meeting was unclear to Justin. All he knew was that the overall topic was the November election, in which the President was standing for re-election. He did not want to be asked, in front of so many people, for a prediction. In fact, he did not want to be asked at all, audience or not. If that is why he was present, those who were waiting for his word were going to be disappointed.

Justin looked at the people around him, trying to figure out who might be who, but it was hopeless. Some of the faces were vaguely familiar, but never having been a fan of television news, names did not come readily to mind.

His reputation as a ‘prophet’ frequently got him into trouble. People were so unreasonable with their expectations. They thought he must be some sort of walking almanac: name the topic, find the page, read the answer. Few people understood that his work was based upon slowly formed links, telepathic or spiritual, with individual men and women, which empowered him to see something of their personal destinies. Foreseeing the future of an entire nation would be something else. "Why have they put me here with all these strangers?" he asked himself, but had no answer.

Five more restless minutes passed, and then someone said, "Please stand" and everyone rose in unison. There was a slight noise at the door behind him, and the same voice pronounced, more loudly, "The President of the United States!"

Heads turned and watched as the great man entered the room and moved to take one of the armchairs by the fireplace. Justin had a clear view of him. He could study his face and listen to his reactions as various people gave reports and answered questions. Had they placed him there with that in mind? Probably. "Remember, I am a portrait painter," he had told Miguel in the car. "That allows me plenty of time to get to know someone, to feel who they really are. I would be unlikely see into anyone's spirit in the course of a casual five-minute encounter."

For almost an hour people talked about the election. Justin was not introduced. No-one asked him to speak, nor did he offer an uninvited opinion. In fact, no-one appeared to notice him at all. Except for the President, that is. He noticed Justin as soon as he came into the room, and as he sat down, he gave him one of his famous smiles. He might even have tried a wink. "You and I have a secret, don't we?" was the unspoken message. The prophet just sat there, watching, listening, thinking, trying to be unphased by the surroundings.

By the time things were over, Justin felt he knew everything he needed to know about the President and his destiny.

When the meeting had been going for an hour, Blue Rinse reappeared. She spoke quietly to the President, who immediately rose to his feet, excused himself, and left the room. Things were brought to a close by his Chief of Staff, a lean, sour looking character with a military bearing, and people started to leave. When Justin's turn came, he was led into a small office where he found Miguel waiting.

"I am afraid you are not quite finished," he was told. "We have to wait for a minute or two."

"What for?" asked Justin.

"The President needs to see you privately."

"I thought he might."

For five minutes Miguel avoided conversation by working with his cellphone. Then, at some unseen signal, he said, "Let's return to the Oval and see what the Great Man has to say."

They entered the celebrated room to find it deserted. Miguel began to fill the time by pointing to the huge desk. "This is the world's most famous desk, given by Queen Victoria of Britain to President Hayes in 1880. It is made from the remains of a nineteenth century sailing ship, the Resolute, and has been used by many Presidents, but not always in this room."

As he spoke a door opened and the President strode in. Walking directly over to Justin, he grinned and held out his hand.

"So, you are the famous Prophet I have heard so much about. Welcome to the nation's capital and its most famous home."

He walked round behind the desk and took his seat, inviting Justin to be seated too. He made some signal to Miguel, who left the room.

"He doesn't want any witnesses for this conversation," thought Justin.

The President leaned back in his chair, arms raised, hands clasped behind his head, totally at ease. "Is this your first time in Washington, Mr. Gates?" he asked. For five minutes he led a casual and friendly conversation about the city and its history, presumably trying to help Justin relax. Then, suddenly, his manner changed. Bringing his arms forward and leaning on the desk, he said, "Now, to business."

Justin looked at him. In his youth, the artist had been taught to revere the presidency, to regard its occupants as men of great stature. Somehow, along with the responsibilities of the job, whoever gets it acquires a mantle of greatness, of enhanced self-importance. Meeting a president for the first time is an overawing experience. The man and his surroundings are enough to intimidate anyone, including the portrait painter from Texas.

Here he was, face to face with the most powerful man in the world, America's Commander-in-Chief, the so-called leader of the free world, the person who had control of its greatest economy and of enough weapons to completely destroy it. Lest he be distracted by these thoughts, Justin reminded himself that the President was just a man, and probably not totally admirable at that. He was an elected politician, probably used to compromising his principles in the pursuit of power.

"I am sure you know why I asked you to come."

"I think so."

"I want to know what you can tell me."

"What would you like me to tell you, Mr. President?"

"You know what I want to hear, Mr. Gates. You have a reputation for predicting the future. My team researched you, and you seem to have a dammed good record. How you do it, I have no idea, and I don't really need to know. I just need you to tell me that I am going to win this coming election."

Justin drew in his breath and plucked up his courage. "And if that isn't the case, Mr. President?"

The other man literally jerked. He thrust his head forward and stared at his visitor.

"I beg your pardon."

"You are wanting me to predict a victory. What happens if I cannot do that?"

"But I am sure you will," came the reply.

"Mr. President, with all due respect, you brought me here to tell you how the election is going to turn out. I can do that, and you can choose to believe me or not. What you cannot do is command what my prediction will be."

"But, dammit man, in a few hours I am going to hold a press conference. The bastards have been hounding me for one, and I need to have something spectacular for them. I want you to stand beside me, on the podium, and say, or at least confirm, that the party is going to win in the election, and that I will remain President for another four years."

"And if I cannot say that?"

The President almost shouted in his exasperation. "Just think about it, man! The publicity! The exposure! You will be seen by a hundred million people. The Prophet will be known around the world. You will be talked about from here to Moscow, from Tokyo to Sydney. You will be famous in every country there is. Your reputation will be made, your future secure."

"My reputation will be un-made, and my future worth nothing, if I fail to tell the truth."

The President added a slightly menacing tone to his voice. "Are you saying that I am going to lose this election?"

"No, Mr. President, I am not."

"So you ARE saying that I will win?"

"I am not saying that either."

"Then what the hell are you saying?"

"At this moment I am not saying anything: not making any prediction, that is."

"Well, why the hell did you come? Just for the glory of pissing off the President?"

"No, sir. I came because you asked me to. But before I can tell you your future, I have to be sure you can handle it."

"Are you crazy? I handle issues of world-wide importance every day, and deal with crises by the hour. Of course I can handle it."

"I apologize if I offend you. That is not my intention, but you do need to understand. In my line of work, I find three kinds of people. There are those who accept what I tell them; those who believe it but won't accept it; and those who think that what I have to say is rubbish. Which are you?"

"That depends on what you tell me."

"Exactly my point. You are asking me to tell you what you want to hear, not the truth."

"I am asking you to tell me that I am right., that I am going to win"

"The only thing I can tell you, Mr. President, is the truth. But first ...."

"Now what?" interrupted the great man, his exasperation boiling over.

Justin refused to be perturbed. "First I must make this plain. I know what the election will mean for you personally. I don't have a clue what it will do for your party. What I do is work exclusively with individuals. If I can connect with them, I will often get an insight into their future, their destiny. I can do nothing for groups of people, let alone political parties. They have no souls."

"What gibberish! Now tell me what I want to hear."

"That might be hard."

"If you tell the world I am going to lose, that could cost me millions of votes. But tell them that I am the winner, and they will climb on the band wagon in droves, and I'll win. That's why I need you. That's why you're here."

"You are wrong, Mr. President. I am sad to tell you that there is no way for you to win."

The Great Man was apoplectic, increasingly despising Justin as he absorbed what had been said. He pressed a button on his console, rose from his seat, barked "Stay right there!", and left the room.

Moments later someone else came in, a short stocky man with a bushy gray beard and bulging grey eyes. He introduced himself as one of the White House lawyers. Dragging a nearby armchair across, he sat down, closely facing Justin, placing a folder on the desk as he did so.

"Listen," he said, "And listen well. Everything that has passed between you and the President in today's private meeting is privileged. That means that you may not speak of it to any other person, whoever they might be, ever. This is a matter of official secrets. If you divulge any part of your conversation, including any opinion or advice you might have offered, you could be charged with a crime and possibly sent to prison. You should not even tell people that you have been here or that the meeting occurred."

Justin swallowed hard and muttered, "That might be hard. I may have mentioned to one or two friends that I was coming."

"That is one of the reasons you were included in the committee meeting. You can admit to that part of your visit, if necessary. But you must refuse to discuss what was said in that meeting, other than the fact that no-one there asked you for a prediction. Do you understand?"

Justin nodded his assent.

"I hope you do. And no-one, repeat, no-one shall ever hear that you had a private, one-on-one meeting with the President. What is more, if the President asked you for an opinion on any matter, that is itself a national secret. If you gave one, that is also a secret, and you may not share it with anyone else."

"Are you saying that, in an election year, I am forbidden from having or expressing an opinion about the outcome?"

"As far as the vote for President is concerned, that is exactly what I am saying."

The bearded attorney leaned across and picked up his folder. He handed it to Justin.

"The President requires you to sign this document. It binds you under the Official Secrets Act, to keep secret the matters discussed with him. Is that a problem?"

Justin sighed, merely glanced at the paper, and asked for a pen.

* * *

Three hours later, the President strode into the East Room at the White House for the long-awaited press conference. The fall election race was heating up, and he had been avoiding the press for some weeks. He stepped onto the podium and opened his folder, the one containing bullet points covering all the likely questions of the day, all neatly sorted and tabbed by subject. He raised his eyes to look at the gathering, intending to invite a first question from somebody safe, like Anthony Walker from NBC, one of his favorites. But, before he could speak, a voice rang out from somewhere in the room.

"Mr. President, is it true that you have consulted the Prophet of Houston concerning the outcome of the election?"

The President looked down at his folder. There was no tab for the Prophet, or for Justin Gates. No-one on his staff had thought, or known, how to prepare notes on that subject. There had hardly been time, anyway. He would have to wing it.

"We did have a meeting in the Oval Office this morning, involving a number of people. Mr. Gates, to whom I imagine you are referring, was among them."

"Did you discuss the upcoming election with him?" asked another reporter.

"That is what the meeting was about."

The original questioner spoke up again, before anyone else could get in. "Mr. President, please answer plainly. Did you or did you not ask Mr. Gates to predict the outcome of the election?"

"He was most encouraging: we expect our performance to be outstanding."

"Would that be your party's performance, or your own personal prospect?"

"The meeting was about the election in general, not specific individuals. Now, shall we move on to another subject." The President looked in the direction of the NBC reporter.

"Anthony?" he said, expecting a favorable question from his favorite reporter. That is not what he got.

"Forgive me, Mr. President, but our viewers will be anxious to know if Justin Gates, whom they know as the Prophet of Houston, and who is renowned for his accurate predictions, expressed an opinion about your own chance of being re-elected."

"You disappoint me, Anthony," said the President, clearly irritated. "I believe I have answered the question already."

"But my station has been informed, by a member of your own staff in fact, that you had a private meeting with Mr. Gates, a one-on-one encounter, after your committee meeting ended. It is hard to believe that you did not ask him if you are going to win or lose in November. Please either deny it or tell us what he said."

The President looked smugly across the room.

"The country will be pleased to hear the word of the Prophet. I did ask him, and he did answer. He said we are going to win."

There was a buzz of muted conversation. The President beamed at the crowd with his most charming smile.

"And our majority will be the largest ever seen in the history of America."

* * *

Justin slid his key card through the mechanism and opened the door. Immediately he heard the television. As he stepped into the room he saw Jenny stretched out on the couch. Whatever else the President's office might have done, they had at least provided him with a great hotel.

"Hello, sweetheart," he said, crossing the room and bending to kiss her forehead.

"Mmm, Mmm," she murmured disapprovingly, and turned up her face. "What sort of greeting is that?" Reaching out with her left arm, she pulled him down until they were able to kiss softly and fully on the mouth. "That's more like it."

"I take it you missed me," said Justin.

"Always. Come and sit beside me."

She wriggled to make room beside her.

"How have you spent your day?"

"I went to the Smithsonian. Or part of it, at least. It is more than vast. Did you know it's the largest museum in the world? Well, it's a collection of museums, really. I went to the Museum of American History. It was fascinating, but it wore me out. I came back here for a rest. Besides, I didn't know how long you might be, and I am impatient to hear about your day. I know you had mixed feelings about it."

"Well, I attended a rather boring meeting about the election, and then had a one-on-one with the great man himself."

"How did that go."

"Not too well. We did not exactly see eye to eye. He more-or-less commanded me to predict a reelection victory for him. I told him I could not do that. He was furious. He stormed out of the room, and sent in a lawyer to make me sign papers saying I would never tell anyone what he and I had said to each other. Then he stood up at a press conference and told the world that Justin Gates, the Prophet of Houston, had predicted a victory. He even said it would be the greatest victory of all time, or something like that."

"How awful! What did you do?"

"Well, of course, I was not actually at the press conference. Once he knew my view he didn't want me anywhere near that. But what could I do? I had signed to say I would keep quiet on the subject."

"So how do you feel about it, then?"

"To be honest, Jen, I am furious. Absolutely furious. Of course, from time to time I make a prediction which the person concerned won't accept. That must be expected. But for the President of the United States to stand up and tell the world that I had said one thing, when I had told him exactly the opposite, well, …… it leaves me speechless!"

"How can you explain it?"

Justin sighed. "It's plain and simple, really. Some people believe what they want to believe, in spite of evidence to the contrary. It's a common failing. But we should expect better of our President."

"Or," his wife responded, "He simply lied. It seems to me that politicians often do." Laying her hand on his arm, she sighed and added, "I suspect that D.C. is full of such hypocrites."

He husband nodded. "I agree. Give me Houston, any time."

* * *

Six months later, Justin found himself in a television studio. It was all Jenny's doing. Ever since the Carne trial and its attendant publicity, the producers at the TV station where she worked had been on her case. Bill kept saying things like, "Your fiancé is a hero. He would have a real following, if only he would do a few interviews and so forth. Can't you persuade him to come out of hiding?"

"He's not in hiding," she would retort. "He just likes his privacy. The bright lights are not for him."

Gradually the pressure got to her, plus the hints that she would get more in-front-of-the-camera work if she persuaded Justin to put in an least one major appearance. So here he was, facing the audience and the lights and, of course, the questions.

"Now that the election is behind us, and the President has lost," continued the late-night host, "Are you going to admit you were wrong?"

"Was I?" asked Justin.

"At his news conference he said you predicted a great victory for him. We have the video to prove it."

"I believe he did say that."

"What do you say?"

"I don't say anything. Anything that passes between me and a client is private. I never reveal such things."

"But either you did say it, in which case it turns out you were wrong, or you didn't, which would mean that the President of the United State is a blatant liar. Which is it?"

"You and your viewers will have to decide that for yourselves."

"Are you ever wrong in your predictions?"

"I don't believe so, although there are times when clients refuse to believe what I have to reveal. Some people would rather deny an uncomfortable truth than face up to it. Just look at all the millions who deny climate change, even though the evidence is staring them in the face. It's a common human failing."

"And you say that the President of this country and the leader of the free world is like that?"

"Maybe he is. After all, he still hasn't admitted that he lost the election. To misquote Jack Nicholson in A Few Good Men, 'The truth? He can't handle the truth'."

"Then what is your message to him."

"I doubt very much that he would want to hear anything from me. But if he did, I would remind him that his fate, and, in fact, the fate of the whole country, is already determined and cannot be avoided. As has been said, 'we often meet our fate on the roads we take trying to avoid it'. That is a lesson we should all remember."

CHAPTER 20

The Wedding

Justin was thirty-one years old when he and Jenny finally tied the knot. Living together in the Sugar Land town house was a joy in many ways, but it was a squeeze all the same.

"We need to look for somewhere bigger," said Justin, "Somewhere where you can have an office and I can have a bigger studio, more suited to welcoming strangers."

They started searching internet, and driving out at the weekends to explore the various communities in and around Houston. The search for their new home brought them even closer together.

One day, one of them said, "Maybe it is time for us to actually get married." Later, they argued about whether he said it to her first, or she to him, but they were in total agreement. "It will be our place," Jenny added. "We can own it together.

* * *

It was a modest ceremony, held in a waterfront garden on the edge of a lake, presided over by the vermillion orb of the setting sun. A golden glow touched the ripples on the lake, the leaves on the trees, and the emotions of the moment. The newlyweds looked into each other's eyes, kissed gently, and absorbed the deep contentment of two souls becoming one.

Twenty people attended, including Justin's mother and sister and Jenny's only living relative, a cousin from Florida. Binnie, now forgiven, was loudly present. Bill, Jenny's boss, had agreed to give her away, which seemed appropriate because she was leaving her job. The only person whose presence Justin missed was his former teacher and mentor, Peter van Leyden, who had died from a brain hemorrhage earlier in the year.

And then there was Tony White.

When the plans for the wedding were being finalized, Justin called his sister in Seattle. He needed to tell her that he had found her father. She was astonished. Speechless.

"He's a great guy, sis. You will really like him," Justin said, hoping for a response.

Finally, she said, "You have to be joking."

"No. It's true. We met some months ago. I've been waiting for the right time to tell you."

"And now is the right time?"

"I think so."

"Why didn't you tell me before?"

"I didn't see how I could tell you without telling mom as well, and I really worried about how she would take it."

"How did you find him? Did you go looking for him? Why would you do that?"

"Actually, it is more like he found me."

"Well, I want to know everything about him."

It was a long phone call, but the whole story came out. Tina was fascinated and excited. "I am thirty-two years old and I'm going to meet my father for the first time!"

"There's one more thing you should know. He is going to be at the wedding."

"Gosh!" responded Tina, adding, as the truth sank in, "And mother doesn't know."

"Correct. I've been hoping you will prepare her."

In the end, everything worked out well. Alice was secretly delighted at the news, although she tried to appear cool and casual. Her brief romance with Tony still stood as her only real experience of love. Although, through pride, she had rejected his offer of help when Tina was young, she had never felt any bitterness toward him. In fact, she was more than more than a little excited at the prospect of seeing him again.

* * *

On the evening before the wedding, Jenny and Justin met Alice in her hotel lobby. She looked stunning in an emerald-green dress and silver high heel sandals. A moment later, Tina arrived, also dressed as if she were going to meet the Queen, or her prince, perhaps. The three of them, too nervous to sit down, stood in a group, waiting for Tony to arrive. The plan was to go to dinner and allow food and wine to ease any awkwardness out of the conversation.

"I want you beside me," Alice told Justin as they waited. "He probably won't recognize me after all these years, but he'll know it's me if I am next to you. And I might not recognize him either. Thirty years is such a long time."

There was no need to worry He showed up precisely on time, wearing the same open, generous smile that she remembered from all those years ago. Three decades of thinking "if only …." were washed away in just seconds.

Later, when she and Justin were alone, she said, "You know, in all these thirty years, I have never forgotten his face, or his smile, or his touch." She blushed when she said that last word. I think it just slipped out. "It felt so comfortable, him being with us this evening," she said. "Thank you, darling, for bringing us together."

For Tina, the evening was one of the most momentous she would ever know. Until Justin had called her with the news about Tony, any curiosity she had about her father had died for lack of nourishment. Alice would simply not talk about him. Her excitement at discovering that he actually existed and that she would be meeting him, was dizzying. When he walked into the hotel foyer and she realized who he was, she stepped back, away from the others, so that she could spend a moment getting used to things. She wanted to look at him, digest the fact of his sudden appearance in her life, before plunging into an actual relationship. All she could do was stare and say to herself, "That's him. That's him." Justin saw that she was immobile, almost in a state of shock, and came to the rescue. Taking her hand, he led her the few steps to where Tony was standing, talking to Alice. Interrupting them as politely as he could, he said,

"Tony, let me introduce my sister, your daughter, Tina."

There were a few moments of silence. Even the normally eloquent Tony seemed overcome. To Justin's surprise, it was his sister who broke the ice.

"If you really are my dad, you ought at least to give me a hug."

Which he did. Then, keeping one arm round her shoulders, he stretched out and pulled her mother into the embrace.

"I never thought this moment would come," he said. "I am so very happy that it has."

When the wedding was over, and the happy couple had departed to an unnamed destination, Alice and Tony were walking beside the lake in private conversation.

"You know," he said to her, "I was always sad that you didn't call."

"Call? How could I. I didn't have your number."

Tony looked at her.

"But I left it for you. On the nightstand. I was sure you would find it."

Alice stared hard at him, and knew he was telling the truth. She shook her head. "Well, I don't know why I didn't," she said.

They walked along silently, until she sighed, "Just think how different our lives might have been, if I had found it."

CHAPTER 21

The Honeymoon

The newlyweds decided to honeymoon in Colorado. An extensive search of Airbnb had found an isolated mountain cabin overlooking a lake.

"It sounds like a wonderful, isolated getaway," Jenny said as she told her husband about it. "We could spend our days walking in the mountains, and our nights being romantic in front of the fire."

He asked, "Does that mean we wouldn't have to deal with other people at all?"

She nodded happily.

"Sounds perfect," he replied.

They spent their wedding night in an airport hotel in Houston, before flying to Colorado and renting a Jeep. Their destination was Lodgepole Valley. Starting as a cleft in the peaks of the Southern Rockies, it drops down from West to East, getting wider and deeper as it goes, until it emerges into the wide open plain of easter Colorado. Over tens of thousands of years, a creek has scoured away at the rock, creating the canyon, leaving it with a near-vertical southern wall and a less steep one opposite. In the nineteen fifties a dam was built across the top end of the valley, to form a lake, one-and-a-half miles long, deep and green and inviting. Below that, the creek was still there, carrying away the water from the dam and its power station. It ran along the foot of the southern wall for about a mile, before turning sharply and heading for the northern slope, isolating the upper part of the canyon and its lake from the rest of the State. Within the space between the dam in the west and the creek in the east, the good citizens of Lodgepole City minded their own business and generally kept the rest of the world at bay.

Justin and his new wife fell in love with the valley as soon as they saw it, as they crossed the creek via the one and only bridge, and drove up Main Street. They had contacted the owner of the cabin, one Andy McGuire, presumably a Lodgepole resident, by email. He had invited them to meet him at the Eagle Eye Café.

"It's half-way up, on the left. You can't miss it," he had written.

He proved correct. They parked outside the café and went in. The place was comfortable and inviting, furnished with plain wooden tables and chairs, and a long glass display cabinet at the back, filled with cakes and other temptations. There was one customer when they arrived, a tall, broad-shouldered man, with a weathered face, an almost bald head, and a rather unruly gray/brown beard. He wore a battered cowboy hat on his head and well-worn Western boots on his feet, clearly a man of the country, of the mountains.

"Hi there, folks," said with a grin, removing his hat and standing up to greet them. "You made it then."

"I hope we didn't keep you waiting," said Jenny.

"Nah. We got time out here. Plenty of it. Come to think of it, time might be the only thing we got too much of."

He invited them to a cup of coffee and a slice of "the best cheesecake in the world." As they ate and drank, he talked about the cabin.

"My father built it in the fifties. Used all local lumber, cutting down the Lodgepole Pines himself. He sunk a well and paid for a power supply, so it has all you need for comfort. Driving up to it is a bit of a challenge, but it is worth it. The location is stunning."

They left the café and headed on up Main Street. Andy led the way in his huge Ford pickup, and they followed. Main Street appeared to be the spine of the town, sloping upward to end at the Square, a large, paved rectangle with room for about twenty cars. On the far side of the Square was the City Hall, elevated and approached by a wide stretch of stone stairs. To the right a narrow country road exited the Square and threaded its way between some houses before curving and climbing up to the top of the dam, more than a hundred feet above the town. The two vehicles came to rest in a wide, flat parking area, and their occupants got out.

"This road continues across the dam and up into the mountains opposite. It's a beast of a trek. I should know. That's my way home. If you keep going you end up in the next valley, but it takes you forever to get there."

"So the only viable way out of Lodgepole City is the way we came in?"

"Correct. Main Street Bridge is it. By the way, you will stand out as strangers if you keep saying Lodgepole City. Everyone here prefers 'Pole City. You might remember that. Anyway, I thought you guys might appreciate looking at things from up here."

He walked them over to the wall at the edge of the dam, and pointed out the City Hall, which was below, occupying the top side of the Square, and facing the rest of the town. Main Street ran, straight as an arrow, from there to the Bridge, dividing the city into two unequal parts. To the right, the south side, the land was sandwiched between Main and the creek, and was never more than an eighth of a mile wide. It was low land, crowded with narrow streets and houses, and one church. By contrast, the north side was much larger, and included a mix of commercial and residential properties, plus another church and a graveyard. The land there rose, gently at first, and then more steeply, to form the valley's northern side.

"It is such a pretty valley," Jenny observed. "Where does the name Lodgepole come from?"

"That's what they call those trees," replied Andy, indicating the crowds of pine trees on the lower slopes beyond the lake. "Good, straight trunks. Great for building and stuff like that."

A stony track led from the back of the parking area further up the hill to the McGuire cabin. Just wide enough for a pickup, and too rough for the average sedan, it crossed a deep gulley by means of a bridge of tree trunks, and ascended sixty more feet to reach the house. It did not go anywhere else.

The cabin looked like something from a travel brochure. It was built of weathered pine logs, with a long porch across the front of the building, and a stone chimney at the back. There were chairs and a table on the porch, as well as a two-person swing, and a small grill for barbecuing. The property was perched on the north slope, facing across the lake, with a view of the dam, below and to the left.

"Wow!" exclaimed Jenny to her husband as she climbed out of the Jeep and stretched. "You have certainly picked a spectacular place."

"Me? You were the one who found it." He smiled at her excited face. "Looks OK, though, doesn't it?"

Andy McGuire led them inside. The layout was simple. There were two bedrooms, each with a simple bathroom. In between them was the long general living space, which included the sitting, kitchen and dining areas, and a wonderful stone-arched fireplace containing a large, cast iron stove with glass doors.

"That thing burns wood. You'll find plenty of logs at the west end of the house. Get it going, and the whole place will feel like a sauna in no time."

He was soon ready to leave. The newcomers stood on the porch, saying good-bye, when he remembered one more thing. "I am afraid that cell phones don't work too well up here. They do much better down by the dam. In any case, I'll be around most days, in case you need anything, and you know the way back to the town."

Left to themselves, they unloaded their suitcases, and put away the provisions which they had brought with them – another piece of McGuire advice. Justin opened a bottle of Pinot Noir, and they settled, side by side, on the porch swing.

"Listen!" said Jenny.

He tried, but heard nothing.

"What to? I can't hear anything."

"That's my point. There isn't a sound. Not even a rustling breeze or a singing bird. When did you ever hear such silence?"

He thought about that one, and was tempted to tease her about the concept, but this was clearly a special moment for her, so he said, "No, I haven't".

"At home there is never such silence. There is always traffic noise if nothing else. This is just lovely," his new bride enthused, snuggling up against him.

"Not too isolated?" he asked.

"Not yet, but I have only been here half an hour," she smiled. "Give me a few days, and we'll see."

"You think?"

She squeezed his hand. "Maybe not.

* * *

The sun sets early in the mountains, and the evening air is cool. Before long they went inside. After a few experiments, Justin managed to light a fire in the cast iron stove. They cooked together, pasta and sauce and shrimp, followed by a bought apple pie, and went early to bed.

"Let's have the room that looks down the valley," Justin suggested. "I think the window in the end wall should catch the rising sun."

"Oh," teased his lover, "Can't wait to wake and get up, is that how you feel on your honeymoon?"

He pulled her against him. "I will show you how I feel on my honeymoon."

* * *

Justin was right. The sun rose and shone into their room long before they were ready for the day, but they managed to ignore it. It was almost eleven before they were eating toast and fruit and drinking coffee on the porch, and studying the view. Apart from the cabin, the only man-made thing they could see was the dam. Below them, the lake shimmered in the midday sun, a light breeze gently disturbing its surface. In the distance, ahead and to their right, there were sparkling snow-capped peaks.

"This is perfect!" said Jenny.

They heard a truck coming up the track. It stopped beyond the end of the house, out of their sight. A moment later, McGuire appeared.

"Just wanted to check on y'all," he said cheerfully. "Anything you need?"

The newlyweds looked at each other and shook their heads.

"This is just great," said Justin. "But we do appreciate you asking. How about some coffee?"

Andy did not mind at all. Soon he was seated, and warming his hands around a steaming mug.

"I have lived here all my life," he told them. "My folks owned this valley, or at least, the pastures in it. Then the mining company came and took it away. They wanted it for a lake. Paid off some folks in the County and got it. All I have left is these green patches of hillside." He shrugged his shoulders. "That's life, for you."

"Why does a mining company want a lake?"

"They need water for their process, I suppose, and for hydro-electric too."

"It is a pretty lake," said Jenny.

"Used to be a darn sight prettier valley."

* * *

For three days, the honeymooners walked in the mountains, and round the edge of the lake. From the house, a steep path led down to the water's edge, where Andy had built a small pier and moored a rowboat.

"I like fishing," he explained. "You're welcome to take the boat and catch a few for yourself. I've brought you some rods and stuff."

Justin hesitated. "I don't know much about either boats or fish," he said.

Andy frowned, as if to say, "How come?"

"Tell you what," he said, "We could take the boat out this afternoon. Spend a couple of hours with me, and you'll be an expert. I have to go into 'Pole for an hour or so, but we could go when I get back."

"That would be great! If you're sure you have the time."

"No worries. I already told you, we have more than enough of that round here. I'll see you then."

True to his word, Andy came back. He came up the steps onto the porch, greeting them with the words, "Are we going fishing, then?"

Justin was keen, but Jenny said she would rather stay in the house, reading, and starting work on the novel she was hoping to write. She watched the two men carry the tackle down to the boat, and called out, "Bring some fish back, and I'll make supper for us all."

"Pretty cute woman, your wife," said Andy.

Before long they were out in the middle of the lake, and Justin was learning to cast his line and feel for the tug of a fish. After a while, his line went taut, and the reel started to spin. With Andy's guidance he played with the fish until he could bring it to the side of the boat. Together, they lifted it in.

"What sort is that?" asked Justin, looking at the quivering silver shape in the bottom of the cooler.

"Him? He's a rainbow trout. Good one, too, by the look of him. Be great to eat."

Justin had never been fishing before. In fact, he expected it to be a rather monotonous activity, but it was not. Fiddling with the rods and lines, the baits and lures, was all new and interesting. Then there were Andy's lessons on how to cast, how to reel in, how to spot where the fish might be: all new notions to be heard and absorbed. And, if ever there was a moment to spare, there were the birds to watch, circling overhead, diving into the lake for fish, or disappearing into the darkness between the trees for whatever their purposes might be. On top of all that, there was conversation. Andy was an interesting companion, full of information about the mountains, the city and, of course, the lake. This all gave Justin plenty of time to study his face, and began to think about asking him to sit for a portrait.

"I live over there," he pointed beyond the dam. "Further up that road."

"So you have to cross the dam a lot," I said.

"Almost every day," he answered.

Justin asked how the dam came to be built in so beautiful a valley. Andy explained that Lodgepole City had begun life as a mining town, in the boom days of the 1890's. It grew and prospered for thirty years, until its own local mine ran out. There was a more successful copper mine in the next valley to the north, and people from Lodgepole either found jobs there or drifted away. Then that mine fell on hard times too, partly because its water supply was dependent on melting snows, seasonal and unreliable. Mining activity had to be cut back frequently, once the melt was over. The business was heading for bankruptcy.

"That'll be the end of Lodgepole," its residents said, but they were wrong. As the lawyers and bankers took over the failing mine, a character called Marvin Garner arrived. An entrepreneur with money and an interest in mines, he offered to save the business, but he had one major demand. The city or the county or the state, he did not care which, had to build him a lake to guarantee year-round water, and allow him to add a hydro-electric generating station. He treated the right officials magnificently. Palms were greased and permits slid right off them onto his desk. The McGuire family was 'persuaded' to sell its pastures in the valley, above the town, and the dam was constructed in record time.

"Mind you," said Andy. "It is not one of those poured concrete structures like the Hoover. It is basically a massive rock wall, with a concrete face on the water side. But at least it works. Water gets piped from the lake into Garner's power plant, right there at the foot of the dam. Then the creek takes it on down to the mine. When it was finished, everyone was happy. The city was saved. The mine and the city got cheap power and plenty of water. There's a lot of people in 'Pole who won't have a word said against it, just as there's a good few think it is an eyesore and was built far too quickly. They are always complaining and campaigning. If you removed it tomorrow, for them, that wouldn't be too soon. Walk into town and start asking people about it: you'll find a lot of strong views. As for me, I hate the bastards who built the dam and flooded the valley, but I would never leave, and there's a good few agree with me. If you start asking people about it, you might stir up trouble for yourself. Folks here don't like outside interference in valley business."

"Dear me," said Justin. "I'll remember that."

He was sitting in the bow of the boat, and Andy in the middle. They were facing each other. When it was time to row back to shore, Andy turned round, and took the oars, leaving Justin to look beyond him at the dam. He could see the place where the mountain road came into sight, curving round a grove of pine trees before crossing the dam. He imagined him, appearing around that bend every morning on his way to town.

That is when the preview occurred. I saw Andy come round the curve from beyond the trees, Suddenly he cried out, "What the hell?" as he slammed his foot on his brake.

The truck squealed to a halt.

"What the hell?" he repeated, and gazed, horror stricken, at the scene in front of him.

The road ended, not a dozen yards beyond where he had stopped. The whole dam had disappeared, had fallen away, turned itself into a massive waterfall There was no town anymore, no streets or houses or churches or shops, just the water, celebrating its freedom, leaping over the rocks, a wild, tumbling series of white-water rapids. And Andy, staring at it all, open mouthed.

"Are you OK?" Andy rested on his oars and looked at his passenger with concern.

Justin heard him, and the strange image disappeared as quickly as it had come. He shook himself back into reality.

"I think so," he replied.

"That's a relief! For a moment I thought you were .... Well, I don't know what I thought, but you did have the weirdest look on your face."

Trying to avoid an explanation, "I guess my mind was somewhere else," he said.

They covered the remaining yards to the pier in silence. Andy frowned as he looked at his passenger, trying to figure him out. Justin didn't know what to say or do. In that moment of revelation, he had seen, quite clearly, that Lodgepole's precious dam was doomed. Should he tell anyone? His preview had focused on Andy McGuire. Should he at least warn him, and leave him to warn the town? But who would believe him anyway? Jenny and he were newcomers to the valley. "Folks don't like strangers coming and interfering in their business," Andy had said.

Justin decided to have a word with his new wife, and see what she thought, before throwing any rocks into the pool of Lodgepole's tranquility.

The two men had caught seven good, edible trout. Andy showed the visitors how to gut and clean them, and Justin got the barbecue going. Before long, the three were seated around the table on the porch, enjoying a feast.

"I've never eaten such fresh-caught fish in my life," said Jenny, her eyes shining as she thanked their landlord for his help.

"That's the trouble with you city folk," he responded. "You don't know what you're missing. I love it here."

Eventually the sun began to slink away behind the peaks. Andy rose from his chair, stretched, thanked his hosts for a pleasant evening, and disappeared. They listened to his truck bumping its way down the rough track, until they could hear it no more. Then Justin took Jenny by the hand and made her sit next to him on the swing.

"Sweetheart, …." he began, and then did not know what to say next. He realized that, although she knew that he had previews from time to time, he had never described one to her in detail. Indeed, many of them could not be described, since they came as sudden thoughts or convictions, without any visual component. In such cases, if asked how he knew something, all he could do was shake his head and say, "I just know."

"Yes, dear?"

"I had another preview, this afternoon, when I was in the boat with Andy."

"Is that a problem?"

"It might be."

"Do you want to tell me about it?"

"I think I need to. I am not sure how to describe it."

"What were you doing when it came?"

"We were rowing back across the lake. Andy says he lives across the lake, beyond the dam. It's funny, really. He curses the day it was built, yet he uses it all the time. It provides the only road between his place and 'Pole City. As he told me about it, I could just see him, appearing at the far end of the dam, by that bunch of pines, and heading out across it. He says he does that, pretty well every day. He painted quite a clear picture of it, for me."

"So?"

"So, in my imagination, I was watching him come to the dam."

"And?"

"And he arrived at the lake….."

"And?"

"It wasn't there."

Jenny turned to stare at her husband.

"What was not there?"

"The dam."

"Not there?"

"Not there," he confirmed.

"What was there, then? In its place?"

"A huge waterfall. A raging river."

"Gosh!" Jenny said in a quiet voice. "What do you think it means?"

" I'm pretty sure it means that the dam is going to burst."

"You can't be serious," she responded, but she saw he was. "That would be an enormous disaster. It could destroy the town."

"That's what is going to happen. There won't be any town left."

"What are you going to do?"

"Do?"

"Yes! Do. You know something is coming which could wipe Lodgepole off the map. You are the only person who knows it. How can you keep that to yourself?"

They sat there, on the swing, in the gathering darkness, both trapped in their own thoughts. After five minutes, Justin said, "You know, Jen, I've had dozens of previews, hundreds in fact, but I have never had to deal with the consequences. That is always up to the people concerned, not me. I'm not sure I should get involved now."

"What about when you got off that flight to Phoenix? Weren't you getting involved then?"

"Yes, but I wasn't trying to change anything, or interfere with what was going to happen. I was simply taking care of myself. When I have a preview, I usually tell the person concerned. From then on, what they do is up to them."

"Well then, since Andy McGuire seems to have been the inspiration for this one, perhaps you should at least tell him."

"I suppose you are right. But can you see him taking me seriously?"

"I don't know," Jenny admitted, "But you have to try. After all, you are the Prophet of Houston,"

"Don't say that! You know how I hate that title."

"Yes! But I also know that you are famous, and your fame makes you credible."

"Hmm."

Getting hold of Andy wasn't easy. They had his phone number, but there was no signal at the cabin. Justin decided to walk down to the dam, where it was much better. From there he got through straight away.

"I was wondering if you had time for a chat," he said, once the greetings were over.

"Sure," said Andy.

He told Justin to wait at the dam, and he would be along in five minutes. He was as good as his word, arriving promptly, driving along the dam to where Justin was standing.

"Hop in," he said. "I'll drive you back up."

Jenny saw them coming and put some coffee on. The two men sat on the porch while she worked on chores inside.

"So what are we going to talk about?"

"I thought you might tell me about the dam."

That surprised Andy. "The dam? I thought we had talked about that already. But, OK, what else would you like to know?"

Uncertain how to begin, Justin asked, "How do you feel about it?"

"Feel? Do I have feelings about it? I suppose I must." He pushed his hat back off his forehead and twisted his mouth into a grimace. "Well, they stole our family's land to build it, so I should hate it. But it saved the city, so I should love it."

He stopped, a frown on his face. "What else should I tell you?"

"I was wondering if it is a good dam. You know. Well built. That sort of thing."

"I admit, there's a lot of differing views on that."

Just then the door opened, and Jenny came out with two mugs of coffee in one hand and plate of cookies in the other.

"Have you told him yet?" she asked her husband.

With a guilty expression on his face, Justin shook his head. She gave him a hard look, put her things on the low table in front of them, and turned to leave.

“Told me what?” asked McGuire.

Jenny looked at her husband while she answered.

“That the dam is going to break.”

With that, she disappeared back into the house, leaving Justin to deal with the fallout.

“What was that?” asked an incredulous Andy.

Justin answered, “She said that the dam is going to break.”

“She has to be joking.”

Slightly embarrassed, Justin said, “Actually, she isn’t.”

This irritated the older man, the native of the valley.

“What does a woman from the city know about our dam here? Is she an engineer?”

Justin felt he had no choice. He tried to explain about his previews, ending with the fate of the Lodgepole dam.

“And you say that all the things you predict come true?”

“Actually, yes.”

After a moment’s thought, the older man stood up, said “’Scuse me,” and went into the house. Several minutes later he came back out, shaking his head.

“She is just as crazy as you are,” he said.

He moved as if he was going to sit back down, then changed his mind. “I don’t know about you two, but I think I had better be going.” He strode off toward his truck. Just before disappearing out of sight he looked back at Justin and called out.

“You could be getting into a whole load of trouble.”

* * *

That afternoon the weather cooled down and dark clouds began to roll in. A chill breeze was finding its way down the valley, and a walk in the hills did not seem such a great idea. Besides, the honeymooners had Justin’s preview on their minds. So they climbed into their rented Jeep and bounced their way down to the town, parking in the Square. Justin was about to open his door when Jenny delayed him.

"Do you think McGuire is going to do anything? About the preview, I mean?"

Her husband shrugged. "How would I know?"

"Well, someone needs to. If that dam bursts and no-one is expecting it, goodness only knows how many people will be flooded, even drowned. It could be a huge disaster."

"But he warned us against stirring up the locals."

"Well, you can stay in the truck if you like. I am going to see what I can do."

She got out of the truck and walked up the steps to City Hall. It was a wooden building, wide, but not deep from front to back. There was a good sized porch, symmetrical, with a pair of benches each side of the double entry doors. Inside, it was dark and cool, but clean and well organized. To the right was a door with a light showing through its frosted glass panel. Jenny opened it and went in.

A small, gray-haired woman sat at a desk, working with a computer. She turned and gave a quick, bright smile.

"Yes?"

Jenny was in no mood for beating about the bush.

"No offense to you, Miranda," she said, noticing the name plate on the desk, "But I was wondering who is in charge of things around here."

"If you mean, things in this office, then it is me, but I doubt that is your meaning. You probably want to know who is the Chairman of the City Council. That would be Charlie Pierce. He works at the mine. You would do better to look for him in the evening."

"Oh."

"Maybe I can help," the other woman said, adding with a touch of acid in her tone, "Even though I am not in charge."

Jenny opened her purse and pulled out a business card. In the month before her wedding she had resigned from her job in the newsroom and started to work freelance.

"I am a news reporter," she said. "Here on a special assignment. We have heard a rumor that your beautiful valley is in danger, and I wanted to check it out."

"Danger, what danger?"

"That maybe your dam is in a bad state, and likely to burst."

Miranda looked horrified.

"You had better be careful. There are people round here who would run you out of town for saying something like that. Who is spreading such a rumor, anyway?"

"Have you ever heard of the Prophet of Houston?"

"I don't think so. Houston is a long way from here. Who is he?

Jenny tried to explain. When she paused for breath, the other woman asked, "And he is the one who says our dam is doomed?"

"That's right."

"Well, I don't know what to say. I can't imagine anyone in Lodgepole buying your story."

With that, Miranda turned back to her work. Jenny took the hint and moved toward the door. When she was half-way through, the woman behind her spoke again.

"I am not saying anything, but you might find a more sympathetic ear in the Eagle Eye Café, down Main Street, on the right."

"Thank you, Miranda. You have been more help than you know."

She found her husband sitting on one of benches in the porch, studying the flat, square fronted properties that lined the square, and slipped onto the seat beside him. The building sheltered them from the wind.

Justin observed, "All you need is hitching rails along the edge of the sidewalk, and this would be perfect for a John Wayne movie."

"Never mind that," she said, "We have much more urgent things to deal with."

She told him about her conversation with Miranda.

"What now, then?" he wondered.

"We may as well walk down to the café. I wouldn't mind a bite and I imagine you are starving."

Wrapping their coats around them, they walked slowly, looking at the various stores and houses along Main Street, until they arrived at the Eagle Eye, where they had first met Andy McGuire. The place was owned and run by a rotund, cheerful, apron-clad woman called MaryAnn. She had curly dark red hair, pale blue eyes, and very pink cheeks. She waddled across the room to greet them.

"You'll be the folks from Texas," she said. "I have just the table for you. Would you like to sit in the window?" Without waiting for an answer, she led them to a table next to the large window that overlooked the street.

"Let me find you some things," she said, and bustled away in search of menus, silverware, and napkins. Justin leaned across and whispered to Jenny, "Your Miranda must have been on the phone. I wonder who else she has been talking to."

The waitress returned, suitably equipped, and talked them into trying the pork chops. While they were waiting, and watching the passersby, a tall, middle-aged woman, dressed in well-worn jeans and boots, came in. She paused, just inside the door, and looked hard at them, and then went to the back of the room and said something to MaryAnn, who nodded in their direction before answering. The two women whispered excitedly to each other for several minutes, and then the newcomer left, staring at Justin and Jenny as she went.

That performance was repeated a couple more times during their meal. Each time the newcomers left without purchasing a thing.

"I think they are just coming in to see who we are," said Jenny to Justin in a low voice.

"I think you are right," he answered.

"That Miranda, she must be the town gossip. I should have guessed."

A pair of real customers came into the café, sat at a table, ordered food, and paid no attention to them. Then a man arrived, a taller than average character, with a figure that betrayed too much good living. He had dark hair above his fleshy, suntanned face. His leather sports coat was well worn but had obviously been expensive when new; his jeans were smart and his boots well-polished. After merely nodding to MaryAnn he strode over to where Jenny and Justin were having their meal, full of self-importance.

"Hi. My name is Charlie, and I would like to welcome you to Lodgepole City."

He reached across to a nearby table and dragged a chair over, so that he was sitting close to them.

"Don't mind me," he said, "Just carry on eating. They have great food here."

Jenny laid her fork down and looked at him.

"You must be Charlie Pierce, Council Chairman. Is that right?"

"Sure is, ma'am."

"What might we do for you, Charlie?" asked Justin.

"Nothing really," was the reply. "I just wanted you to feel at home in our little community."

"That's kind of you," said Jenny, unconvinced.

"The folks round here are really proud of their city," he went on. "They want you to have a good time, enjoy the scenery, have fun on the lake, do some fishing, that sort of thing."

"Which we are doing."

Charlie nodded approvingly and rose from his chair. "Great. And how long do you plan on being here?"

"A couple of weeks."

"Well, that's alright. I guess I'll be seeing you around." He began to move away, then sat down again, and said in a less friendly voice, "A word of advice. Don't be going round unsettling folks with talks about their dam. Some of them are a mite touchy on the subject."

"But if it's the truth …." said Justin.

"It isn't." Charlie leaned forward, speaking quietly, as if he were revealing a secret. "Let me tell you about that dam. It's been here sixty years. They built it, and it saved the city. Then, almost ten years ago, some out of town preacher guy appeared, big bible under his arm and a voice loud enough to wake the dead. He started telling folks that the dam was breaking, and that it would collapse by that year's end. He was a powerful speaker, and a lot of people believed him. Some upped and left town. The population went down by ten percent or more. We had a bunch of bad storms that year, and the dam did not burst, although it did develop a slight leak. But the damage was done. Lodgepole's reputation was shot. No-one wanted to risk buying a house here. Property values fell by a third. It ruined some families financially, and a few of our best citizens just never returned. It's taken all the years since for things to recover. No. Lodgepole doesn't need another false prophet saying the dam is doomed."

He stood up again. Looking down at them, he forced a smile, said "See y'around," and left.

The honeymooners looked at each other. "What was that about?" Justin asked. His wife just shook her head.

MaryAnn squeezed her ample self between the tables and stood, looking down at them. "Charlie Pierce get himself on your case, did he?"

Justin raised an eyebrow. "I didn't know we had a case."

"I hear you are worried about our dam," the waitress said.

Miranda really has been talking, thought Jenny.

"Charlie wouldn't like that. He does whatever Garner wants, and Garner doesn't like people talking about the dam."

"Why is that?" Jenny asked.

"There are plenty of us who never did like it in the first place. We think it was built too fast and too cheap and likely not too well. We got together and hired someone to look at it, a consultant he called himself. He said it is already getting old and weak, and something's wrong with the concrete. I don't know much about it all, but each time we have a big storm and the water level rises, water leaks out around the bottom of the dam."

"That sound serious," Justin suggested.

"The only way to fix it is to empty the lake, or spend thousands on special engineering of some sort. And Garner, he doesn't want to do that."

"So, what do you think is going to happen?" asked Jenny, slipping into her news reporter mode.

"Things will go on getting worse until, one day, the dam will burst. That's what we think. Right now we are trying to raise money to hire an attorney, one to persuade the county or the state to do something."

"And Mr. Garner doesn't like that? Right?"

"Right. He gets mad. Any time we try to have a meeting about it, to get folks involved, he sends his guys to disrupt it. He made Charlie ban us from having our meetings in City Hall. We had one in here …." She waved her arms around the room. "… but his thugs came and broke that window where you are sitting. I can't keep affording new windows. Last time we met at the Baptist Church, but the pastor there said, 'Not Again'. I guess they got to him too."

She looked at her guests, shaking her head sadly.

"It's good of you to care about us, but you might be wiser if you kept your thoughts to yourself."

Justin said, in a quiet but convincing voice, "Whether or not we keep quiet, MaryAnn, that dam is going to burst, you know. There is no way to stop it."

MaryAnn stared at him, absorbing what he had said. Her face crinkled, and she began to cry. "I was born in 'Pole," she said through her tears. "Went to school here, got married and had kids here. All I want to do is to end my days here, too. I love this place."

The Prophet and his wife walked back up Main Street, studying the view of the dam way back beyond City Hall.

"What would happen if it burst?" Jenny asked.

"When it does, you mean," corrected her husband.

"Ok. When."

"I'm no engineer," Justin went on, "But if it collapses all at once, I imagine the town will be wiped out. All that water; it's probably enough to wash away every building in the valley."

"So what are we going to do?"

"We could just pack up and go home. I don't see how we can help here."

"Maybe we should have told MaryAnn about you being the Prophet."

"Don't call me that!"

"Well, we have to find some way of persuading people to listen to you, and you do have a great reputation. They just need to hear it."

They arrived in the Square and climbed into the Jeep. As they drove up the hill, Jenny asked, "Don't you have any idea when it'll happen?"

"Not really, but it could be soon, I think. In the past, previews as sharp as this one usually foresee imminent events."

"Perhaps we should go round town, knocking on doors, telling people they need to leave."

"Can you see anyone going? Two strangers from Texas come and tell them their town is going to be destroyed, with nothing but my word to back us up. We would be laughed out of town."

Frustrated and anxious, the newlyweds arrived at the cabin. Justin lit the fire, and they sat in front of it, talking and reading and worrying. Eventually they went to bed, but sleep was slow to come. When they did drop off, they both slept very soundly, and were still not awake when there was a loud banging on the front door. Jenny was the first to hear it, and she nudged her husband. "Wake up! Someone's here."

Still half asleep, he said, "Perhaps they'll go away."

The banging continued, loud and insistent. On top of that, a male voice started to shout, "Mr. Gates, get out here," over and over again.

Justin struggled into his jeans and headed for the door.

There were two men standing on the porch. Aggressive types, dressed in jeans and all-weather jackets, with Western hats on their heads. One was dark haired and one blonde. Apart from that, they could have been twins. Each of them wore a holstered handgun, and each carried a short black rifle.

Justin silently named them Darkie and Blondie.

Darkie was in charge. He stepped forward, thrusting his rifle toward Justin.

"You and your woman, you are out of here."

How do I reply to that? Justin asked himself.

"D'you hear? You are to get out of here."

"Why? We have this place booked for another ten days."

"That don't matter. You gotta go."

"Who says?"

"Mr. Garner. That's who."

"And why does he say we have to go?"

"Hell if I know."

Before Justin could answer, Jenny arrived on the scene, clutching her pink satin robe around her. She pushed herself to the front, stepped right up to Darkie, pushing his gun aside, and looking into his face from not more than a foot away.

"Get off our porch. And tell that Mr. Garner of yours this. If he has a message for us, he had better bring it himself."

Taken completely by surprise, Darkie stepped back, momentarily lost for words, but clearly readying himself to take matters further. His partner looked at him anxiously.

"The boss said nothing physical."

"I guess you're right."

Blondie waved his gun toward the couple on the doorstep.

"You have 'til sundown," he said.

"Tell Mr. Garner to come and tell us that himself."

"No-one tells him what to do," said Darkie.

Blondie jerked his head in the direction of their waiting truck and said,

"C'm on. Let's go."

CHAPTER 22

The Storm

The weather had taken a turn for the worse. Heavy black clouds were piling up beyond the mountains to the north and west, and in the east, the morning sun had already disappeared behind more, and yesterday's chill wind had renewed itself. Jenny, dressed only in pajamas and robe, shivered. She and Justin went inside. Breakfast on the terrace was clearly a bad idea. He went to work on reviving the embers in the stove, while she dressed and set about preparing the food. They would eat off trays as they sat in front of the fire. That is where they were when someone knocked on their front door, not as violently as had Darkie, but still enough to make them jump. They looked at each other, sudden anxiety on their faces, and exclaimed simultaneously, "Garner!"

"It can't be," guessed Jenny, "Not so soon. His henchmen have not been gone long."

The visitor knocked again. Justin rose and went to the door, opening it warily. With a sigh of relief he called out to Jenny, "It's OK, it's only Andy McGuire."

She replied, "Invite him in. He's welcome!" She rose from her seat and took the trays to the kitchen.

"Coffee?" she called to the newcomer, who was still outside.

He shook his head and called back, "Thank you, no." And then, in a more normal voice, he continued. "This is going to be a busy day. I just wanted to come round and check on y'all. I know you don't have TV here, and I'm not sure if you would spend your honeymoon watching the news anyway."

Jenny joined the two men on the porch, looking anxious, sensing trouble in the wind.

"What are we missing?" asked Justin.

Andy replied, "It's the weather. Have you noticed how dark it is? And there is a nasty west wind. It all spells trouble, I think."

"How much trouble?"

"Can't say. The TV says we could be in for the worst storm in decades. It could rain three or more inches an hour, up here in the hills. That's what they said this morning."

"Will we be OK, up here, like this?" asked Jenny.

"Oh, I should think so," Andy answered. "This house has survived worse in the past, much worse. But you will be wise to stay indoors. If the rain gets really bad you won't want to be driving down that track to the dam. That could get tricky."

He looked down at the lake, in the direction of the dam. "You know what?" he said, "That lake is already dam full, if you'll pardon the pun. It can't take too much water before it overflows."

"How much water will a storm like this give it?"

"Can't say for sure. Maybe three feet or so, or even more. The storm could easily last a day or two. Then the rain will stop, and you'll think it's all over, but you'll be wrong. See all those mountains? They'll catch huge amounts of water, which will keep on running down the slopes and through the gullies and creeks until it gets here. However much the lake rises by during the actual storm, we could see as much go up by two or three times as much more after it is over. Watch and see."

Jenny asked anxiously, "But the dam, will it be OK?"

McGuire looked at Justin as he answered her.

"You'd better ask your husband."

Was he being sarcastic? She couldn't tell.

The three of them stood, silently contemplating the incoming storm and what it might mean. Then Justin changed the subject.

"We had visitors this morning."

Clearly surprised, Andy asked, "Who would that be? Hardly anyone even knows you are here."

"Two gun toting goons. Garner sent them."

"That's not good. What did they want?"

"They told us to leave."

"Did they indeed? Marvin must be really upset with you."

"Why? I wouldn't have thought we were a nuisance to him, much less a threat."

"Oh, I can see why he's mad. You are stirring up trouble about the dam. The last thing he wants is to be forced to fix it. To do that, he would have to drain the lake and refinish its concrete. It would cost millions. Even if the state footed the bill, it would put his mine out of business for at least a year. His whole business empire could be in jeopardy, not just the mine."

"But people's lives are at stake. If the dam should burst .... when it does, I mean, it will spell total disaster for the town, and people might die."

"You don't realize the hold he has over Lodgepole folk. He provides their jobs, pays their wages, and supplies them with cheap electricity and free water. No-one wants to fall out with him. They know he is a ruthless operator. When he says jump, they do."

Jenny cut in. "He told us to jump, and we didn't."

"He'll not like that. Nor will he leave it. You will hear from him again, for sure."

Justin said, "You should have seen the way Jenny stood up to them. Right in their faces. Told them to get lost. Said Garner had better come and deliver his message himself. I was proud of her."

Their visitor stared at the couple for a long moment, then shook his head.

"I wouldn't want to be in your shoes. You had better watch out. Anyway, I have to be off."

With that, he said good-bye, and turned to leave.

Justin put his arm protectively around his wife's shoulders. "See you again soon," he called. They watched him climb into his truck and move off. As it bumped its way down the track, Jenny felt the arm around her suddenly tighten. She looked up at her husband's face, and saw a far-away look in his eyes, far-away but sharply focused on something she could not see.

"Sweetheart ... " she began, but he wasn't listening.

He was whispering, just to himself, "This is it. It is ready to happen."

Back in the cabin, she asked him, "Are you really sure?"

He nodded. "Before this storm is done, that dam is going to collapse."

"Then what shall we do?"

"We could just sit tight. We are high enough above the lake to be safe. Or we could pack up and leave altogether." He gave a bitter laugh. "At least that would please Mr. Garner."

"But we can't abandon these people. We should warn them. They need to get away while they can."

"But if we go back to town, who can we talk to? Who will believe us, enough to respond?"

"Maybe we could start with MaryAnn in the café. At least we know she is sympathetic."

Jenny turned to go into the kitchen, and then stopped.

"Listen!" she said. "What's that sound."

There was a noise, as if someone was dropping pebbles on the cabin's metal roof. Lots of pebbles.

"It's rain," said Justin. "Heavy rain."

They listened as the noise increased. It became deafening, as if the house was being bombarded with rocks, not drops of water. Never having heard rain like it, they went out onto the porch to see what it looked like. The mountains across the lake had completely disappeared. Even the surface of the water below them was unrecognizable, being torn up by the wind and pounded by the huge drops of rain. The wind came roaring down the valley and tearing along the length of the porch, trying to sweep them off their feet and throw them down the slope into the lake.

"There is nothing we can do while it storms like this," Justin said.

They retreated into the house.

"As soon as the weather improves, let's go down to the town, and hope we're not too late."

The pounding on their roof was deafening. Conversation was hard. Concentration on any meaningful task was impossible. In the end, they wrapped themselves up warmly, and went out onto the porch, to watch the anger of the storm. There was clearly no way for them to leave the house. Water was rushing off the slopes and pouring down the track, turning it into a foaming river. They were marooned, trapped in the cabin until the rain eased up, and maybe even longer, until the drive was usable again.

"It is lucky we are on our honeymoon," said Jenny.

"It will certainly be memorable," her man replied.

The rain pounded down relentlessly for more than two days. Its intensity let up a little, from time to time, but it never got near to stopping. The hillside around the cabin was waterlogged. When the dam could be seen through the downpour, it was clear that the water level was rising. Without television or cell phone service, the couple were unable to learn if the dam was damaged.

"I wonder which threat is greater," mused Justin. "Water spilling over the top or the increased pressure on the broken concrete."

On the third day, about noon, the rain gave up and the clouds began to drift away. By four o'clock the sky was patchily blue, and the sodden grassy slope began to steam. However, the track down the hill was still a river as water found its way down from the heights around them. They decided to wait until the next morning before venturing out. They kept looking at the dam. It looked undamaged, although the water was only inches from the top. They remembered Andy McGuire's words about how much more it would rise after the storm was over.

"It's still very scary," said Justin. "And trouble is coming. I just know it."

So, on the fourth morning, they wrapped themselves in their boots and waterproofs and headed for the Jeep, which was parked with its front bumper against the house. Justin drove. He reversed in a tight turn, and then moved forward into the top of the track. Immediately, he jammed his breaks on, making Jenny lurch forward, her seatbelt saving her from hitting the windshield. In front of them, half way up the track and blocking it entirely, was a huge dark green, high riding pickup. It wasn't moving.

"What on earth …." He began to speak, but stopped as he saw the truck's two occupants open their doors and climb out. Blondie and Darkie!

"Oh no!" groaned Jenny. "What now?"

Marvin Garner's two thugs stood in front of their truck, brandishing their ugly weapons. No one moved.

"They are forcing us to go to them," she concluded. "Do we have any choice?"

"Probably not," replied her husband. "I think I had better see what they want.'

"Do be careful. They look really mean. I don't like this situation at all."

Justin patted her hand and told her not to worry. To appear cooperative, he walked round to the front of the Jeep, and leaned against its radiator.

"Let them make the next move," he told himself.

The stalemate only lasted a couple of minutes, but it felt like an hour. In the end, the thugs became impatient. Being almost a hundred feet away, too far for conversation, they began to slowly walk up the hill. Justin began walking down toward them, trying to match their speed. When they were only about thirty feet apart, he stopped moving and shouted, "What do you two want now? We told you to tell your boss to come himself, if he had a message for us."

Blondie laughed. "Tell Mr. Garner. That's a joke. He don't take orders from no-one."

"Shut your mouth," Darkie snapped quietly, before calling out, "He sent us with a new message."

Justin wished he was closer. He would have liked to read the other man's eyes.

Darkie continued. "You'll like this one. The boss says you are welcome to stay and enjoy your honeymoon."

"And just what does that mean?"

"Can't you hear? It means what I said. Stay up here in your cabin and have a great honeymoon."

"Well, that is good of Mr. Garner, although I can't see why we should need his permission."

"He said for my mate and me to stay here and see that no-one bothers you while you are…. "He searched for words, and Justin was sure he heard Blondie say something very indecent indeed. "While you are finishing your vacation."

"You mean, to stop us leaving? To stop us going into the town?"

"You've got it. That's just what he means. And he said that, when you're ready to go, we should give you a real safe escort until you are on your way."

By this time, Jenny had joined her husband. "That's kidnapping," she shouted. "You go and tell your boss that he can go to hell." She tugged on Justin's arm and said, "Let's go."

Darkie replied, "Can't do that. We're not allowed to leave here, not until you're ready to go."

Husband and wife turned their backs on the intruders and walked back up the slope. Justin opened the Jeep's door, preparing to get in, but his wife stopped him.

"Let's leave this here. At least it will stop them getting too close to the house."

They locked it up and went back onto the porch.

"What do we do now?" asked Justin.

"I'm not sure. But we will think of something. We can't be beaten by Garner and his goons."

"Meanwhile, the dam could give way, and flood the town."

"We'll think of something first," she insisted. "For the moment, I just don't know what."

Back in the cabin, Jenny set about brewing some fresh coffee while Justin worked on reviving the fire in the stove. He was interrupted by her hand on his shoulder.

"Let's go fishing," she said.

"Fishing? Are you crazy?"

"No, Jus. Think about it. They are not going to let us drive down the track and go to town. Garner told them to let us have our vacation here, so long as we don't try to leave. So that is what we will do. Have a vacation. Take the rowboat out onto the lake and go fishing."

"And how will that help to save the people of Lodgepole?"

"While we are in the house here we can't do anything. We can't even phone anyone, but our phone works down by the lake. And that means on the lake, too, I would think. We can go fishing, and while we are on the lake we can call for help."

"Call who?"

"Who is the one sympathetic person we know in Lodgepole?" Jenny asked, and then answered herself. "MaryAnn. That's whom we should call."

Justin looked at his wife in admiration.

"You know, you are brilliant," he said. "Without you I would just be sitting here doing nothing."

"Without me," she replied with a smile, "You wouldn't be here at all."

They collected the fishing gear together and headed down the path to the lake.

As Justin took the oars and pushed off from the shore, he looked up at the two thugs.

"You can bet this is making them nervous," he said. "They are sure to be keeping a close eye on us."

"At first, I'm sure," Jenny observed. "But I'll bet that they get bored pretty soon, and lose interest."

"I hope so," he replied.

Darkie and Blondie saw them heading down the path, rods and other gear in hand. They did not like the fishing idea, suspecting a trick of some sort. Using their short-wave radio, they called for instructions. "Let them go, but keep a damn close watch on them," they were told.

Once out on the water, Justin and Jenny started fishing, or at least, making a pretense of it. Fortunately, there was almost no breeze or current, to push the boat around. Using the oars, Justin kept it angled so that Garner's men could not see Jenny using the phone, and he watched her face as she made contact with the owner of the Eagle Eye Café.

"MaryAnn?...."

"This is Jenny Gates, from Texas ….."

"That's right. ……"

"You remember we were talking to you about the dam …."

Justin watched his wife, with growing pride. She was so urgent, so anxious, so passionate, as she explained her concern to the other woman, his and her concern really, for the people of 'Pole City. Over the years, he had seen clients talk about their dying children with less urgency. She explained the fix they were in, and their refus al to be beaten by Marvin Garner and his bullies. To Justin, she sounded like a Joan of Arc, ready to mount her horse, sword in hand, and ride off to save the world. He was stunned to realize what strength of character she possessed. He knew he already admired her, but this was something more.

The call ended. She looked at Justin and nodded.

"She is going to come and pick us up at the end of the dam. I told her we will be there in exactly thirty minutes. I hope you can make it without attracting trouble from our friends on the hill."

"Friends?" he said, glancing at the green pickup and its occupants. "Yes. With any luck, they won't notice until it is too late. Anyway, what are they going to do? Shoot the bottom out of our boat? Didn't Garner say 'nothing physical'? Once MaryAnn arrives, they will have to leave us alone. They would not want to do anything violent in front of a witness."

The plan almost worked. Justin maneuvered the boat so that it drifted, without being obvious, toward the end of the dam by the parking area. It was about three minutes away from the rendezvous with MaryAnn before it was noticed.

*   *   *

In their big green pickup, Garner's men were thoroughly bored. The radio was tuned to a rock music channel, but they were parked on the side of the mountain and reception was terrible. Darkie was taking a nap while Blondie, supposedly on watch, was picking away at his fingernails. Every now and then he glanced out of the window to check that the rowboat was still on station. He did not notice the gradual movement toward the shore, not until it was almost there. Sitting up with a jerk, he shouted, "Shit!", which woke his partner.

"You fucking idiot," Darkie said. "You were supposed to be watching."

"I was watching. They just moved so fast. What'll we do now?"

"You have to ask? For God's sake! Turn this truck around and let's get after them."

Blondie tried the starter – once, twice, three times. The third was the magic. The engine roared to life. He picked first gear and started up the hill, thinking to turn round in the wide, flat area beside the house. Of course, as he got close, he realized that the Jeep was blocking his way. A three-point turn seemed the only solution. He swore a string of oaths and wrenched the wheel to the left. The nose of the truck swung off the rocky path, which was hardly wider than the vehicle anyway. As soon as both wheels were off, he pulled hard to the right and brought the truck to a stop. Selecting reverse, he attempted a tight turn to bring the truck into position, facing down the hill. However, the torrential rain had tuned the grassy surfaces beside the track into a slimy sponge. As he completed the turn, his back wheels ran off the road and dug themselves into the mud. Furiously, he switched to forward gear and revved the engine hard. The wheels spun themselves in deeper, until the truck was stuck fast, totally blocking the track.

Blondie looked at his partner. "What do we do now?" he asked pathetically.

"What I am going to do," replied Darkie viciously, "is shoot you." But he didn't. Instead, he reached for his radio. "Garner's going to be a raging bull when he learns about this. Maybe he'll do the job for me."

"I nearly didn't make it," MaryAnn told her passengers as they climbed into her Chevvy Tahoe, Jenny in the front and Justin behind. "The dam is leaking badly. Maybe it is starting to overflow too. The Square is already covered with water." Glancing down at Jenny's feet, she added, "It's lucky you are wearing boots. You are going to need them."

They entered the Square in its northwest corner. It was deserted except for one parked Range Rover. City Hall was to their right, the only building on that side of the square.

MaryAnn stopped her Tahoe and exclaimed, "Good Heavens!"

Jenny looked at her anxiously.

"What is it?"

"All that water. There is never that much."

The water wasn't deep, probably less than an inch, but it covered most of the paved area. It was flowing from the direction of the dam, round both sides of City Hall, and across the Square toward Main Street, the only down-slope exit.

"For the past ten years or so," she continued, "During storms, the dam has leaked a bit, most of the water finding its way into the river. I have never seen it overflow like this." She shook her head and made a worried face.

"How does it leak?" asked Justin.

"God knows. Maybe water leaks into the dam through the cracked concrete, and works its way through the rocks until it comes out on this side."

"You know, this is just the beginning," said Justin. "The whole thing is going to give way. Soon."

"I pray you are wrong," was the fervent response.

"I wish I was."

Jenny added to her husband's words. "But he's not."

There was silence in the cab for a minute, then Justin said, "We have to get out."

"What are you going to do?"

"I don't know. Find some way of warning people, I suppose. Before it's too late."

"Listen," MaryAnn said, "You will have to do whatever you think best.

You are welcome to hang out in the Eagle Eye, but I am sure you won't want to do that. But let me tell you. After you phoned, I made some calls of my own, to people who share our concerns about the dam. They are going to come to the café at four o'clock. I told them about you guys, and they want to hear what you have to say. I hope that works for you."

"It certainly does," said Jenny. "You are the best, MaryAnn. We would not have a chance without you."

"Nor would 'Pole City," echoed Justin from the back seat, starting to open his door.

MaryAnn said, "I hate to let you go like this."

"Don't worry," he said. "We'll be alright. We owe you hugely for getting us out of that mess up on the hill. I wonder why those idiots haven't chased us down here."

"Be glad they didn't."

"Oh, I am. It is odd, 'though."

Jenny was already outside the pickup. She looked back in.

"Thank you so much for all you have done. We'll see you at six, safe and dry."

"I didn't do much. Glad to help, really, but now you are on your own. Watch out. Not everyone is going to be so pleased to see you."

She drove away.

Justin looked at his wife.

"What do we do now?"

"We start there, I guess," she said, indicating City Hall.

As they turned to walk in that direction, Justin grabbed Jenny's arm.

"Wow! Look at that dam," he said.

From where they stood, the face of the dam could be seen quite clearly, beyond the building.

Its rock wall face had changed. Water was running down over the face of the stones. Its central portion was becoming a vast, ornamental waterfall.

Jenny and Justin stood together in the middle of the Square and gaped, until the urgency of the situation hit them. Then they ran up the steps, pausing at the top to look back at the town, spread out before them like a map. Main Street ran, straight as an arrow, from where they stood to the bridge. To the right, on the south side of Main Street, was a low-lying area of narrow streets and houses, as well as a church. How many people lived there, we wondered? When the dam burst, their homes would all be submerged. No doubt about it.

To the left of Main Street, the land rose up, gently at first and then more steeply until it encountered the steep slope of the mountain. There were more streets, houses and businesses there. Those close to Main were also sure to be flooded, but the ones further back might be safe. Time would soon tell.

The door behind them opened and an angry voice demanded, "What the hell are you two doing here?"

Justin turned to see the angry face of Charlie Pierce.

"Have you seen the water?" he asked.

"Of course I have," came the irritated reply.

"Doesn't it alarm you?"

"Nah. The dam leaks like that in every storm."

Jenny joined in. "Like that? Really? I bet this is the worst it's ever been."

Pierce gave her the courtesy of a moment's thought before he answered.

"You may be right, but it always dries up in the end."

"Not this time," Justin said. "Look at the face of the dam."

Before Pierce could turn to do that, his cell phone rang. He pulled it out of his pocket and touched the screen.

"This is Charlie ……"

"Yes, Marvin ……."

"As it happens, they are right here now ….."

"That would be a problem ……"

"Well, I don't have any deputies here right now ….."

"I'll have to do what I can ……"

Jenny grabbed her husband's arm.

"We had better get out of here, fast."

They ran.

Charlie Pierce shouted,, "Hey, you two….", which only made them run even faster..

In seconds they were across the Square and sprinting down Main Street. Charlie was neither young nor fit, and wasn't about to run anywhere. He turned to close and lock the door behind him. Cursing loudly, he headed for his Range Rover. By the time he had it started, they were out of sight. They didn't know where they were heading, but nor did he. Garner had told him to restrain them in some way, and they weren't going to allow it.

The rain started again, cold and unpleasant. The streets were almost deserted, people being either at home or in church. Jenny and Justin sheltered in the doorway of a hardware store, out of view of anyone passing down Main, and discussed options.

"Don't doubt me, Jen. That dam is going to go, probably today."

She looked at Justin, holding his gaze, willing him to be determined. "Then we have to warn people. Let's split up. I'll take the south side if you'll start on the north. When I've finished, I'll come across and join you. Let's knock on every door we can. Speak to whomever will listen. Try and recruit people to believe and help. But above all, tell them to get out of town. Our cell phones should work, so we can keep in touch. In any case, let's plan on meeting back at the Square at three o'clock. That's the highest point in town."

As she ran toward the nearest street on the south side, her husband did likewise on the north. Picking streets at random, he tried every door. Most of those who answered did at least listen, although some mistook him for a salesman or a Jehovah's witness, and shut their doors in his face. People who were already concerned about the dam were quickly convinced and started to prepare for the coming disaster. A larger number were skeptics and told him to go away. Some did this patiently and politely, but not all. At one house, the husband heard him talking to his wife and came out brandishing a pistol.

"Get out of here, and leave us alone," he hollered.

And, all the time, water continued to gush out of the face of the dam.

On her side of the river, Jenny worked her way around the first couple of blocks and came to the church. She crept up to the front door and listened. Inside, a man was speaking loudly, probably preaching a sermon.

"If I could get in there and speak to everyone at once," she thought, "I might persuade them all to go home and save what they can before evacuating."

She opened the door and slipped inside. One or two faces turned toward her, but most were intent on the preacher's message. Or asleep. What should she do now?

The church was about half full. There were about a hundred worshippers. At the far end a preacher stood in the pulpit, holding forth about the evils of the day. She started to walk down the aisle toward him. Someone came up behind her and tugged her sleeve, whispering in her ear. She refused to stop. The preacher watched her approach and stopped his message.

"It seems we have a visitor," he announced, "Perhaps she is in particular need this Lord's Day. Can we help you, young lady?"

He was small, skinny and middle-aged, with a kindly face and a gentle smile. Jenny wondered that he could preach in such a loud voice. She nodded, and just kept walking.

"How may we help?" he asked. "Are you needing prayer, perhaps?"

"More than prayer," she responded, speaking loud and clear. "Far more."

By now she had reached the steps in front of the pulpit. Turning to face the people and speaking as loudly as she could, she announced, "You all need to save yourselves. The dam has started to leak and it is going to burst. The streets are already flooding."

Suddenly, the sanctuary was full of noise. People were talking, shouting, standing up and looking around.

The preacher asked Jenny if she knew what she was saying.

"Oh yes! I do. And if you look outside, at Main Street, you will see it has already started."

He looked at her intently for a moment, then called to one of his elders.

"Jim, step outside and go to the corner. Look down to Main Street. If she's right …."

He didn't need to finish. Jim was already through the door. In far less than a minute he was back.

"There's water in Main Street," he shouted at the top of the voice, and the panic started. People pushed, pulled, shoved, and shouted. Someone screamed. Everyone tried to leave through the same narrow doorway at the same time. Those who got through started running to their houses or climbing into their cars. Many worked their cell phones, frantically trying to contact loved ones and share the warning. In their houses, those who had believed the warning, urgently crammed children, pets and other essentials into their vehicles and tried to escape.

The church was on the south side, but most of Lodgepole's dwellings were on the north. Going home meant wading across Main, whose sidewalks were already under water. Pedestrians could still walk splashily across, but it was a real challenge. Jenny discovered an elderly lady in a motorized wheelchair, immobilized at the edge of the street, watching it become a river. She had covered her face with her hands, and was praying.

"Do you need help?" Jenny asked, startling her, and feeling foolish for asking when the answer was so obvious.

The woman lifted her head and smiled tearfully.

"Not much you can do, my dear. I am here and I live over there." She pointed across to the north side.

"Wait here. I will try and find someone."

Jenny ran back toward the church, where the pastor was standing at the door, talking to Jim and another man. Breathlessly, she explained the problem. The two men immediately sprinted down the block, plucked the old lady out of her chair, and carried her across the flooded street. Leaving her leaning heavily against a street-side trash bin, they returned and brought her chair across too. By the time they arrived back at the church both men were wet up to their knees.

* * *

It was exactly one mile from the Square to Main Street Bridge. In that distance, the ground dropped fifty feet. Water was rushing down the gradient toward the river, where it created a wide pool of uncertain depth. The road disappeared into this water, rising again twenty yards farther, to climb up and over the bridge. Although the escapees were familiar with the place, many hesitated before driving into it. A major traffic jam built up, increasing the general panic. And, all the time, the water kept rising.

Although Main Street Bridge was the usual exit from the town, there was also the small road from the Square up to, and across the dam. Attempting to avoid the chaos at the bridge, and seeing that the dam had not yet collapsed, a number of families headed in that direction. The road was both steep and narrow, and it, too, became its own bottleneck.

Jenny saw the water creeping up the side streets. The whole area between Main Street and the church was about to be flooded. She went back and joined the preacher, standing on the top of the steps outside the sanctuary doors, and called Justin.

"Have you seen Main Street?"

He had not.

"It's much more full of water," she told him. "It could be over my knees by now."

Justin stepped round a corner to look. A frustrated Charlie Pierce was driving back up toward the Square. The water was up to his hub caps, and flowing fast.

"I see it," he said. "Things are getting bad in a hurry. Maybe you should come over here now."

"There are still a lot of people in homes who don't know what's happening. I need to keep on finding them."

"I am worried about you, sweetheart."

"I'll be OK. See you at the Square."

"Well, OK, but let's make it in just one hour. Things are going to be pretty wild by then."

"One hour it is."

Justin could not help worrying. "Do be careful. Stay safe. I love you."

"And I love you too."

From her elevated position on the church steps, Jenny could see between the houses toward the dam, about a quarter mile away. Through the cold drizzle, she could just make out what was happening. At several points in its center section, jets of water were shooting out of the dam, deluging the roof of the power station beneath.

"Oh my God!" she muttered, then noticing that she was standing next to the preacher. "Sorry Reverend," she added. She knew she should be running among the streets, knocking on doors and shouting to everyone she saw, but she was transfixed.

"Even He won't be able to save us now," the preacher replied.

His words spurred her into action.

"Then we have to warn people."

She ran down the steps and started rousing more people in their homes. Above her head, someone started ringing the bell in the church's tower.

Soon after that, the dam started to break. Some of the huge rocks which formed its face became dislodged. The pressure of the water behind them gradually pushed them out of place, and they began to tumble to the ground. Large jets of water spurted out of the holes they left behind. Pretty soon, the water in Main Street was above everyone's knees. People were panicking. Some insisted on trying to get to the bridge, which was hardly accessible now. On the north side, many were hauling their families and their possessions up the streets which led toward the steep mountain slope, although there was nowhere particular for them to go. On the south side, between Main Street and the creek, the land was generally flat, and the only escape routes were staircases to upper floors.

For thirty minutes, Jenny worked like a woman possessed, ringing doorbells, or beating with her fists when there was no bell, and shouting until she was hoarse. She decided to stay ahead of the rising water for as long as she could. It was dryer and safer that way, she reasoned. If she had to wade through the flood she would be slowed down and reach fewer homes. Without thinking about the passage of time, she drove herself on. If, during all this exertion, her phone rang, she did not hear it. Gradually the water level forced her up what slope there was, until she arrived back at the church, which had been built on the highest point around. The preacher was still standing on the top step, which was just about the only dry place in sight. He stretched out a hand and helped her up.

"You are a marvel," he said. "A real angel. Now, come with me. You deserve to be somewhere safe. He took her round the outside of the building to the base of the bell tower. Using a key, he opened a small door and showed her the staircase inside.

"Go on. You'll be safe up there. I have to see who else I can help."

She hesitated.

"Go on," he said. "I'll be sending others to join you."

Not knowing what else to do, she began to climb, until she found herself in a small, open sided gallery, with a roof and a huge bell hanging among the rafters above. She walked over to the rail on the side facing the dam and gazed in horror. The massive rock wall was being torn apart, boulder by boulder, by the force of the water. Rocks, some as big as cars, were being flung out, crashing down onto the building below. Not more than ten or twenty feet above the ground, an opening had formed, large enough to drive an eighteen-wheeler through. Water was gushing out of this with such force and in such an amount that it was pummeling the power station to death.

* * *

On the north side, Justin continued to run from house to house, gradually working his way up the slope as the flood spread itself among the streets behind him. After fifteen minutes he turned to look back toward Main Street, and then at the dam, and realized his mistake. He and Jenny should not have separated. She had argued that they could cover more ground by working separately. Maybe she was right, but it was a terrible decision, and he should have seen that at once. Things were deteriorating much too quickly. By the time three o'clock arrived, there was not going to be any way for her to cross Main Street to him on the safer side, nor for either of them to make it back to the Square. He pulled out his phone and tried to call her. She didn't answer.

He looked across at the south side, but could not see how far the flood had advanced over there. One thing was clear: there was no hope for that side of town. It would be totally inundated. Every single building there would be under water before long. The only question was, to what depth? Perhaps the upper floors would remain dry. That was the best hope. There would be no other refuge.

He tried to call Jenny again. Perhaps, if she came right then, she could still get across.

She did not answer. He had no idea why. Probably it was a bad moment. She might have been talking to homeowners or something like that. He gave her five minutes, and tried again.

No answer. He dialed once more. Still no answer.

"Come on, Jenny! Pick up! Where are you?"

Justin was so worried about her that he could hardly concentrate on his own mission. It took real will power to keep going from door to door, when all he wanted to do was to find his wife. His brand-new wife.

* * *

Leaning over the wooden rail in the bell tower, Jenny looked down at the streets below. Main Street was full of water, racing downhill, becoming quite impassible to anyone and everyone. The water was approaching windowsill level. She lifted her eyes and saw crowds of people squeezing their way up the streets on the hill opposite. How many people were over there, she wondered? A couple thousand perhaps? She had no real idea. And, among them but out of her sight, was her sweet husband. Not normally a religious woman, she made an involuntary prayer. "O God! Let Justin be alright." Her throat tightened and she began to cry.

Things were about to get worse. A faint rumbling sound began, gradually increasing in volume until everyone in Lodgepole could hear it. It increased until it reached an ear-splitting crescendo, sounding like the roar of a thousand Jurassic beasts. Justin, on the north side, was part way up a sloping street, at an intersection. He had a clear view, and watched in horror as the dam seemed to swell, thrusting its abdomen out toward the town. New splits appeared in its stretched surface, each one producing a fresh jet of water more fierce and destructive than the one before it.

In the streets which climbed the north slope, the escaping crowds turned to gaze at their dam: the dam which had given their city its power and water and made its life possible. They watched as, with slow, patient determination, it tore itself to pieces.

* * *

There were half a dozen vehicles on the road up to the dam. The first, a van driven by a thirty-year-old librarian, carrying his wife and three kids, was followed by his in-laws and the family pets in a small SUV. They convoyed safely across the dam. Next came an elderly couple in their minivan, who somehow thought they would be safer if they drove slowly. Behind them were two more families, desperate to escape while they could, and cursing the speed of the couple in front. The convoy was still creeping across the dam when it finally gave way. The surface of the road began to crack, becoming a crazy jigsaw puzzle, with widening fissures between its pieces. Below, unseen by the luckless escapees, the rock wall, which had supported the road for fifty years, simply disintegrated. With a cataclysmic explosion, the dam's concrete face, whose job was to keep the water of the lake in place, finally surrendered. A one-hundred-foot wall of water leaped out of the canyon and dumped itself on the waiting town.

Everyone who was out in the streets either watched in terror or ran for his life. The entire center section of the dam simply disappeared. Concrete, rocks and three cars, with their screaming occupants, were hurled outward, riding on the top of the unimaginable tsunami. Lodgepole Lake tried to empty itself, to destroy the community for whom it had been created. Billions of gallons of water were forcing their way between the remaining walls of the dam, tearing at them, ripping them apart as if they were made of cardboard.

Down below, Main Street had totally disappeared, replaced by a torrent of white water, which furiously tore the fronts off buildings as it roared down toward the bridge. Cars, which had been parked on or near it, were bobbing like corks, being swept to goodness knows where. Chaos reigned. City Hall was destroyed, water bursting in through the double doors at the back and out through those at the front. Suddenly, the walls on either side of the porch gave way and the clock tower on the roof above started to lean forward. The entire building seemed to twist and tremble, before it took a proud step forward, off its foundation and fell, face down, into the Square.

All over Lodgepole, people were running crazily, trying to reach higher ground. A few pick-ups and SUV's, crammed with families and their belongings, were driving here and there, but there was no way out of the valley. All the streets, on both sides, eventually led back to Main, or connected with the now destroyed road across the dam.

In time, most of the crowds on the north made it up the slopes to safety, but those on the south were not so lucky. Sandwiched between Main Street and the river, the ground did not rise more than ten feet at best. They had to seek refuge indoors, in the upper floors of the houses, and hope the structures would withstand the force of the flood.

From her elevated position in the bell tower Jenny studied the crowds on the slope opposite, desperately hoping for a glimpse of her new husband, but the people were so distant, so small and so crowded together, that it was almost impossible. Her tears didn't help, although she kept wiping them away. Justin had to be there somewhere. If only she could see him. If only he could see her.

He couldn't see her, of course, any more than she him. The ache was unbearable. Of course, he had always loved his mother, been crazy about his sister, and had genuine fondness for his grandparents. He had also treasured the friendships of his mentor, Peter van Laden and his college pal, Nehal. And there had been Emmy, of course. But his love for his sweetheart was something entirely new to him. They had been the lights of his life until he discovered her. She became his bright sun, lifting his journey out of the ordinary into the spectacular. Now, suddenly, she was in danger, out of reach and out of sight. His inability to help brought him close to panic. There was an intense, physical pain in his chest. He felt like someone who is gagged and cannot call for help, or tied up and unable to move, or blindfolded and incapable of seeing. The desperate need to do something was fighting against the certainty that there was nothing that could be done.

Many years before, PV had encouraged him to paint what he could not see, to visualize feelings. Now, in that devastated mountain city, that ability became his curse. Not knowing what was happening to his bride, he could see the worst possibilities, one after another, cascading before him. Was she trapped, perhaps under a fallen tree, while the water rose around her? Was she flailing uselessly as the raging current swept her away? Perhaps she was sitting on some rooftop, soaked to the skin and shivering, hoping for help. Most dreadful of all, he envisaged her drowned body floating up to the surface, deathly white, only to be sucked down again.

And there was nothing he could do!

Justin had no way of knowing that, at that moment, Jenny was high and dry, safe in the bell tower of the church. She was the first to arrive there, but others began to join her. A young couple, the husband carrying a baby, came first. Then two tired looking women arrived, probably in their sixties or seventies, and looking as if they had hardly had time to get dressed. Before long the little platform was full, yet people kept arriving. A large, bullish man in his thirties was trying to force a way for himself and two teenagers.

"There isn't room!" protested one of those already there.

"Sure there is," he responded, squeezing and pushing.

The crush made one of the older men cry out, "Stop pushing. We're being crushed to death here."

The bull kept pressing on people, dragging his kids in behind him. Suddenly there was a loud cracking sound, and several screams. The pressure between the people in the tower proved too much for the hundred-year-old timbers. The wooden rail gave way, and the young couple with the baby began to fall. Quick as lightning, the husband threw the baby at Jenny.

"Save her," he begged as he disappeared downward.

Instinctively, Jenny reached out. She was at the very limit of her balance. She scooped the precious bundle to her breast with one hand while reaching out for something to hold onto with the other. Her fingers grasped the broken end of the wooden rail, which was still attached to the tower, and gave her the leverage to swing herself back toward safety. But there was no room. The crush of people had filled her space. She looked imploringly at a kindly looking woman and thrust the child at her, just as the rail splintered and gave way. Jenny overbalanced completely and fell, unable to save herself. She landed on her head and blacked out.

Jenny's life was saved by a woman who had died twenty-five years before. The Rev. Sam Piggot had been the pastor of the church for five decades when he died. He had come to Lodgepole during the Depression, gathered a few believers together, and started work. By the time he had his fatal heart attack, the cause had several hundred members, every one of whom loved, or at least admired him. Money was raised to construct a bell tower in his honor, and he was buried in a plot close by. Winifred, his widow, planted bushes to shield him from the cold winter winds, and placed a sturdy wooden bench between them. Every day, come rain or shine, she would visit him, sitting on that seat and telling him about the fortunes of his flock. Eventually, she too died, and was placed beside him. She no longer needed her bench, but it remained where it was in case anyone else should need it.

When Jenny fell from the tower, she landed, headfirst, on one of the bushes, and toppled over onto the bench, where she lay, a strangely twisted form with her head at a wrong angle. She didn't move. It wasn't clear if she was even breathing. If anyone had seen her, they would probably have taken her for dead, but no one did. Gradually the waters rose around her. If the fall had not killed her, she would surely drown. But that is not what happened. As the flood deepened, and began to envelop her body, the wooden bench started to float, and the swirl of the tide swept her away.

CHAPTER 23

Survival

The helicopters began to appear in mid-afternoon, vultures circling around a carcass. They buzzed in from the open end of the valley, and flew up to the dam, then hung around, hovering, salivating over the disaster. On their sides were the logos of various television channels and news organizations. The earliest of them arrived in time to see the dam rip itself open. Their producers were delighted about that. The live streamed images made spectacular TV. "These images may be difficult to watch" they said gleefully. Soon after, a military helicopter arrived, bearing the insignia of the Colorado National Guard. It circled, looking for somewhere to land. With the city itself being increasingly submerged, the only practical site was the parking area at the north end of the dam. A team of medical and other personnel disembarked. Carrying stretchers and other medical equipment, they started to walk down the narrow road toward the town. Before long they were meeting with Charlie Pierce and other civic leaders. Obviously the entire city would have to be evacuated, although it was too late to do anything that evening, except transport some really urgent cases. The power station had been flooded soon after the dam started leaking, and was now submerged, leaving the City without electricity. This meant that the water supply had to be cut off, since its pumps no longer worked. In any case, as the flood increased, so did the likelihood of water pollution.

The dam burst on Sunday afternoon. All that evening the water continued to pour onto the city, arriving more quickly than it could escape. The flood deepened, and kept doing so long after nightfall, when it was no longer possible to watch it or see what was happening. There were no electric lights, of course, and the moon was hiding somewhere, too terrified of what it might reveal. But there was light of a sort. There always is, even on the darkest night. Eyes get used to it and learn to interpret the shadows.

It was the worst night of Justin's life. He was trapped on the north side, backing up the slope as the water rose. All he could do was stare across to the south side, as its entire surface disappeared, every street flooded. Jenny had to be there somewhere, but where? He had no idea, no way of knowing. Perhaps she was in a house, hopefully with some kind people, secure on an upper floor. Goodness knows how many times he tried to call her. Not once did she answer. He tried leaving messages, but there was no response, no call back, no text, nothing. Finally, his battery died. His phone became as useless as he felt himself.

His spirits fell with the increasing darkness, until he could not see the south side, let alone any sign of life on it. The entire city was without power. A few homes seemed to have their own sources of light, usually dim, but not enough to help. What was he to do? Finally, recognizing his need to take a break from worrying about his bride and think about himself. Where was he going to spend the night?

"If you need somewhere to go, you would be welcome in here."

He was walking past a building whose windows revealed a dim, flickering glow. The speaker had a warm and compassionate voice. Justin made out his silhouette, taller and broader he was himself.

"I am Larry," the stranger continued. "This is my bar, The Splintered Pole. There are quite a few people in here already. Of course, there is no service, just a place to sit down in the warm. At least it's dry and safe, and we do have candles." So Justin went in, and found a seat in a booth with a married couple, retired teachers who had moved to 'Pole two years before, in fulfilment of their retirement dream. The wife kept bursting into tears, and her husband tried to divide his efforts between comforting her and making conversation with him. Sleep was impossible, and it was a relief when the light of dawn started to appear. Despite his denial of service, the owner of the bar managed to produce a mountain of wrapped cookies, bags of chips, various other cold foods, and an abundance of soft drinks. The sight of this feast made Justin realize how hungry he was, and he took full advantage of it.

As dawn broke, a woman in some sort of military uniform came into the bar. She asked for attention, and proceeded to explain that the National Guard were preparing to evacuate the town. She asked those who were fit enough to make their way up to the car park by the dam, where the Guard had set up a post.

"We need to record everyone's name and address, and make a list of all those who are missing. Then you will be taken by helicopter to a new emergency shelter which is being opened in the High School. You will be safe and dry there, and able to look for loved ones. And you will be able to start making plans for the future."

Justin wasn't sure if he wanted to go. All he wanted was to find Jenny, or find out that she was alright. It was tempting to stay in Lodgepole, where he would at least be near where she had been when he last spoke to her. Escaping to safety would feel like abandoning her. However, the soldier explained that there would be three ways for people to escape. Mobile people on the north side could climb the hill to the parking area and be lifted out by helicopter. Those who were trapped on rooftops and other high points could be rescued by smaller, more maneuverable choppers. Then, when the waters steadied, boats would be brought in, somewhere near Main Street Bridge, and used for search and rescue, especially on the south side. He was more likely to find her at the High School. Everyone they found would end up there.

* * *

Evacuations had started at dawn. A pair of troop-carrying helicopters began ferrying Lodgepole's citizens from the dam parking lot to the County High School ten miles away. There they were provided with cots to sleep on, food to eat, clothes to wear, and counselors to talk to. Representatives of FEMA were expected, to help them plan for the longer term and the repair of their flooded homes. All school activities were cancelled for the next seven days at least.

For the whole of Monday, the flow of water from the ruined lake prevented the use of rescue boats, but by Tuesday morning things had improved. Teams of volunteers started arriving at the Bridge. They came from outside the City, some from many miles away. Mostly, they towed their own boats, which they launched into the flooded streets, and started searching for people trapped in the various homes and businesses. As they puttered among the houses, they were greeted by calls for help and other signs of life from the survivors. People were rescued from upstairs windows, garage rooftops, and other high points. In each case, they were ferried back to the Bridge area, where they were set on dry land and whisked away in bus loads to the High School. Teams of trained and qualified helpers went from house to house, looking for survivors who were too weak to shout and too frail to move. There was obvious concern for anyone who did not make it upstairs. Sadly, some had died where they sat or lay.

Eventually, Justin arrived at the dam parking lot. He spent forty minutes standing in line before it was his turn. There were several tables, each occupied by someone in uniform, who was recording information and entering it into a computer. As Justin learned, each of those devices was linked wirelessly to a server at the emergency center. At one station he provided his own details and verified them before they were consigned to the central computer. Then he moved on to a second station where a surprisingly young, female captain was working furiously with a laptop, entering details of people who might be missing and checking to see if they had already been found. In his extreme anxiety, he could hardly speak as he tried to talk about Jenny.

"Is there any news of her?" he asked, once her name had been recorded. The captain touched some keys and studied her screen.

"Not yet, I'm afraid. There is no-one called Gates among the survivors we know about, but nor is she among the list of those who didn't make it. It is still very early in the process. If I were you, I would take the helicopter to the school. That is where everyone is going to end up. It will be your best chance of finding her as soon as she is rescued."

Still reluctant to abandon Jenny, Justin walked over to the ruined dam. Someone had strung plastic tape to prevent people getting too close, but he ducked under it. No one stopped him. Leaning on what remained of the wall, he looked down into the ruined city. Jenny was somewhere there, wasn't she? Or had she been helicoptered out? Or had she succumbed to the flood, and been drowned? Or was she safely in the upper floor of a south side home? Was she alright? Was she injured? Was she sick? Was she dead? Not knowing was the killer.

The officer, to whom he had given Jenny's details, had made a promise. "We will call you the moment we hear anything" and Justin had replied, "Thank you. That would be wonderful."

Only when he was leaning on the wall at the dam did he remember: he no longer had a working phone. How was anyone going to reach him with whatever news there might be?

Being so close to the cabin, he was tempted to retreat there for a few hours. He could snatch some much needed sleep and change his clothes. There wouldn't be any electricity, of course, but he could recharge his phone in the Jeep. How long would that take, he wondered. With a last look down into the devastated valley, he set out up the hill. Ninety minutes later he was back at the parking lot and standing in line for a helicopter ride. His phone was working again, and he felt refreshed by a cold shower. Sleep, he had decided, could wait.

Once at the High School Rescue Center, he lay down on a camp bed in the gymnasium and fell into an exhausted sleep. For almost two days he remained at the school, sleeping in the gym, eating in the cafeteria and exercising on the sports field. Socializing did not appeal, although he was sure he could have had some interesting encounters. The place was full of anxious people, every one of them facing an uncertain future. He could have had a harvest of previews, but he had no interest in doing so. All he wanted was an insight into how and when Jenny and he would be together again. He would have gladly exchanged all the previews that were to come in his remaining years for that single one right then.

*   *   *

The Rescue Center, was a noisy and busy place. There were at least two thousand people, coming or staying or going. Various officials and help agencies were trying to assist the desperate, homeless citizens of 'Pole City. The school had a public address system, which was constantly making announcements. The one everyone wanted was, "Will Mr. and Mrs. So-and-so come to the front office." That usually meant that someone's relatives had been found, or their transport away from the valley had arrived, or some hoped-for assistance was available.

Late on Wednesday morning, it was Justin's turn. He was sitting at a desk in a quiet classroom, listening through an open door for the announcement which would mention his name. His mind wandered back to that day, long ago, when he had been sitting in another classroom, and his chemistry teacher had caught him drawing her picture, and marched him off to see the head of the art department. That was the moment when his life as an artist had really begun, under the watchful eye of Peter van Leyden. He remembered the days of self-discovery while he was at UC Berkeley, and the ways in which Emmy and Nehal had each, in their unique way, helped him to become his own person.

Closing his eyes, he saw again the faces of some of the people he had helped over the years as he became 'the Prophet of Houston'. The creased and weathered face of Hank, the rancher, who wanted a painting of his favorite horse. The beautiful and excited Maddie Brewer, who could not stop talking about a wedding that would never take place. The neurotic Betsy Something from whom he took away the fear of cancer. And, of course, the girl in the airport who looked just like his sister and turned out to be exactly that.

As he remembered Bella, his thoughts turned to the confusing issue of the FlyWay air disaster and his role in it. The question still bothered him, whether he should have said nothing, and allowed Bella and the rest to carry on to Phoenix. Presumably Michael Kahn would still have been waiting with his missile in Palm Springs, and FlyAir 439 would still have been destroyed.

And, of course, he pictured again, that sweet, intelligent reporter with the unforgettable smile who appeared on his doorstep and tried to interview him about the crash and ended up winning his heart. The love of his life, who might have survived the storm or perished in it; he had no way of knowing. And that hurt, probably more than anything had ever hurt in his life before.

Justin sat at a student's desk, leaning his shoulder against a wall, with his eyes closed and his vision full of memories.

"Will the following people please come to the main office." The loudspeaker in the corridor outside the classroom's open door announced four names. "Mr. Justin Gates" was number three.

For two days Justin had been hearing such messages. At first, his pulse would race as soon as the announcer began to speak, but repeated disappointments had dulled his response. It took him several seconds to realize that his time had come. He clumsily leapt to his feet, pushing the desk out of his way, and headed for the front office.

"Have you found her?" he asked, before the girl with the Red Cross badge had even lifted her head to look at him. "Is she OK?"

She ignored his question. Instead she said, "Please give me your name and date of birth."

She was following procedure.

He told her who he was, and impatiently watched her work her computer.

Looking at the badge on her shirt, he said, "JoAnn, just tell me where is she?"

The girl consulted the record on her screen.

"It says that there is someone in St. Francis Hospital in Colorado Springs who matches your wife's description, but they have not yet been able to confirm who she is."

Justin felt his throat tightening with anxiety. "Why not? She hasn't told them?" Even as he spoke, the truth dawned. "She can't speak? Please, tell me she is at least alive."

JoAnn looked at her screen again, then at Justin's face.

"This person, who sounds like Mrs. Gates, is in a coma."

Justin drew in a deep breath as he tried to absorb what this could mean.

"Is that all you can tell me?"

"Let me read you what it says here. Her condition is stated to be 'Comatose. Significant head wound. Various other bruises on upper torso.' And then there is a note. 'Monday, 1 pm. Subject was spotted floating on a wooden bench, which was caught in a tree close to Main Street. Removed by helicopter. EMTs unable to revive her during flight. Signs of concussion and near drowning. Taken to St. Frances.'"

* * *

It took Justin four hours to get to the hospital, begging lifts and waiting for buses, but he made it. A chubby African-American nurse, with a deep, gentle voice and kind eyes, took him to Jenny's room.

"We don't have an identity for her," she said. "Let's look through the window first."

They approached the door with its glass panel. Justin was trembling, afraid of what he might see.

"This is the one," said the nurse, stepping aside so that he could easily see inside. He took in a deep breath for courage, and held it as he stepped forward.

There she was! She didn't really look like herself. There was no color in her cheeks nor in the exposed skin of her neck and arms. She lay on the bed, listless, eyes closed, mouth drawn down at the corners. But it was Jenny. His Jenny. No doubt. Still breathing, it seemed. Connected to life by a collection of sensor wires and plastic tubes.

He breathed normally again. Tears in his eyes, he looked at the nurse and nodded. Then he grasped the doorknob and let himself in.

For two days, Justin hardly left her side. He stroked her hand, kissed her forehead, and talked to her often.

"There is no certainty that she will wake up," the doctors said, "But we believe she will. It might take hours, or days, or even months. No-one knows. But your presence gives her the best chance."

" The voice of a loved one is often what it takes," the nurse told him.

Sitting in that quiet room, for long, quiet, seemingly endless hours, I thought about my life, the life I had persuaded Jenny to share, the life which I no longer wished to live without her. I looked at her, calmly and sweetly asleep, unaware of what she had been through and what I was still going through. All I wanted was to take her home, content to be nothing more than a 'struggling artist' for life. But I had my peculiar gift, and so long as that was true, I knew that quiet normalcy was beyond my reach.

Why had I been given my peculiar gift, I wondered. Did I really want it? During those long hours in the hospital, watching my sweetheart endure her coma, I doubted it.

A long time before, Shivangi had told me that my gift was a privilege, that it added a quality to my life which few people possessed. By sharing my previews, whether they were troubling or exciting, I could enable other people to walk taller, feel stronger and cope better with their journeys through life.

But what about Jenny? And what about me?

I could not help thinking that she had almost died because I had previewed the collapse of the dam. Without that foresight, we would not have been running around the streets of the doomed city, and she would never have been trapped on the south side, nor gone into that church, nor taken refuge in the bell tower. But then, it was another preview, about the fate of an airliner over Palm Springs, that led to Jenny entering my life in the first place. The same gift had brought us together and then nearly torn us apart. I could hardly make sense of it all.

Justin slept in the recliner next to her bed, and only went away, briefly, to eat. Doctors and other white coated beings came and went. They tried to encourage him with their platitudes, but he knew as well as they that her recovery was not guaranteed. He thought a lot about the irony that he, the Prophet of Houston, was quite unable to predict the future for his loved one, nor indeed, for himself. Caring about what he might see blocked his ability to see it.

There weren't many people that Justin needed to call. His mother came first on the list, and then Tina. They were both full of concern and compassion, and sad that they could do so little to help. Each offered to come and keep him company during his vigil. He thanked them but said he was fine. He was about to call Becky when a call came in. It was Tony White. Alice had called him as soon as she heard the news. He asked what had happened and how Jenny was doing and if there was anything that he could do to help. Again, Justin said he appreciated the offer, but the only thing to do was be patient and wait.

Late on the Friday evening, Jenny opened her eyes. It was a small, silent event, but it changed Justin's world. At the time, he was talking quietly to the nurse, and it was she who noticed.

"Look!" she whispered, nodding toward the patient in the bed.

"Oh my God!" Justin exclaimed, jumping up and leaning over so that Jenny could see him.

"Good morning, Sweetheart," he said, quite forgetting the time of day.

"Welcome back."

The doctors kept Jenny where she was for three more days, carried out various tests, including an MRI of her brain, and pronounced her almost back to normal. She could go home. Justin called his mother to share the good news. Without being asked, Alice then called Tony, who called Justin immediately.

"No arguments about this, Justin," he said. "I am sending Andrew and the jet. They will take you back to Houston."

Exactly eight days after the disastrous flood, Tony White's Pilatus PC-24 lifted off from Runway 17L at Colorado Springs Airport, taking the honeymooners home. Jenny looked down at the front where the mountains met the broad, flat Colorado plain, searching for a sight of Lodgepole. At her request, the pilot had arranged to pass over that area before heading off toward Houston.

Suddenly she spotted the valley, three thousand feet below. She could just make out the ruined dam, now holding back but a remnant of its former lake, and below that the city, its streets presumably now dry. From that height, the buildings seemed very tiny, but they did appear remarkably intact. After a moment of searching, she spotted a speck on the green hillside, high above the scene of the disaster. That had to be their cabin.

"Look, Jus," she said, "There. It's Lodgepole. That's where we were."

"Where you nearly died," he responded in a quiet voice.

She leaned forward and took hold of his hand.

"But I didn't."

"Thank heavens," he replied, with such feeling that it brought tears to her eyes.

Silently, they gazed down at the scene, each lost in private and confusing thoughts, with grief and relief and gratitude swirling around together.

Speaking half to herself, half to her husband, Jenny said, "I wonder how many people survived."

"And how many didn't," he responded.

"I wonder what would have happened if we hadn't been there, if you hadn't had your preview. A lot more people would have died, I'm sure."

Justin pursed his lips as he thought about this.

"You know, Jen," he said, "I did have the preview. That's true. But it was you who made me do something about it. If you had not insisted that we go down to warn people, we would have stayed safely in the cabin, hidden away from the storm, and left things to Andy…"

"Who didn't believe you and wasn't going to get involved. I think we were fated to be there when we were needed."

"Fated?"

"Yes, fated. Perhaps our decision to honeymoon in Lodgepole, and to stay in the cabin above the dam, was more than an accident. Perhaps some mystical force, one we are hardly aware of, pushed us to be in that place at that time. Maybe life is more than a patchwork of predictable events. Maybe there is purpose to it all,"

"But what would that purpose be?"

Jenny looked into her husband's eyes.

"That, my love, is something for you to figure out. After all, it is you who is the prophet. I am just lucky enough to be your wife."

* * *

Up front, Tony's pilot sighed and said to his co-pilot, "Well, I hope that was what she wanted. We need to go." He shifted the controls, and the plane accelerated, climbing into a wide turn, and headed south, toward Houston.

Message from the Author.

Dear Reader,

Thank you for reading my story. I hope you enjoyed it. Whether you did, or not, I would like to know. Please email your comments to david@fraseroz.com

Made in the USA
Middletown, DE
29 December 2022